THE LATE NIGHT HORROR SHOW

BRYAN SMITH

GRINDHOUSE PRESS

For all the late night psychotronic movie weirdos out there. You know who you are. Blood, guts, and beer forever.

Other titles by Bryan Smith

PART 1

COMING ATTRACTIONS

ONE

There was something odd about that music. The sound was discordant. Jarring and shrill. But that wasn't the odd thing about it. What was odd was how tantalizingly familiar it was. The defining element of the music was the sound of seemingly one thousand tortured violins being violently assaulted by an army of escaped mental patients bent on wringing the soundtrack of hell from their undoubtedly stolen instruments. Rapidly repeated stinging bursts of sudden, sharp sounds, followed by longer and more ominous-sounding notes in a lower register.

The overall effect was so like something he'd heard a million times before, with perhaps a couple of minor variations, perhaps wedged between the more familiar notes as an afterthought, a way of warding off a copyright violation lawsuit.

Yet . . . he couldn't quite put his finger on why it was so damn familiar.

What the hell is *that monstrous noise?*

John Dorsey stirred from his semi-doze and squinted at the fuzzy images on the television in his living room. There was nothing wrong with the picture. And his eyesight was usually fine. The fuzziness was instead a result of the many beers he'd consumed since his breakfast earlier that morning. Wait . . . was it still morning?

He swiveled his head slowly to the right, squinting harder than ever now.

"Ah."

Sunshine was visible through the half-drawn blind above the buzzing air conditioner. Didn't quite solve the mystery. Could be late morning, still. Could be afternoon. Could be early evening. But something about the glaringly bright quality of the sunshine made him doubt the latter possibility. It was still relatively early, though not so early that he hadn't had time to put a respectable dent in that case of Pabst Blue Ribbon.

Speaking of . . .

He glanced down at his dangling right hand, which was hanging over the arm of his recliner. The top of the can was held very lightly by the tips of his fingers. Even the slightest lessening of his grip would send it tumbling to the carpeted floor. He frowned and got a more solid grip on the can. He then sat up straight and again trained his eyes on the television.

Little less fuzzy now.

Huh. Interesting.

A woman on the screen was attired in a very skimpy bikini. Nice body. Long, black-as-sin hair flowing over milk-white shoulders. She was screaming and running down a long, shadowy hallway. Someone was chasing her. A dude, naturally. Very large, of course, and wearing some kind of freaky mask. It was easy to see why you'd want to run away from him. Partly it was the ugly mask, but mostly it was because of the huge, whirring chainsaw held high over one of his shoulders.

"Jesus. Not another fucking *Chainsaw* sequel."

This one looked to be the worst yet. The production values were clearly far below the norm for the series. This one looked like one of those schlocky shot-on-video pieces of garbage that had a tendency to sit unrented for years on the shelves of failing video stores everywhere. And the chainsaw-wielding psycho on the screen didn't look right at all. The mask looked cheap. A flimsy piece of plastic shit you might buy for a buck at Wal-Mart the day after Halloween. Nothing at all like a mask stitched together from dead human flesh. And the guy lacked the classic Leatherface physique. John's mouth curled in disgust. Clearly this was a case of some hack with a camera "rebooting" or "reimagining" the franchise. The only question was how in

God's name these obvious amateurs had managed to wrest away the rights to . . .

He frowned again.

"Huh."

The woman had reached the end of the hallway. The door there was locked. Of course. It had to be locked. Otherwise she couldn't turn to the camera, as she was doing now, splay a hand across her mouth, and scream again as the dude with the chainsaw at last got close enough to begin the butchery.

A title in wavy yellow letters splashed across the screen.

Chainsaw Maniac!

John raised the can of Pabst to his mouth. "The fuck is this?"

Of course. Should have been obvious from the beginning. Not an official *Chainsaw* sequel, but instead a cheap rip-off. As the faux-Leatherface character raised his weapon and began to lower the whirring blade toward the cringing babe, the tempo of the music increased again. Now that he'd come out of his beer-induced stupor, his synapses were firing faster and he was able to place why the music was so familiar.

He snapped the fingers of his left hand and jabbed a forefinger at the screen. "*Psycho!* You cheap bastards are ripping off Bernard Hermann's score!" He chuckled and raised the can to his mouth again. "Hell, of course you are. So many others have done it, so why not you, right?"

He laughed some more.

The laughter cut off abruptly as it dawned on him that there was a disturbing lack of refreshing *cerveza* streaming down his horribly parched throat. He scowled at the empty can as he shook it. "Someone has stolen my beer. This offense cannot be tolerated. I declare global thermonuclear war as just retribution." He chuckled. "Unless, of course, a diplomatic solution is hastily arranged." He pitched his voice higher and jerked his head toward the kitchen. "Marie! Another beer! Stat! The fate of the world hangs in the balance."

He laughed some more. Then he frowned again. This wasn't like him. This . . . jocularity. This delirious good humor. No. No. That wasn't quite fair. It was what he'd once been like, a lifetime ago, or, in normal people terms, approximately five months ago. Which, imagine this, happened to coincide with his layoff from the well-paying job he'd held for nearly a decade. Yes, a thing like that, especially in today's barren job market, was enough to crush any man's spirit.

So . . . why was he feeling so good?

He kept frowning for a moment. Then he smiled and shrugged. "Whatever. Life is full of mysteries."

The images on the screen shifted. The wavy yellow letters blurred and spread across the screen, giving way a moment later to new images of horror and destruction. A post-apocalyptic world. Burned-out buildings and piles of debris in smoky, smudgy streets. Hordes of drooling, slack-jawed people in tattered clothes lurching around in the streets, most of them bearing evidence of grisly wounds. The music was different now, too, the derivative symphonic sounds replaced by a bludgeoning, staccato heavy metal beat and rumbling, growled vocals. He couldn't place the song, but the band sounded kind of like Disturbed. Only it wasn't Disturbed. It was some sound-alike outfit, some anonymous group of nu metal douchebags whose tunes were undoubtedly far cheaper to license. A black helicopter flew high above the lumbering throngs of the dead, the whir of the chopper blades intermittently audible between bursts of metal riffery. A man clad in a helmet, goggles, and military armor leaned out of the 'copter, an M-16 clutched in muscular hands. But he didn't fire his gun. It would obviously be a waste of ammunition. There were just too many of them.

Too many zombies.

Another set of wavy yellow letters splashed across the screen.

Rise of the Dead!

The production values on this one were obviously higher. Still not up to big studio, A-List Hollywood standards—some of the zombie make-up was too obviously fake—but clearly several notches above the ridiculous chainsaw thing. And yet, the seamless transition from those scenes to these, along with the identical font used for the movie titles, implied an obvious connectedness. John's instinct to snarkily pick apart cheap movies yielded to a genuine interest.

John belatedly realized a stentorian-sounding voiceover announcer was speaking. He made himself focus on his words: "*Chainsaws. Zombies. The undying lust of the undead. Blood flowing thick as a river through dirty city streets. Women in danger and the maniacs who crave their demise—*

John giggled.

He couldn't help it.

Crave their demise?

The ad copy for this thing sounded as cheap and cheesy as the movies themselves.

—all of these dark wonders and more will be on display all weekend at the Late Night Horror Film Festival at the Sunshine 6 cineplex in Murfreesboro. Doctor Ominous presents six masterpieces of horror. See them all . . . if you dare."

John giggled again.

But wait. Who was this "Doctor Ominous" character? It had the ring of a moniker a cable TV horror host might use, though he was unaware of anyone with a local host gig going by that name. Not that it mattered much. It was just strange.

And also . . .

"*If* I dare? Ain't no 'if' about it, motherfuckers."

He realized the truth of the statement as he spoke it. The movies looked bad, but bad movies could be their own kind of good time. Especially if enough booze was consumed, which would most assuredly be the case if he had anything to say about it. Suddenly he had a plan for the evening that involved something more than slowly rotting in front of the television. Sure, it wouldn't involve anything productive or particularly positive, but at least it would get him out of the apartment, out from between these too-close-together walls, this grim, Kafkaesque space he had begun to suspect was not an insubstantial contributing factor to his slow decline. He would get out and breathe, enjoy the simple pleasure of just being around other people again. He would feel human again, and maybe, just maybe, that wouldn't be such a small thing at all.

It might even be the first necessary, small step toward getting his life back on track.

He stared at the empty beer can in his hand and was reminded of something.

"Oh, yeah. Need a refill."

He turned his head slowly to the left, stared beyond the partition that separated the small apartment's living room from the cramped kitchen. Marie usually sat at the little table there and read books or magazines while he sat in front of the television and drank himself into oblivion. They hadn't been interacting in any meaningful way since just after the layoff. She didn't nag him or cry or get hysterical. She just sat in there in deep, uncharacteristic silence.

Brooding.

He often thought things might be better if she did show some signs of losing her patience or temper. It would prove she still cared. It might give him just the kick in the ass he needed to get out and find some kind of job, even if he had to humble himself by taking some position that paid very little and was obviously beneath him. Fast food. Convenience store clerk. Car wash attendant. Something. Anything. He hoped like hell he could convince her to go with him to the film festival. He smiled at that. A real date. How long since they'd been anywhere together socially?

Months?

A year?

Too long, in any case. A night out might make her smile again. He'd give anything to see that.

But—

Where the hell is she?

The apartment was small. She could only be either in the bathroom or their bedroom. He shifted his weight, feeling the bloat of who-knew-how-many beers in his tender belly, and leaned forward in the recliner. "Marie?"

There was a faint note of panic in his voice. He recognized it and told himself it was stupid. There was no good reason to worry. She was lying down, taking a nap, or maybe was in the bathroom, taking a shit. No reason to worry. It quickly became a mantra.

No reason . . . no reason . . . no reason.

He made his voice even louder. "Marie!?"

Still no answer.

His heart was beating faster now, thudding heavily in his chest.

No reason . . . no reason . . .

"Shut up," he muttered as he hauled himself out of the recliner. The beer can slid from his shaking fingers and landed softly on the carpeted floor as he staggered toward the open bedroom door.

"Marie?"

His voice sounded weaker now, full of fear.

He stepped into the bedroom.

Marie was there, stretched out on the bed, and it became instantly clear why she had failed to answer his multiple entreaties. She was naked, her body very still and covered in blood. Her mouth hung open and her eyes stared up at nothing. Her hair was matted with sticky gore. It was easy to see why. Someone had used the heavy brass base of the nightstand lamp to smash in the back of her head. And she had been stabbed. A lot. More times than he could even begin to count.

She was dead.

Unmistakably, irreversibly, undeniably, completely fucking dead.

After a long moment's silence, a shrill, strangled sound issued from John's throat. He staggered closer to the bed, the strangled sound growing louder and more distraught with each step. Everything became more crisply defined. He saw how pulped her cheekbones were. He saw the crookedness of her previously perfectly straight nose. He saw white fragments of teeth amidst the dark gore on the bed sheet.

"Ohhhhhhhhhhhh . . ."

John's eyes rolled back in his head and his body pitched forward as he fell unconscious across his wife's bloody corpse.

TWO

Kira Matthews was in her usual mid-afternoon spot behind the counter at Mondo Mocha. She was leaning over the counter, her bare elbows propped on the scuffed and stained old wood of the counter top. The tip of a forefinger moved slowly over the screen of her iPad as she surfed over to another page of the horror festival's rather dinky website. Kira was no web designer, but even to her untrained eye the site's design seemed amateurish. Stock graphics combined with a clumsy, non-intuitive interface to render navigation a supremely irritating experience. Any site with multiple pages needed an all-purpose menu allowing quick navigation back to any page within the site, but the geniuses who'd put this thing together hadn't bothered. The only menu was on the main page, a very long column of links down the left-hand side of the page, which included links to pages with plot overviews, individual actor bios, director bios, and reviews. She'd surfed back to the main page somewhere in the neighborhood of six trillion and ten times. Just a rough estimate. If anything, that was lowballing it. The site triggered vague memories of early websites from the 90s, when she'd been a kid. She couldn't figure out whether the site's primitive design was an intentionally cheesy homage to web design of a bygone era or if it looked so bad simply because the designers really were that inept.

She had read nearly every page within the site at this point, lingering longest on the pages devoted to *Blood Lust,* a vampire film. It looked every bit as cheesy as the rest of the festival's roster of schlock, but she had a particularly fondness for vamps. The fascination had its roots in a youthful exposure to the film version of *Interview with the Vampire.* Thus began an obsession that occupied much of her teenage years. She devoured everything related to bloodsuckers, both in film and literature, accumulating an impressive collection of books and DVD's that encompassed all the classic works of the subgenre to all the cheesiest shitfests ever made and everything in between. Including the *Twilight* books, a thing she rarely confessed to these days.

Her exhaustive review of the horror festival's site was a testament to how monumentally bored she was. Most of her friends were out of town. Some just for the weekend, but most had scattered to the four corners of civilization for the summer. Today was Sunday, the day before Memorial Day, and most of the Mid-South University student population had cleared out of town shortly after finals a couple weeks back. The little coffee shop was campus adjacent and was a popular place for laid back studying and web surfing when classes were in session. Customer traffic would be light until the students began to return in mid-August. Right now, in fact, the shop was empty. The last paying customer of the afternoon had shuffled off almost a half hour earlier. The only other person in the shop at the moment was Miss Mildred, the owner. She was in the back doing some sort of half-assed inventory.

The bell above the door jangled as someone came into the coffee shop. Kira glanced up from her iPad and smiled when she saw Lashon Miller stroll up to the counter.

"Hey."

"Hey."

Lashon set a book on the counter and yawned as she stretched her arms over her head. Kira glanced at the book. *Wolves of the Calla* by Stephen King.

"Haven't you read that already?"

"Yeah."

"Don't you have any new books to read?"

Lashon shrugged. "Bored. Nothing new appeals right now. So I'm reading some shit I like again. Hook me up with a large caramel latte, please."

Kira set to work making the drink. "What are you doing tonight?"

Lashon flipped dark hair out of her face with a toss of her head and shifted her posture so that all her weight was balanced on one leg. She turned the little wire rack of folk CDs that sat on the counter. "Don't know. The usual, I guess. Sit at home. Be fucking bored. Unless, like, I go on an epic fucking killing spree down at the square. Still haven't ruled that out."

"So . . . still haven't patched things up with Greg?"

Lashon continued to slowly spin the wire rack. "No."

The monotone reply worried Kira. Lashon and Greg Nelson had been a hot item for over a year. They had been mad for each other, the kind of couple given to frequent public displays of affection, the super inappropriate, borderline-foreplay kind that made people uncomfortable. About a month ago it had come to an abrupt end. Lashon had refused to talk about it and so it had become a subject of gossip and speculation among the others in their circle.

Kira finished the drink and set the brimming plastic cup on the counter. Lashon picked up the cup and took a small sip, making a soft sound of satisfaction. "Mmm. I don't have any money."

"What?"

"I don't have any money."

Kira sighed. "For fuck's sake, Lashon."

Lashon took another sip of her drink and said nothing, but stared levelly at Kira.

Kira rolled her eyes. "Whatever, bitch. I'll pay for it."

"Thank you."

Kira forced a smile.

Right. Like I had a choice. Jesus.

Kira had precious little money of her own, but what else could she have done? With the possible exceptions of Jason and Monroe, Lashon was the closest friend she had made since moving to Murfreesboro after high school two years ago. She couldn't refuse her service or kick her out for non-payment. Nor could she just let her have the drink on the house. Miss Mildred was funny about that kind of thing, and you could never tell when she was watching you on that black and white security monitor in the back. The money was coming out of her pocket and that's all there was to it.

Lashon was looking at the CDs again.

Kira fumed the more she thought about it.

Something had to be said.

"Look—"

Lashon sighed. "He hit me."

"What?"

"Greg. He hit me."

Kira's expression softened. "Oh." Then her face hardened again. "That fucking asshole."

"Yeah."

Kira stared at her friend and thought back over the last month. She couldn't remember seeing any bruises on her face, but that didn't mean anything. He might have hit her where it wouldn't show. "I'm sorry."

Lashon's expression was strangely blank as she removed a CD by Ani DiFranco from the rack, flipped it over, and looked at the back. "Why? You didn't hit me."

Kira stared at her friend. There was something more than a little odd about her demeanor today. The drink thing was out of character. The timing of the abuse revelation was also questionable. It almost seemed as if it'd been meant to distract her. And, perhaps most disturbingly, she knew damn well Lashon Miller didn't give the first shit about Ani DiFranco or anyone else among the selection of NPR-approved artists on display on the little spinning rack.

"Will you put that fucking CD back please?"

Lashon looked at her again, her expression staying blank a moment longer. Then a corner of her mouth tilted upward in a cautious smile. "Okay."

She returned the CD to the rack.

"Happy?"

"Yes. Look—"

"I'm sorry I'm mooching a drink off you, okay?"

Kira smiled and felt something inside her relax. "Okay." Then she frowned again. "But what's this about Greg hitting you?"

Lashon took another sip of her drink, wincing as her lips pursed around the thin straw. She licked her lips after releasing the straw. "Okay. I sort of lied."

Now we're getting to it. About time.

Kira leaned against the counter. "So there was no physical abuse at all."

"Didn't say that. There was. I hit him."

Kira gaped at her. "What? Are you fucking serious?"

11

"Yeah."

Kira was reeling.

What . . . the . . . FUCK?

"Why? What did he do?"

"Nothing much."

Kira didn't know what to say. She just continued to stare at her friend in open-mouthed astonishment.

Lashon's expression now was somber instead of carefully blank. "It was all my fault. It was around finals time. I was so stressed the fuck out. And he was just frustrating me, pissing me off no matter what he did or said. Finally, I just snapped and hit him."

"When you say you 'hit' him . . ."

Lashon shook her head. "I know what you're thinking and I'm not talking about a slap or any fucking little love tap. I punched him. In the face. As hard as I could. I mean, I really let him have it." Moisture brimmed in her eyes. She made no move to wipe it away. "And, shit, I did it more than once. He just took it. I wish he'd hit me back."

Kira felt sick. "Jesus."

"Yeah. I chipped one of his teeth on my engagement ring." She held up her left hand and wiggled the bare fingers. "Which, by the way, I no longer have." She laughed softly as a tear rolled down her face. "So, no, I haven't patched things up with Greg. Or, rather, he hasn't patched things up with me. And I don't blame him. I don't know how to explain it. I just had a . . . mental break. I guess."

Kira couldn't believe what she was hearing. It went against everything she'd ever assumed about her friend. She would never in a million years have guessed Lashon possessed the potential for that kind of violence. And yet, there was none of that sense of awkward falseness she'd exuded before. Her gut told her this wasn't just more bullshit. It was the truth. Which was so fucked up on so many levels she couldn't even begin to wrap her head around it. "I just . . . I guess I never suspected you had that kind of rage inside you."

Lashon wiped tears away. "I'm just lucky he didn't call the cops. Do you hate me now?"

Kira shook her head. "I . . . no. I'll be honest, I don't understand this. It disturbs me, but I care about you."

Lashon smiled. "At least someone does. Are you . . . afraid of me?" She laughed too loudly then. "Hell, I know I'd be if someone unloaded a story like this on me."

Just say it. What she needs to hear.

"No. I'm not afraid of you."

Lashon looked grateful. "Oh, good. I'm glad. That means a lot. You're the only person I've told. It feels good to sort of . . . confess. Now if I could just stop feeling like I should step in front of a speeding bus and be done with all this misery."

Kira flinched. "Don't say things like that."

"Don't tell you how I really feel, you mean?"

Awkward silence time again.

Kira glanced at her iPad, noticing the horror festival's site for the first time since Lashon walked through the door. "Go out with me tonight."

Lashon smirked. "What, like on a date?"

Kira turned the iPad toward her. "I'm checking this out later. Jason and Monroe are going, too."

Lashon glanced at the screen, then looked at Kira, a corner of her mouth curling up. "*Those* guys." She rolled her eyes, but her attention returned to the screen. She touched the screen and navigated to the page for *Blood Lust*. That didn't surprise Kira. One of the things they'd first bonded over was their shared enthusiasm for all things vampy. "Shitty site."

"Shitty movies, too, probably. Super low-budget indie films made by nobodies. We'll get really drunk and make fun of the movies. It'll be fun and you could use a distraction. What do you say? You don't really want to stay in by yourself, do you?"

Lashon continued to scroll down the page and began to smile. "Maybe not. I, uh, still, you know, don't have any money."

"I'll pay."

Lashon beamed and stood up straight. "Fabulous. I'll go home and get myself ready."

"Pick you up at six?"

Lashon picked up her book and started toward the door. She raised her latte cup in a salute. "Sounds good."

Then the bell above the door jangled again and she was gone.

Kira stared after her for a long, pensive moment. Then she reached under the counter for her purse and took out her wallet. She extracted a sufficient amount to cover Lashon's latte and opened the register.

~

Hidden behind a corner of the liquor store on the other side of the street, Greg Nelson watched her come out of the coffee shop and start off at a brisk pace down the sidewalk, going in the opposite direction. Clad in black tights and a clingy black t-shirt, the willowy, dark-haired girl cut an angular figure against the glare of the bright sunlight. There was an extra spring in her step that hadn't been there prior to her entering the coffee shop. He'd even caught a glimpse of a smile on her face before she'd turned and gone in the other direction.

The change in her demeanor wasn't too hard to figure out. Her closest female friend, a flaky little blonde named Kira Matthews, worked at Mondo Mocha. The apparent lifting of Lashon's spirits had something to do with an exchange between the two, no doubt. He didn't like Kira much. She was a little too weird, with her interests in obscure music and movies no normal person had ever heard of. And—he could admit it—she was a little too smart. He had never been able to comfortably converse with her in any sort of depth on just about any subject. He didn't hate her, necessarily, but she was sort of like an alien life form. Too different and, ultimately, unknowable, at least for the likes of him.

He watched Lashon until she turned down a side street and disappeared from his sight.

His car was parked at the curb.

He got in and used an alternate route to drive to the apartment building where she lived.

THREE

The gun boomed and the bottle perched at a wobbly angle atop the rotting old tree stump exploded in a spray of green glass fragments. Silence descended over the rocky rural setting again as the gun's report faded in the shooter's ears. The field was a gentle slope, descending toward a line of green trees. It was at the southern perimeter of the many acres of rural land owned by the McKinley family for generations. Tucked away in a remote corner of Rutherford county, the property was just about as private a place as one could hope for in modern America. The nearest neighbors were miles distant and not apt to complain about the sound of gunfire even if they could hear it from here, which wasn't likely.

Brix Harris took aim at another green bottle. This one was balanced on a large rock some thirty yards down the slope. She dipped her head, squinted down the sight of the gun, and squeezed the trigger. Another spray of green glass fragments suddenly littered the countryside.

She smiled tightly in satisfaction. "Let the bodies hit the floor."

In her mind, it wasn't green glass flying across the landscape. Instead, she saw red. An explosion of it. Blood and brain matter blowing out of exit wounds, each squeeze of the trigger resulting in a flawless head shot. There were more empty bottles spread across the sloping field. Some were propped on rocks. Some were on tree stumps. Others were wedged into various spots on the ground. Until a few minutes ago, a row of gleaming green bottles had lined a slightly warped wooden plank balanced atop two old sawhorses. Her bullets had knocked them down with impressive precision. Not a shot was wasted. Again, though, she didn't see bottles, not in her mind. She saw bodies staggering backward down the slope, crashing clumsily into the ranks of lurching zombies behind them. She imagined the zombie horde slowly advancing on her, moaning and drooling with their hands extended in her direction, their decaying forms moving clumsily up the rocky incline as the relentless hunger that drove them propelled them forward toward their doom.

She squeezed the trigger again.

BOOM!

Again.

BOOM!

She heard a crunch of booted feet traversing the rocky ground behind her as she paused to reload. She slapped the fresh clip in and spun on her heels to aim the Glock dead-center between the interloper's wide blue eyes.

Trevor McKinley held up his hands. "Don't shoot."

Brix didn't lower the gun. "On your knees, motherfucker. Now!"

Trevor gingerly lowered himself to his knees and stared up at her. "Please don't kill me."

"Why not, bitch?"

"Because I love you."

She squinted at him. "Something crazy just came out of your mouth. What did you say to me?"

"I love you."

"Wow. You're pretty dumb. You know that?"

"Yeah."

She lowered the gun and engaged the safety. "Get up."

"You didn't have the safety on?"

A corner of her mouth curled up in a wry grin. "You ever know me to let a gun go off without meaning to?"

Trevor got to his feet and pulled her into an embrace. "Not unless you count my dick as a gun. A *love* gun. I think that's gone off earlier than you'd like a time or two."

She smiled and kissed him. "Yeah. You're getting better about that, though."

Trevor brushed a long lock of her blonde hair away from her face, tucking it gently behind an ear, then he tilted his head slightly and stared at her with that familiar mix of worshipful adoration and intense desire. He was constantly telling her how he couldn't believe a girl as pretty as her was interested in him and there were times she detected a quiet desperation in these soulful gazes of his. It was as if he was convinced their time together came with a pre-stamped expiration date and that he had to savor every moment like this one to the fullest, just drink in as much of her as he could before she inevitably moved on to someone more worthy. He was selling himself short, but she'd just about given up trying to make him believe that. She wished she could make him understand that, as far as she was concerned, this relationship was for keeps. It didn't matter that they were so young, with her still a teenager at nineteen and he having just turned twenty. Nor did it matter that most everyone she knew changed partners with a frequency that made her head spin.

She raised up on her toes slightly and moved her face closer to his, dropping her voice to a breathy whisper: "Brix plus Trevor, together forever." She kissed him softly on the mouth, eliciting a slight shiver from him. Then she kissed him again, leaning into him. "Forever and ever. And ever and—"

This time what she elicited from him was a lustful grunt. His arms wrapped tighter around her as he kissed her with an abandon that stole her breath and weakened her knees. But she didn't let go of the gun the whole time. The hand holding it stayed at the small of his back, aiming the weapon carefully away from him. They made out for several minutes more before she placed the palm of her free hand flat against his chest and pushed him gently away.

She stared intently up at him. "Your folks home?"

"Yeah."

"Shit."

He nodded toward the woods. "We could do it out there."

She shook her head. "No. I'm not gonna have a bunch of bugs crawling all over me while we fuck."

"What then?"

She smiled. "We'll drive out to the lake and do it in my car, like last weekend. That was nice, wasn't it?"

He was smiling, too. "Yeah, it was." Then his smile faltered. "Um

. . ."

She frowned. "What? Spit it out."

His shoulders sagged. "You remember my friend Monroe?"

"Your high school buddy."

"That's him. Anyway . . . he invited us out to Murfreesboro. There's a horror film festival playing at a theater there this weekend and tonight's the last night. They're gonna party and catch a couple of the movies. I sort of said we might do it, but I'll call him back and tell him—"

"Hold on. Would I know any of these movies?"

Trevor was shaking his head before she finished the question. "No way. They all look like FearNet rejects, barely better than home movies, but one of them's a zombie thing."

"Zombies?"

Trevor was unable to suppress a reluctant smile. "Yeah."

She sighed. "I love zombies."

"I know. So . . ."

"We haven't been to Murfreesboro in a while."

"That's true."

"And I don't have to work tomorrow."

"And I don't work at all, which I totally know I need to do something about, but the point is that—"

"We're going."

"Okay then." But now Trevor's brow creased. "But what about . . . you know . . ."

She smirked. "The fucking?"

"Uh, yeah . . . that."

She pressed the Glock into one of his hands and made him curl his fingers around the grip. "Kill a zombie for me. Just one. And we'll go do it in the woods, bugs be damned."

Trevor's frown deepened as he moved away from her and took aim at the nearest green bottle, which sat atop the largest rock in the field some twenty yards straight down the slope. She'd intentionally been saving that one for him. Trevor didn't have her natural gift for sharp-shooting. Even this one gimme shot wasn't actually a given. He took a deep breath and let it out. He was taking his time, making sure of the shot he was about to take. His arms were as steady as she'd ever seen them. He took one more deep breath, slowly exhaled, and then squeezed the trigger. The bullet went wide and chipped bark off a tree at the bottom of the slope.

"Shit!"

Brix smiled. "It's okay. We'll do it any—"

He shifted his weight and swung his arms slightly to the left, taking aim at another bottle farther down the slope. The gun boomed again. The bottle remained intact. His face became a twisted mask of frustration. Brix took a step toward him, concern etching her features.

He didn't look at her. "Stay back."

She stopped in her tracks. "This really isn't important. It's just a game. Let's go have some fun."

He forced his jaw open and let out another big breath. "You're wrong. It is important."

He squeezed the trigger.

The bottle exploded.

Brix pumped a fist into the air as a big grin curved across her face. "Yeah! *Fuck* yeah!"

She ran to him and jumped into his arms, making him drop the gun in surprise. Then he was grinning too as he swung her around one time before setting her back down on the ground. They kissed with renewed hunger and urgency for several moments, until Brix broke the clinch, quickly scooped up the fallen gun, and seized him forcefully by the hand.

"Let's go."

She started tugging him down the slope.

Toward the woods.

"Come ravish me, you badass zombie killer."

Trevor required no further prompting.

FOUR

The theater was adjacent to a little strip mall that had seen better days. Half the storefronts were shuttered. The businesses that were still open included a pawnshop, a car title loan company, and a cash lending service. That most of the current mall tenants were the sort that existed primarily to prey upon the misfortunes of low-income families was just one of a number of clues this wasn't one of the ritzier parts of town. The unpleasantly fragrant homeless dude sprawled out on a bench in front of the pizza buffet next door to the pawnshop was another. Ditto for the used car lot on the other side of the street. It had plenty of colorful pennants flapping in the breeze, but this did nothing to distract one's attention from the uniformly shabby condition of the decrepit vehicles on display. It was one of those tote-the-note places, where you could get a car without a credit check. Trouble was, all the cars were unreliable crap. Not one of the vehicles on display had been manufactured in this century.

Monroe Taylor leaned against the side of his friend Jason's own second-rate ride—a poorly maintained 1978 Chevy Malibu—and took a slow sip from a jug of hunch punch as he surveyed the squalid urban landscape. He remembered his mom bringing him to this mall as a kid. A K-Mart had been the mall's anchor tenant, the big draw that pulled in crowds, a healthy percentage of which trickled down to other then-profitable establishments like the Blockbuster video store and the cool record shop where he'd spent hours browsing the wide selection of metal and punk albums. But K-Mart had pulled up stakes a decade ago and the record store followed not long after. The formerly halfway nice area then descended into an apparently irreversible pattern of decay. This was the first time Monroe had visited the area in years.

This being early evening on a Sunday, the mall's parking lot was mostly empty. The parking lot of the Sunshine 6 cineplex was only marginally fuller. Maybe a dozen and a half cars were scattered across the lot. Monroe took another sip of from the plastic jug of hunch punch. It was a berry-flavored punch mixed with a generous dose of Everclear, 190 proof pure grain alcohol. He was already feeling a mild buzz. That was good. He wanted to do a slow burn, go in feeling a little tipsy and then get steadily hammered throughout the night. It was the last night of the three-day festival, which would run into the wee morning hours. His plan was to see three of the six movies before all was said and done. He thought he'd start with the zombie picture, because it looked like the best of the bunch and he wanted to be at least mildly sober for it, then move on to that crappy-looking chainsaw thing, and then wind up the night with either that vampire movie or that haunted house ghost thing.

He took yet another sip of hunch punch.

Something kicked the car window behind him.

Someone screamed.

Monroe grimaced. "Jesus."

His best friend, Jason Tatum, was fucking Nikki Carson in the back seat of the Malibu. That was probably her foot kicking against the window. She screamed again and kicked the window again. Monroe sighed and pushed away from the car, walking off a few yards out of annoyance. But he didn't begrudge them their good time. He'd be doing the same thing if a willing sex partner happened to be handy.

He drank more hunch punch and stared out at the street.

A silver Hyundai rolled up to a stop at the intersection, pulled through it, and turned left into the theater's parking lot. Monroe smiled as he recognized the car. It belonged to Kira Matthews. Someone was with her. Another girl. As the Hyundai drew closer, Monroe took a closer look at Kira's passenger and realized he knew her.

Lashon Miller.

Huh.

Lashon was all right, but she could come across as a little stuck up. She definitely thought she was a better class of person than Monroe. Which was sort of true. She was smarter and better educated (Monroe having dropped out of college after his first disastrous semester), and she sometimes let him know this in not-so-subtle ways. Which stung, but she was also often nice to him. She was a hard girl to figure out, but Kira really liked her and that was good enough for him.

The Hyundai pulled to a stop a space over from the Malibu. Kira's window rolled down and she smiled out at him. "Hey."

"Hey."

"Been here long?"

"Maybe fifteen minutes."

Lashon leaned over from her seat, stared up at him through the window. "What's that you're drinking?"

"Berry punch and Everclear."

"Gimme some."

"Sure."

He sauntered over to the Hyundai and passed the jug through the window. Lashon took it and knocked back a sizable gulp. She licked her lips. "Yum."

Monroe stared at her. She looked really cute tonight, wearing a short black skirt and a clingy, shoulder-baring black top. Her shoulder-length black hair looked like it had been done recently. It looked glossy and perfect. Kira looked good, too, in denim cutoffs and a white tank top. It was hard to say which one he might have the better shot with, in romantic terms, just theoretically speaking. Kira was a friend. Their relationship was formed initially out of a mutual fondness for British television and Japanese horror movies and he'd never put the moves on her out of respect for the friendship. Still, he'd always found her attractive.

A faint scream rang out.

Lashon shifted in her seat to peer past him at the Malibu. "What's going on over there?"

"Jason's fucking Nikki Carson in the Malibu."

Lashon unclipped her seatbelt and opened the door on her side. She climbed out and peered at Monroe over the roof. "Let's harass them."

"Uh . . ."

Lashon gave him a quick once-over as she came around from the other side of the Hyundai. "You look good, Monroe. You've lost weight."

"Uh . . ."

Strange comment. Point of fact, he hadn't lost any weight since the last time he'd seen Lashon. Hell, he was pretty sure he'd put on a couple pounds. Not that it mattered. He was a pretty skinny dude, so he could afford to gain some. She was just being purposefully flattering. He wasn't sure whether that was a good or a bad thing. With a girl like Lashon, you could just never tell. It could be a totally innocuous comment or she could have some kind of weird, unknowable ulterior motive.

She passed the punch jug to him and continued on toward the Malibu. Monroe glanced at the car and saw the sole of one of Nikki's small feet pressed flat against the glass. Then he looked at Kira as she got out of the Hyundai and threw her door shut.

"Lashon says I've lost weight."

Kira looked him over, then rolled her eyes. "You might get lucky tonight. She and Greg are finished, for real."

"Really?"

"Yeah."

"Wow."

Monroe wondered if he could bum a rubber from Jason. Just in case. He'd have to be smooth about asking, being sure to do it when Lashon was out of earshot. Of course, it was highly unlikely he'd actually wind up getting with her, but it couldn't hurt to be prepared.

Kira scowled at him. "You don't have to be so excited."

Monroe made his smile go away. "I'm not excited."

"Are, too."

"Whatever."

Huh. What if Kira and Lashon both wanted him?

That'd be a tough motherfucking dilemma.

Lashon leaned over the back of the Malibu and peered through the rear windshield. She rapped her knuckles on the window and giggled at the shriek this elicited from Nikki. A dim shout of "You bitch!" could be heard from the interior of the car.

Lashon giggled again and kept peering through the window. "Ooh, look, Jason's got a big pink pimple on his left ass cheek. That's nasty."

More shouts from the car.

Lashon gave them a cheery wave and came back to where Kira and Monroe were standing. "That Nikki chick is kind of hot. How did a loser like Jason get with her?"

Monroe shrugged. "I, uh . . ."

"Never mind. Let's have some more of that fucking punch."

Monroe passed the jug back to her and she took another healthy swig. "Mmm. Man, I plan on getting good and fucked the fuck up tonight. And maybe get laid." She pressed the jug into Kira's hands. "Stop looking all scowly, bitch. We're here to have fun. Drink up."

Kira accepted the jug with obvious reluctance. "I only want to get a little buzzed. I'm driving, remember?"

She started to pass the jug back to Monroe after a tiny sip, then stopped, frowning. "That really does taste good."

She took a bigger drink.

Lashon laughed. "Rock on. Fuck moderation. Hey, you never know when the world might end. It could happen tonight, while we're in that dump of a theater. A fucking nuclear bomb could drop right on our heads while we're watching shitty movies. We could all just suddenly die. Like *that*." She snapped her fingers. "So you might as well party like there's no fucking tomorrow. You don't want to have been all boring and responsible and shit in the last moments of your existence, do you?"

Kira took one more big swallow and passed the jug back to Monroe. "Oh, whatever. Last thing I want is a DUI. That should do me for a while."

Monroe said, "The possibility of all-out nuclear war is really kind of remote these days anyway."

Lashon looked at him. "Is that right?"

Monroe nodded. "Yeah. And even if it happened, I seriously doubt whoever was attacking us would waste a nuclear warhead on fucking Murfreesboro. Those things are expensive and there's nothing worth wiping out here anyway."

Lashon's expression turned pensive. "Huh. You've got a point. I'm not sure the rest of the world would even notice we were gone."

"Probably not. And if anyone did notice, they'd be all like, 'Whoa, Murfreesboro got flattened by a fucking nuclear bomb. Never heard of that fuckin' place.'" He smirked. "Hell, I'm not sure it'd even really count as an attack on America, per se."

Lashon snatched the hunch punch jug from Monroe. "You're a

funny motherfucker sometimes, you know that?"

Monroe grunted. "Yeah. I know. Shit."

They heard a creak of rusty hinges as the Malibu's passenger side door swung open. The seat on that side was shoved forward and Jason Tatum emerged from the car wearing only his jeans. A couple of empty tall boy beer cans fell out of the car and clattered on the asphalt. Jason had a muscular build and a moderately hairy chest. He had shoulder-length brown hair and looked like he hadn't shaved in at least a day. A cigarette was wedged into a corner of his mouth. "Any of you peeping Tom motherfuckers got a light?"

Lashon dug a plastic Bic out of her little handbag. "Here ya go, stud."

Jason lit the cigarette and blew smoke at her. "Enjoy the show?"

Lashon smiled. "Mixed review. Good energy, but your performance could use a little work. I'd be happy to give you some pointers."

Jason passed the lighter back and stared at her.

Monroe frowned.

Huh.

"He doesn't need any pointers, bitch."

Nikki had come out of the car. She was a short but very curvy girl. The tight white shorts and baby-doll t-shirt she wore emphasized a full figure that was just plain distracting. Monroe usually tried to avoid looking right at her. Otherwise he'd stare and drool and that would be awkward.

Lashon directed another smile at Nikki. "Relax. I'm just joking around."

Nikki wrapped her arms around Jason, mashing her enormous breasts against his ribs. She glared at Lashon. "Better be."

Lashon kept on smiling. "If I know what's good for me, right?"

Monroe started to get a twitchy feeling. *Uh-oh. This could get ugly.*

Kira cleared her throat. "Uh . . . maybe we should go get our tickets."

Jason smiled and draped an arm around Nikki's shoulders. "Nah. Movies won't start for an hour yet. Let's hang and party some more first."

The gesture of physical affection from Jason seemed to relax Nikki. A lot of the tension went out of her posture as she smiled and said, "Yeah, I wanna get fucked up. Gimme that jug, bitch."

Lashon reluctantly surrendered the jug.

Monroe glanced at Kira. "Yeah, let's hang a while. Besides, we're still waiting for someone."

Kira squinted at him. "Who?"

"Old buddy of mine. We were tight in high school. Trevor McKinley. I've mentioned him before."

Kira nodded slowly. "Yeah. I think I remember."

"Anyway, he and his girl are coming. Apparently she's crazy for zombies. They'll be seeing *Rise of the Dead* first, which is my plan as well."

Kira blew out a petulant breath. "Hmph. I want to see *Blood Lust* first."

Monroe grinned. "You and your vampires."

Kira made direct eye contact with him, holding his gaze for a long moment. "See it with me."

"I, uh . . . sort of promised I'd see the zombie thing with Trevor first."

Kira suddenly gripped him by the hand. "See it with me." She squeezed his hand and smiled. "Please?"

Lashon laughed. She already sounded a little drunk. "Dumbass. Say yes, or you're even dumber than you look."

Kira squeezed his hand again.

Monroe swallowed hard. "Uh . . ."

Fuck.

His head was spinning. The world had turned upside down. Although he'd vaguely entertained romantic notions regarding Kira, he'd never taken them too seriously, figuring he was the kind of guy she'd like for a friend but never anything else. He was a fun goofball she could pal around with and that was that. Except, apparently, he'd been dead wrong.

He didn't know what to think, scarcely knew what to say.

He sighed. "Trevor will be pissed."

Kira smiled. "He'll get over it. And we'll see whatever they want right after. Sound good?"

Monroe found himself smiling, too. "Yeah. It does."

A black Ford F-150 pulled into the theater's parking lot and headed in their direction. The truck parked behind the Malibu and both doors swung open. The guy who emerged from the truck's passenger side was Trevor McKinley, his friend. The girl, who had been driving, was blonde-haired and strikingly pretty, but she looked kind of country in her denim jacket, tight blue jeans, and boots. That didn't surprise Monroe. Trevor still lived with his folks out in the sticks. His friend looked kind of country himself in his crisp, freshly-laundered blue jeans and buttoned-up flannel shirt.

Jason favored the newcomers with a sideways grin. "You must be the infamous Trevor McKinley. Heard a lot about you from my bro. Good to meet ya."

He removed his arm from Nikki's shoulders and extended a hand.

Trevor shook the proffered hand. "Same."

The girl was wearing a *Dawn of the Dead* t-shirt under her denim jacket. It showed a hollow-eyed bald zombie over the title, an image from the original version. Monroe realized she was looking right at him. She was smiling but had a peculiarly intense vibe about her. She approached him but didn't offer her hand. "You're Monroe."

"The name they gave me, yeah."

"I've seen pictures, that's how I know who you are. Trevor really loves you."

Monroe felt suddenly uncomfortable. "Uh . . ."

Kira laughed. "Damn, girl, you can't say shit like that to guys. They have manly images to protect."

The girl looked at Kira. "Yeah, but I don't care about shit like that and so Trevor doesn't either. I'm Brix, by the way."

She kept looking at Kira. She still didn't offer her hand.

Lashon laughed. "Brix? As in bricks, the building material?"

The girl's oddly intense smile vanished. "As in B-R-I-X. It's my name. Got it?"

Lashon exchanged a guarded look with Kira. "Uh, yeah . . . got it."

Monroe sensed Kira's discomfort. He couldn't blame her. The girl was pretty, but there was something undeniably off and weird about her. He was sort of glad now that he wouldn't be seeing the first movie with them.

Monroe belatedly realized that Jason and Trevor were laughing and talking, apparently oblivious to the strange tension Brix was generating in everyone else. Even Lashon had fallen silent, which was unlike her, especially when she had some booze in her. It was cool that Jason and Trevor seemed to be hitting it off. He'd been worried about that.

Jason barked loud laughter about something, then walked over to the Malibu, where he reached into the back and fished out a Slayer t-shirt and his shoes. He pulled the t-shirt on and stepped into the shoes as he continued talking to Trevor. Once he was fully dressed, he reached into the car again and pulled out a cooler. Monroe heard the sloshing sound of partially melted ice. Jason flipped the cooler's lid open, pulled out beers, and started passing them around.

Monroe capped the jug of hunch punch before accepting a can of PBR. He passed the jug to Jason, who shoved it down inside the cooler. The buzz of conversation grew more boisterous as the booze continued to flow. Brix even seemed to warm to the rest of them a little after pounding a couple cans of brew. Before they knew it, it was time to head up to the theater.

As they started in that direction, Kira gave Monroe a little nudge in the ribs with her elbow.

He looked at her. "Yeah?"

Her brow was slightly creased. "It's funny. I was sure this place had closed a long time ago."

"Huh." Now Monroe was frowning, too. He stared at the theater marquee, where the titles of the movies were spelled out in black block letters. He didn't spend a lot of time in this part of town, but he did come through here once a week or so en route to other places. He tried in vain to recall the last time he'd seen the marquee lit up like this. "Maybe they just reopened."

"Maybe."

She didn't sound certain. There was even a small hint of wariness in her tone. Which was silly. It was just a movie theater. What was there to worry about?

~

A few more cars pulled into the theater's parking lot shortly after tickets went on sale. Two of the late arrivals were John Dorsey and Greg Nelson.

John parked his Camry in a remote corner of the lot, far away from any other cars. He sat slumped behind the steering wheel. His eyes were red-rimmed and puffy. He'd been crying almost non-stop for hours, ever since he'd regained consciousness to find himself sprawled across his wife's bloody corpse. He'd been acting irrationally from that moment forward. Rather than calling the police, he'd changed out of his bloody clothes and into clean ones. And then he'd left the apartment and started cruising aimlessly around the city with an open twelve-pack of Coors in the seat beside him. He didn't believe he'd killed his wife. He simply wasn't capable of it, not even in a drunken stupor. As implausible as it sounded, the only explanation was that some maniac had come in and savagely slaughtered Marie while he was passed out, inexplicably leaving him alive. He believed with all his heart that this was what had happened. And yet, instead of acting in a sane way, he was doing illogical things authorities would undoubtedly perceive as the actions of a guilty party.

But he couldn't seem to help himself. He wasn't in his right mind at all.

He choked down one more beer and got out of the car.

As John staggered toward the theater, Greg Nelson watched his drunken progress with a disdainful fascination. The drunk was weaving badly. Twice he bumped into parked cars and nearly tumbled to the ground. The man was pathetic. Clearly a late-stage alcoholic.

Not that Greg cared.

He had concerns of his own, after all. He spied Kira's silver Hyundai almost immediately. It was empty. She and Lashon were already inside the theater. He parked on the other side of the lot and turned his car's engine off.

He made no move to get out of the car.

He would wait another ten to fifteen minutes, long enough for the feature presentations to begin. Then he would go up to the box office and purchase a ticket, just another late-arriving fright film fan. According to Lashon's blog entry from this afternoon, the movie they'd be seeing first was *Rise of the Dead*.

The was so helpful of her, posting her plans for all the world to see.

She would never know he was in the theater with her.

FIVE

The man in the ticket booth had a swarthy complexion and eyes that looked too big for his head, the orbs bulging from their sockets in a deeply unsettling way. He was slender and wore a rumpled and ill-fitting tuxedo. He greeted each customer with a tersely uttered and oddly formal "Good evening, sir" or "Good evening, madam." His accent was vaguely foreign but not immediately identifiable. A pencil-thin mustache made him look like a silent film actor, as did slicked-back short black hair. Rings of varying types and sizes adorned each of his fingers. The rings struck Monroe as odd. In his experience, men who were not mobsters or rap stars did not wear rings, unless they were to signify marriage, successful completion of high school or college in a particular year, or fraternity affiliation.

Jason, being devoid of tact, of course had to comment as soon as he stepped up to the ticket window. "Dude. What's up with all the fucking rings?"

"Do you wish to buy a ticket?"

A snort. "How did you guess? *Two* motherfucking tickets, pal. What are you, some kind of gypsy fortune teller?"

The ticket seller pushed a button and two paper tickets popped out of a slot on the metal counter. "I am not a gypsy. Two tickets is fifty dollars."

"Fifty fucking dollars? Are you for real?"

The man's strange smile did not falter. "One ticket buys access to all movies. You may see one or you may see them all. Do you wish to pay or not?"

Jason brought out his wallet, a black cloth thing emblazoned with the words BAD MOTHERFUCKER in block lettering, like Samuel Jackson's wallet in *Pulp Fiction*. Which happened to be his favorite movie. He counted out bills and pushed them through the slot in the ticket window. "Are you sure you're a dude?"

The ticket seller pushed the tickets through the slot. "You are holding up the line, sir. Please move along so that I may service the next customer."

Nikki, standing beside Jason, giggled. "*Service.*"

Several people in the vicinity also tittered.

Jason snatched up the tickets. He took Nikki by an arm and began to steer her toward the entrance. But he couldn't resist one last snide shot at the weird ticket seller. "I'm curious about your sex change operation. I've got a general understanding of how the man-into-a-woman process works, but the other way around's a mystery. What did they use to make your dick?"

"Move along, sir. Please."

"Oh, and what's up with your eyes? You should see a doctor about that."

"Sir, if you don't—"

Jason's loud laughter cut him off. "It's cool. I'll leave you alone now. Whatever you are."

Nikki giggled again and then they were pushing open the glass door to the left of the ticket booth and stepping into the theater. Monroe reached for his wallet as he and Kira stepped up to the window. Kira gripped his arm lightly and spoke in an emphatic tone: "No. I'm paying."

Monroe frowned. He didn't know how to feel about that. For one thing, he wasn't sure if this qualified as an official date. On dates, guys were expected to do things like buy tickets and pick up the check at restaurants. It was one of the rules and everyone knew it. On the other hand, he didn't have a lot of money currently and it was tempting to let Kira pay.

"Look—"

Kira looked him in the eye. "I'm paying. Seriously. It's no big deal. I already told Lashon I'd pay her way in and, because you're my date now, I'll get your ticket, too."

"Um . . ."

Lashon sighed behind them. "Will you just let her do it? You know you can't win arguments with her."

Monroe did know that. "Okay. Whatever."

Kira stepped up to the booth and purchased three tickets. Monroe noted a flyer taped to the booth's glass window. It read, *Doctor Ominous presents The Late Night Horror Show!!!*

"Who the hell is this Doctor Ominous dude?"

Lashon snorted. "Who cares?"

Moments later they were inside the theater. Another slender, tuxedo-wearing man with a swarthy complexion stood at a metal stanchion to the rear of the booth. He took their tickets, tore them in half, and wished them a pleasant evening. Monroe glanced back at him as they moved further into the lobby and approached the concessions stand. Then he looked at Kira. "This must be a family business."

"Yeah."

"Those dudes look exactly alike. I mean *exactly*."

"I know that. I have eyes of my own, you know."

"I'm just sayin' . . . it's fuckin' eerie."

Kira shrugged. "Maybe they're twins."

Lashon slugged him in the shoulder. "Try triplets."

Monroe followed her eyes and did a double-take when he saw the man standing behind the concessions counter. This man wore a bow tie and a black satin vest over a starched white shirt, but physically he was another virtual clone of the ticket seller, with the same slender build, complexion, thin mustache, and slicked back hair.

Monroe leaned close to Kira to whisper in her ear. "What'd I fucking tell you? *Eerie*."

Kira squinted at the guy in the bow tie. "Yeah. Okay. Maybe you're right."

Jason and Nikki were already at the counter. Jason caught Monroe's eye and grinned. He jerked a thumb at the man in the bow tie, whose back was turned to them at the moment. He was scooping fresh popcorn into a large bucket. "You see this shit?"

Monroe stepped closer to his friend and kept his voice low. "They all look alike."

"*Exactly* alike."

"That's what I said."

"It's weird."

"Weird as *fuck*."

Brix Harris abruptly moved into Monroe's field of vision, stepping right up to Jason and getting in his face. She and Trevor had been behind Lashon in the ticket queue. Her body language was visibly hostile. "Jason."

He frowned at her. "Yeah. What's your problem?"

"I just like to know what kind of people I'm hanging out with. I'd like to know if you always act like a retarded monkey in public."

"The fuck are you talking about?"

His tone was harsh, but she didn't back off one bit. "That obnoxious display at the ticket window. Did you think you were funny?"

His frown slowly transformed into a crooked smile. "Shit. I *know* I was funny."

"You sounded kind of like a bigot."

The frown returned. "What?"

"You heard me."

"Goddamn. How the fuck did you get that out of anything I said?"

"I've got transgendered friends. Think about it."

Jason, looking incredulous, stared at her. "It was a *joke*, for fuck's sake. And I've got a hard time believing you have friends."

"Fuck you."

"Fuck *you*."

Brix's acid tone seemed thick with the threat of real violence. "You're an idiot. And you better watch yourself."

Jason shook his head. "Are you seriously scolding me, like I'm some kind of little kid? I'm just having fun. You're not my mama, so piss off with that shit. And knock off the stupid threats. You don't scare me. Got it?"

"Just mind your damn manners so I don't have to kick your ass."

The man in the bow tie cleared his throat. Jason blinked and looked at him. The items he'd ordered were on the counter. He picked up the popcorn bucket and passed the over-sized fountain soda cup to Nikki, who was glaring at Brix. Jason looked at Monroe, then at Trevor. "I could say a lot of things here, but I'm just gonna keep my fuckin' mouth shut, out of consideration to my friends."

He and Nikki walked away.

Brix glared after him for a moment before returning to the back of the line.

Monroe leaned close to Kira. "Awkward silence."

She responded with a grunt and spoke under her breath. "Yeah."

Monroe shrugged the weirdness of the moment away and approached the counter. They ordered popcorn with extra butter, candy, and large sodas, then headed off to the theater showing *Blood Lust*. Lashon accepted the candy and soda purchased for her by Kira and went off by herself to the theater showing *Chainsaw Maniac*, having abruptly decided she didn't want to be in the same theater with Brix Harris. And she thought it'd be nice to give Kira and Monroe some space while they watched the vamp movie, making it more like a real date for them. At least for the first movie. She'd catch the second screening of the zombie flick with them, avoiding the weird Harris girl altogether.

Though he'd been the focus of Brix's hostility, Jason wasn't about to let that sway him from seeing the first screening of *Rise of the Dead*. Given the number of people present, the theater would be mostly empty anyway. He and Nikki would just sit far away from the weird hicks, making out for ninety-some minutes while the end of the world played out on the big screen.

The initial screening of *Blood Lust* was lightly attended, to understate. Monroe and Kira had the back row of the theater to themselves. Another couple sat in the row closest to the screen, a world away. They had the place virtually to themselves. The theater lights went down and the requisite safety announcement appeared on the screen. Kira leaned closer to him and dipped a hand inside the large bucket of popcorn propped on his lap. Monroe put an arm around her shoulders and she leaned even closer. An MPAA advisory appeared on the screen and the first coming attractions trailer began soon after.

Monroe smiled.

The real fun was about to begin.

SIX

John Dorsey took no note of any oddities regarding the theater employees. He was too off kilter physically and emotionally for such things to register. The employees, in turn, opted to ignore the pint bottle of whiskey shoved down his right hip pocket, though the outline of the bottle was very plain to see. At any other theater on any other night, the bottle would have been confiscated by theater staff before he was allowed in. He was so drunk many theaters might have barred him from entering at all. But the Sunshine 6 was no ordinary theater and, despite appearances to the contrary, the employees were not actually human. He purchased his ticket and entered the theater with no complications. He staggered over to the concessions stand, purchased a fountain soda, and promptly reeled off in the direction of the nearest auditorium, which turned out to be the one showing *Chainsaw Maniac*.

Some fifteen minutes later, Greg Nelson got out of his car, walked up to the ticket booth, and purchased a ticket. Unlike John, he was absolutely sober and therefore noticed the employees' similarity in appearance along with a few other odd little quirks, including the way their dark complexions masked somewhat the flawlessness of their flesh, which was devoid of any wrinkles or blemishes. Their skin had an almost artificial quality to it, as if they weren't quite real at all. Greg dismissed this as fanciful nonsense as he entered the theater, where he bypassed the concessions stand and headed directly for the auditorium showing *Rise of the Dead*.

~

The lights had gone down in each auditorium in the Sunshine 6. The theater safety announcements and lame commercials were over. Trailers for all six films that were a part of the Late Night Horror Festival were being screened now.

Brix Harris and Trevor McKinley were kicked back in seats in the approximate middle of the auditorium screening *Rise of the Dead*. Brix had her right leg up, with her foot wedged into the space between the two empty seats in front of her. She munched on a piece of popcorn and watched the trailer for *Blood Lust*, which looked boring as hell. It was the usual angst-ridden vampire nonsense. This impression had nothing to do with how pissed she was that Trevor's friend had opted to see it first with that hipster chick Kira rather than sticking to the original plan. She loved horror in general, but vampires were her least favorite of all the major monsters. Modern authors and filmmakers were too prone to portraying them as objects of desire or as potential romantic partners. *Puke*. The old vampires were all right. Bela Lugosi and Christopher Lee. All those old Universal and Hammer Films classics. But the angsty shit?

Fucking . . . PUKE.

The *Blood Lust* trailer ended at last, mercifully. A trailer for something called *House of the Damned* began a few moments later. It looked better than *Blood Lust*—almost anything would—but it stirred no real excitement in her. It was a haunted house thriller. There were scenes of people dying in weird accidents apparently caused by hostile poltergeist activity. The main characters were introduced in a series of quick cuts. They were ghost hunters or something. It looked like a tedious rip-off of *Paranormal Activity*.

Whatever.

The trailer ended.

Kim smiled.

Just two to go and then—*ZOMBIES!*

She glanced at Trevor, who was watching her in his standard adoring way. As usual, he was far more interested in her than anything else that was going on. She leaned over for a kiss and felt his tongue flick between her lips. The physical contact sent a delicious shiver through her body. She couldn't help thinking back to the wild abandon of their coupling in the woods this afternoon. When she was with Trevor, it was as if the rest of the world didn't exist at all. She bit down on his lower lip, making an animal sound deep in her throat and eliciting a groan from him in return.

She abruptly broke the clinch and popped another piece of popcorn into her mouth. She smiled. "*Zombies.*"

He chuckled. "Yeah. Yay, zombies. I just wish Monroe was here. Then I could relax and watch the movie without being distracted by your hotness."

Her expression darkened. "Monroe needs a better class of friends."

"We don't really know them."

Brix grunted. "I know all I need to know. Fuck them."

Trevor didn't say anything this time, but his discomfort was palpable. She knew he thought she was too judgmental. What he didn't understand was that life was too short to waste trying to accommodate assholes. She didn't have room in her life for obnoxious clowns like Jason Tatum, end of story. The same went for his dimwitted busty girlfriend. Kira and Lashon weren't as bad, but they both irritated her in different ways. They were the kind of chicks who thought they were better than regular people because they were in college. Smarter and more sophisticated. The hell with both of them.

So status quo. The only person she gave a damn about was Trevor.

And he was right here with her.

She squeezed his hand.

Another trailer was starting. The very last one before the feature presentation.

Brix grinned in anticipation.

The zombies were almost here.

~

A quick scan of the auditorium showed maybe as many as two dozen people seated and waiting to see *Rise of the Dead*. Given the paltry number of cars in the parking lot, Greg deduced that a large majority of the paying customers had elected to see this film first.

The door swung shut behind him as he moved further down the aisle. It was too dark to identify any individual from this distance, but he could see that most of the audience was comprised of couples on dates, with one largish group of perhaps five or six people seated together in the front row. From the noise they were making, he assumed they were drunk teenagers. A few other people sat alone at various spots throughout the auditorium, usually well removed from anyone else. In his effort to locate Lashon, Greg elected to ignore the singles and the large group up front. He took a few more tentative steps down the aisle and attempted to study the rest of the attendees without being obvious about it. Despite his efforts at subtlety, a pretty blonde girl in a denim jacket caught him looking and flipped him a middle finger. Her expression made it clear she was not to be fucked with and he quickly moved along.

~

Lashon was having second thoughts. The decision to see *Chainsaw Maniac* had been made hastily. She hadn't wanted to be around that weirdo Brix and had tried to do something nice for her friend by giving her some space. The latter was admirable, she supposed. The kind of thing a real friend just did now and then. Considering she'd abused her friendship with Kira lately, it was no doubt the *right* thing to have done. But here she was. Alone. *Goddammit.* She did not care for this shit at all.

Here I am, she thought. *Sitting by myself in a smelly old decrepit theater waiting to see a movie about a chainsaw-wielding asshole butchering young virgins. I am not a pimply sixteen-year-old boy with a head full of fucked up slasher fantasies, so what's wrong with this fucking picture?*

"The hell with this."

It was time to swallow her pride and get out of here. She still had just enough time to get to the theater showing *Blood Lust* before the final trailer ended. She wouldn't even have to bother or intrude on Kira and Monroe. She could maybe sit a few seats down from them. Close enough to her friend that she didn't feel so alone while still allowing her some space. She grabbed her purse, stood up, and smoothed out her skirt. She made her way down the row of seats to the aisle. The half dozen other people in the theater all turned their heads to look at her. It made her skin crawl. She was the only girl seeing this flick. She felt a distinct sense of unease as she reached the aisle and started toward the door, doing her best to hurry along without seeming panicked.

She reached the door and grasped the handle.

She pulled on it. It didn't budge.

"What the fuck?"

She pulled again. Same result. She peered through the narrow vertical window inset at the edge of the door and saw one of the strange theater employees staring in her direction. She pounded the base of a fist against the door, rattling it in its frame. Someone in the theater made a shushing noise. She ignored this and banged her fist against the door again. The employee tugged at his bow tie and came closer. He was grinning.

"*Hey, asshole!*" She pitched her voice as loud as she could and banged on the door yet again. "*Open this fucking door! It's locked!*"

He came closer still, almost right up to the door, but he made no move to open or unlock it. He was still grinning. Lashon's heart hammered as she realized the expression had a mocking quality to it.

I see you in there, the expression said. *And you are not getting out, no matter how much you scream and shout.*

People in the auditorium were hissing at her and telling her to sit down and shut up.

The man in the bow tie was laughing now.

Lashon's sense of panic and exasperation gave way to genuine fear.

What the hell is happening here?

Lashon turned away from the door and raced down the aisle to the bottom of the auditorium, where she veered right and headed straight for the emergency exit. Which was also locked and would not budge no matter how hard she threw herself against it.

A burly man near the front of the theater came out of his seat and approached. The expression on his puffy face was a mixture of agitation and concern. "Lady, what the hell is wrong with you? Are you having some kind of fit?"

Lashon reeled away from him and lifted her face toward the screen.

The trailers were over.

The movie was starting.

The man came after her. "Hey, calm down. Do you need help?"

Lashon sobbed and dropped to her knees. "We're trapped." She said it over and over, the anguish in her voice rising every time. "We're trapped. *We're trapped.*"

On the screen, a metal door banged open and light spilled into a darkened hallway. A man wearing a mask stepped through the opening. In his hands was a big chainsaw buzzing at high rev. Lashon stood and backed away from the screen as the masked man started down the hallway.

She felt a hand at her back.

Heard a voice in her ear, a low, throaty tone.

She opened her mouth to scream.

~

By the time the final trailer was over, Monroe was at peace with missing the chance to catch the zombie movie with his old friend. Kira's body felt so warm and soft beneath the arm he'd draped around her shoulders. She had kissed him once already. Which had made him realize how much he'd been repressing his true feelings for her. Being her friend was nice. He'd derived a not insignificant degree of fulfillment just from that. She was the only truly close female friend he had. She'd shown him different ways of looking at things, viewpoints he didn't get from his male acquaintances. And yet, some hidden part of him clearly had always desired more, something deeper.

The movie was starting. He could tell by the sudden swell of ominous music. But he couldn't bring himself to watch the screen. He was entranced by Kira. Everything about her suddenly seemed so perfect. The soft, round shape of her face. The small nose. The slightly plump lips. Eyes so big he could imagine falling into them.

She sensed his scrutiny and looked at him.

There was a long moment of electric tension. Nothing was said, but much was communicated in that shared gaze.

Kira set the popcorn bucket on the sticky floor, then she seized a handful of his shirt and pulled him toward her.

Monroe kissed her.

Slid a hand up one of her bare thighs.

And then there was an abrupt crash of amplified thunder. Monroe jumped. There was a flash of bright light. Lightning? That had to be it. It was storming in the movie. The movie he didn't give a shit about right now, a sentiment apparently shared by Kira. She gripped the hand on her thigh and urged it further up her leg.

She moaned softly, whispered his name. It was a delicious thing to hear from her lips.

There was another bright flash.

And then another, brighter now, almost blinding. Monroe blinked and felt suddenly woozy. His head felt thick, his body distant, his thoughts fuzzy. The light flared brighter still, blotting out the world. For a long moment, he seemed to exist only in a sightless, soundless void, a place of pure white. He couldn't even see his own body. A thought drifted out of the formless ether. He had died. Some sort of sudden attack. This was the afterlife.

The moment passed.

He heard another huge crash of thunder.

Then he felt rain pattering on his head.

He opened his eyes. Opened his mouth. Felt water touch his tongue. He was lying flat on his back on asphalt. He could feel its rough texture beneath him. He stared up at the sky, at the black clouds drifting high above him, moving fast and occasionally obscuring a luminous full moon.

He sat up, took a look around.

"What the fuck?"

He was in the parking lot outside the theater. He got to his feet and staggered around in a slow circle. The Sunshine 6 was dark. There were no movie titles on the white marquee. The only vehicle in sight was Kira's silver Hyundai. Every other car, Jason's Malibu included, had vanished.

His first thought was of Jason Tatum.

Motherfucker put something extra in the punch. Acid or some shit.

How else to explain this?

He heard the sound of an engine approaching. A huge vehicle of some sort came screeching into the parking lot. Its bright headlights pinned him as it rocketed toward him. He held up his hands against the glare and was able to discern the huge outline of a Hummer. It squealed to a stop six feet away and doors on both sides popped open. Two muscle-bound men clad all in black emerged.

One pointed at him. "Get him."

Monroe gaped at them. "Whoa. Hey. Just hold the fuck on. I don't know what the hell's going on, but—"

Both men came at him.

Monroe belatedly realized that full-throttle retreat was by far his best option. He staggered backward a few steps, then turned to flee at full speed, but by then they had him. He struggled against them, but they held on to him with grips of iron. One of the men opened one of the Hummer's back doors and tossed him inside.

Kira was there.

A man with the coldest, blackest eyes he'd ever seen was seated next to her.

Kira whimpered, her eyes bulging with fear. As Monroe watched in stunned helplessness, the man opened his mouth, displaying elongated incisors. *Fangs ... my God, those are fucking fangs.* An animal rumble issued from the man's throat. Then his head snapped toward Kira's throat, his fangs ripping into the tender, exposed flesh.

Monroe felt nausea at the sight of the suddenly spurting blood.

Kira's blood.

He felt light-headed again. He pitched sideways in the seat, unconscious.

~

The door wouldn't open.

Greg frowned and tried it again.

Same result.

Lashon wasn't here. He couldn't understand it. He tried to think. Kira's Hyundai was outside. That was undeniable. So *she* was here. But perhaps Lashon had changed her mind about coming. Maybe she'd opted to mope around her apartment again instead. It was what she did most days.

Then again . . .

There was one other possibility. He knew from Lashon's blog that Kira was seeing the vampire movie first. Perhaps she had decided to stick with her friend and see that one. The prospect of searching another auditorium didn't excite him. Yet he felt he had to do it.

But this situation with the door was getting in the way.

He reached for the handle again, but this time his hand fell limply upon it and slid slowly off the slick metal. He felt woozy and screwed his eyes tightly shut in time to miss that first flash of blinding white light. When he opened them again, the auditorium doors were still right in front of him, but something was different. He felt sick. Nauseated. But his curiosity overrode these physical symptoms a moment longer. Long enough to peer through the door's vertical window.

The lobby was dark.

Completely dark.

He could make out a dim outline of the concessions stand and a portion of the ticket booth. And something was moving out there. A man. Probably one of the weird theater employees. But even this person was just a vague outline, a form that was becoming dimmer with each passing second. Wow. That was just really strange. It was almost as if the world outside the auditorium was . . .

. . . *fading away.*

The world grew fuzzier as he staggered backward down the aisle. So strange. He felt almost high. Stoned. Like he was floating away on a silky-soft white cloud.

There was yet another flash.

And then he felt nothing at all.

For a while.

~

The first flash of white vaguely troubled Brix. It seemed to originate from nowhere and wasn't a part of what was unfolding on the screen. The movie was just beginning and what was happening there was happening in near total darkness. And she had never been to a theater where the house lights would produce that kind of sudden, blinding flash. Given the absence of any logical external source of the light, this left the possibility that it had been triggered by something internal. Something in her brain. Synapses misfiring. That was scary as hell, but when she glanced at Trevor she saw him staring blankly up at the screen, his face twisted in an expression of confusion and worry she suspected mirrored her own.

Her body tensed and all her senses went on full alert. She had shifted into fight mode without even thinking about it. It was the way she'd taught herself to react and it was second nature by now. She had long believed an apocalyptic event of some nature was just around the corner and that it was every right-thinking person's duty to prepare themselves for survival in a world gone wrong. She had no evidence to indicate anything of the sort was happening now, but that didn't mean it wasn't. She thought of her Glock, shut away now in the glove compartment of the F-150. Never in her life had she more wanted to feel its reassuring weight in the palm of her hand.

Trevor looked at her. Opened his mouth to say something.

And that was when the second flash came.

Someone screamed.

As the second flash passed, Brix became aware of a deep wooziness. She also felt mildly sick. Jesus, something was really fucked and wrong about that flashing light.

Need my gun. Got to go . . . get it . . .

She tried to stand.

Then the flashing light blinded her again and the world went away for a little while.

PART 2

FEATURE

PRESENTATIONS

SEVEN

But not for long.

Brix also woke up flat on her back in the parking lot outside the theater. But this was not the same version of the parking lot in which Kira and Monroe found themselves after the bright flashes that interrupted the screening of *Blood Lust*. Here it was not raining and there were no vampire predators prowling the area in enormous automobiles.

But that didn't mean danger wasn't present.

She heard something strange. A kind of . . . *groaning*.

Was it Trevor? Was he hurt?

Brix's eyes snapped open. She saw the dark sky above and knew at once this was no dream or hallucination. Somehow those bright flashes in the theater were connected to her inexplicable relocation to the parking lot. She knew intuitively no one had carried her out here. What had happened was more akin to teleportation. Which was the kind of thing you saw all the time in cheesy science fiction movies, but, so far as she knew, teleportation technology did not actually exist. Or if it did, it was the kind of ultra top secret Area 51 thing few people knew about. And the government sure as shit would never deploy the technology in a dinky theater in a nowhere town showing cheap-ass horror movies. Unless . . .

The groaning sound came again.

What the fuck *was* that?

She knew she should get up and check that out. She should also get a fix on Trevor's location pronto. And she meant to do those things in just a second. But the troubling thought that had flashed through her mind wouldn't go away. Because maybe a nowhere town was *exactly* the kind of place government black ops types might decide to conduct risky experiments with potentially hazardous and unpredictable new types of technology and/or weaponry systems.

Shit.

"Brix?"

Trevor!

Brix was up and on her feet in the next instant. She had already locked on the direction of Trevor's voice and was turning that way when she froze and stared off into the distance. It was nighttime in Murfreesboro. The college town was no Manhattan, but it was a metropolis compared to where she lived. It was big enough that she should see a sea of electric lights in any direction. There *was* light in the distance, random flickers here and there punctuating the darkness, but the source of it was not provided by the power company.

Those were fires burning in the distance.

Fucking *fires.*

Brix gaped at the twisting columns of flame for a long moment.

Holy shit. What the fuck?

"Brix!"

Trevor again, sounding panicked this time.

And then a scream.

Brix gave herself a mental slap.

Get your head in the game, bitch!

She completed the turn toward the sound of Trevor's voice and got moving. She saw him on the ground some twenty yards from her. It was especially dark in that corner of the parking lot, but she could see that her boyfriend was scooting rapidly backward, desperately trying to get away from a shadowy figure that had emerged from behind a black SUV. The figure took another lurching step toward Trevor, drawing close enough that she could see he was a man attired in a ragged black suit. His hair was a mess and his face looked haggard in the pale moonlight. Some drunk asshole. She wasn't sure yet why

Trevor should be so afraid of someone like that, but he *was* afraid and that was all she needed to know.

This was one lousy drunk who was about to get his ass handed to him.

Hard.

By a *girl.*

That last bit was a point she always relished driving home after dealing with pukes like this. Some people were just in especially dire need of having their egos squashed. Mostly bullies and fake hardasses. She considered it a public service, like holding doors for people or helping old ladies across the street. Brix moved past Trevor just as he was finally getting to his feet. He clutched at her as she went by, his fingers sliding off the sleeve of her denim jacket. "Brix! Don't! Stay away from him."

"Don't worry, baby. I've got this."

A scream came again. The timbre of it was the same as the previous scream. It had a distinctly feminine quality to it. And now someone else was yelling. A guy. She heard terror in that voice. But she kept her focus on the task at hand. One crisis at a time. She would help those people as soon as she'd dealt with this dumb asshole.

She was very close to him now, mere yards away.

He took another lurching step in her direction.

And . . . groaned.

Brix frowned, faltering just the slightest bit.

Um . . .

Yet another lurching step. And now the smell assailed her. How had she not noticed it in the first place? The stench was so foul it made her eyes water. He smelled like a pile of rotting meat left out in the sun all day.

Another staggering step closer.

Almost within kicking distance.

She was maybe letting him get a little too close, closer than she normally would when squaring off for a fight with someone, though she wasn't overly worried. His gait and his lopsided stance were strong indicators he would be dead meat the moment she went into attack mode. There was a remote chance he was faking her out, but she doubted it. Bottom line, she didn't perceive this clown as a real threat. And yet, something was very wrong with him. Her curiosity was piqued.

She wrinkled her nose and scowled at him. "Dude. What the fuck?

You smell like you slept in a fucking sewer."

The man's mouth hung open. It opened marginally wider still and another low groan emerged.

"What was that? Sorry, I don't speak stupid. Try English, okay?"

Another grown, louder this time.

He lifted a hand, reaching for her. Brix took an instinctive step backward. She didn't like that. Not at all. It went against everything she believed. Backing down made you look weak. That was a lesson her father had instilled in her at an early age.

Trevor yelled at her again. "Get away from him! Jesus, Brix!"

Another of those instinctive backward steps.

Dammit.

She heard sounds of violence nearby. Heavy thuds. More screams and more yelling. That Nikki chick and her asshat boyfriend, she was pretty sure. Obviously Stinky here wasn't the only threat in the vicinity. The reality of how much trouble they were potentially in hit home again. Yes, something immensely strange had happened in the theater. But something even stranger was happening out here in the parking lot. She needed to stop trying to figure this guy out. There were bigger mysteries that needed solving.

She squinted at him, the extent of the ragged condition of his clothes becoming apparent for the first time. His suit had been nice once upon a time. But now it was badly stained and torn in many places. He wasn't in such great shape, either. He was gaunt and his eyes were a strange milky white. And, holy shit, one of his ears was missing. There was an ugly wound where it had been. The really weird part was the wound wasn't leaking blood.

The guy looked sort of . . . *dead.*

Like a—

No. Shut up, Brix. That's crazy. You've seen too many bad movies, that's all.

Still . . .

The man who looked like a walking dead thing took yet another staggering step toward her. Brix now stood frozen in place, gawping at the lurching impossibility right in front of her. Trevor grabbed her by an arm and tried to jerk her backward. She yelped and yanked her arm free. She opened her mouth to say something, but the words went unsaid as she sensed something rushing toward her from the right. She tensed, bracing for a collision or a blow, but neither came.

Jason Tatum appeared in front of her, wielding a heavy, old-fashioned tire iron. His arms were already in motion, swinging the length of heavy metal straight at the head of the rotten-smelling one-eared dude. Brix flinched in anticipation of the sure-to-be devastating blow. Punches and kicks she understood. They were how you fought and defended yourself against bad guys. Unless they were armed, which this guy wasn't. But this was something else altogether. This was assault with murderous intent. The tire iron connected with devastating force, cracking the man's skull and sending him toppling to the asphalt. Jason then fell atop him and shifted his grip on the tire iron before raising it high above his head.

It came down again.

And again.

The sound of cracking bone was sickening. He was pulverizing the poor bastard's skull. It freaked her out. She was witnessing a murder. She wasn't a stranger to violence, but this shit was on a level beyond anything in her experience.

Except . . . was it really murder?

Jason got to his feet again, rounding on Brix with eyes wide from adrenaline. "The fuck is up with you?"

Brix was embarrassed by how ineptly she had handled the situation. She covered this by reacting with hostility of her own. "The fuck's up with me? The fuck's up with *you*? I didn't need to be rescued by your sorry ass."

"Didn't look that way to me."

Brix fumed. She curled her hands into tight fists. "I would've handled it."

"Right. Whatever. Looked to me like you were about to be zombie dinner."

Zombie.

So there it was. The word some reflexive part of her subconscious hadn't allowed her to acknowledge until now. Maybe because doing so meant being forced to acknowledge something far more disturbing. More disturbing even than the possibility of having stumbled into a government experiment with teleportation technology. Not just more disturbing, but far weirder. She couldn't begin to fathom how it had happened, but she could no longer deny it—reality itself had been inverted.

Or this was some kind of different version of reality altogether.

A world where . . .

Her shoulders sagged and her hard expression melted away.

"Fuck."

She shook her head and turned away from Jason to stare at the darkened movie theater. A theater that, in this world, had never played host to a festival of cheap horror flicks. It was a boarded-up, abandoned wreck of a place. Just one more dead thing in a dying world. She stood still and let it all fully register. The smells. The fires in the distance. Rubbish and (probably) piles of bodies burning. Other hints of death and decay. And there were more groans out there. More *hungry* groans. She could see more shadowy figures shuffling toward them. A dozen. Two dozen. Maybe many more.

She laughed, but it was a bitter sound. A hopeless sound. "Fuck. *Fuck.*"

Trevor tentatively touched her shoulder. "Brix? What is it?"

She turned to look at him. She glanced at Jason. Nikki was beside him now and his arm was around her slender shoulders. His look of wired hostility was gone. She acknowledged this with a terse nod, knowing somehow that he understood what she knew, as well.

She shook her head. "This is so fucked. So many years of fantasizing about this shit and here it is. Goddamn."

Trevor frowned. "What are you saying?"

Brix's expression sobered as she again looked directly at the guy she loved. The guy she would now have to fight tooth and nail to protect if they were to have any hope of survival. "We're in the movie, baby. We're in fucking *Rise of the Dead.*"

EIGHT

The first thing Lashon Miller was aware of was being wet all over. Droplets of rain pattered her face. She opened her eyes and saw a night sky filled with huge, dark clouds. A flash of lightning followed an ominous rumble of thunder. She dimly recalled checking the forecast before heading out for the evening. There had been no suggestion of thunderstorms. It was supposed to have been a clear, warm night. Instead she was soaked and shivering. Other odd things penetrated as her head cleared and she became more aware of the world around her.

Things such as the odd abundance of tall trees everywhere she looked.

Lashon sat up and drew her knees toward her chest. She sat there rocking and shaking on the soggy ground, her head turning this way and that as she searched the small clearing she was in for clues as to how she had wound up here.

But there was nothing.

Just a lot of trees and that creepily impenetrable darkness beyond them.

The last thing she remembered was being at the theater. Had

someone abducted her from there and brought her to this place? Maybe. She had been in attendance at a lurid movie about a chainsaw-wielding maniac. Maybe one of the guys in the audience was a for-real psycho. He had spotted her and hadn't been able to help himself. He snatched her, somehow spirited her out of the theater, and brought her to this wooded locale. The perfect place to have his perverted way with her. To rape and murder her. To butcher her body the way he'd seen so many of his favorite movie killers do it to all those pretty actresses.

Thunder crashed above her again, making her flinch. A subsequent burst of lightning, far brighter than the first, lit up the sky.

Lashon sucked in a sharp breath.

The flash at the theater.

That weird grinning dude in the bow tie.

She remembered it all now. She hadn't been abducted. Not in any normal world sense, anyway. Something very wrong and very strange had happened in that theater. Something connected with those blinding white flashes. Those weird theater workers, all of them so nearly identical to each other, were somehow responsible for this. She couldn't begin to understand how that was possible, or even what the larger implications of it might be, but she knew in her gut it was the truth. Just as she knew the theater workers hadn't actually been human. She didn't know *what* they were, but she knew that. And did it really matter? They were weird and dangerous. Those were the only relevant facts, in her view. And whatever had happened, at least one good thing had come of it.

She was nowhere near any of those weird bow tie-wearing fucks or their dumpy, rundown theater.

Which nonetheless left her with the reality of figuring out where she was and doing something about it. The sooner the better, too.

Now, in fact, would be a good time.

She uncrossed her arms, braced her hands on the wet ground, and got unsteadily to her feet. Once she was upright she crossed her arms again, hugging her body as tightly as she could as she continued to shiver. She did a slow turn in the clearing, looking for any indication of a good direction to begin her journey out of this godforsaken place. She scanned the ground for signs of tracks in the muddy earth. If someone had carried her to this place and then walked back out of the clearing, there should be ample evidence of that, but there were no footprints anywhere, at least none that were visible here in this deep darkness. It was almost as if some unknowable power had scooped her up and set her down in this place. A crazy notion, maybe, but it would account for the lack of tracks in the wet ground. And the idea was impossible to dismiss, given the profoundly odd nature of the things she remembered from the theater.

She thought yet again of the theater workers. Those mysterious creatures wearing their masks of false humanity. Who and what were they? Where did they come from? What were they trying to accomplish by doing what they had done?

Questions without answers. At least for now. And maybe for always. She could live without answers, if she could somehow manage to get home and survive this night.

And if I can do that, she thought, *I'm never going to a goddamn horror movie ever again.*

She thought about that a moment longer and amended the resolution to include any movie of any type. Why take chances? She preferred books, anyway.

There was a spot at the edge of the clearing where there was a larger than usual gap between two of the tall trees. Might a path back to something resembling civilization lie within the darkness beyond that gap? Maybe. Maybe not. Lacking any other obvious options, it was as good a place to start as any. She started toward the gap but had taken no more than two steps when she heard the first heavy footfall directly behind her. The sound pinned her to the spot for a moment, making her heart race madly while she waited to hear the sound again, praying all the while it had only been her imagination the first time.

But then she heard another heavy footfall. Closer now.

And something else—the sound of heavy breathing. But it was a muffled sound, as if it were coming from behind a . . . mask?

Her heart hammered even harder at the thought. And though the rational part of her brain knew the only sensible thing was to take off running right then and there, something more primal within her caused her to turn around and take a look at the person stalking her.

A thing she recognized as a massive mistake an instant later. She screamed and staggered backward, nearly tripping over her feet as the soles of her shoes sank into the soft, yielding ground.

The man standing perhaps six feet from her was tall and powerfully built, hugely muscular beneath dirty overalls and a sopping-wet flannel shirt. A bland white mask obscured his face. The mask reminded her vaguely of those worn by killers in several horror movie franchises. The kind with sequels nearly numbering in the double digits. But this mask was really the kind worn by imitation killers in the even cheaper knockoffs of those more successful movies. While there was nothing distinctive or very noteworthy about it, it would subtly remind audiences of iconic horror villains, a subliminal marketing tactic that might bring in just enough suckers to help make back the film's undoubtedly miniscule budget.

This mask, in fact, looked very much like the mask worn by the killer in *Chainsaw Maniac*. She had seen images from the movie on the horror festival's website while idly checking it out on Kira's iPad. Even more disturbing, however, was the chainsaw gripped in the man's huge, meaty hands.

Though she was terrified beyond measure, Lashon couldn't help voicing the question that sprang immediately to mind: "Is this some kind of sick fucking joke?"

By way of an answer, the masked man yanked at the chainsaw's starter cord and its blade instantly roared to full, buzzing life. The man raised the chainsaw over his head and squeezed something near its handle to push it to an even higher rev. Lashon's immediate impression was that he looked very much like a man striking a deliberate pose.

Like, say, an actor in a movie.

A movie like *Chainsaw Maniac*, perhaps.

Lashon felt for a moment like a person locked inside an especially disturbing dream. This was all just too weird to be real. But that impression was a trap and she quickly recognized it as such. Every other piece of sensory input told her this was all absolutely real and that she was in danger of suffering a nasty, painful death within moments.

The man revved the chainsaw again, then as he began to advance on her. Lashon snapped out of her paralysis and began to stagger backward, nearly tripping more than once. She knew she should turn and run right now, but the thought of turning her back on the chainsaw-wielding psycho was too terrifying. It was too easy to imagine that whirring blade sinking into the flesh between her shoulder blades once her back was to him.

Please, God, she thought. *I don't want to die. Not today. Not ever. Please . . .*

The man moved closer still and the end of the nastily buzzing blade was perhaps a foot from her face when she glimpsed a flash of movement at the edge of her peripheral vision. Something big was rushing straight at the masked man, who appeared not to sense the oncoming threat. Maybe it was the noise of the chainsaw that made him oblivious. Maybe he was just fucking stupid. Lashon didn't care. All that mattered was that someone was apparently coming to her rescue. In the last moment before impact, she recognized that some-one as the slightly heavyset man at the theater who'd come out of his chair to ask her if she was all right.

He collided with the masked psycho, jolting the chainsaw out of his hands as he drove the bigger man to the ground. The chainsaw thumped to the ground, where the blade dug for a moment into the soft earth before going still. Lashon stared at it for a shocked moment before shifting her attention to her rescuer. The guy was sitting astride the masked man and was hammering away at his hidden face with two big fists.

He sensed her scrutiny and glanced up at her, his face twisting in a desperate grimace as his eyes locked with hers. His face was red from overexertion and slick with rain. He was breathing heavily, but managed to push out a single word: "*Run!*"

One of the masked man's big hands shot upward and clamped tightly around her rescuer's throat.

Lashon screamed.

And then she heeded the stranger's advice.

She turned away from the scene of struggle and plunged into the deeper darkness of the woods.

NINE

Kira awoke with a gasp and sat bolt upright, breathing heavily and hearing the amplified beat of her overdriven heart pounding in her ears. The dream was over. She was safe and sound in a comfortable bed. There were no vampires here. No one was assaulting her. And, really, given her tastes in literature and movies, it was a wonder she had never had that kind of dream before. She had long prided herself on not scaring easily, but, apparently, even the most hardened dark fiction addict could eventually pay a price for constant indulgence in the stuff.

She swept the thick comforter away from her body and swung her legs over the side of the bed, intending to get up to take a pee. Instead, she sat there on the edge of the bed, suddenly struggling to understand some things. This was a four-poster bed with an ornate wood frame. A gauzy canopy hung above her. She couldn't remember ever having slept in a bed like this one. Moreover, she was relatively certain she didn't know anyone who had a bed like it. But that was far from the only off-kilter detail about her current circumstances. Another odd thing was the very flimsy blue negligee she was wearing. It was see-through and had a very short hemline. She didn't have much in the way of sexy lingerie and knew she had nothing quite like this thing in her wardrobe.

There were other things, too. The room she was in was not at all familiar. It was big. *Really* big. There was what looked like a real fireplace at the far end of the room, complete with a stone hearth. Very old-fashioned. Indeed, all the furniture in the room looked like antiques. She turned her head side to side in open-mouthed amazement, doing a slow survey of the contents of the room. A large steamer trunk sat at the foot of the bed. It was secured with a very big and very old-looking padlock. A roll top desk sat against the wall opposite the bed. It looked sort of fragile in the way of many very old things. Fragile and quaint. She could imagine Charles Dickens sitting at that desk, scribbling away at *Hard Times* or some damn thing. A tall wardrobe cabinet stood in a corner of the room. Like the bed, it was almost exquisitely ornate, with much painstakingly carved detail.

The windows in the room were all painted black. Weird.

She got up and went over to the wardrobe, hoping to find something more suitable to wear. She pulled at one of the rickety doors and the knob came off in her hand as the door creaked open. She frowned as she peered in at the handful of items dangling from wire hangers. They were all very tiny pieces of lingerie. She glanced at the knob in her hand, her frown deepening for a moment, and then she screwed it back on and pressed the wardrobe door firmly shut.

She moved numbly to the center of the room and took it all in again.

A single, obvious conclusion soon took center stage in her mind—*I have to get out of this room and out of this fucking house, wherever the hell it is, as soon as I can.*

If that meant fleeing into the night in this silly little excuse for a nightgown, so be it.

There was a door to the right of the Charles Dickens desk. It was the only door in sight and had to be the way out. She took a single, determined step toward it and then stopped.

She frowned.

And put a hand to her neck, feeling for the marks she prayed were not there.

But they were.

And suddenly her heart was off to the races again. Her legs felt weak. She was woozy and felt as if she might pass out again. Passing out was even sort of an attractive option, though she knew her chances of escaping whatever kind of prison she was in depended on remaining alert. The bad dream hadn't been a dream at all and had nothing to do with her fondness for fictional vampires.

A *real* vampire had bitten her.

And had drank deeply of her blood . . .

—ohmygodohmygod—

She raced to the door and yanked it open, intent on getting herself out of this place as fast as she could, but two massive men with blond crew cuts dressed all in black stood outside the door, flanking it on either side. They turned toward her as the door came open, their enormous bodies filling the doorframe.

Kira felt like crying.

No escape. No escape. Oh, God, there's no way out . . .

One of the blond behemoths smiled tightly at her. "You are not to leave."

"Says who?"

The other one remained stone-faced as he said, "You are to stay in this room until further notice by order of The Master."

"The what now?"

The creepily smiling one said, "The Master."

Kira nodded. "Right. That's what I thought you said."

But what kind of total whack job has his employees refer to him as "The Master?"

She kept that question to herself, figuring it could lead to nowhere good and that, anyway, there could be no sensible answer for it.

The smiling one glanced at her chest and then looked her in the eye again. "You should return to bed and await the honor of The Master's presence. He is anxious to drink of you again." His sinister smile broadened. "And to partake of your beauty in other ways, of course."

Kira nodded again. "Uh huh. You talk exactly like you're in some weird 70s Euro Vampire movie. You realize that, right?"

The smiling one became The Frowning One. "I do not understand."

"I know you don't. Okay, so . . . I'm gonna, like, take your advice and go await the presence of this Master person." She moved back a step and began to swing the door shut. "Later, guys."

She stared at the closed door a long moment.

It was painfully obvious now that she was completely trapped.

Goddammit.

So she returned to the bed and waited for the vampire to come calling.

There was nothing else she could do.

~

One of the black-clad brutes kicked a door open and shoved Monroe roughly through it. His shoulder banged off the doorframe, sending a shock of pain down his left side as he staggered to the edge of a small landing at the top of a spiral stone staircase. The only light available spilled in from the mansion's huge restaurant-style kitchen, through which the thugs had just dragged him en route to this place. The staircase twisted down into utter blackness. Monroe gulped. His first thought was it looked like a path straight down into the heart of Hell itself. But just as he was thinking that, torches mounted in sconces on the stone wall at descending intervals of approximately a dozen feet sparked to life. The flickering tongues of flame pushed back some of the darkness, enough that one could descend the staircase without taking a blind tumble, but the light was too hazy to glimpse the bottom, which at a guess had to be at least a hundred feet or more below the surface of the earth.

"Bloody hell. How is this even possible?"

By which he meant every aspect of his current situation. The abduction by vampires. The inexplicable lighting of the torches. What the fuck was that? Magic? And, perhaps the most pressing matter of all right at the moment, the mystery of whatever awaited him at the bottom of this medieval staircase.

He turned around to gape at the big thugs as they glared at him from the other side of the open door. "There any chance I could come back in there?"

"No."

"I was afraid you'd say that."

One of them curled one of his big hands into a fist, then gripped and squeezed it with his other hand, cracking the knuckles. A gesture meant to intimidate. It was effective, too. One side of the knuckle-cracker's face twitched in a sneer. "Go down the stairs. Do not stop until you reach the bottom. Do not attempt to come back up."

"What happens if I disobey?"

"You die."

"Right. Well, I don't want that, so . . . okay then."

He moved away from the sneering thugs, took a deep breath, and took his first step down into the darkness. A moment later he heard the door slam shut behind him, followed by the sound of a deadbolt clicking into place. It was hard not to hear a bone-chilling finality in that sound. He now fully expected never to see the outside world again. As he descended the next dozen or so big stone steps, he began to perceive distant, barely audible sounds. He couldn't identify them immediately, but another dozen winding steps down brought the sounds into slightly clearer focus and he felt another chill. This one went deeper, sinking its icy tentacles right into the very center of his trembling soul.

Moaning.

Screaming.

These were the things he was hearing.

And they were getting louder with every downward step. Monroe had a fleeting thought that maybe he should just pitch himself off the staircase. A fall to his death right now might well be a far better thing than meeting whatever was waiting for him down there. It would be easy enough to do. The staircase had no banister or railing. He could just stop right here and step over the edge. It would all be over quickly. He considered it only briefly, though. He really didn't want to die. The only real option was to continue down to the bottom and hope for the best once he got there.

So he kept going.

And the sounds of torment kept getting louder.

FIRST INTERMISSION

Greg Nelson regained consciousness an indeterminate time after the flashes of white light. Unlike everyone else in attendance that night, however, he did not wake up somewhere outside the cineplex, although he did not initially realize this as the appearance of the building's interior had changed dramatically during his time of unawareness. He woke up face-down in one of the sloping aisles between sections of seats. Except that the worn and stained red carpet he remembered had been replaced by a series of rectangular white panels. The panels were translucent and he could make out vague shapes of some form of machinery beneath, the purpose of which he could not begin to divine. Things were moving down there in a kind of clockwork synchronicity. There was light, too. And it was moving, a pulse of diffused brilliance that rotated slowly from the top of the aisle down to the bottom and back again. Over and over. For many hazy minutes Greg stared at the light and the dimly perceived rotating gears, almost feeling hypnotized by the strange sights. But then, as his mind continued to clear, it occurred to him how very odd this all was. And as the last of the mental fog dissipated, he began to freak out a little.

He braced his hands on the panel beneath him and propelled himself upward, staggering backward a few clumsy steps as his feet fought to find purchase on the slippery panels. He eventually got himself properly righted and turned in a slow circle, gaping as he took it all in, marveling in terrified wonder at a transformed auditorium that looked like a sleek and ultra-futuristic chamber in the kind of starship that only existed in science fiction movies. The sections of seats were arranged precisely as they had been prior to the consciousness-obliterating flashes. There were double doors inside recessed alcoves at the top of each aisle. A large screen occupied the exact space one would expect. But any resemblance to any movie theater he had ever patronized ended right there.

Every seat looked as if it had been formed from the same seamless mold. There were no interlocking parts. No cushions that went up and down. He glanced down and noted that the seamlessness included where the legs of the seats met the floor. You couldn't unbolt the things and remove them because they appeared to melt right into the floor. Also, they were all the same flawless shade of bone-white. As was practically everything else in the theater, with the exception of the translucent floor panels and the screen. A kaleidoscope of slowly swirling color patterns danced lazily across the center of the screen. Lines of color extended outward, growing steadily thinner as they reached toward the edge of the screen before collapsing in upon themselves. An instant later, the pattern began to repeat. Like some kind of old school computer screensaver.

Odd.

Very, very odd.

The first thing he inferred from all this strange sensory input was that the theater he remembered hadn't existed at all. Instead it had been a highly realistic illusion of a decaying cineplex, an extraordinarily tactile skin image projected over this white skeleton beneath. The second thing he gleaned from all this information was that it would likely be in his best interest to get the hell out of this place as soon as possible. Another thing hit him before he could act on that undoubtedly very intelligent impulse.

He was the only person left in the theater.

Everyone else in attendance had vanished. Where had they gone? And why had only he been left behind?

"Why me?"

He hadn't intended to speak out loud. It had just happened, the words popping out before the thought had even registered. He regretted the utterance immediately. The sound resonated disturbingly in the empty space, echoing and bouncing back at him, making him cringe as if he had screamed the words instead of uttering them in his normal speaking voice.

Run, he thought. *No more thinking. Just run.*

NOW.

And so he did, spinning away from the screen to race to the top of the aisle and the double doors there. He seized one of the door handles, intending fully to yank it open and just keep running. But yet another disturbing thought flashed through his mind before he could do that. *The theater workers.* He had forgotten about them, but now he was remembering, oh yes. All of them so strangely identical. So weird looking. There had been something off about them. The one part of the illusion that hadn't been perfect, perhaps? He thought so. More than that. He *knew* it. He didn't know who or what those guys were, but they were not human.

And they might still be lurking out there in the lobby of this strange pseudo-theater.

Shit.

He pressed his face up close to the door's vertical window and peered out at the lobby. At first he thought there was nothing out there, just a formless white void, but then he began to make out shapes. A short hallway led to the space that had functioned as the theater's lobby. However, like this auditorium, it had been stripped of its illusory skin. From his vantage point, he could see a corner of what had been the concessions stand. A translucent panel hung on the wall behind it. Once it had displayed the prices of refreshments, but now it was a blank slate. His eyes flicked to the hallway floor and he saw another series of translucent panels, where another pulse of diffused light repeatedly made the circuit from one end of the hallway to the other and back again. That impression of being aboard some unfathomably advanced starship returned, this time as a perhaps very likely explanation for what he was seeing rather than some fanciful notion based on movies. Which would mean the theater workers were imperfectly disguised members of an alien race. Some kind of weird research team that had come to earth to perform behavioral experiments on unsuspecting humans. He thought he was really on to something there, but he couldn't see what use the insight was to him. He wasn't a hero in a movie. It wasn't up to him to save the day or anything like that. He was just a regular guy with an unfortunate fixation on a girl who had hurt him, a stupid thing that had caused him to become caught up in a situation he couldn't possibly solve. He couldn't help any of the people who had disappeared from this place. Not even Lashon. No one was moving around out there. It was time to stop cowering behind this fucking door and make a run for it.

Before he wound up trapped here forever.

Or killed.

He sucked in a big breath, slowly released it.

And then he pulled the door open.

TEN

They were coming closer.

The zombies.

Drawn from the shadows by the smell of fresh meat, appearing singly and in groups of two or three or more. A few looked fresh, as if they had just turned. But most more closely resembled the one Jason had put down. Their clothes were dirty and ragged. Their flesh bore evidence of old wounds, a few of which were especially hideous. Ripped open stomach cavities and ruined faces. One lumbering figure approaching from Brix's left wore the uniform of a policeman. He was missing an arm. A fragment of bone protruded from the stump. But Brix's gaze went to the empty holster attached to the belt around his narrow waist. She assumed the man had lost his sidearm during his own struggle for life. Which was too bad for him, but it reminded her of something important.

Like really, *really* fucking important.

The Glock in the glove compartment of the F-150.

Panic jolted her as a horrible thought flashed through her mind. This was a different version of reality from the one she had inhabited until a few moments ago. Did the big truck her father had passed down to her even exist in this world?

Shit.

She got a quick fix on her relative location in the parking lot and turned in the direction that should point her toward the truck—assuming it was even there.

There it is!

Her truck was parked right where she had left it, over by Jason's shitty old Chevy Malibu, a couple dozen yards from where she stood now. She took off running, propelled forward by instinct, paying no mind to the startled voices calling after her. They were surrounded by zombies. Enemies. Creatures intent on killing and devouring them. They needed some form of protection. More than that, a means of fighting back. She would feel better—more in control—with the reassuring weight of the Glock in her hands. None of this was anything she consciously thought. They were things she understood on a gut level. The enemy had the greater numbers. The enemy would be relentless and unafraid. Her Glock 17's magazine contained 17 bullets. Not nearly enough to permanently beat back an enemy as vast as the one they likely faced, but it was better than nothing. It was a start. A fucking fighting chance.

But something was wrong. She saw that too clearly as she drew closer to the hulking outline of the old F-150. She stopped short, her heart sinking as she saw that its windows had been blown out. But that was hardly the extent of the damage. Black scorch marks marred the truck's exterior. The tires had melted. But the moment of despair was short-lived. There was no time to wallow in it. She shoved away the reflexive self-pity. A deep-seated anger took root in its place. Someone had violated her property, an act constituting an assault against her personally. Something like that could not go unpunished. She couldn't hit back against the specific individuals who had trashed her truck, but she had another target in mind—the mysterious creatures who had caused this reality split or whatever the hell it actually was. *They* were the ultimate responsible party here, and *they* would pay. Somehow.

She heard feet pounding across the asphalt behind her. More panicked shouts. Brix ignored this and got moving once again. Seconds later she reached the truck. The door on the passenger side was cool to the touch. She seized the handle and gave it a yank. Locked. Of course. She never left it otherwise. Her purse was back in the theater in that other reality, so she didn't have her keys. But given the condition of the truck, that wasn't really a problem. She slithered in through the open window, a pile of safety glass on the floorboard crunching beneath her booted feet as she situated herself in front of the glove compartment.

Just one problem.

The fire had melted the truck's entire dash, including the glove compartment's door. The melted plastic had congealed around its edges. She gripped the mangled handle and pulled on it with all her might, but it wouldn't budge.

She thumped a fist against the ruined dash.

"Shit!"

"What the fuck are you doing in there?"

Jason Tatum, his voice right next to her.

Brix glanced out the window and saw him standing next to the truck. His eyes were wide and his chest was going up and down, a result of chasing her across the lot. He looked scared. She couldn't blame him. He was still holding the tire iron. It was the old kind, a long, rust-flecked piece of metal with a socket for turning lug nuts and a pronged end for popping off hubcaps.

Brix leaned through the window and snatched it from his hands.

His face contorted in a mix of surprise and fury. "Hey! Give that back!"

"Sorry. I need it."

She poked at the edges of the glove compartment's door with the pronged end of the tire iron, feeling for an open space where she could insert the metal. She finally found an opening in the melted rubber, albeit a very small one, and then gritted her teeth as she tightened her grip on the tire iron. Calling upon every ounce of strength she possessed, she drove the thing deeper into that tiny hole. The hole widened and she began cranking the tool up and down. There was a cracking sound as some of the melted plastic began to give way. Still, the marginally wider opening wasn't nearly big enough. She had to keep working at it. So she tightened her grip again and redoubled the effort, nearly screaming through her gritted teeth at the strain it was causing in her arms and shoulders. Jason had fallen silent. She could feel him watching her, probably wondering what on earth could possibly be worth this kind of effort, especially in the midst of this much danger.

"My gun."

"Say again?"

At least he sounded somewhat calmer now.

"My gun. My Glock. It's in the goddamn glove box."

"Oh."

"We need it."

A pause, followed by a sigh. "Right. Okay. I get that. Really. But if you can't get to it in the next few seconds . . ."

He let the rest of it hang there.

Brix didn't need to hear the words. She knew well enough what the stakes were. Either she would get this damn thing open and get to the gun *right now,* or it was time to accept defeat and get out of here and get running again.

She shifted her position on the barren seat bench, folded one leg beneath her for greater leverage, and screamed again as she again cranked the tire iron up and down. The cracking sound was louder this time and an instant later the pronged end of the tool slipped all the way into the compartment. Brix shifted her body around again, pressing the sole of a boot against the tire iron while she gripped the socket end with both hands. She shoved downward ferociously and was rewarded with the loudest crackling of yielding plastic yet. The compartment door dropped open and there was the Glock. She nearly cried at the sight of that lovely, shiny nickel plating.

She heard the others now.

Trevor yelling at her.

That Nikki idiot gibbering in terror.

She tossed the tire iron through the open window and heard Jason Tatum gasp in surprise. The tool clattered on asphalt. Jason cursed. No matter. Everything was cool now. Well, relatively speaking.

Brix grabbed her gun and slithered back out through the window, dropping to the ground a moment later and turning to face the terror-stricken faces of the others. Strike that. Trevor and Nikki were terror-stricken. Jason was scared, too, but he also looked composed and ready to fight. Good. She thought she could count on him when things turned tough. Which would be any fucking second now. It grieved her to think it, but she couldn't say the same for Trevor. His safety would have to be damn near her top priority from here on out, because otherwise he wouldn't survive.

There were even more zombies now.

Dozens of them.

The closest was maybe ten feet away, closing on an oblivious Trevor from behind. Brix brushed past him, took aim at the zombie's head and squeezed off a single shot. A single shot was all she needed. Her aim was perfect, as always. A hole punched through the center of the thing's forehead and an explosion of bone and brains blew out the back of its skull.

That's one down.

She listened to the groans of the shuffling, rotting animated corpses.

And a hundred to go.

But she amended the thought in the next second. The threat they were facing wasn't limited to what they could see here. There were likely thousands more of these dead things out there. Maybe millions of them. Perhaps even *hundreds* of millions. All over the world. At least if what they were dealing with here was a global apocalypse, a *Dawn of the Dead*-type scenario. And she thought it was. The sheer scope of it felt suddenly oppressive. Suffocating. Her breathing quickened at the thought of it. But she couldn't afford to lose control. Not now. Things seemed hopeless. But that didn't mean she could just give up.

Still, the enemy's strength in numbers was a real issue. The Glock's clip held sixteen bullets now. She could use them all and be bang on target every time and it still wouldn't be nearly enough. They had to retreat. Find shelter, some place where they could regroup and figure out a survival plan.

She turned away from the line of approaching dead and looked at Jason. "Your car looks like it hasn't been fucked with. Get us the fuck out of here."

He dragged a set of keys out of a hip pocket. "Shit. Let's give it a shot. But it's a tricky fucker sometimes. I get stranded a lot."

The 1970-something Malibu was parked near the F-150. Miraculously, it appeared to have escaped whatever calamity had befallen her truck and some of the other nearby vehicles.

Jason hurried over to his car, keyed it open, and slid behind the wheel, leaving the door ajar as he inserted the key in the ignition. Fearing the worst, Brix held her breath as he gave the ignition a twist. She let the breath out as the engine rumbled to full, throaty life. He gave it the gas, revving the engine higher a moment, and then twisted in his seat to look at her. "We're in business."

Brix couldn't help it—she was grinning. "Great. Let's haul ass."

The rest of them converged on the car as Jason leaned toward the passenger side door and thumbed its lock open. Nikki opened the door and made for the shotgun seat. An understandable instinct. Of course she'd want to ride next to her boyfriend.

Brix seized her by a bicep and held her still. "No."

Nikki scowled. "No? What the fuck do you mean *no?*"

Brix kept her expression neutral. No sense in escalating the hostility here if at all possible. "I'm sorry. I really am. But I'm the one with the gun and I need to ride up front. I can't be pinned in the back if shooting becomes necessary."

"She's right, babe. We'll all be safer this way."

Jason, being the voice of reason. Again. Brix was having to revise her initial impression of the guy on the fly. She still thought he was an arrogant ass, but maybe this was a situation in which being an arrogant ass wasn't necessarily a negative.

But Nikki was still glaring at Brix. "Let go of my arm, bitch."

Trevor moved into position next to Brix. "Hey, she's just trying to help."

Nikki rolled her eyes. "More like trying to help herself to my man."

Brix began to lose her cool. They couldn't stand here arguing with the zombies getting closer by the second. Nikki was being stupid. And Brix wasn't about to die because of someone else's stupidity. She reached past Nikki, shoved the seat forward, and pushed the suddenly screaming, indignant girl into the back. Brix stepped aside, glanced at Trevor, who gave her a nod and crawled into the back with the screeching brat.

Brix dropped into the passenger seat and pulled on the interior door handle. It closed with a resounding thunk. She looked at Jason. "Burn fucking rubber."

He worked the Malibu's gearshift. "Whatever you say, boss."

And Brix couldn't help it when she grinned, though she turned her face away from Jason to hide the expression. There was a world of zombies out there. A world teeming with unimaginable horrors. A world in its death throes. She had every reason to feel nothing but overwhelming despair. But she did not. Now that she had some sense of her bearings and they were taking some kind of action, she was able to admit she was almost excited. A part of her was eager to face the challenge of surviving in this world overrun with animated dead. This wasn't something she would admit to the others, not even Trevor. They would think there was something wrong with her, perhaps even be disgusted by her.

In a way, she'd been preparing herself for precisely this moment since childhood—since her first ever illicit midnight viewing of *Night of the Living Dead.*

Jason gave the Malibu the gas again.

And the car leapt forward.

Into the night.

Toward their destiny. Toward whatever awaited them out there. Brix tightened her grip on the gun in her lap.

ELEVEN

John Dorsey couldn't breathe. The masked man's big hand was locked tight around his throat, constricting the airway down to nothing. He wheezed and clawed at the man's hand, digging his fingernails into the rough skin and drawing thin trickles of blood. But the effort was to no avail. Just as he was on the verge of succumbing to panic, he had a brainstorm. He allowed himself to go limp, feigning unconsciousness. He couldn't match this behemoth's strength, but maybe he could outwit him. It was a long shot. Odds were his opponent would keep the pressure on at least long enough to ensure genuine unconsciousness or even death. It was what John would do in his position. And it was the smart thing to do.

But maybe the masked psycho wasn't so smart, because the moment John went limp the guy let go of his throat and shoved him away. John hit the ground hard and didn't move. He desperately wanted to gasp for breath after the long seconds of excruciating deprivation, but, aside from a single big intake of oxygen as he was tossed aside, he managed to keep his mouth shut. Maintaining the illusion of unconsciousness, at least for the next several moments, was key to survival. He still wasn't at all certain the big man was buying his performance. But he did know any kind of miscue now would seal his doom.

He heard the man get to his feet and then stand there breathing heavily behind his mask for a few moments. John didn't know which direction the man was facing, but he pictured him staring straight down at him, black eyes flicking behind the eye-holes of the mask as he watched him for signs of life. John could almost feel those eyes on him, boring into his flesh. It made his guts curdle. At last, though, he heard the man moving away from him, the wet ground squelching beneath his booted feet. He then heard the man grunt and let out a big breath. It wasn't hard to guess what he was doing. He was retrieving his fallen chainsaw. John tensed at the realization. Any second now the chainsaw would roar to life. John couldn't help it—this time he did begin to panic. He couldn't just keep lying here in the mud, waiting to die. Still, he was scared to move. The maniac was still very close. But a moment of truth was coming. John decided that if he heard those footsteps start back in his direction, he would get off his ass and start running.

The man did start moving again . . . but the sound of his footsteps soon receded. He was headed in another direction. John opened one eye, risking a peek at the retreating figure's broad back. The glimpse was enough to verify two things—that he had indeed retrieved the chainsaw, and that he was going after the girl John had at least temporarily saved. That big gap between two of the trees he disappeared through was proof of that. The girl had gone that way, John was sure of it.

And he was just as certain of something else.

The maniac would catch her.

The man likely knew these woods well. It was a reasonable assumption, anyway. He wouldn't be randomly walking around out here with a chainsaw. But John reminded himself that this was regular world logic. Those rules might not apply to . . . wherever the hell this was. The dude was like something out of a cheap slasher flick. The kind where there was no kind of real logic at all. Just a series of excuses to knock off scantily-clad starlets in the most gruesome ways possible. Could be he and the girl had been sent to some twisted alternate reality governed by a similar lack of logic. Could also be the guy's whole reason for existence was to chase pretty girls through these damp woods.

Jesus, it made his head hurt just thinking about it. All he really knew was he had to help that girl. He thought of Marie, lying there butchered and nude on their bed. Brutally murdered by some other psycho motherfucker while he'd been passed out drunk. He would never forgive himself for that. Marie was dead because he had failed her.

He wouldn't fail this time.

Or if he did, he would die trying to do the right thing. For once.

He got to his feet and took off running.

~

Darkness swallowed her. It was as if instead of running into the woods she had run straight into the enormous mouth of some great beast. A beast that had now closed its mouth and soon would suck her down its gullet to its stomach. It was an easy enough thing to believe thanks to how all of existence seemed to have been replaced by a formless, endless black void. The impression was unsettling, but she didn't allow it to slow her down. Though she couldn't see anything, she could still feel the ground beneath her feet. That was enough to keep her anchored to reality—or to what was passing for reality now. And the still stark memory of what she was running from was more than enough to keep her in motion. Unfortunately, she couldn't go nearly as fast as she wished. The darkness was impeding her speed, of course, but so were the stylish shoes she was wearing. They simply weren't designed for running blindly in the dark. She kept slipping on the wet ground, but she mostly managed to remain upright by flailing for—and grabbing onto—the abundant low-hanging branches of the many tall trees around her. Sometimes, though, her hands grabbed nothing but air and she would go tumbling to her hands and knees. But every time she was able to claw her way back to her feet and get moving again. She was even able to establish a decent half-running pace after a while. She was moving fast enough that for the first time she began to feel the first real ray of hope. If she could just stay focused and keep moving, she might survive this insane night after all.

Then she ran into the tree.

The blackness was so complete she never saw it looming in front her. She ran right into its wide base at a pace just short of an all-out run. The collision blasted the breath from her lungs and sent her tumbling backward to the ground. The impact when her body hit the ground was painful enough, but it was made worse by the sharp rock that gouged the small of her back. An edge of the rock cut through the lacy fabric of her camisole top and sliced into her flesh. Blood from the wound stained the ground beneath her as she cried out in agony and rolled onto her side to escape the sensation of the rock digging into her flesh. The movement was too soon after so hard a blow, though, and triggered another jolt of even more intense pain. This time it brought tears to her eyes and she cried out again, louder than before.

Stupid, she thought. *So stupid.*

You have to be quiet.

He might hear you.

She didn't know whether the masked man was still after her. It was possible the stranger who had come to her rescue had subdued him. Or even killed him. The latter didn't seem likely. The stranger was kind of beefy, but the clear overall strength advantage belonged to the muscular masked man. She recalled how, in the last moment before her dash into the woods, the man's big hand had clamped hard around the stranger's throat. No, she had to assume the stranger was dead and that the psycho in the mask was on her trail again. And that meant she had to keep as quiet as possible, even when she felt like screaming from hurting so much.

So Lashon set her jaw and bit back the next scream as she again struggled to her feet. Once she was upright, that sense of directionless disorientation was worse than ever. But she couldn't just stand there so she held out a hand and took a few cautious, exploratory steps straight ahead. The palm of her hand soon touched the rough texture of tree bark. She moved her hand over the bark, enough to discern that it was a *very* big tree. She was certain it was the one that had knocked her to the ground. So she felt her way around the tree and got moving again, this time at a slower, more cautious pace. She still detected no sounds of pursuit, so it was probably okay to move a bit more deliberately now. She hoped so, anyway.

After a few more minutes of blind groping and forward motion, a thing that felt nearly like a miracle occurred. The thick canopy of leafy tree branches overhead began to thin out some, letting in a bit of diffused moonlight. The downside to this was that more rain began to patter her head again, but that was okay because at least she could fucking *see* now. Just a little, it was true, but it was better than nothing.

As she kept moving, her thoughts returned to her rescuer. She knew nothing about him. Who he was. What his name was. Not a damn thing. And he knew the same nothing about her. She was just a stranger to him, as well. And yet he hadn't hesitated to put himself in harm's way to help her. It was even possible he had given his own life to save hers. Which was really brave and admirable and all, but it was also kind of fucked up, because if she survived this she would always feel guilt for the sacrifice he had made. Didn't mean she'd change anything about what had happened even if she could. She wanted to live, even at the expense of someone else's life or safety. She didn't much like what that said about her, but not liking it didn't make it any less true.

The trees continued to thin out as she pressed ahead. The rain also tapered off and soon stopped altogether. She glanced upward now and then and was pleased to note that the sky seemed to be clearing. It was warm and humid now that the rain had passed. But the still-damp camisole top felt plastered to her skin. A change of clothes would be one of the first items on her agenda should she manage to escape this place. She was still hearing no evidence of pursuit. The cautious optimism she had felt before began to return. The feeling intensified significantly when she began to discern noises from somewhere ahead.

Boisterous voices.

Music.

Laughter.

All very faint, but getting louder with each few steps forward. The sounds were heartening. They were like signals from the normal world, that wonderful place where chainsaw-wielding masked men existed only in movies. She couldn't make out anything being said yet, but something in the timbre of the voices made it very plain these were young people in good spirits, a family or group of friends partying a bit and . . . having a good time . . . in the woods. Which struck her as sort of strange considering how nasty the weather had been until just a few minutes ago and for other, murkier reasons she couldn't quite pinpoint.

A few dozen yards further along, she began to perceive the dim outline of a house through the trees. The sight of it spurred her to a faster pace. The house sat in the middle of a sizable clearing in the woods. It came into sharper focus as she neared the line of trees at the edge of the clearing. It was a two-story wood house with a long porch in front. External lights lit up the area around the house well enough that she could make out a narrow dirt road that dead-ended at the clearing. The road wound away into another section of the woods somewhere off to her right. There were multiple vehicles parked outside the house, including an SUV and a jeep with big, mud-flecked tires. The sight of these things brought tears to Lashon's eyes. Her blind flight through the treacherous woods had brought her to the perfect place. Ahead of her was a real, tangible path out of this nightmare. Someone here could drive her to the nearest hospital or police station. She couldn't believe her luck. If she had turned in a different direction after her collision with the tree, she wouldn't have happened upon this place or these people. She might still be fleeing sightlessly through thickening darkness.

I'm meant to live, she thought. *God wants me to live. It's fated.*

The thought triggered an eruption of grateful tears.

Several people were hanging out on the porch. A few with beers in their hands were standing at one end near a grill. Others were sitting in chairs or leaning on the porch railing. No one had noticed her yet because she still hadn't entered the clearing. Lashon paused just inside the line of trees, studying the strangers and wondering what she might tell them. Hers was a pretty wild story. If she told them everything, they might think she was crazy. No, clearly some level of fabrication was in order. But she would have to do her damnedest to convince them that some crazy man had been chasing her through the woods. There was real danger lurking out here tonight and they needed to know that.

She let out a breath and took a step toward the line of trees. A sound somewhere behind her made her gasp. She whirled about and scanned the gloom-shrouded woods. She saw trees and the blackness between them. And nothing else. No sign of a masked man in dirty overalls. And yet she had heard *something.* A sharp, cracking sound. The kind of sound, say, that a booted foot might make when stepping on a fallen branch. And although she couldn't see anyone out there in the gloom, it was possible her pursuer—if he was out there at all— might be lurking behind one of the big trees, waiting patiently for her to turn her back to him again.

It was a creepy thing to think and she tried to dismiss it.

But she couldn't.

Several moments passed.

And then the sound came again, closer now, from somewhere off to her right.

Fuck this, she thought.

She spun around again and ran into the clearing.

TWELVE

Kira stared blankly at the stone fireplace at the opposite end of the room and tried to think what she might do next. She didn't like the idea of just sitting here and waiting for this "Master" person to show up and take another bite out of her neck, but she didn't appear to have any other options. A significant block of time passed. Perhaps as much as a half hour. Long enough to start feeling bored. Lacking anything else to do, she stood up and walked over to one of the black-painted windows. Nailed shut. An inspection of the other windows showed they had all been secured in the same manner. Seeing this did nothing to calm her nerves. She was a prisoner and there was no way out. She could maybe try to smash through one of the windows and climb out to drop to the ground below but that would make a lot of noise. The big blond guys would kick the door open and be on her long before she could get outside. She had locked the door from the inside, but the door was made of wood and the lock was hardly imposing. It wouldn't delay the blond goons more than a second or two. Not nearly long enough. And the guards were far from the only complicating factor. She had no idea how high up this room was, whether it was on a second or third story. It could be quite a drop from the window to the ground below.

It was hopeless. There truly was no way out.

Kira wandered over to the full-length oval mirror mounted on a stand next to the wardrobe. She stared at the image of herself in the tiny blue nightie. She frowned. She hated to admit it, but she sort of liked the way she looked in it. The cut of the flimsy garment emphasized the jut of her breasts and the swell of her hips in a baldly erotic way. She turned a little for a side-view of her figure, admiring the flatness of her belly and her slender, toned legs. She had taken up running at the beginning of the latest semester and it had shown some serious dividends in terms of her physical appearance. It was something she had known in a vague way for a while, but until now she had not fully appreciated the extent of the improvement. She really looked kind of . . . hot.

She felt good about it for maybe five seconds.

Then she frowned again.

Awesome, she thought. *Congratulations. You turned yourself into a hottie. And now you've attracted the attention of a vampire with a naughty nightie fetish.*

It was the stuff of kinky fantasy. Unfortunately, now it was also real life. Sort of. She still hadn't worked out just how "real" this alternate world was. So much about it seemed too ridiculous, like things staged for a cheap movie. The room reminded her of sets from old European horror films she had seen on Netflix. The guards were caricatures of B-movie villain henchmen. And yet it all looked and felt real enough. No matter how fantastical it all seemed, she was convinced this was no elaborate put-on. Nor was it a hallucination. No hallucination could ever be so finely detailed. All she really knew was that whatever had happened to bring her to this alternate world was beyond her understanding.

She turned away from the mirror and returned to the bed, suddenly unable to bear looking any longer at her sleek and, yes, very lovely body. Just as she was about to sit, she heard the sound of a key being inserted in the bedroom door's lock. She turned away from the bed and stared in sudden, wide-eyed terror as the knob rotated. She heard the click of the bolt as it retracted and then the door creaked open on hinges in dire need of oiling.

The vampire strode into the room, pushing the door shut behind him.

Kira's heart slammed in her chest. She sucked in an involuntary breath and just stood there, shaking like a scared little kid in the presence of a hulking, abusive father. She was in the presence of a for-real fucking *monster*. Oh, he didn't *look* like a monster. His physical appearance was that of an attractive man in his mid-thirties. He stood maybe a hair over six feet. He had penetrating dark eyes and a chiseled jaw line, as well as thick, wavy brown hair, a hank of which fell rakishly over his forehead.

"You need not fear me." His English was fluent, but he had an accent she couldn't immediately identify. It was vaguely European. "I mean you no harm."

Kira at last managed to swallow the lump in her throat. "I . . . I don't think I believe you."

The peered at her in a quizzical way. "Oh? And why not?"

Kira touched the marks on her neck. "This, for one thing. I do tend to fear men who take actual *bites* out of my flesh." Her frightened expression shifted, hardening into a kind of fearful anger. "And then there's the whole abduction thing. Really, I've got a whole list of reasons to be afraid of you. Also, what have you done with my friend?"

The vampire laughed softly and took a step toward her.

Kira took a matching step backward.

The vampire ceased his advance and held up a placating hand. "Please. You must relax. I merely wish to talk to you and explain what's happened and why you are here."

Kira couldn't help it . . . she laughed. "Oh, yeah? That's gonna take some serious explaining. Because I'll tell you right now, there's nothing you can say that'll make me okay with this bullshit."

The vampire smiled. "That remains to be seen. All I ask is you reserve judgment and listen to what I have to say. I suspect your attitude toward me will change significantly once you understand the true reasons for your presence here."

Kira grunted.

Not likely, you bloodsucking freak.

"Whatever. It's not like I really have a choice."

Another smile.

But this time he didn't dispute her assertion.

"Hey, asshole. Another question for you."

His smile faltered.

Good. Got to you. Finally.

It was nice to see the smug bastard off balance, if only for a moment.

"Why am I dressed like a fucking whore? Seriously. This is another of those teensy little things that don't do a whole lot to reassure me about your intentions."

There was an accompanying dark twinkle in his eyes as his smile returned, a hint of his true predatory nature. Instead of answering her question, he strode across the room to a waist-high cabinet set against the wall between two of the blacked-out windows. The cabinet's top was comprised of two sliding panels. He pushed these apart and reached inside, pulling out a bottle filled with some type of brown liquor and two cocktail glasses.

He waggled one of the glasses at her. "Drink?"

Kira's instinct was to decline, but she hesitated. She realized she was thirsty. And a drink of something strong did sound kind of nice right about now. She was trapped in a bizarre and inexplicable situation with no obvious way out. She stared at the bottle and the shimmering liquid within.

She shrugged. "Sure. Fine. Whatever."

"I'm afraid we have no ice. I could have some brought in if you like."

"Just pour the fucking drink, please. Um, and some ice and water later would be nice. If you could arrange that."

He unscrewed the cap from the bottle and poured more than an inch of booze into each glass. After returning the bottle to the cabinet, he approached her again, holding out one of the glasses for her. "Of course I can arrange that. You can have whatever you want." Yet another creepy smile. "Within reason."

Kira accepted the glass and took a tentative sip from it. "Um . . . wow. That's really good. What is it?"

"A very fine one-hundred-year-old bourbon."

Kira nearly gagged on her next sip of the delicious liquid. "Seriously?"

The vampire peered at her in that vaguely amused quizzical way of his. "Excuse me?"

"Come on. You're seriously telling me I just drank something a century old? You're shitting me, right?"

"It is the absolute truth, I assure you. I'm particularly fond of this batch. An extraordinarily limited quantity was produced especially for me. This is one of my last remaining bottles. I deem precious few of my guests worthy of it."

Kira mulled this over for a few moments rather than instantly applying. Of course she caught the implication that he had been alive a hundred years ago, despite possessing the physical appearance of a youngish man. It jibed with one of the most basic elements of vampire folklore, that of the ageless immortal bloodsucker. She guessed many other clichés of vampiric literature and film would be rooted in reality in this world. Reality, again, being relative. Here, just as in many movies from her world, vampires might fry in the light of the sun, fear crosses, or cringe at the smell of garlic. Or be killed with a wooden stake through the heart or via decapitation. There was no good reason to believe any of this, other than the way things worked here conformed to the way things worked in the low-budget film *Blood Lust* and its countless antecedents. There were probably even actual vampire hunters in this world. Real Van Helsings. Real Buffys. Which, if true, would be sort of awesome.

She found herself smiling at the thought.

The vampire's expression turned quizzical again. "Have I amused you in some way? I assure you I'm not exaggerating."

"Say what?"

He nodded at the glass in her hand. "Regarding the bourbon. I truly do almost never share it with guests."

"Huh. So why did you have it stored in an unlocked cabinet?"

"I had it stored here shortly after your arrival, while you were still unconscious. I knew even then I'd be sharing it with you."

Kira nodded. "Right. Because I'm special or something."

He smiled. "Indeed you are."

Another nod from Kira.

Right. Of course I am. Because I'm the fucking star of this story.

Another absurdity. But it happened to fit in smoothly with all the million other little absurdities coloring her current circumstances, so she could hardly dismiss the notion as nonsense.

An idea occurred to her. It was sort of crazy, but such was the strength of the compulsion that she had no choice but to take the chance.

She held out her glass. "Could you hold this a second?"

The vampire's expression was wary, but he took the glass. Despite the wariness, there was amusement in his eyes. He was indulging her because he was utterly unafraid of her. And why would he fear her? From his perspective, she was just a helpless human girl.

Kira smiled. "Thanks. Just need to test a little something."

She extended her hands toward him and positioned her index fingers in the form of a cross. The vampire cringed away from her. The glasses slipped from his hands and shattered on the hardwood floor, spilling precious ounces of priceless aged bourbon. He hissed at her and bared his teeth. The incisors at the corners of his mouth instantly elongated into fangs. The hair on his head thickened and stiffened and his brown eyes turned a menacing shade of midnight black.

Kira gulped.

Uh-oh.

The knowledge that she had fucked up in a very serious way hit her with breathtaking force. She had made the critical mistake of treating this like a game. The world she was in did seem strongly informed by the rules of fiction from her world, but this world *was* real. She was no actress in a corny stage play. Everything about this situation was ridiculous on the surface, but that in no way diminished the genuine danger she was in just by being here.

She pulled her hands toward her chest and her expression turned apologetic. "I'm sorry. I didn't mean anything by that. Really. I just had to . . . to . . ." She was shaking and it was becoming harder to push the words out. "Had to . . . see . . ."

She stopped.

There was nothing she could say that would make any sense to him. And nothing to do but throw herself on his mercy.

"Please don't hurt me."

She pulled her fingers apart and dropped her hands.

The vampire continued to regard her warily, perhaps gauging whether she might have any other nasty surprises for him. His fangs were still extended and his hair was still doing that strange fright-wig thing. But his posture was more relaxed and his eyes weren't quite so black. For a long moment, Kira was almost able to believe there would be no serious consequences for her stupid stunt.

Then he hissed at her again.

Oh, shit.

She never had a real shot at defending herself. He was too fast. Blindingly fast. One second she was standing there and the next his hands were on her. Then she was flying backward, her feet leaving the ground for a moment before she began to descend. Her back hit the canopied bed's plush mattress and then he was on her again, his unbelievably strong body pinning her to the bed and rendering her immobile. He snarled at her and bared his teeth again, rearing his head backward as his mouth opened impossibly wide.

Kira's eyes filled with tears. "Please. No."

His head snapped toward her neck and his fangs pierced the tender flesh of her throat, causing her to cry out in anguish and pain. She whimpered and trembled uncontrollably as he began to drink from her. But then a strange thing happened. As he continued to drink of her blood, the pain began to fade and then, finally, stopped altogether. Even stranger, the sensation of her blood being drawn into his mouth turned pleasurable, almost unbearably so. She was turned on. She was too overcome by the delicious sensations to puzzle much over the oddity of this development. Her nipples stiffened. She moaned. When she became aware of the massive erection straining the crotch of his jeans, the moans gave way to animal grunts, primal expressions of the most intense desire she had ever known.

The vampire raised himself up and tore the flimsy nightie from her body with a single vicious swipe. She was screaming for him by then. And he obliged her. His clothes came off quickly and then he dove inside her, making her scream again. She screamed many more times before it was over.

And then, after a while, she had occasion to scream yet again.

~

When Monroe reached the bottom of the winding stone staircase, he arrived in a very small room with a dusty wooden floor and stone walls. There was a big door set in the middle of the wall directly facing him as he came off the final step and set foot on the floor. Wood planks creaked beneath his feet as he moved further into the room. He approached the black door, but stopped short of it, frowning. The door was made of iron and had a closed port at approximate eye-level. Torches mounted in sconces to either side of the door blazed brilliantly. His head swiveled this way and that as he took a look around the room. Except for the top half of an ancient human skull wedged into a corner, there wasn't much to see. The skull was disturbing, sure, but he was unsurprised to discover someone had died down here. The only mystery on that count was what had happened to the rest of the poor bastard. The big iron door was the only way in or out of the room. Unless you counted the tall staircase he'd just descended. And given the dire warning he'd received about attempting a return journey, you couldn't count that at all.

So, then . . . this door.

He couldn't stand here staring at it forever. The guards had told him precious little about what to expect once he reached the bottom of the staircase. He had expected some form of demented arrival party. A gaggle of capering, leering goons, some kind of old-time horror movie shit like that. It was possible his imagination had run a little wild over the course of the long descent down the stone steps. Of course, he wasn't too upset about the lack of capering goons. That would have been a whole lot of no fucking fun at all. But, coupled with his dearth of knowledge about how to proceed, the room's emptiness was somehow more ominous. The moans and screams issuing from somewhere on the other side of the heavy iron door weren't too reassuring either. He wondered whether he was expected to open the door himself and walk on through into whatever chamber of horrors awaited him on the other side.

Probably.

Monroe listened to the screams a while longer. After several minutes, he turned away from the door and walked back to the foot of the stone staircase, where he took a seat on the bottom step and crossed his arms over his knees. Because fuck it, maybe there really was no way out of this shit. That didn't mean he had to offer himself up on a goddamn platter for these assholes. They could damn well come out here and drag him inside themselves.

Whoever "they" were.

He didn't have a clue on that point either. Could be there were more vampires on the other side of that door. Or maybe some skulking, Renfield-like servant goons. He didn't know and he didn't care. All that really mattered was that people were being tortured in there. And what he was hearing was the sound of his own future. As he sat there, his head filled with an array of medieval torture scenarios. Thumbscrews. Racks. Red-hot branding irons. And so on and so forth. The thought of enduring that level of agony, especially over a drawn-out period of time, was inconceivable. He would be begging for death, just like all those miserable bastards he was hearing now.

After a while, it was too much. He clapped his hands over his ears to shut out the sickening sounds. He shut his eyes and tried to imagine he was somewhere, anywhere, else. Some tropical beach paradise, maybe, or front row and center at a Led Zeppelin reunion concert. That would fucking *rule*. Man, he could just picture it. The crowd roaring, going wild. Jimmy Page ripping into some gargantuan riff. The air thick with the pungent odor of pot, like at all the wild 70s shows he'd read about. It was so vivid, so crystal clear, it was almost like—

His eyes snapped open at the sound of a heavy bolt being thrown back. He jumped to his feet as the big door began to swing open, giving serious consideration to a mad dash back up the stairs, regardless of the warnings he'd received.

Then a guy who looked like a taller Tom Cruise peered around the edge of the door at him. He frowned. "Dude. What are you doing over there?"

"Uh . . . um . . ." Monroe blinked rapidly for several moments before giving his head a hard shake. "N-Nothing. Not doing much. Just . . ." He blew out a breath and rolled his eyes toward the ceiling for a moment before looking at Tom Cruise again and shrugging. ". . . hanging out."

The guy laughed and came out into the room. "Hanging out?"

Monroe bounced up and down on the heels of his feet. He was feeling jittery. "That's about the size of it."

Tom Cruise laughed again. "Hilarious."

This was some weird shit. Weirder even than capering goons or more vampires. Tom Cruise was wearing khaki shorts and a polo shirt with the collar popped up, like in some cheesy 80s movie.

What the fucking hell is up with this shit? Have I died and gone to fucking Ferris Bueller land?

Tom Cruise laughed yet again. "You crazy stoner bastard."

Monroe flicked his long hair out of his eyes and rocked back on his heels again. "Oh. Right. Sure. *I'm* the crazy one. And meanwhile, there you are, standing over there looking like Mr. 1985."

"1986."

"Say what now?"

Tom Cruise flashed a gleaming, movie-star grin. "I've been down here since 1986."

"How's that? You don't look any older than me."

Tom's mega-wattage grin widened some more. Fangs popped. "Vampire."

Monroe gulped. "Oh. I see. Well . . . don't really know what to say to that."

Tom's fangs retracted. He shook his head and chuckled. "Come along with me now. You know you've got no choice."

Monroe sighed, feeling a deep resignation. Tom Cruise was right. He really did have no choice. So he came off the bottom step again, shoved his hands into his hip pockets, and slouch-shouldered his way across the creaky floor.

Tom Cruise shook his head again. "Relax, pal. It's not gonna be so bad, I promise."

"Right. The screams say otherwise."

Tom's perma-smile slipped a notch. "Oh, that. Sorry. Hold on."

He turned away from Monroe and slipped through the door. Monroe followed him into a room that bore no resemblance to any medieval chamber of horrors he'd ever seen in movies. This room was more like the rec room of some insanely wealthy family's lavish vacation home. It was big, for one thing, about the size of the cafeteria back in high school, with completely modern fixtures and furnishings. There were bubbling Jacuzzis on an elevated space at the far end of the room. Girls in bikinis were in the water, all of them holding cocktail glasses with wedges of lime stuck on the rims. Behind them a mural depicted an ocean view as seen from the bay window of a beach house. There were several other people lounging about on sofas, swayback chairs, and beanbag chairs. Some were talking and nursing frothy drinks, while others were reading or napping. There was an area for pool tables and foosball tables. Old school arcade games lined one wall. A full bar dominated another wall, complete with a tuxedoed bartender in a bowtie, who was flipping bottles around in a showy way like . . .

Like motherfucking Tom Cruise in that other goddamn movie. None of this can be real. It's just not possible. I must have fallen and hit my head when I reached the bottom of those stairs. That's the only explanation. I'm dreaming this crazy shit.

Except . . . it didn't *feel* like a dream. At all.

Tom pulled the door shut once Monroe was inside and moved to a control panel mounted on the wall next to the door. He grinned again at Monroe as he pushed a button, silencing the screams.

Monroe stared slack-jawed at him for a long, long moment. "Motherfucker."

Tom clapped his hands together once and laughed long and hard at that. "Oh, man. You should see your face. You look *pissed.*" Then he gave Monroe a jocular slap on the shoulder. "Relax, bro. Just a little hazing thing we like to do with the new arrivals. The guards call down and tell us ahead of time to expect someone and I turn on the screams to round out the whole Hammer Studios horror vibe of the descent. No harm intended, though. It's all in good fun."

Monroe shrugged away Tom's hand and took a cautious step backward, regarding him warily and not trusting that affable smile in the least. There was a monumental disconnect between the terrifying experiences of earlier in the evening and the strange revelations of this room. It was as if someone had spliced together random scenes from two totally disparate films, so jarring was the difference. *The Satanic Rites of Dracula* meets fucking *Risky Business*.

Please, God, dude . . . if you're out there, get me out of this bizarro world and I promise I'll never do anything bad again. I mean, you know, within reason. I'm not about to become a monk or anything, but I'll definitely make an effort.

Monroe waited.

He glanced up at the high ceiling.

Nothing.

Tom was sort of frowning now, while still somehow maintaining his smile. "What are you looking at?"

Monroe shrugged. "Nothing. Nothing at all."

Tom nodded. "Right. Well, I can tell you're scared, but for real, you can relax. You don't know it yet, but you're among friends here."

"No offense, but I find that hard to believe. I was attacked and brought here against my will." He tapped his chin with the tip of an index finger, as if he'd just thought of something super important. "Oh, yeah, and I was threatened with death. So you'll just have to cut me some slack if I find it a little hard to believe a goddamn thing you say."

Tom's expression sobered some more. "Right. I understand. Totally. You've been through a lot, but the worst is over. Well . . . nearly over."

"What's that supposed to mean?"

"Well, there are one or two little bits of mild unpleasantness we have to deal with before we can move on to the fun stuff."

"Such as?"

Tom's expression was mildly pained. Even so, the smile never entirely went away. How was that even possible? It was creepy as fuck.

"Well, and I apologize in advance for this part, but there's simply no way around it . . . we do have to kill you."

Monroe made a dash for the heavy iron door, seizing the handle with both hands and tugging at it with all his strength. There was no thought in this. Just instant reaction. Surrender to primitive instinct and panic. A wild and uncontrolled drive to escape, regardless of how impossible it seemed.

The door didn't budge.

Monroe screamed. "*SHIT!*"

He tugged at the handle again, screaming some more.

Behind him, Tom was laughing again. "Door's electronically locked. That sound you heard in the waiting chamber of a bolt being thrown back? Another sound effect."

Gotta get out, gotta get out, gotta get out—

Tom chuckled, right behind him now. "All right, enough of that nonsense."

He seized Monroe by a bicep and pulled him away from the door with astonishing ease. Then he spun him around and started dragging him across the room toward the elevated space where the Jacuzzis and bikini-wearing girls were. Monroe flailed and struggled to tear himself free from Tom's grip, but the guy's strength was inhuman. Which made sense, what with him being a goddamn vampire.

The girls all turned smiling faces their way as they reached the Jacuzzis. Some were sitting on the edges of the Jacuzzis, while others were fully in the water. Even in his terrified state, Monroe couldn't help noticing how gorgeous they all were. Each was gifted with Playboy centerfold racks and curves. Theirs were the faces of perfect, slutty angels.

One of the girls, a stunning brunette with flowing shoulder-length hair and eyes a brilliant shade of blue, swiveled her hips on the edge of the nearest Jacuzzi, turning herself to face them fully. "Who have you brought us tonight, Tom?"

Despite everything, Monroe couldn't help laughing.

Tom.

Well, that's fucking convenient.

"His name's Monroe. Be gentle with him, girls. Don't make him all the way dead. Monroe's a special case. He's to become one of us."

The blue-eyed brunette beauty smiled. "Wonderful. About time we got some new blood in here."

Monroe looked at Tom. "Dude, I don't wanna be a vampire."

Tom's grin took on a wicked aspect. "Tough shit."

He grabbed Monroe with both hands, lifted him as easily as he'd lift a child, and tossed him into the nearest Jacuzzi. Monroe plunged into the water, his head sinking fully beneath the surface for an instant before several sets of hands seized him at once and pulled him back up. He gasped for breath, blinked water out of his eyes, and stared around him at the bevy of curvaceous, dripping wet bikini beauties.

They were all smiling very broadly.

Too broadly.

Fangs popped at the corners of all those lovely mouths. And then they were all tossing their heads back and doing this totally unnerving, weird hissing thing.

Aw, crap.

And then they were on him.

It felt like heaven at first. All that soft, jiggling female flesh pressing against him from every angle.

And then it hurt.

A lot.

THIRTEEN

Stalled and wrecked cars choked the streets of the ruined city. Jason was nonetheless able to navigate his way through by using sidewalks and road shoulders, as well as by occasionally exploiting gaps in the unmoving sea of automobiles. There were bodies in varying stages of decomposition in some of the cars, while others were empty. Other corpses were splayed across medians. Still others had fallen in the road. Jason frequently had no choice but to drive over the ones in the way. This made all of them, even Brix, a little queasy each time it happened. There were more zombies everywhere she looked. Not huge throngs of them like in a lot of movies. Their ranks were thinner than that. But they were numerous enough to present a significant problem. The shambling forms would stop at the sound of the approaching engine noise and turn in that familiar clumsy way to eye them hungrily. And then they would stagger in their direction. Some moved in a steady yet relentless gait. Others fell over after a step or two. The ones that fell often had trouble regaining their feet, but even these refused to give up the scent of the fresh flesh that had entered their vicinity, crawling or using their hands to pull themselves forward.

For Brix, it was all a little unnerving, but she was staying mostly calm now.

Nikki, however, was becoming completely unhinged. She bounced up and down in the back, occasionally pounding her fists in frustration and uncomprehending rage against the back of Jason's seat. She cried. She screamed. And over and over, she asked the same maddening, unanswerable questions.

"What's going on? How did all this happen while we were in the theater? It doesn't make any sense. Nothing makes any fucking sense. Why isn't anyone explaining this fucking shit to me? How did this happen? *How-how-how-how-how-how-how*—"

Enough.

Brix turned in her seat and aimed the Glock at Nikki. "Shut up. Now."

Sudden, shocked silence.

But only for a moment.

Nikki reared back and kicked the back of Jason's seat with the flat of a foot, hard enough to make Jason lose his grip on the steering wheel for a moment.

Jason's head snapped backward for a second as he leveled an angry glare at his girlfriend. "Knock that shit off, Nikki! You almost made me crash."

Nikki kicked the seat again, harder than before. "*Fuck you, Jason! That bitch is pointing a gun at me! Fucking make her stop right fucking now!*"

Everyone cringed at the volume she was able to generate that time.

Jason shot an apologetic look Brix's way. "Um . . . could you maybe stop pointing that at her? Just, you know, so we could have a more peaceful ride."

"I ought to blow her brains out. *That* would make things more peaceful."

Jason looked pained. "Hey, come on . . . she's my girlfriend."

Brix snorted. "You poor bastard."

Nikki laughed. "Wow. What an unbelievable cunt you are. You were treating Jason like scum before all this went down. Now you're all fucking *interested* in him all of a sudden. Don't even lie, bitch, I can see it in your eyes."

"You're crazy."

Nikki laughed some more. "I'm not. And two can play this game."

She scooted closer to Trevor and put her hand on his knee,

maintaining eye contact with Brix the whole time. Trevor had been sitting there in stunned silence, looking shell-shocked at being so close to all that noise and rage. Now he just looked startled and scared, almost like a mouse suddenly cornered by a pouncing cat.

Brix glared at her in simmering fury for a long moment. Then she pulled the gun away so that it was no longer pointing at Nikki. "There. You happy? I've done what you wanted. Now get away from *my* boy-friend."

Nikki smiled as she turned away from Brix, wrapped her arms around Trevor's neck, and leaned into him to press her mouth against his, thrusting her tongue between his parted lips. The kiss went on for several seconds while Brix fumed and Trevor made muffled noises of protest.

Jason had noticed what was going on and now he sounded pissed. "Jesus, Nikki. Cut that shit out right now."

Nikki broke off the kiss and smiled darkly at the back of his head. "Or what?"

"Or this." Trevor shrugged free of her embrace and shoved her roughly away from him. "Let that be the last time you lay your skeezy hands on me, bitch. I wouldn't want you if you were the last girl on earth."

Brix smirked. "That's my boy."

Nikki glared hatefully at him for a moment.

And then she erupted again, screaming yet again and kicking the back of Jason's seat with both feet. The seat rocked forward with tremendous force, startling Jason and sending the steering wheel spinning out of his grip. Instinct made Brix drop the Glock and lurch toward the steering wheel, but by the time her hand locked around the molded plastic, it was too late. The Malibu slammed into the side of a stalled U-Haul trailer, resulting in a grinding, ominous crunch of metal. The impact ripped her hand from the steering wheel and threw her against the dash, causing her to cry out in pain. Jason was thrown against the steering wheel and cried out, too. There was screaming from the back as Brix fell awkwardly back into her seat. She was momentarily too stunned to act when Nikki surged forward and reached between the seats to snag the fallen Glock. Brix's eyes went wide as the barrel came level with the center of her face. One glimpse of Nikki's grim, snarling expression was all she needed to know the girl was about to kill her. She was already squeezing the trigger. There was nowhere to run. No cover to seek. She was fucking dead, that's all.

Or she would have been had Jason not interceded. He fell back from the steering wheel and saw what happening just in time to swat at Nikki's hands, throwing her aim off. The report of the gun was very loud inside the car, obscuring some more screaming. Thanks to Jason, the bullet punched harmlessly through the passenger side window instead of making a mess of Brix's head. But the crisis wasn't yet over. Nikki still had hold of the gun and she was correcting her aim to take another shot at Brix. But the delay allowed enough time for Jason and Trevor to attack Nikki simultaneously. Their hands guided her arm away from Brix again and the next shot went through the windshield. Nikki spewed indecipherable, screaming venom and squeezed the trigger yet another time. Brix knew it was her turn to act, and she had to do immediately, while Nikki's arm was immobile. She stiffened her hand and chopped at the other girl's thin wrist with as much brutal power as she could muster. Which was a lot. And then she did it another time.

The pain caused tears to burst forth from Nikki's eyes. She dropped the gun and Brix snatched it up again and pressed the barrel against her forehead.

Jason barked a single word at Brix: "Don't!"

Brix was shaking. Her finger trembled on the trigger. She didn't want to admit it, but the narrow escape had traumatized her. Her heart was going so fast she thought it might explode. She struggled to hold back tears of her own as she stared at Nikki's anguished, moisture-streaked face.

"Brix." Trevor. His tone soothing, gentle. "Listen to him. Don't do this. It's over. You're in control again. You don't need to kill her. And you don't really want to. That's not you."

Brix wrenched the gun away from Nikki's forehead, but glared murderously at the other girl. "I'm gonna sort shit out with you later. Believe it, bitch." She looked at Jason. "We've got bigger things to deal with now. Can you get this heap going again?"

Looking as relieved as a man who'd just narrowly escaped a date with the reaper himself, Jason heaved a breath and let go of Nikki. He reached for the ignition and gave the key a twist. Nothing. No grind of an engine struggling to come to life. Just that repeated ominous click as he turned the key back and forth several times.

He stopped trying and looked at Brix. "It's dead."

"Shit."

"Yeah."

Trevor also relinquished his grip on Nikki and turned in his seat to stare out the back window. "Um, guys . . . we're about to have a big fucking problem."

Brix followed his gaze and saw at once what he was talking about. Maybe the streets weren't quite choked with the living dead, but there were enough of them about to cluster into a small, deadly crowd given enough of an opportunity. And that was precisely what had happened after the crash and the ensuing struggle. The crowd of walking corpses was closing on the Malibu with deceptive speed. Another few moments and escape would be impossible.

"Everybody out!" Brix screamed the words. "Now!"

She got the door on her side open and emerged from the car just in time to put a bullet through the head of a zombie less than six feet in front of her. The zombie staggered backward and toppled over, knocking another hissing animated corpse to the ground with it. More screaming emanated from inside the car. A quick glance told the story. The door on Jason's side was stuck, the metal crumpled from the crash, and they were all struggling to get out through the passenger side door. Brix moved a few extra steps away to make room. It took several more seconds—precious time they could ill afford to lose—but the rest of them eventually managed to exit the crashed car to stand in slack-jawed terror behind Brix. They were moments away from total defeat. From agonizing death. They all felt this down to their bones. But, while the others allowed their terror to paralyze them, Brix realized it was down to her to act and be the leader.

A quick scan of the surroundings revealed they had crashed at the edge of a four-way intersection. More cars and corpses everywhere. She saw buildings. Convenience stores. A doughnut shop. Fast food restaurants. A full-service auto repair garage looked like potentially the most secure building, but it was too close and there were too many zombies in the way. Brix's head snapped rapidly this way and that, desperately seeking the way out. Then she locked on a distant row of houses, a residential area a hundred yards or so beyond the nearest convenience store.

A quick glance over her shoulder. "Follow me!"

She shot the next nearest zombie through an empty eye socket and took off running, hoping like hell the others had enough of their wits about them to follow immediately.

More zombies peeled off from the crowd and gave chase. These were the fresher ones. They were faster than the ones who had been rotting a while. Two more headshots took out two of the fleetest. She had lost track of how many rounds had been fired from the Glock's single clip. Too much confusion. But for sure the rounds wasted by Nikki during the struggle in the car didn't help matters. She needed to outrun these fuckers, not waste her remaining ammunition. No problem. She was young. She was fit. She could fucking fly when she felt like it. Her legs and arms pumped hard and her booted feet pounded the pavement as she blew by the convenience store and kept going. A one-legged zombie was lying in the street up ahead. It moaned and reached out to her with a badly rotted hand missing some of its fingers. Brix stutter-stepped around him and returned to full-speed in the space of maybe a second. She heard other running feet on the pavement behind her. Whether they were Trevor and the others or more zombies giving chase, she did not know.

As she zoomed into the residential area, she noted significantly fewer cars lining the street curbs. She took this as an indicator that most who lived here had chosen to flee the city. But to where? Refugee centers? Out to the countryside where there was more open space and less chance of being cornered by the living dead? She hadn't been here when the shit had gone down, so she couldn't know. But it would be a good thing for them—at least right this moment—if most of the survivors had scattered far and wide. It meant most of these homes would be empty. And empty houses meant a lower likelihood of a potentially deadly struggle with homeowners reluctant to allow entry to a group of desperate strangers.

She didn't slow down as she ran past the first block of houses. Nor the second. She heard voices yelling at her. Shrill and beseeching. Hard to make out most of what they were saying, but she got the gist of it. The others wanted to try one of the first group of houses, but Brix knew that was a mistake. What they needed was some distance between themselves and that little pack of dead. She jogged left when she reached the next crossroad and for the first time risked a backward glance. They were all still back there, struggling to hang close to her. Even Nikki, unfortunately. If anyone was in dire need of being ripped to pieces and devoured by flesh-hungry zombies, it was her. Alas, fate was on the idiot's side. Most of the zombies appeared to have abandoned the chase. Even the fastest of them couldn't keep pace with a healthy living human running flat-out.

Brix spotted a house with its front door standing slightly ajar. She slowed as she neared the house and ran across its patchy front lawn, stopping just short of the small porch.

"Hello?" she called out, after taking a moment to catch her breath. "Is anyone in there?"

This was a potentially tricky situation. Entering a house through an open door was obviously an easier proposition than trying to break into one that was locked down tight. The problem was that the house might not be empty. There could be other survivors inside. Armed people with understandably twitchy nerves. Or there might be more zombies lurking somewhere in there. But they were in desperate need of a place to hole up for a while and regroup.

"Hello?" she called out again, taking another cautious step closer to the porch. "If anyone's in there, we're not dangerous. We just need some kind of shelter for a while."

She heard the others come jogging up behind her. They were huffing and puffing as they moved into position to either side of her, staring with curious expressions at the open door.

Jason glanced at her, brow furrowing. "So what do you think? We go in?"

Brix stared at the beckoning door a beat longer. There had been no answer, nor had there been any kind of audible noise from inside. No creak of floorboards under lightly treading feet. Nothing discernibly furtive at all.

She approached the porch, raising the Glock as she cast a quick glance over her shoulder. "Hang back while I peek inside."

The house was old and the porch was wood over a cement foundation. It creaked loudly as she climbed the stairs and advanced toward the door. Holding her breath, she leaned close to the opening and peeked inside. The interior was a shambles, from what she could see. There was debris everywhere. A sofa cushion had been shredded. She saw empty bottles and cans. Fast food wrappers. A bookcase had been knocked onto its side. A haphazard pile of old paperbacks stood near it. She let out her breath and called out one more time. Still no answer. So she nudged the door with the toe of her boot and pushed it slowly open. The wider view revealed more evidence of sloth and disarray. Whoever had occupied the place most recently had lived like pigs. The little house didn't have a second floor. Probably only had a few rooms in total. From here she could see virtually the entire living room, a small dining area beyond it, as well a glimpse of what had to be the kitchen through an archway. She still couldn't be entirely certain the place was empty, but things were looking good.

She studied the mess a moment longer.

Relatively speaking.

She stepped into the house and backed away from the open door. She then raised the Glock and moved in a wide semi-circular arc until she could see there was no one lurking behind the door. That done, she moved further into the house, still keeping the gun in front of her. She heard a creaking behind her and glanced back to see the others entering the house.

"Trevor, shut that door. Lock it if you can."

He nodded and did as asked.

A careful but short search of the rest of the house revealed a kitchen as filthy and debris-strewn as the living room and a short hallway leading to two small, dingy bedrooms. The place was a dump for sure, but it was empty.

Brix rejoined the others in the living room.

Trevor looked at her. "Door's locked. Regular lock and deadbolt."

She nodded. "Good."

Nikki leveled a murderous glance her way before she took off running, disappearing down the short hallway. A moment later they heard a door slam.

Brix almost laughed.

Well, there's one way of avoiding the reckoning you've got coming, bitch.

But it would come, one way or another. Oh, yes.

Trevor tilted his chin at Jason. "Maybe you should check on her."

Jason laughed heartily. "Right. After the shit she pulled? Girl almost got us all killed. Fuck it. She's on her own." He squinted at something on the wall behind Brix. "The fuck is that?"

Brix turned and saw a single word spray-painted in large, squiggly red letters on the expanse of dingy drywall:

PARTHENOGENESIS

Brix puzzled over the word for a few moments, thinking she had heard it somewhere before, but then she shrugged and shook her head.

"No idea what that means."

Trevor frowned. "Wow. Kind of fucking random. A big fifty cent word like that spray-painted on the wall of a shithole like this."

Brix shrugged again.

The little mystery wasn't worth their time. They had bigger

concerns at the moment. She turned away from the wall and stared at the windows at the front of the house. Any curtains that might once have hung from the rods above them were long gone. For now, the bright moonlight shining through them was the only source of illumination available. But if they were still here by sunrise . . .

"We'll need to cover those windows in the morning."

Jason grunted. "I'll check the bedrooms for sheets and blankets."

After he was gone, Trevor smiled and approached Brix, drawing her into an embrace. "You did good."

Brix grunted. "I guess."

"No guessing about it. You took action while the rest of us were standing there with our thumbs up our asses. You saved our goddamn lives tonight, Brix."

This earned him a reluctant smile. "Yeah. I guess I sort of did."

This time he kissed her and it lingered—maybe a little longer than appropriate under the circumstances. But she didn't fight it. It felt nice. And it was good to feel something nice after so much horror.

But darkness encroached on her thoughts again and again anyway.

Because the horror was far from over.

FOURTEEN

Lashon sprinted between the vehicles parked outside the house and came to a gasping stop in front of the porch. She looked up at the young people gathered there and saw a range of expressions that conveyed varying levels of surprise, fear, and cautious amusement. She thought about how bedraggled she must appear to them after her flight through the woods, what with her formerly nice clothes now torn and plastered to her skin by sweat and rain, her hair in disarray, and the scratches on her skin caused by her multiple falls in the dark. No wonder some of them, the girls especially, looked wary. But there was nothing for it. These people were her only hope.

"Please. You have to help me."

One of the guys approached the edge of the porch. He was about her age and kind of cute, with wavy brown hair and an earnest-looking face. He squinted at her, eyeing her up and down, but in an appraising way rather than a leering one. "What happened to you?"

He had a deep voice and she thought she heard real concern in it. She hoped her perceptions were on the money. With her luck so far tonight, she wouldn't be surprised if these people scoffed and told her to fuck off somewhere else. "Someone was chasing me. A . . .

man. He was trying to kill me."

"What?" She heard a bark of feminine laughter. A curvy blonde girl in denim cutoffs and a bikini top was the culprit. Lashon glanced at her. Perfect hair. Perfect nails. Perfect skin. Perfect everything. Except that the skeptical, sneering expression twisting her face made it obvious she was kind of a bitch. "Are you fucking kidding with that shit?"

"No. I'm dead serious."

The girl laughed again. "Get outta here. You're fucking with us."

The guy who had initially addressed Lashon glanced at the blonde. "Pretty sure she's not fucking with us, Mercedes. Look at her. Something serious happened. We should help if we can."

Lashon liked what she was hearing from this dude, but for just a second it was hard to focus on that because . . . *Mercedes?*

Are you fucking kidding me?

It was all she could do not to roll her eyes.

Mercedes executed a perfectly withering eye-roll of her own. Lashon was certain the girl had spent a significant portion of her bitch life practicing the bratty expression. "What-the-fuck-ever, Grant. Waste your time with her lying ass, I don't care."

Another of the girls, a brunette in tan shorts and a white halter top, peeled away from the other girls to stand next to Grant. She was lovely, with perfect, unblemished white skin, startling blue eyes, and the face of a goddess. Jesus. All these people looked like they were straight out of Central Casting. Of course they did. If they were characters from *Chainsaw Maniac* somehow made flesh, they sort of were. But this girl was more like Grant. Lashon saw what looked like very genuine empathy in her expression.

The brunette tilted her chin at Lashon. "What's your name?"

"Lashon."

"Unusual name."

For a white girl, she finished in her head.

That was the unspoken part. Many thought it, few said it.

"I know."

I've only had it my whole damn life.

The brunette smiled. "I like it. I'm Ashley."

Lashon forced a strained smile. "Nice to meet you, Ashley."

Now please stop blathering and help me out.

"Likewise." Ashley glanced at Mercedes, who'd apparently opted to ignore Lashon's existence and was now engaged in conversation with another girl about nail polish. She looked at Lashon again and lowered her voice. "Pay no attention to her. I don't."

Lashon's smile became marginally more genuine. "Yeah. Thanks."

Grant coughed. "Back to the whole guy trying to kill you thing . . . maybe you should start from the beginning. Tell us what you were doing in the woods and what happened."

Lashon turned away from them for a moment to scan the line of trees at the edge of the clearing. Talking to these people, it was easy to be lulled into the fantasy that none of it had actually happened. But it had. And she had to convince them she was telling the truth. That was the tricky part. She couldn't tell them everything. Then they would all think she was messing with them and would probably send her on her way. She looked at Grant and Ashley again, took a deep breath, and told them a version of the truth.

"I was out with some friends earlier tonight. We went to a movie. But I got separated from them and . . . something happened. That part's kind of fuzzy . . . I was drunk . . . but I think I was abducted. I woke up out there . . ." She indicated the woods behind her with a hand gesture. "There was a man in a mask. He had . . . he had . . ." Lashon's heart started beating faster as she recounted this part of her ordeal. It was all still so fresh. The terror she'd experienced still so close. But she swallowed and made herself continue. "He had a fucking chainsaw. He came after me with it. I got up and ran. I ran and I fucking ran. I don't know how, but I lost him out there. But I think he might have caught up. I think I heard him stalking after me right before I came running up here."

One of the other guys, a jock type with muscles and rakish blond hair, moved away from the grill to stand next to Grant. He took a swig from a nearly empty bottle of Newcastle and peered out at the edge of the woods. "What do you think, man? Should we check it out?"

Lashon gasped. "No. That's a bad idea."

And of course Mercedes dialed back into the conversation at that pronouncement. "Of course it is. You're afraid your goddamn lie will be exposed."

The jock glared at her. "Shut up. You're just being a bitch, like always. This chick's been through some real shit. Anyone with eyes can see that."

Mercedes' expression turned hard. Almost murderous. "Fuck you, Rick." Her gaze shifted from him to another guy by the grill, who was good-looking but more slightly built than either Rick or Grant. "You gonna let that asshole talk to me like that, Blaine?"

Blaine looked nervous. "Um . . ."

Mercedes did the withering eye-roll thing again. "Of course you are. Pussy."

Lashon sighed. "Enough fucking drama. Didn't you people hear me? The psycho motherfucker has a *chainsaw*. We need to get inside, right now, and call the goddamn cops."

Blaine laughed. "Good luck with that. We're way out in the sticks. There's no landline and cell service is spotty. You won't be able to reach anyone."

Lashon groaned. "Right. Of course. Why would it be any other way?"

Mercedes made a face again. "What's that supposed to mean?"

It means, you dumb cunt, that I'm in a slasher movie come to life and of course there's no phone service out here because that would be inconvenient to the needs of the fucking script.

But she couldn't say that, of course.

"Nothing. It's just my luck, I mean. Which, tonight, is all fucking bad."

Mercedes made a show of looking her over again, her face continuing to convey nothing but disdain. "Story of your life, I bet."

Lashon had an array of equally catty things she could say in response, but she was done sniping with the girl for now. She had bigger things to worry about. They all did, even if they didn't quite believe it yet.

Rick put the Newcastle bottle to his lips and knocked back the last swallow before dropping the empty in a large metal trash can by the porch rail.

He tilted his chin at Grant. "I'm checking shit out. With me?"

Grant nodded. "Let's do it."

Lashon's eyes widened as they came down the porch steps and stepped purposefully past her. "Wait, wait, no, you can't do this. Please listen to me."

Still more snide laughter from Mercedes. She ignored it and turned to follow the guys as they marched across the clearing. Rick glanced back at her and winked. "I'm not worried. Show ya why."

He headed toward the big red Jeep as he dug into a pocket of his shorts. He pulled out an electronic key fob attached to a ring of keys. The Jeep's headlights flashed once when Rick pushed a button on it.

He opened the door on the passenger side and leaned inside. Lashon moved around him and lifted her chin for a better look at what he was doing. She saw him open the glove box and remove a very large handgun.

Rick threw the door shut and showed her the weapon. "Desert Eagle. .45 caliber. If your chainsaw guy is out the door, he should be scared of *us*."

Lashon frowned. "This is still a bad idea. Please don't go out there."

Rick placed a hand on her shoulder. It was a light touch, but she could feel the strength in his grip. This was a big, strong guy. He had confidence in spades. Too much, really. He was the kind of guy who thought nothing could hurt him because nothing ever had. "Relax. It's gonna be okay." His smile was nearly disarming enough to make her forget what was happening. "I promise."

She heard a car door thump shut and turned to see Grant approaching them from the direction of the black SUV, another gun in one hand and a big flashlight in the other. He and Rick exchanged nods and started off toward the line of trees.

Lashon followed them for the first several yards. She was nearly overcome with frustration, but by this point she realized there was no stopping them. "Guys . . . please be careful. Don't get yourselves fucking killed."

Another smiling backward glance from Rick. "We'll be fine. Wait there, okay?"

Lashon gave up. She stopped following them and stared helplessly after them as they continued across the clearing and then disappeared through the line of trees. She caught shadow glimpses of them moving around out there now and then. The flashlight beam was intermittently visible, as well, darting from place to place in a seemingly random way.

She gasped as someone came up beside her and placed a hand gently between her shoulders. A glance to her left showed Ashley standing beside her. She relaxed a little. The lovely pale-skinned girl smiled and said, "Why don't you come inside while they look around? You could clean up and have a drink. Maybe change into some clean clothes. I have some things I think would fit you."

Lashon stared in silence at the line of trees for a long moment. She could still hear the guys thrashing around out there, but she could no longer see the flashlight beam.

She sighed. "Maybe I should do that."

"Come on, then."

Ashley's hand moved to the crook of Lashon's arm and tugged at her, a gentle nudge to steer her back toward the house. Lashon allowed herself to be pulled in that direction. It really would be nice to get inside a nice, warm place and into clean clothes. It might make her feel human again. Normal. Maybe things would be all right, after all. Perhaps *Chainsaw Maniac* really had provided the basis for this world. But did it necessarily follow that everything that happened here would occur as it would in a typically idiotic cheap slasher film? She was no longer so sure about that. This was a real world. Tactile. Tangible. These were actual, flesh and blood people.

Ashley gave her arm a reassuring squeeze. "Things are gonna work out fine. Don't you worry."

Lashon managed a tired smile. "Maybe you're right."

And, of course, that was when the first ear-piercing scream rang out from the woods.

FIFTEEN

Kira stared at the mirror and screamed.

At first she thought the impression a trick of the light, but now she had gotten right up to the mirror and was holding her mouth open wide. There was no denying the disturbing reality. She felt for the sharpness, carefully, with the tip of her tongue, lightly touching a protrusion that had not been there before. Frowning, she just as carefully probed the other side of her mouth and found an identical protrusion.

Fangs, she thought. *Fucking fangs.*

I'm a goddamn vampire.

She turned away from the mirror and glared at the smiling creature who had turned her into a monster. He was still shirtless, but he had slipped back into his trousers and was sitting on the edge of the bed.

"What have you done to me?"

He stood and padded across the hardwood floor toward her on his bare feet. He kept smiling and gently brushed one side of her face with the back of a hand. "Mmm, you are exquisite."

Kira didn't shrink away from his touch. Despite her anger, the touch triggered an echo of the overpowering arousal she'd experienced earlier. "I know. I'm a fucking goddess. Now how 'bout you answer my question, asshole?"

He shrugged. "Isn't it obvious what I've done?"

"I think you should spell it out anyway."

"Very well. During the course of our lovemaking—"

She snorted. "Lovemaking? Is that vampire code for rape?"

His expression darkened. "I did not rape you. You loved every second of it. You cried out for more. *Begged* for more. I know you remember."

She *did* remember. Very well. She felt more echoes of desire as a series of vivid images flashed through her mind. The vampire poised above her, his muscled torso shifting and twisting as he rode her harder than she ever had been before, making her scream herself hoarse with each devastating thrust, driving her nearly mad with ecstasy.

He brushed her cheek with the back of his hand again. "Yes. I see that you do."

She pushed his hand away and brushed past him. She kept going until she reached the other side of the room, where she intentionally put the bed between them. Then she folded her arms over her bare breasts and glared at him some more. "You're right. I remember everything. I also remember I had no control over any of it, including how my body reacted to you. You have powers. Vampire fucking *powers*. And you used those powers to make it happen. Which means you forced yourself on me. Which means—"

"ENOUGH!"

His booming voice startled Kira. The force of it made her stagger backward a step. It was the first time she had seen him display undiluted anger and it was a fearsome sight indeed to behold. He crossed the room so fast he was an almost invisible blur.

Kira gaped as he materialized in front of her. "Holy shit. That was . . . freaky."

He seized her wrists and pulled her close. She found herself focusing, at least for a moment, on the pale blue hue of his lips. Despite the apparent danger—and despite the terror she felt—she found herself wanting to kiss those lips. To draw the especially ripe bottom one into her mouth and chew on it. For starters.

She tilted her head slightly, blinking rapidly as she stared up at him.

Damn. Seriously, what's wrong with me?

Because though she was fighting hard to hold on to her anger and her misgivings, she wanted him again. More than that. She *needed* him. How could she still be so weak, now that she was no longer human? He put a hand on her throat. Lightly, without squeezing. Regardless, the touch rendered almost senseless with renewed desire.

He seemed to sense her thoughts. "I am your maker. You will always want me, just as you will always serve me. So enough with your impudence. It is not becoming in a new bride."

"New . . . bride?"

His hand moved from her throat down to her breasts, which he caressed for a moment before dragging his fingertips down the length of her belly to the moist spot between her legs. His touch electrified her, made her twist and moan. He leaned into her and bent down a little to kiss her on the neck, his lips grazing the spot where the now-vanished puncture wounds had been. Then his mouth moved to her ear and he whispered things that frightened her even as his roving hands continued to stir her lust.

"Yes, you are my bride. My first true bride in many years. Others have come and gone, but they were trifles, never intended to rule beside me as a near equal. But you are special. I sensed it when I first set eyes on you. You have great potential. I will teach you the pleasures of blood and ruthlessness. And you will learn to love it all. To revel in the pain and pleadings of the lesser beings. Our pitiful playthings. The stinking humans."

It was quite a speech. And she might have giggled at it under other circumstances, say if it had been a piece of dialog in a cheesy old movie. But mirth was the furthest thing from her mind in that moment. Because she knew he was telling her what he truly believed. And, worse yet, she believed what he was saying. Believed it totally. She was almost eager for it. She should have been appalled by the notion, but she was not. A dim part of her hoped this was because she was so turned on rather than the more unsettling possibility that her conscience had deserted her along with her humanity.

She climbed up on the bed, crawling backward until her arms were splayed across the pillows bunched against the massive headboard.

He stared down at her and smiled again. "You desire something, bride?"

She just stared at him, her eyes blazing with erotic need. "You know what I fucking want."

He did.

And he gave it to her.

~

Monroe came to flat on his back on a narrow twin bed. The mattress was hard and uncomfortable. The ceiling above him was concrete painted white. He was still quite woozy upon waking and opted for the moment to remain in his prone position. He rolled his eyes around a bit and saw that the walls were decorated primarily with rock band posters. The Cure, Bauhaus, Killing Joke, The Cramps, Fugazi and the Misfits. There were also posters for the movie Eraserhead and something called The Church of the Subgenius. A frown slowly dawned as Monroe absorbed all this. The punk and alternative décor would all have been very cutting edge a quarter century ago. Perhaps he had somehow been transported back in time to 1987 or whatever. Time travel was an absurd notion on the surface, but it made as much sense as anything else that had happened.

He stared at the ceiling again, focusing this time on its solidity. On its undeniable *reality*. After several minutes of this, he shifted his focus back to the rock band posters, noting the creases in them and the way most of them seemed to curl up a bit at the corners. These were old posters. They had been folded and put away for a time before being displayed again on these dorm room-like walls.

Though he still hadn't moved, he could see enough of the room to determine that it was very small. Yet another poster, this one showing a collection of imported beer bottles, adorned the closed door to the room. Against the wall directly in front of him was a small desk, upon which was an assortment of books, papers, and an old-fashioned dual cassette boombox. A wrinkled postcard-sized image of Axl Rose was pinned to a bulletin board on the wall directly above the desk.

1987, Monroe thought. *I am definitely in 1987. Somehow. God help me.*

He tried to think of any reasonable way of explaining his current situation. Other than time travel. Nothing immediately presented itself. Then his brain tripped across a random fact he found immediately perplexing. He had been bitten numerous times. His flesh had been fucking ripped into. So he should still be in some degree of pain, right?

Right. Fucking A, right.

But he wasn't in pain. At all. In fact, despite still feeling a touch groggy, he actually felt pretty damn good.

Well, shit. That's weird.

He started probing at his flesh with his fingers, feeling for places where he clearly remembered being bitten. There should be holes. Gashes. Wounds still weeping blood. But all he felt was perfectly smooth flesh. Weirder and weirder still. In the course of his probing, he also determined he was wearing a garment of some sort he hadn't been wearing before. The texture of the material was all wrong. He lifted his head slightly and saw that he was wrapped in a blue bathrobe with the sash cinched shut at his groin. He also saw his bare feet sticking over the edge of the small bed. He couldn't help noting how very pale his feet looked, with a faint tinge of blue around his toes. This made him frown again, because his first thought was of autopsy scenes in television crime shows. Tie a tag around one of his big toes and he'd be a dead ringer for a corpse splayed on a stainless-steel autopsy table. Because those feet definitely looked like the feet of a dead man.

This triggered another memory flash, Tom Cruise telling him he was sorry but they had to . . . had to . . .

Monroe gulped.

They had to kill me before turning me into a goddamn vampire! Oh, Jesus! Oh, shit! I'm a goddamn bloodsucking fiend!

This thought obliterated the remaining vestiges of his stupor, and he sat bolt upright in the bed and screamed. And then screamed again. The sound resounded explosively in the little room, making him cringe. He regretted the primal reaction immediately. It was so loud it would surely bring some other undead denizens of the fucking night running in here to check up on him.

I have to get out of here, he thought. *Have to escape.*

But before he could turn his thoughts to the practicalities of making that happen, he was distracted by another sound in the room.

A whimper. Somewhere off to his left.

He frowned yet again. The sound was small and pitiful. Barely audible at all. And short-lived. He immediately recognized that whoever had made the sound was striving hard not to make it again. Something else odd struck him. He could smell the person. Not just their scent, but their fear, too. It was rolling off her in waves. Yes, it was a female. Somehow he knew that without even looking at her.

He turned his head and saw her cowering in a rear corner of the room. She was nude and she was chained to the wall. She was slim, but with a nice figure, hips that swelled pleasingly and breasts that were large but not quite into porn star double-D territory. Her lank blonde hair hung to her narrow shoulders and looked like it had not been washed in days. She had a pretty face. The kind of face that looked beautiful even without makeup. Big blue eyes, striking cheekbones, and full, ripe lips that practically begged to be kissed. She was trembling. Her whole body was. It made her look like an animal trapped outside in the cold. She was in a squatting position, with her back pressed hard into the corner. Monroe's mouth hung open as he stared at her. His mind went sort of blank for a period of time as he drank in everything about her. It was only when he felt thick droplets of drool collecting in the corners of his mouth that he snapped out of it. But he remained entranced by her. Not just by her physical beauty, but also by her obvious terror of him. He was disturbed to discover he found her fear arousing.

He glanced at the closed door and frowned, surprised that his screams had brought no one running. There could be no doubt someone out there had heard him, yet they were choosing to leave him undisturbed. Which caused him to wonder whether this whole scenario might be some kind of game the other vamps were running. Some kind of twisted initiation rite.

He looked at the girl again.

She cringed and let out another helpless whimper.

What he was thinking made sense. In a fucked up way, of course. She was a gift to him. He was meant to take her. To use her as he saw fit. Which, being a vampire, likely included a wide array of unsavory and depraved acts.

Part of him *really* wanted to do depraved things to her.

He felt a reflexive pang of guilt at this realization. But it wasn't as sharp as it should have been. The change had done something to his conscience. He believed he still had one, but it felt weakened at the very least. It made him angry. He hadn't asked to become what he was now. It was better to be human. Better to have compassion. Better to be normal and live in the sun rather than some skulking night predator.

Wasn't it?

He rose from the bed and crossed the room to squat in front of the cowering girl. She cringed again and tried to press herself further into the corner. An effort in vain, of course. There was nowhere for the poor thing to go.

He peered curiously at her. "I think I'm sort of meant to, uh, you know . . . rip your throat out and feast on your warm blood, or some shit like that."

Sudden tears spilled from the corners of her eyes at this statement. "Please . . ."

Monroe felt a twitch at his crotch and had another disturbing revelation. The begging of a helpless victim was also a turn-on. He supposed this was a common thing in all vamps. It was messed up as hell and he did feel a slightly more intense stab of guilt at the knowledge—but the guilt didn't make the feeling go away.

He wanted her.

In every way possible.

He wanted to fuck her.

And he wanted to tear her apart and wallow in her blood.

But he wanted to scare her some more first.

He touched her chin, relishing the way she jerked away from him.

Then he thought of Kira.

And the warped smile gave way to yet another frown. *Kira. Jesus.* He had almost forgotten about her in the midst of all this madness. She was still out there somewhere. And perhaps was going through something very similar to what he was experiencing. Except maybe she was on the other side of the equation. Maybe she was naked and chained up in some other room, cowering and crying while another vamp sadistically toyed with her.

He stared at the crying girl in front of him, feeling very cold inside now.

It took a tremendous effort of will, but he made himself stand up and walk away from the girl. He sat on the edge of the narrow bed and looked at her again, this time feeling little of the lust that had nearly overpowered him moments ago.

She sniffled. "Please don't kill me."

Her voice sounded very small and frightened, almost like a child's. Its fragility made him wince. He shrugged. "Part of me really wants to kill you. Like, really, really bad. But I'm gonna try hard not to."

This sent more tears sliding down her face. "Please . . ."

"Don't beg!" His voice made her flinch. "I'm sorry. I didn't mean to be so sharp. It's just that the begging makes it worse. The craving. Look . . . what's your name?"

She sniffled again. He saw her throat working as she struggled to speak. The tenderness of the flesh there was excruciatingly tempting. He couldn't help thinking of how it might feel to take a bite out of it. She apparently sensed the direction of his thoughts because she at last managed to push out the words. "Marnie! My name is Marnie. Please don't kill me."

"Jesus. What did I tell you about that? No begging. Not if you want to live."

"I'm sorry."

"Shit, girl, don't apologize either. None of this shit is your fault." He frowned. "Also, try really hard to stop crying, okay?"

Yet another sniffle. "I . . . can't help it."

"Yeah. I get that. Just try, okay?"

She met his gaze for a long moment and at last managed a small nod. "Okay."

Monroe couldn't help savoring the exquisite lines of her body again. She really was quite a beauty. It'd be a shame to destroy such a work of natural art. The vampire part of his nature would delight in it, of course. He would have to work very hard to hold the beast at bay.

But why?

This is what I am now. I can't change it. Why fight it?

His desires and cravings would only intensify over time. He understood this instinctively. This girl's only chance for survival depended on him somehow getting her out of this place very quickly and then sending her on her way, urging her to get as far away from him as she could as soon as possible.

The effort was almost certainly doomed to failure, but he had to try.

Right?

The voice of his vampiric nature whispered insidiously again: *Wrong. So wrong. Kill her. Fuck her. Rip her apart!*

Monroe screwed his eyes shut and cried out as he slapped his hands against his ears. "*Shut up, you bastard, and get out of my fucking head!*"

Some moments later he opened his eyes and noted Marnie's startled expression. "Um . . . sorry about that. I'm having some . . . issues."

She nodded, but didn't say anything.

Monroe gave his head a hard shake. "Okay. Okay. I think I've got it under control again. For now. Can't make any guarantees for ten seconds from now, but I give you my word, I'm doing my fucking best."

Her demeanor underwent a drastic change. She sagged against the wall, allowing her shapely butt to slide to the floor. "I believe you. I do." He heard the deep resignation in her voice and knew almost word for word what she'd say next. "But it doesn't matter. It's like you said. You're meant to kill me. They won't allow anything else. I'm fucked."

Yep, he thought. *Total truth.*

The girl was fucked as fucked could be and there was no getting around it. And yet he still felt compelled to make the effort. Why, he couldn't say. Or maybe he *did* know. An image of Kira formed in his head again. Kira and Marnie even sort of looked alike. Blonde. Similar body types. He just couldn't hurt this girl. It'd be like killing Kira by proxy.

"Maybe you're right. Probably. Shit, I won't lie. But I'm gonna try to help you anyway."

She shook her head. "But why?"

"Been asking myself the same question. I don't have a good answer, except that you remind me of a friend."

Marnie grunted. "I guess I can buy that. Makes as much sense as anything. So . . . how do you mean to help me?"

"I haven't the faintest fucking idea."

"Great. Awesome."

Monroe glanced at his lap and fiddled for a moment with the sash of the bathrobe. Clearly he couldn't make his getaway attired so goofily. He stood up again and began a further examination of the room. In another corner near the desk was a closet with an accordion-style door. He pulled this back and peered in at an assortment of clothes. T-shirts dangling from hangers. Multiples pairs of jeans folded and sitting on a shelf. He checked tags on both and they were close enough to his size for comfort. He grabbed one of the pairs of jeans and pulled a Butthole Surfers t-shirt off a hanger. He also grabbed a battered pair of Nikes from the closet floor.

Marnie stared at him curiously as he pulled the jeans on up under the bathrobe. A corner of her mouth quirked in amusement. "What? Couldn't get naked in front of me?"

Monroe's own expression was deadly serious. "Don't tempt me."

Marnie sobered at once. "Right. Sorry."

Monroe removed the bathrobe and pulled on the vintage rock shirt. Then he sat on the edge of the bed again and shoved his feet into the shoes, which were a little tight for comfort but not excruciatingly so.

Then he looked at Marnie again. "Right. Well. I have no idea what to do next. I mean . . . I'm just one guy and . . ." He waved a hand at the closed door. ". . . there are all those undead fuckers out there. The odds are, well . . . kind of long."

She made a face at that. "No kidding."

He scratched his chin. "Let me think. There's gotta be something . . . some kind of way . . . if only . . ."

Marnie cleared her throat and coughed. "Um . . . well . . . I can think of one way you might be able to save me."

Monroe's face crinkled in confusion. "Say what now?"

Marnie managed a small smile, but there was a deep, obvious sadness in it. "I'm telling you I have an idea. A solution. Something that could really work."

Monroe's confusion deepened. "Huh. So what is it?"

She hesitated only a moment. "You can turn me into a vampire."

Monroe laughed. "You're kidding."

But Marnie was shaking her head. And her expression betrayed a disquieting earnestness. "No. I'm not. Think about it. You're totally right. There's too many of them and only one of you. You could never fight your way through them all, and they sure as shit won't let you just walk me out of here." She leaned toward him a little, her expression becoming more severe as her voice took on a more intense edge. "You have to kill me. And then you have to turn me. Just like they did to you. Just like they did to my friend, Lisa. It's the only way I can survive."

"Is that what you want? Really? To become a fucking monster?"

"It's the only way." Her voice remained resolute even as her bottom lip trembled. "I don't want to . . . cease to exist. I can't bear it. Please. Do this for me."

"What did I tell you about begging?"

She made an exasperated sound. "I don't care anymore. Kill me. *Turn* me. If you're really serious about helping me, you'll do it."

Monroe stared at her in stunned silence for many long moments. Then he shrugged. "Listen . . . I only just became a vampire. I didn't know I was one until I woke up here. I've never drank anyone's fucking blood before, much less turned anyone. I don't know how to do it."

Marnie pushed away from the corner, stood up, and approached him. She came as close as the length of the chain allowed. "Just do it. I figure it's gotta be instinct, right? Decide you're gonna bite me and turn me. Just do it."

She lifted her chin and tilted her head to one side, extending her neck to the furthest extent possible.

Fuck.

Monroe didn't want to do it. What she suggested was crazy. And yet ... she was sort of right, wasn't she? There really was no other way, at least none that was obvious. He stared at the beating pulse in her neck and felt his arousal return.

Let instinct take over. Just do it.

Marnie's eyes rolled toward him as she kept her neck extended. "Do it. Kill me. Turn me. And then fuck me after if you want."

Her last statement crushed what remained of his resistance and inflamed the resurgent cravings. His mouth snapped open to an unnaturally wide degree as he came at her and tore into her delicious neck. The blood spattered his face and filled his mouth with warmth. She screamed once and then sagged against him as he drank greedily and snarled and writhed against her. Drinking her blood and feeling her life force begin to fade was the most exhilarating thing Monroe had ever experienced.

He felt exultant.

Somehow more alive than ever, despite technically being dead.

And he kept drinking from her tender, cooling flesh until she was dead, too.

SECOND INTERMISSION

The door swung shut behind him as Greg Nelson eased out into the hallway. The way to his right led to more auditorium doors. Clearly not the way to go. Or was it? He frowned as he reexamined his options. He'd set out with the intent of heading straight for the front doors of the cineplex. After all, the obvious way out was the way he had entered the place. But maybe it would be smarter—and safer—to seek a rear exit. The lobby and concessions area had a lot of open space. He thought of how exposed and vulnerable he would be if he went that way. His heart began to race faster as he imagined it, a fresh surge of panic threatening to overwhelm him until he was able to coax himself back to an acceptable level of calm.

Once he had himself under control again, he crept quietly to the other side of the hallway and put his back to the wall. He again glanced in each direction. There was still no indication of alien presence either way. That the strange theater workers were aliens remained his working theory. It was, he was certain, a reasonable assumption, given the evidence all around him. The translucent floor panels beneath him were identical to the ones in the theater aisles. He frowned again at the diffused light making the circuit from one end of the hallway to the other and back again, over and over. He wondered whether there might be aliens somewhere beneath him, maybe looking up at him right now. A disturbing possibility occurred to him. Perhaps observation and study of his actions as he attempted to extricate himself from this situation was an integral piece of some fucked up alien experiment. And the whole thing with the movies was only a component of something larger. He hoped not. Because it would likely mean he had no real chance of escape at all. And it would mean that to them he was little more than a dumb lab rat struggling to make his way through an impossible maze. The scenario seemed all too plausible.

Okay, he told himself. *Okay. It doesn't matter whether they're watching you. Or whether you're caught up in some weird experiment. You've got no control over that. You don't even know if it's true. Either way, it doesn't change what you've got to do. Get out of here. Or die trying. Pick a direction and GO.*

A smart idea, no doubt, but Greg made himself stay where he was a bit longer as he tried to logically weigh the pros and cons of heading toward the lobby or seeking a theoretical rear exit. A rear exit might not exist at all. Yes, in a real cineplex there would be one, but this was not a real cineplex. There *might* be a rear exit anyway, but he couldn't take it for granted. Yet that didn't mean he had to go charging into the lobby heedless of any potential danger lurking there either. There was another option.

Calm, he thought. *Calm.*

Inhale.

Exhale.

Center yourself.

There.

Now GO.

Keeping his back to the wall, he began to move slowly in the direction of the lobby, sidestepping carefully to avoid a potentially catastrophic stumble. As he neared the end of the hallway, he glanced back the way he had come and saw nothing to alarm him. He was still alone. And though it was hard to trust the impression, it was beginning to feel like the whole place was empty of any other living presence, alien or human. Other than the dim hum of the strange machinery beneath the floor, the only other audible sound was that of his own breathing.

The end of the hallway was only a few steps away now. He reached the edge of the wall and turned slowly to peer around the corner with one eye. His lungs expelled a tremendous breath. It was the loudest sound he'd made since exiting the auditorium. He simply couldn't help it. There was no one in the lobby. No one he could see anyway. He supposed it was possible aliens were hunkering down behind the big white block that had been the concessions stand—or were crouched down inside the nondescript four-sided cubicle that had been the ticket booth—just waiting for the right moment to spring up and scare the ever-living shit out of him.

Well ... it was possible. Hell, *anything* was possible. If he had learned nothing else tonight, he had sure as shit learned that. But whatever. This was his best shot at getting clear of this craziness. Back to normality. Back to the real world ... or at least back to a world that made sense to him, unlike this freaky phony cineplex.

There was no real choice here.

He pushed away from the wall and stepped into the lobby. His whole body was shaking now with live-wire energy. This lasted until he advanced past the concessions stand and reached the middle of the lobby. Nothing was happening. No alarms were going off. No aliens were racing after him to seize him and drag him off to some nightmarish anal probe chamber of doom. So he stopped and turned in a full circle to stare in wonderment at the empty lobby. He knew he should be running for the door while he had the chance, but some strange impulse compelled him to take a moment to take it all in. A bank of video games had stood against the far wall opposite the concessions stand. But, like everything else, the video games had been false impressions. Illusions. In their place stood tall booths oddly similar in appearance to the games they had mimicked. The booths were molded shapes protruding seamlessly from the walls, similar to the way the theater seats had seemed as one with the floor. Each booth was outfitted with screens and a white control panel. Each control panel had a single toggle control and a surrounding set of buttons. On the screens odd and colorful geometric patterns swirled against a sea of darkness. Again, Greg was reminded of the theater, this time of the strange patterns he had seen on the "movie" screen. Only this wasn't quite the same. It was more random. The shapes stranger.

He wanted very much to take a closer look.

To maybe play with the controls and see if anything happened.

But then his common sense kicked in. The impulse was a lunatic notion. Probably nothing would happen. But maybe something would. Possibly something very bad. This was alien technology. Messing with it couldn't produce any good result and might even raise the alarms he'd been fearing.

So he turned away from the bank of strange machines and headed straight for the front entrance. No more fucking around. The sooner he got out of here, the fucking better. He was there in a matter of seconds and pressed his hand against a white bar in the middle of one of the doors, pushing on it carefully, a considerable part of him expecting it to be locked down tight. Surely it wouldn't yield easily to a simple touch. Getting out of an incomprehensibly advanced alien facility or ship couldn't be so easy.

Except that it was.

The door opened smoothly and Greg stepped out into the crisp night air.

SIXTEEN

Brix came out of the kitchen after spending some time poking through the drawers and cabinets and saw Jason standing in the middle of the living room. He had his chin cupped in one hand and was staring thoughtfully at the mysterious word spray-painted on the chipped and filthy drywall. It was an oddly thoughtful pose for someone with such a self-consciously snide and tough exterior. She walked over to where he was standing and turned toward the wall to ponder the word herself.

PARTHENOGENESIS

An earlier search of the kitchen had turned up a box of cheap candles and matches. Several candles blazed now in equally cheap plastic holders arrayed around the filthy living room. The candles provided ample illumination, but Brix had fretted some over whether the light might draw unwanted attention from zombies staggering through the street outside. Yet no one, herself included, wished to stumble around half-blind in the dark.

Jason grunted. "That word. It rings a fucking bell. It's driving me a little crazy."

Brix nodded. "Yeah. Me, too."

They looked at each other, made lingering eye contact for a long moment that soon turned uncomfortable. Brix forced her gaze in another direction after she felt a faint flush touch her cheeks. There was a strange little spark of something between her and Jason now. Nikki was a bitch of the highest order, but that didn't mean she was dumb. She'd picked up on it right away, long before Brix had even sensed it or been able to acknowledge it herself. A lot of it undoubtedly had a lot to do with Jason being the only other person in their group able to pull his shit relatively together right from the outset of all this craziness. It was situational and didn't mean anything deeper.

Trevor was standing over by one of the windows at the front of the house. He had a finger hooked around the edge of one of the thin bed sheets they'd pilfered from the bedrooms to use as makeshift curtains. He was staring out at the street with a slack expression that could have been the result of either delayed shock or exhaustion.

Brix moved away from Jason and approached her boyfriend. "Anything happening out there?"

Trevor kept peering through the little gap between the edge of the bed sheet and the window frame. "I saw a couple of zombies go by. Didn't even look this way."

"Well . . . that's good."

"Yeah."

Brix stepped closer and put a hand against the middle of his back. She pressed a side of her face against his shoulder. "I think we got far enough ahead of that pack that they lost our scent. Or whatever. If we stay quiet in here, we might be able to hole up until we can come up with a long-term plan."

Trevor shifted backward slightly, settling against her.

It felt nice.

But then he made a sound of frustration that was close to a whimper. It broke the pleasant spell of intimacy. Trevor turned away from the window and looked her in the eye. "A long-term plan? Really?" He laughed, but the sound was strained, evoking desperation more than humor. "Come on, Brix. You've seen the way it is out there. The world's in flames. It's just like in all your fucking movies you love so much. The world is *over*. What kind of long-term plan fixes that? How can we hope to survive more than a day at a time?"

Brix was a little taken aback and was trying hard not to show it. It was one of the few times he'd ever spoken so harshly to her. She took care to remind herself that he'd been through a lot and was just exhibiting predictable symptoms of stress. She couldn't blame him for it and she certainly couldn't reply with reciprocal harshness. She had to project a sense of calm and steadiness. And hope he could connect with that and draw power from it. From her.

She clasped hands with him and said, "Look, you're right. I know. It looks bad. Really bad. But we don't know all the facts about what happened here yet. For all we know this is a localized incident. And even if it isn't, there are things we can try."

"Like what?"

She nodded at the window. "There are other cars out there. A lot of them. We can jumpstart one of them, maybe, and—"

Another of those strained laughs from Trevor. "So now you're a car thief? Do you even know how to jumpstart a car?"

Jason loudly cleared his throat and spoke up. "I do. But they gotta be older models, like from twenty years ago or earlier."

Brix kept her gaze on Trevor. "See? Don't know if you noticed, but this neighborhood isn't exactly Beverly Hills. We'll find a car Jason can start. And we'll get out of here and head for the country, maybe even out to my dad's property. It's rural and dad has a ton of guns. There won't be many zombies at all out there and we can defend ourselves."

Trevor visibly relaxed as she said all this. Her strategy was working. She needed to keep him away from that panicky edge. She had no real world experience in dealing with apocalyptic scenarios, of course. She was no different from anyone else in that regard. But she thought she had pretty good instincts, as well as a very level head on her shoulders. She was just naturally better equipped to deal with a crisis than a lot of people. This didn't mean, though, that she had no doubts of her own. She had no idea, for instance, how closely this world mirrored their own. Did a version of her father exist in this place? No way to know. Ditto for the property he owned and all his badass weaponry. But these concerns were all things beyond her control and therefore there was no reason to share them with Trevor. He was calm now and she wanted to keep him that way. The rest of it would take care of itself one way or another. They would go out to where her father's property should be and either it would be there or it would not. And if not, they'd just figure out where to go from there.

"I've got it!"

Jason.

His loud exclamation made Brix flinch. She let go of Trevor's and turned to look at Jason. "What have you got?"

He shook long locks off his forehead and grinned. "The fucking *word.*" He waved a hand at the defaced drywall. "Fucking *parthenogenesis.* I knew I'd heard it before. I had this sort of goth girlfriend a couple years back. Name was Mona. Or Moira. Some shit like that. Anyway, there was this song she liked called "Nemesis" by a band called Shriekback. That big goddamn word is in the lyrics."

Brix glanced at the spray-painted word. "Hey. Yeah. Now that you mention it, pretty sure that's how I know it, too. Can't remember where I heard the song, though."

Jason laughed. "Shit, who cares? Bottom line, mystery solved. Somebody here was a Shriekback fan."

Brix eyed the spray-painted word curiously. "Huh. I guess." She looked at Jason again. "So . . . any idea what it actually means?"

"Don't know, don't give a fuck."

Brix moved toward the center of the room again. "Yeah, I guess we've got bigger—"

An ear-piercing scream rang out and Nikki came dashing out of the hallway that led to the bedrooms, wielding a huge handgun that looked almost as big as she did. The gun's massive barrel looked like a cannon and was aimed right at Brix's face. Brix grabbed for the Glock shoved into the waistband of her jeans at the small of her back. But things were happening too fast. Nikki's face was a contorted mask of rage and her finger was already squeezing the big gun's trigger. Thoughts zipped through Brix's mind like flashes of lightning as her hand closed around the Glock's grip and yanked it free. She was about to die. She had been in this very position less than an hour earlier and she liked it no better this time. And she guessed that Nikki had found the weapon during a search of the room she'd shut herself in, either stashed away in a drawer or up on a closet shelf. Brix felt stupid for allowing the bitch the privacy and time she'd needed to find a weapon. Stupid. So fucking stupid. And there was nothing she could do to change it now. She was just fucked.

Just as she was bringing the Glock up—albeit far too late to aim and squeeze off a shot before Nikki could kill her—there was a flash of movement in her peripheral vision.

And then Trevor was standing right in front of her.

Blocking the path of the bullet as the report of the gun resounded in the little living room. Brix stared in helpless horror as blood exploded from a big hole between her boyfriend's shoulders blades. The high-caliber slug passed right through him and ended up somewhere else. Brix never saw the bullet of course, only recognized that she wasn't hit. The blast propelled Trevor backward. His body collapsed against her, knocking her off balance and sending her stutter-stepping to the left. There was another report from the big gun. Another miss of Nikki's intended target. Trevor had saved her again, albeit unintentionally this time. Brix was still off-balance but managed to swing the Glock around and squeeze off a shot. She got lucky. The bullet took Nikki in the shoulder. There was a bright bloom of red and then the girl was screaming in agony. The sound was music to Brix's ears. She had never heard anything so righteous. All she wanted in that moment was to make the bitch keep on screaming—right up until the moment she killed her.

Nikki staggered backward a few steps and slumped to her knees. The big gun was no longer in her hand. Brix couldn't see immediately where it had landed. The important thing was that her adversary was unarmed. She was wounded and defenseless. And she was in the last moments of her worthless life.

Brix stepped right up to her and put the barrel of the Glock to her forehead. "Say goodbye, you fucking whore."

Nikki let out a wail of agony and stared up at her with shiny eyes. More tears ran in rivulets down her face, streaking her makeup. "Please, please . . . no. I'm sorry. I'm sorry. Please."

Brix sneered. "You're fucking sorry? Seriously? Tough shit."

Her forefinger tightened around the trigger. Her entire body was shaking. Rage unlike anything she'd ever experienced consumed her. She felt completely devoid of pity. Felt nothing at all like compassion as she stared down at Nikki's anguished face. This person was less than human to her. This person deserved nothing like mercy.

"Get ready to die."

Nikki wailed again.

Brix put more pressure on the trigger.

And then Jason said, in a quiet but steady tone, "Don't."

Brix glared at him. "You must be kidding. She killed my man, so I'm killing her. God help you if you try to stop me."

Jason held his hands up in a palms-out placating gesture. "I won't. I get it. I do. But I wanna talk you out of it."

Brix frowned. "Why?"

He gave her the most earnest expression she'd ever seen from him. "Because I don't think this is you. Not really. Yeah, you've taken out a bunch of zombies. But they're not *people*. Not really. This is different. Killing Nikki will make you feel better for about five seconds. But Trevor will still be dead and you'll still have to deal with that. *And* you'll have to deal with the fact that you killed another human being. A *defenseless* one. I know it's hard right now, but try to think ahead a minute. How will you feel about it later? It'll haunt you, I think. I think you know it, too."

Brix didn't say anything to this right away. But she was thinking hard about it, because she recognized the several grains of truth in what he said. He was right. It *would* haunt her. She broke eye contact with Jason and stared down at Nikki again, whose tears kept pouring down her already very wet face. She was trying to speak but instead was blubbering incoherently, her bottom lip trembling uncontrollably. In that moment, Brix did feel a flicker of something almost like pity. But it was very faint. She couldn't take looking at Nikki much longer. It was making her sick. She glanced over her shoulder at Trevor's unmoving, very still corpse.

She stared at him for maybe a full minute, tears stinging her eyes. Then she looked at Nikki again. "Fuck it."

She squeezed the trigger and the Glock jumped in her hand a little as it expelled a bullet that punched through Nikki's forehead and blew out the back of her skull in a spray of blood and brains and bone matter. The girl's body toppled backward, twitched once on the floor, and then went still.

Brix heard Jason let out a hitching breath. She recognized the emotion. She was feeling it herself after all.

She looked at him. "So what now? Is it your turn? Are you gonna try to avenge that murdering bitch?"

He stared somberly at her without speaking for a long moment. Then he shook his head. "No. I don't like this. I won't lie. But . . . Nikki brought that shit down on herself."

"Damn right she did."

Jason said nothing at all this time.

Brix kept looking at him, taking measure of him during the long, tense silence. It was possible he was lying. That he might take the first opportunity to attack her, that he was just waiting for her to let her guard down to make his move. Maybe. Maybe not. There were a lot of damn maybes in this equation. Too many.

Brix turned fully in his direction, took one cautious step toward him before stopping.

He met her gaze and still said nothing.

The Glock felt heavy in her hand. But it was more than just the actual weight of the weapon. She was thinking about using it again. Thinking about raising it and aiming it at Jason's face. The most ruthless part of her was telling her it was the smart thing to do. She was sure she could survive better on her own anyway. There would be no one else to account for, no one else to slow her down.

And she wouldn't have to watch her back night and day for fear of reprisal.

Now Jason did speak. "If you're gonna kill me, just go ahead and get it over with. I'm tired and who wants to live in a world like this anyway?"

There was a space of maybe two seconds during which it almost happened.

She came so close to raising her hand and squeezing off a shot.

But she didn't. "Can I trust you?"

After another silent, tense moment, he gave her a terse nod. "Yeah."

"How do I know that for sure?"

"You don't."

Brix grunted. "At least you're honest."

Jason nodded again. "Yeah. That I am. So ... what happens now?"

And so they had come full circle. Brix had asked the same question of him only minutes earlier. Now she shrugged. "We start thinking about what to do next. Whether to stay here or go somewhere else."

Jason's head swiveled slowly left to right, again taking in the grisly sight of the fresh corpses splayed across the debris-strewn floor. Brix did the same and felt a fresh stab of heart-rending anguish at the sight of Trevor's slack face. She thought of all the dreams they'd shared of their future together. The outlandish plans they'd made. All of it gone now. Erased from existence. *Murdered.*

Jason cleared his throat. "If we stay here, I say we at least get the bodies into one of the other rooms. Don't know about you, but I don't like looking at them."

"Why not drag them out back? If we're here much longer, they'll start to stink." Brix hated speaking of the body of the one she had loved so bluntly, but this was an area in which emotion had to be set aside. "And there'll be flies and maggots, all that nasty shit."

"That'll take a while." Jason glanced at Nikki. His brow creased and he quickly looked away, focusing on Brix again. "Look, there's a lot we don't know. If we drag them out back, there's a chance zombies could be drawn to the house by the smell of fresh meat. The other thing is I don't think we ought to stay here much longer."

"Oh?"

He nodded. "Yeah. You were right when you were talking to Trevor, you know. We gotta get out of the city. Out to your dad's place sounds like a good idea to me."

Now Brix was nodding, too. "I was just trying to reassure him, but I do think it's the best move. Won't be easy, though. Might even be impossible. We could get killed long before we ever make it out there."

"Maybe, but we should try anyway. What the fuck else have we got to lose now?"

Brix stole one more glance at Trevor's body.

Jason had a point there.

She looked at him again. "All right. So let's do like you say and get them into one of the back rooms and then start talking about—"

There was a loud thump from the direction of the kitchen.

Brix gasped as her head jerked in that direction.

She heard fear in Jason's voice as he said, "What the fuck was that?"

Then there was another thump, louder still.

And then another.

They exchanged worried glances. Jason said, "Do you think—"

Brix was already nodding. "Zombies. Beating on the back door. Drawn by the gunshots, maybe."

More thumps in rapid succession, as if to affirm what she had said.

Jason moved away from her, keeping his head down as he scanned the floor. She guessed what he was looking for an instant before he scooped up the gun Nikki had used to kill Trevor. The sight of it made her physically sick. But they needed all the protection they could get.

Jason cocked his head toward the front door. "Let's go."

Brix frowned. "Now?"

"Yeah. We don't know how many are out there. Some might be out front already. I didn't want to go yet either, but it's fucking time."

He was right. There was no denying it. And even as she recognized this, something primal inside her fought against it. She didn't want to go back out there. Not yet. Not ever. Didn't want to have to face the ghoulish sight of all those reanimated corpses. The reality of it was so unlike the distance of the movies. No movie ever made could accurately convey what it felt like to fight for your life against forces beyond your control.

She heard something from out front.

A creak of clumsy footsteps on the wooden porch.

Jason started toward the door. "Out of time. We're going right now."

He was right again.

Brix followed after him, then picked up her pace and brushed past him to seize the doorknob, turn it, and pull the door open. A badly decayed walking corpse missing most of the flesh from one side of its face stared dumbly right at her.

It reached for her with a shriveled, shaking hand.

Brix shot it in the head and ran outside.

SEVENTEEN

The first thing she was aware of as she struggled toward consciousness was the sound of running water somewhere nearby. She thought she was somehow still in the woods and had fallen asleep close to a rushing creek. But then some other things occurred to her, memories that were fuzzy at first but soon gained crystalline clarity. The clearing. The house. The rich kids with their rich kid names. Her failed attempt to talk Rick and Grant out of venturing into the woods. And the last thing she remembered was the scream that rang out of the woods. Lashon frowned with her eyes closed, not yet fully awake.

Because, no, wait . . . that was *not* the last thing she remembered.

The *last* thing she remembered was a sudden, sharp sting in her side, followed by an immediate and overpowering wooziness. She had then stumbled away from a smiling Ashley, taking two or three clumsy steps before dropping to the ground. There had been a final moment of bleary consciousness before everything went black. She had looked up and seen Ashley again. And there had been something in her hand. A little plastic tube, which she now belatedly realized had been a syringe. And whatever it contained had been very powerful, because she had gone from wide awake to out inside of five seconds.

Lashon's eyes snapped open.

She was no longer in the clearing in the woods. She was in a bedroom, presumably inside the house where all those young people had been hanging out on that porch. And the source of the running water wasn't a creek, but rather was issuing from an open faucet on the other side of a closed door to her right.

Lashon tried to sit up, but the effort made her head ache fiercely. So she stayed flat on her back and stared at that closed door, wondering what was happening on the other side. It sounded like someone was running a bath. She turned her head and saw another closed door opposite the foot of the bed. No one else was in the room with her, but she assumed that wouldn't remain the case for long. Which meant it was imperative she get up and attempt an escape while no one was around to stop her. She was still weakened from whatever drug she had been injected with, but she had to somehow fight through it, get up, and get moving. She had no clue regarding the bigger picture of what was going here or why Ashley had drugged her, but she was a smart girl, smart enough to know it wasn't a good idea to hang around and try to find out.

She braced her hands on the mattress and tried again to push herself up. This time her head hurt even worse and a sudden tide of nausea made her sick. Her teeth chattered and a thin sheen of sweat formed on her brow. But she didn't give up. The stakes were too high. She gritted her teeth and redoubled the effort. By the time she finally got herself into a sitting position, her heart felt like it was going a million miles an hour. Still, she had made progress and couldn't stop now.

She glanced at the side of the bed.

Next step, swing your legs over—

The sound of running water abruptly stopped, and this was followed by the loud squelch of a faucet being shut off. Lashon's heart started going even faster. Someone was in there. And any moment now whoever it was would come into the bedroom. She had very little time left to make this happen. Setting her teeth again, she extended her right leg toward the side of the bed. This triggered another surge of nausea, but she remained determined. She got her right leg over the edge of the bed and shifted her hips in order to start swinging her other leg around.

And that was when the bathroom door swung open.

Ashley stood there framed in bright light, with her hands on her hips. She was naked and had a big hunting knife in her right hand. The lack of clothes and the weapon were startling enough, but the change in the young woman's demeanor was even more surprising. Gone entirely was the open, friendly Ashley who had greeted her so warmly after her catty exchanges with Mercedes. She wasn't smiling at all, for one thing. Her expression was very hard and there was a dead coldness in her eyes that made Lashon want to whimper.

Ashley strode into the room, brandishing the knife. "Where do you think you're going?"

Lashon cringed away from the blade, which cut through the air maybe three feet from her face as Ashley waved it at her. "What have you done to me? Why did you drug me?"

"So you wouldn't get away. Obviously. What are you, stupid?"

Lashon frowned. "But . . . but you were going to help me."

Ashley laughed at this, but there was no warmth in it at all. Her eyes remained just as cold and dead-looking. "I guess we fooled you then. Like we've fooled so many before you."

"I thought you were nice."

"You thought wrong."

Lashon's frown deepened. "But . . . those guys . . . Rick and Grant . . . they were gonna look for the guy who chased me. Why would they do that if . . ."

Ashley arched an eyebrow as she trailed off. "What? You don't get it yet?" Another cold laugh. "That guy with the chainsaw. That was my brother, Barry. He likes to play at being Leatherface while chasing girls through the woods. It's how he gets his kicks. You're not the first he's chased right back home. And you're not the first we've pretended to help."

"Why would you do that? What's the point?"

"Isn't it obvious? It's *fun*. We live in the middle of nowhere, for fuck's sake. We've gotta make our own entertainment."

"But . . . your friends. They all seemed so . . ."

"Normal?"

"Yeah."

Ashley smirked. "More play-acting. We've had a lot of practice. And oh yeah, those other people you met. They're not exactly my friends, really. They're my brothers and sisters. And the names they gave you were all fake. Mostly."

"And you all live out here together?"

"Yep."

Lashon wasn't sure why she kept asking the girl all these questions. Mostly, she guessed, because she was willing to talk and the longer they talked the longer they were putting off whatever unpleasantness these people undoubtedly had in store for her.

"What was that scream I heard?"

Ashley giggled. It was a weird and unnerving sound coming from a mentally unbalanced naked girl with a knife. "Oh. *That*. My brothers did find somebody out there in the woods. A stranger. Some middle-aged pudgy guy."

Lashon got a sick feeling in her gut.

The guy who saved me.

She swallowed hard. "Is he . . ."

"Dead?" Ashley smiled in a way that was as unnerving as the giggle had been. "No. Not yet. But he's probably wishing he was right about now. My brothers had to rough him up some and now they're, uh . . . *working* on him."

"What do you mean?"

Ashley kept smiling as she came a step closer and waved the knife around some more. "You know, *working* on him. *Doing* stuff to him. Fun stuff." Yet another step closer and another slow wave of the knife. Then she jabbed the point of the blade at Lashon's face, making her gasp and cringe backward as Ashley laughed at her reaction. "I'm gonna start working on *you* pretty soon."

Lashon's eyes misted with tears as she shook her head. "No . . . no . . ."

Ashley knelt in front of her and crossed her arms over Lashon's knees. Lashon felt the girl's bare breasts push against her legs. The girl lightly poked the tip of the big knife against her stomach. She was still wearing the ruined black camisole top, but she could feel the sharpness of the blade through the fabric. She held her breath and stared down at the knife. Then she made eye contact with Ashley, holding her gaze for several long, silent moments, knowing they were both thinking much the same thing—how little pressure it would take to push that blade through the fabric and into her flesh.

Ashley poked the tip of the knife against her belly again, a little harder this time. "Time to take your clothes off."

"No."

Ashley smirked again. "Didn't you hear me filling the tub? I'm gonna put you in it and do some stuff to you in there before I start cutting on you. You'll need to be naked."

Lashon made no move to remove her clothes. "What kind of stuff?"

Ashley poked at her stomach a couple more times with the knife. The second time the tip of the blade did pierce the fabric and she felt the cold steel against her flesh. Ashley didn't pull it away this time, apparently content for the moment to let Lashon feel its potential lethality so intimately. "Well, not sex stuff, if that's what you're thinking. At least not to start." Another of those unnerving giggles. "No, I have this little game I like to play with the girls we get. It's called The Drowning Game. I fucking *love* The Drowning Game."

Lashon's breath started coming in quick gasps as she edged toward panic. She tried to speak, to beg the way people in her current position probably always did, but the words wouldn't come. In their place, strangled, inarticulate croaks.

Ashley laughed some more as she struggled. "That's it. That's good. I like that panicky shit. Girls are the best for that. That's why I always play *this* game with them. I like the screaming. It just goes on and on and on sometimes. What I'm gonna do is, I'm gonna hold you under the water until you start to lose your breath. Then maybe I'll pull you back up and let you get your breath back so we can start the game over." She gave the knife another little push and Lashon felt it slice into her skin. It hurt. *Bad.* "Or maybe I won't. Maybe I'll just hold you under until your mouth opens and your lungs fill with water. Maybe you'll never come back up. Alive, that is."

Lashon at last found her voice. "What's wrong with you people? Why would you do this?"

Ashley pulled the knife away from her stomach and licked a speck of her blood off the blade. "Hurting people is fun. That's why we do it. You'd see that if you ever tried it yourself."

Lashon couldn't help thinking back to that night she'd punched Greg in the face. Twice. As hard as she could. She'd never done anything like that until that night. Had never thought of herself as a violent person. It had surprised and frightened her. She had been under so much pressure then and Greg had gotten on her very last nerve one time too many. Yes, she'd felt bad about it almost immediately after, but when she was being ruthlessly honest with herself, she could admit to having derived a very brief, nasty sort of satisfaction from hurting him. But that was different from what this unhinged girl was talking about. Wasn't it? An unplanned outburst like that was worlds apart from torture and murder.

Yes. Obviously.

But maybe you're getting what you deserve, she thought. *Maybe this is some kind of weird cosmic justice or payback for what you did.*

She recognized this as an irrational notion.

But the knowledge made her feel no less guilty.

For the first time since that awful night, she wished she could see Greg again and give him the sincere apology he deserved. She didn't want to reconcile with him. But, yes, he deserved that gesture from her at least.

Now, though, it almost certainly would never happen.

Ashley abruptly poked the knife at her again, harder than any of the previous times. The blade pierced the lacy top and cut her again, drawing blood as she cried out and Ashley laughed.

"Did that hurt?"

Another helpless, frustratingly pathetic whimper. "Y-yes."

"Good. I'm thinking maybe you should start practicing your screaming before we start the Drowning Game. Get your lungs good and warmed up."

Another hard poke from the knife.

Another cut. More blood.

Ashley was yelling at her with each jab. "Go on, bitch! Scream! Fucking *scream!*"

The door to the bedroom came open and the guy Lashon had initially known as Grant poked his head in. His wavy brown hair now looked a little less perfect and he had an abrasion on one of his cheeks. Apparently the "middle-aged pudgy guy" had put up a fight.

He looked at Ashley. "Hurry up and play your stupid little game. We all want a turn with this bitch, ya know."

Ashley flipped him off with her free hand. "Get the fuck out of my room, Dylan. You'll get your goddamn turn. Don't rush me."

Dylan snorted. "Yeah, yeah. Just don't damage her too much before the rest of us can have some fun."

Ashley waved the knife at him. "Get out of my fucking room, asshole."

Dylan laughed. "I'll go. But don't take too much longer or we'll come get her."

He backed out of the room, but before he closed the door Lashon heard a shrill scream issue from some other part of the house. The scream was so loud and piercing it was impossible to determine the person's gender. It could have been some other poor girl they were torturing. Or it might be the guy who had saved her in the woods. She suspected the latter. It made her sick to think what they might be doing to someone who had acted so selflessly on her behalf.

Ashley was leering at her. "You heard that, huh?"

Lashon choked back bile and nodded. "Yeah."

"They're probably pulling his fingernails out."

Lashon's stomach lurched.

Ashley giggled. "Rob, that's the one you know as Rick . . . anyway, that's how he likes to start shit. Or maybe Heidi is sawing things off. That's her thing. Fingers. Toes. Noses. Hands. Dicks. You name it. Then a torch to cauterize the wounds so the fucker don't bleed out."

"You're a bunch of sick fucking assholes."

Ashley smiled. "You say that like you think it's an insult. We're sick and proud, bitch." She stood and held out her free hand. "Come on. Get up. Time to start the game."

Lashon just sat there and stared up at her. "No."

"Do what I say or I'll kill you."

"No. You won't."

Ashley's expression turned hard again. "What? What the fuck did you just say to me, little girl? Do you know how hard I can fuck your world up?"

Lashon shook her head. "You won't kill me because the rest of them would be pissed at you for not letting them have their turn."

Ashley's face contorted with rage as she seized a handful of Lashon's hair and jerked her off the bed. Lashon cried out in pain as Ashley dragged her toward the open bathroom door. But her legs still felt a touch rubbery from the drug and she dropped to her knees after just a few steps. Ashley spewed more insults and epithets as she grabbed her by the hair again and yanked her up. This time, though, Ashley was off balance and Lashon fell into her with her full weight, knocking her to the floor. The big knife went flying out of her hand and into the bathroom. From somewhere seemingly far away, Lashon dimly heard more screaming. Scream after scream in rapid succession.

They're probably pulling his fingernails out.

Rage consumed her as Ashley's sickening words flitted through Lashon's head again. She didn't know if she could do anything to help that poor man. Probably not. But she did know this might be her last chance to help herself and she meant to take full advantage of it. She had fallen on top of Ashley and the other girl was flailing away beneath her. She struggled to keep her pinned down as she raised her head and looked into the bathroom. She saw the knife. It was no more than a few feet inside the open door. What she had to do was clear—get to it and bury it deep inside Ashley's body, probably multiple times, before one of her other twisted family members put in another surprise appearance.

Ashley clawed at her face and screamed.

"Too much noise, bitch."

The next time one of Ashley's hands raked across her face, Lashon seized it and clamped her teeth down around her wrist, biting down as hard as she could. Blood quickly filled her mouth. It was like biting into a tough but extremely juicy steak. Lashon jerked her head side to side twice and tore off a piece of the girl's flesh. Ashley was wailing now. She hadn't solved the noise problem, but it probably didn't matter. Anyone else hearing it would likely assume Lashon was the one screaming so much, and maybe begging for mercy during the "Drowning Game." Blood spilled in bright red streaks from Ashley's wound. Lashon experienced a moment of nasty satisfaction eerily similar to what she had felt in those first moments after hitting Greg. She thought about spitting the girl's flesh and blood in her face, but some nameless, unfathomable impulse made her swallow it.

Oh, sick.

I hope that bitch doesn't have any weird fucking diseases.

She balled up a fist and drilled Ashley as hard as she could dead center in the face. There was an audible snap of bone as her nose broke, triggering another gusher of blood. Adrenaline was burning away the last effects of the drug. She felt at full strength again. More than that. Supercharged. And possessed with a desire to exact vengeance. After two more hard punches to Ashley's already broken nose, Lashon disengaged herself from her adversary and crawled hurriedly into the bathroom on her hands and knees. She grabbed the knife with both hands, stood up, and turned around with the knife held out in front of her as she heard Ashley come running at her.

They stood pressed against each other, standing almost still.

Their faces were only a few inches apart.

Lashon had an odd impulse to kiss the girl on the mouth. So she did. And Ashley wheezed in pain. Lashon made a sound of triumphant satisfaction. "I guess I ought to thank you for impaling yourself on your own knife. You made this so much easier for me."

She pulled the big knife out of the girl's stomach.

And then rammed it back in again up to the hilt.

And again.

Lashon stepped back and Ashley dropped to her knees. The cracking sound her knees made when they smacked the hard tiles was music to her ears. That had to hurt. Not as bad as big knife wounds to the gut, but definitely painful. And right now there wasn't much she liked better than the idea of this girl in wretched, awful pain.

Ashley looked up at her. "Please . . ."

"Look who's begging now."

Ashley whimpered. "Please . . ."

"Okay. I'll be merciful."

Lashon slid her free hand into Ashley's long, silky hair, wound it around her hand, and pulled the girl's head back.

Then she ripped the knife across her tender neck.

Yet another gusher of blood, this the most explosive so far.

Ashley toppled over and bled out all over the tiles. Lashon looked down and saw the blood pooling around her bare feet. Which reminded her that she needed to find footwear of some kind before making her getaway. There was also one other thing she wanted to do. It was foolhardy and meant wasting valuable time, but the impulse to do it was undeniable. Brutal struggles like the one she had just survived apparently fucked with a person's psyche in some strange fucking ways. She could scarcely believe the things she'd done in the last few minutes. The flesh-eating. The mouth kiss for a girl she'd just mortally wounded.

And now this.

She set the knife atop the nearby toilet and began hauling the fresh corpse over to the brimming tub. Then, huffing and puffing mightily from the effort, she hauled the dead girl up over the edge of the tub and dropped her in with a loud splash. Lashon reached into the water and turned the body so that it was facing up.

Then she stood and stared down at her former tormentor.

She smiled. "Hey . . . about your game, Ashley? Looks like I won."

She lingered another moment longer and then walked back into the bedroom to search for shoes. She soon found surprisingly cute and comfortable ones and put them on. That done, she retrieved the knife from the bathroom and tried to decide what to do next. The screaming was still coming from another part of the house. With any luck, the rest of these twisted fucks would be preoccupied with their other catch long enough for her to slip away. But even if this were the case, leaving the bedroom to look for a direct path out of the house was almost suicidally risky.

The bedroom's one window was the only viable exit.

She had taken one step toward it when she saw the bedroom doorknob start to turn.

EIGHTEEN

The fresh blood jetting into her mouth was the most divinely delicious thing she had ever tasted. She sucked at the pulsing wound with an animal ferocity she would have found appalling only hours earlier. She just couldn't get enough blood. It sort of felt like she could *never* get enough. Her instincts urged her to drain the slender girl of every remaining drop in her already limp body. She knew giving in to that urge meant the girl would die, but right now she didn't care. No. Scratch that. She *did* care, just not in the moralistic way she would have prior to the change. She wanted the girl to die. Wanted to feel her life slip away as she held her feather-light body easily in her arms and greedily sucked down all that wonderful blood. Oh, the blood. It was a delicacy like no other. The most wondrous thing in all of creation.

She felt a tug at her shoulder.

Victor, her vampire lover, spoke. "Kira? Release her."

Kira hissed at him, then went back to suckling at the wound. Which, she realized with dismay, was yielding substantially less of the crimson delight than only moments ago. In fact, the flow was down to the merest trickle.

Another tug at her shoulder. "Kira. Darling. She's dead. Let go of her."

With great reluctance, Kira relinquished her grip on the now very still body of the girl whose life-source she had consumed. She experienced a moment of emotional numbness. But it was short-lived and bore only the faintest resemblance to anything like real regret. The girl's body hit the hardwood floor with a dull thud. She hadn't weighed enough to make a big noise. Weighed even less now. An insight that made her giggle.

She wiped blood from her mouth with the back of a hand and turned to look at Victor. "Have them bring me another one. I'm still thirsty."

Victor beckoned two of his black-clad security men forward with a raised hand. They instantly abandoned their positions to either side big drawing room's main entrance, rushing forward to scoop up the corpse and take it away.

Kira giggled again. "Do you have, like, an official corpse disposal room?"

A corner of Victor's mouth twitched. He looked faintly amused. "We use an incinerator."

"Far out. And didn't you hear me? I want another one."

"Your hunger is nearly overpowering, I know. This is common in new vampires. But you must be careful not to overfeed."

"Why? I'm a fucking vampire. Drinking blood is pretty much the whole job description. It's not gonna kill me." She frowned. "It's not, is it? Please tell me it's not."

Victor shook his head. "It will not. But overfeeding so soon after the change *can* make you very ill. Your system is still adjusting. Still changing. Too much blood too soon will make you wish you could die."

"What happens?"

Victor's smile contained a hint of smugness. "Violent, uncontrollable spasms. They can go on for hours upon hours. And then, of course, there's the explosive, seemingly endless fits of vomiting. And—"

Kira held up a hand. "Enough, you've convinced me. No more blood for now. Which sucks. How long do I have to wait?"

Rather than answering immediately, he gently grasped her by an arm and steered toward the center of the room, guiding her to a very plush-looking leather sofa. He indicated she should sit with a sweep of his hand and she reluctantly complied. Everything in Victor's house was ornate and appeared obscenely expensive. The word "house", in fact, was woefully inadequate. Regular people lived in houses. People in slums sometimes lived in things called houses. Victor was about as far from a regular person as you could get. He was a handsome aristocrat, a perfectly preserved relic from a long-gone era, and the building he lived in was a fucking mansion. Multiple floors and wings, with who-knew-how-many rooms. It was a home fit for a king. Or a dictator. The latter felt closer to the truth. This place was a palace, a living shrine to the unassailable grandeur of its master.

And now it was her home, too.

Or so he had told her.

She remained dubious about that. Could she really trust him? Even now?

Victor clapped his hands and a man in a butler's uniform appeared through another door at the far end of the room. He approached Victor and clicked his heels together like a German soldier addressing a superior in some old World War II movie. Then he bowed minutely at the waist and said, "How may I serve you, Master?"

Kira couldn't help it. She giggled again. "Master."

Victor looked like he wanted to roll his eyes, but he somehow was able to refrain from a gesture he no doubt believed beneath him. It would be *uncouth*.

Silly old vampire.

Kira covered her mouth, but was unable to stifle still another giggle.

Victor sighed and addressed his servant. "Yes, Crowley. My bride and I would each like a glass of the special crimson Dom. "In fact, bring an entire bottle."

Another crisp, long-practiced click of the heels, followed by another small bow. "Yes, Master."

Crowley went off to fetch the wine and Victor seated himself next to Kira on the sofa. "You'll enjoy the crimson Dom. It's a very limited Dom Perignon vintage created especially for vampires. It's laced with trace amounts of human blood, a small enough dose that you will not get sick, yet will ease your hunger considerably."

"Dom Perignon makes a wine just for vampires? You seriously expect me to believe that?"

Victor just smiled.

Kira shook her head. "Crazy. Tell me, does Rolls Royce also make cars for rich old vampires, with specially tinted windows maybe?"

Victor kept smiling. "Of course."

"Wow."

Victor took one of her hands in his and gently squeezed it. "You'll find that much of the world is structured to serve the most elite elements of vampire society."

"So are there just regular scumbag vampires, bloodsuckers without a penny to their names who scurry around in dark alleys and nosh on skuzzy old bums? I mean, they can't all be fabulously wealthy like you. Can they?"

This earned her a rare laugh from Victor. "Of course there are regular scumbag vampires, as you put it. However, our paths rarely cross."

In a few moments Crowley returned with a dark, heavy-looking bottle and two glasses. He set the glasses on a small table in front of the sofa and used a corkscrew to open the bottle. After pouring a bit of very dark red wine into each glass, he set the bottle on the table.

"Will there be anything else, Master?"

Victor sipped from his glass before replying. "Nothing now, Crowley. You may take your leave of us."

"Very well, sir."

Another click of the heels and then Crowley was gone.

Kira took her first sip of the wine, savoring the taste on her tongue for a moment before swallowing. "Yummy." She took a larger sip. And then another. "*Very* yummy."

"The blood hunger should begin easing shortly."

He was right. Another few sips and she was feeling decidedly less edgy. Which was a relief, of course, but the memory of what she had done still electrified her senses. She shifted a little on the sofa as she remembered the first plunge of her fangs through warm and yielding human flesh. In the past she had imagined what being a vampire might be like, but none of her fantasies had even closely approximated the reality. Vampirism wasn't a curse. It was a gift. There was no angst. Taking life was a joy like no other, generating an almost sexual thrill in the moment it happened.

She finished off her first glass of the blood wine. "More, please."

Victor slipped the glass from her fingers and filled it for her again. He looked at her with a curious expression. "What are you thinking about?"

"When can I kill someone again?"

He frowned. "I thought I explained—"

She shook her head as she interrupted him. "No, no, no. I know I need to wait a little to drink again. I'm talking about just killing someone. Can I do that?"

"You are bloodthirsty in more ways than one."

She smiled. "Yeah. It's weird, isn't it? I was a good person before you turned me. What I used to think of as good anyway. A moral person. I never hurt anyone. Wouldn't step on a bug, not even a spider. But now I can't think of anything I'd rather do."

Victor had another small sip of wine before setting his glass on the table. "We do not keep an inexhaustible supply of victims on hand. Usually no more than a half dozen or so humans are imprisoned here at any time. Purely for practical reasons. Too many missing people in too short a time could eventually draw the wrong kind of attention. Ideally, the humans I do keep here will last several months before expiring."

"You mean before you kill them."

Victor shrugged. "I am not a new vampire. I've been around for a century and a half and I rarely kill for the sheer thrill of it anymore. No, when my humans die, it is usually because their bodies are simply worn out."

Kira pouted, pooching out her bottom lip. "So I don't get to have *any* more fun tonight?"

"I didn't say that."

Kira's eyes widened dramatically and she abruptly sat up straighter. "You mean . . ."

Victor nodded. "This is your first night as my new bride in blood. I have merely explained how things normally are here. And how they will continue to be in the future. But this is a special occasion. And so I will allow you one more treat." He clapped his hands sharply together. "Crowley!"

Crowley appeared through the servants' door within seconds. "Yes, Master?"

"Fetch us another human morsel."

"Yes, Master." The butler arched an eyebrow. "Any preference, Master?"

Victor glanced at Kira. "Darling? The treat is for you. Any special requests?"

Kira thought about it a moment.

Then she smiled.

146

"Bring me the prettiest girl you have."

~

Monroe held Marnie's face cupped in his hands for many long moments after the feeding had finished. Her blood-flecked lips were soft and delicious. He was possessed by a sudden desire to gnaw them off her face and suck the tasty slivers of flesh down his throat. It struck him just as suddenly that something was very off here and so he opened his eyes.

He stared at her slack features for a long, silent moment.

His shoulders sagged. "Whoops."

Her head was in his hands.

And the rest of her blood-spattered body was sprawled awkwardly on the floor.

After a few moments reflection, what happened became obvious. He had gone into a kind of frenzy once the first drops of her blood shot into his mouth. Things became a blur. He recalled growling like an animal and thrashing his head about as he drank from the big severed vein in her throat. He drank and drank with lustful, greedy abandon. He was like a full-blown alcoholic let loose at the wildest happy hour spot in town with a fistful of cash. And just like a drunk, he could remember very little of what had happened after those first heady, delirious moments. Somehow it had ended with him ripping her head off her shoulders. He looked at the ragged stump of her neck and reconsidered. It looked like he'd *chewed* it off her body, which was about seven thousand different shades of fucked up.

He stared at her horribly still face some more and felt faint pangs of remorse. "I am seriously sorry about that. Didn't mean to . . . you know . . ."

And then it occurred to him that it was a few additional shades of deeply fucked the fuck up that he was continuing to clutch a lifeless human head in his hands—while attempting some kind of half-assed, lame fucking apology. He let go of the head and it hit the floor with a heavy thump. He frowned. "Huh." For some reason he'd expected it to maybe bounce a time or two like a basketball. Of course that made no real sense. Human heads weren't made of rubber. He giggled a little at that and it struck him that he must look and sound like a crazy person. He was still half-drunk on the poor girl's blood.

He glanced down at the head and frowned again.

It was sort of freaking him out now. He kicked it and it went sailing across the room at a high rate of speed. The top of the head hit the far wall hard enough to crack the skull in multiple places, through which promptly oozed what he could only surmise must be brain matter.

"Um . . . damn. And yuck."

Okay, so this was one obvious new thing he was learning about being a vampire. He was super fucking strong. And a killer. Not on purpose. Not this time at least. He'd honestly meant to do as the girl had asked, to feed from her and somehow turn her, make her into what he was by just letting his instincts take over. And so there was yet another obvious fact about being a new vampire—his instincts were for shit and were clearly not to be trusted.

He jumped at a knock on the door. The door was already opening as Monroe turned in that direction and tensed for some kind of confrontation. He was on edge and frightened, but a part of him was almost eager for a fight. He guessed this was another part of vampiric instinct, a natural aggression that came part and parcel with the hunger for blood.

A thin guy with pale skin and black hair came into the room. He wore black clothes, combat boots, and a black trench coat. His hair was longish on top and was swept upward in a weird kind of ridge cemented in place with an absurd amount of gel. A hank of it flopped across his forehead. So here was another guy who looked like he'd stepped out of an 80s movie. *Valley Girl* or *Say Anything* this time.

The guy's blank expression barely changed as he took in the corpse and the wild sprays of coagulating blood, except that a corner of his mouth twitched once. "Damn, dude."

Monroe remained wary. "Who the fuck are you?"

The guy smirked. "I'm Lloyd, that's who the fuck I am. And you must be Monroe."

Monroe didn't say anything. He just stared at Lloyd with the hardest expression he could manage, waiting for him to speak again or make some kind of move.

Lloyd reached into an inner pocket of his trench coat and pulled out a silver flask. A wolf's head was engraved on its side. He screwed off the cap, drank deeply from it, and offered it to Monroe. "Drink? It's good shit, man. Blood-laced top shelf liquor. Helps take the edge off. And brother, you look like you've got an edge in dire need of some smoothing down."

Monroe wasn't quite ready to let his guard all the way down, but he was getting no sense at all that this guy was looking for a fight or was at all angry about what he had done to the girl. He eyed the flask warily for a couple seconds longer, then snatched it from Lloyd's out-stretched hand.

The first splash of liquor lit up his taste buds in an unexpected way. He took a few more much larger gulps before wiping his mouth with the back of a hand. "Holy fuck."

Lloyd's knowing expressing indicated he was much amused. "Hits the spot, don't it?"

Monroe nodded as he took one more long swig. "Hell yeah, it does. Damn."

Lloyd gestured for his flask and Monroe reluctantly handed it back. He screwed the cap back on and slipped it back inside his trench coat. "So . . ." He moved his head, pointedly taking in the carnage before again meeting Monroe's gaze. "Had a bit of a mishap, eh?"

"You could say that."

Lloyd shook his head in an easy way that conveyed a mild dis-pleasure but no real rebuke. "We don't like to waste the food. Pro-curing tasty morsels like Marnie can be complicated. But, hell, this shit's always a risk when indoctrinating the new blood."

"So that's what this was? An indoctrination?"

"Call it what you like. Indoctrination. Hazing. It's a bit of both, I guess. You gotta prove you have what it takes. Get your feet wet." A brief glance at Monroe's feet, followed by a chuckle. "Or bloody, in this case."

Monroe's brow creased as he gave himself a belated once over. "Damn. I've sort of got blood all the fuck over me."

"You'll want to clean up and change clothes again before heading out with the rest of us tonight."

"Heading . . . out? Where are we going?"

"Hunting, Monroe. We'll be visiting a neighboring town to prowl for food."

"Huh." Monroe stared at Marnie's headless corpse. Again, he felt those remote feelings of remorse. It wasn't that he didn't feel bad about what he'd done. He did. It was just that those feelings seemed way more distant than they should. He had some semblance of a con-science remaining, evidently, but not enough of one to trouble him more than mildly. "By food, I'm guessing you mean people."

"You catch on fast."

"I don't know how I feel about that."

Lloyd smirked again. "Yeah, you do. It's just there's a part of you holding on to what's left of your humanity. It won't last long. Listen, out the door here and down the hall to the right are some shower stalls. Get cleaned up and changed, then come on out and meet the rest of the gang." He grinned. "Properly, this time. And get cracking, okay? It's getting to be prime hunting time."

Monroe indicated the corpse and the great splashes of blood with a tilt of his chin. "What about . . ."

Lloyd laughed. "Don't worry about it. We got people to take care of shit like that. Get a move on, son."

And then he was out the door and gone.

Monroe stared at the closed door for a long moment, his face twisting slightly in confusion. So strange. He wondered whether "newbie vampire greeter" was Lloyd's official role in this odd cadre of youthful-looking vamps. Apparently so, but the far more puzzling question was why the vamp-in-chief upstairs maintained this subterranean residence for vamps of presumably lesser stature at all. He couldn't think of any way it made any sense.

He shook his head.

Just stop thinking about it. It'll be easier that way.

And so that's what he endeavored to do, at least for the time being.

He found a fresh change of clothes and left the room in search of the shower stalls.

NINETEEN

The Glock went boom one more time. There was a spray of blood and bone fragments out the back of a head and another zombie toppled over in the middle of the street. Brix shifted aim as she kept running and fired again. Another rotting animated corpse hit the asphalt. Jason was in front of her, firing wildly with the .38 Nikki had used to kill Trevor. One round from the revolver took a zombie in the shoulder and spun it around, putting the thing temporarily out of commission but failing to kill it. Every other shot Jason squeezed off went well wide of its target. Brix heard his roar of frustration as the weapon soon clicked empty. He shifted his grip from the handle to the barrel and whipped it across the face of the next zombie that came within range. This knocked the thing over but earned him a jagged scratch from the flailing creature down the underside of his arm.

Brix wanted to scream at him. He was being stupid and careless, so much the opposite of how he had behaved at the outset of this madness. And now that it was just the two of them, she needed him to keep his head in the game more than ever. As she watched in helpless anger and frustration, he took another swipe at the next zombie in his path with the butt of the gun's handle rather than veering around it. This time the gun bounced off the top of the thing's skull and went flying out of Jason's hand. He earned more scratches for his trouble, this time three livid red marks across a cheek.

Shit.

Fucking idiot.

She saw that he had something jammed into a back pocket. It was hard to tell on the run like this, but it sort of looked like a screwdriver. He'd have better luck using that thing as a weapon than the empty revolver. A quick jab to a temple and it'd be lights out for any of these living dead motherfuckers. But the jackass had clearly stopped thinking straight the instant they'd come flying out of the house.

The zombie he'd wounded with one of his last bullets was struggling to its feet again. Brix took care of it with a calmly placed round to the center of the forehead. She stayed on the move as she aimed and fired. Anything else would mean death. There were just too many of the things around now. They'd had time to amass in numbers while they'd been holed up in that fucking death trap of a house. And now they were spilling out of the spaces between the houses to her right, a great, shambling horde of rotting, upright corpses.

Three of the faster ones were converging on her now from that direction.

She swung her arm out, took quick, careful aim.

Click.

BOOM.

Click.

BOOM.

Click . . .

Shit, goddammit!

The one clip she'd had was finally empty and suddenly she was a lot more scared. With a loaded gun in her hand, she felt capable of taking on and vanquishing any adversary. Now that her weapon was useless, she was all too aware of how vulnerable she truly was. She turned on the speed instead and soon closed the gap between herself and Jason. But then, as they neared a street corner, he abruptly veered diagonally across an overgrown, trash-strewn yard. She saw him skid to a stop next to an ugly beige-yellow compact car.

She screamed at him. "The fuck are you going!?"

For an answer, he peeled off his Slayer shirt and wound it around a fist, which he then used to slam repeatedly at the car's driver's side window. The glass began to splinter and give way. Then his fist punched through and glass clinked as it tumbled to the seat. He kept the shirt wound around his hand and knocked away more glass fragments before reaching inside to grab the door handle and spring the lock.

He peeled the shirt off his hand and tossed it into the car.

Against her better judgment, Brix risked a backward glance.

Oh, fucking hell . . .

There were even more of them now. A virtual sea of rotting flesh advancing on them like a column of drunken soldiers stumbling across a battlefield.

Brix looked at Jason. "Mind explaining yourself? And make it fast, because we're about to be fucking dead, man."

Jason pulled the screwdriver from his rear pocket, smiled grimly at her, and dropped into the car behind the steering wheel. "This is a trick my dad taught me. Sometimes works with older cars like this ugly-ass piece of shit."

Her brow furrowed with doubt as she watched him fit the slotted screwdriver in the car's ignition. He worked it in as far as he could and then began cranking the thing back and forth. The first few times only yielded dispiriting dead clicks. She was sure it wouldn't work. No way could it work. Their luck was too bad for that—

The engine sputtered to life.

Jason let out a whoop of triumph, which was promptly drowned out by the loud rock and roll rattling the car's tinny speakers. It was a song she recognized instantly because it was one of her favorites— Wednesday 13's "I Walked with a Zombie."

Even with imminent, teeth-gnashing death bearing down on them at any moment, this was just too much.

"Are you fucking kidding me?"

A zombie song. Seriously. What were the fucking odds? And wasn't this just how it'd be in some low-budget cinematic walking dead extravaganza?

Of course it was.

It made a fucked up, twisted kind of bizarro sense.

Jason pulled the door shut and leaned over to unlock the door on the other side.

Brix didn't need further prompting.

The front line of zombies was more than halfway across the litter-covered yard at the corner. She hurried to the other side of the car, yanked the door open, and got in just as Jason was putting it in gear. A zombie fell across the hood and reached for them with a gnarled, clawing hand in the same second Jason stomped on the gas pedal and sent them flying backward in reverse. The zombie's twisted brown fingers grasped one of the windshield wipers and it was able to hang on for a long moment. The wiper blade peeled away from the windshield and the zombie slid backward a few inches down the hood, until Jason stomped down on the brake pedal, bringing the car to a wild, fishtailing stop in the middle of the street. The tagalong zombie slalomed sideways across the hood in a violent motion. The wiper blade broke off in its hand as the creature tumbled to the street and rolled a few times before hitting the curb.

Brix's gaze remained riveted to the road ahead. The desperate backward flight had put some distance between themselves and the still-advancing zombie horde. The nearest zombies were still some twenty yards away. But they were closing fast. Faster than she could ever have imagined. She stared at their dead eyes and their reaching, grasping fingers, listened to the wheezing din of their groans—audible even over the music still blasting from the car's stereo—and the thing she sensed most strongly was desperation. A terrible, gnawing hunger that could simply never be sated. It was consuming them, driving their decaying bodies ever forward in search of warm food even as rotting pieces of them gave way and dropped to the street.

Closer.

Fifteen yards.

That terrible groaning, louder all the time.

Jason hit the gas again and cranked the wheel hard to the right, causing the car's rear tires to bounce over the curb. Brix let out a cry of surprise as her head bumped the ceiling. Then Jason was shifting gears and cranking the wheel hard in the other direction. He gave it another burst of gas and the car bounced back over the curb with an alarming scrape of metal. He leaned over the wheel and kept the pedal to the floor with a grim, determined look on his face. They flew through a four-way stop without slowing down and kept on going.

Brix twisted in her seat and saw the zombies receding in the distance.

She heaved a sigh of immense relief and turned back around, reaching for the stereo's volume control to squelch the blaring rock music.

Jason looked at her, a wild grin that was equal parts relief and lingering terror stretching across his face. "Shit. Shit! Holy shit!" He smacked the steering wheel with a fist. "I can't believe we got out of there."

Brix couldn't believe it either. They'd had some other close calls, but none quite so narrow as this latest. And yet there was no time to waste in exulting in the moment.

"We have to get out of this town."

"Believe me, I know."

"It's like I said. We have to get out to the country, out to the wide-open spaces."

Jason took a right turn at another four-way stop. Then the engine roared again and they shot down to the end of the next street, pausing only briefly at yet another four-way stop. As they rolled through to the other side, Brix saw a lone zombie standing in the middle of a yard in front of a little house missing its front door. A chain-link fence ringed the yard. The zombie started toward them, its hands stretched outward in the standard I-am-seriously-fucking-hungry-right-now living dead way. Brix turned her head and tracked his progress as long as she could, somehow unaccountably mesmerized by the lone creature. She thought maybe it was because they seemed more pathetic observed individually, rather than as part of some overwhelming, mindless force. And more sad, too. The zombie hit the chain-link fence and stopped in its tracks, unable to go any further. Its head turned in their direction and it stared dumbly after them.

Brix faced the front again. "Poor fucking things."

She expected reflexive anger from Jason at this statement. But instead he nodded and said, "Yeah. It's fucked up."

They rolled up to another stop sign. This time it was a three-way stop. They could go left or right. Brix had a vague idea where they were now. A left would take them deeper into the old part of town. A right would eventually take them out toward the university.

Jason cranked the wheel to the right and went that way.

He looked at her. "Quicker way to the interstate."

Brix grunted. "Suits me."

They rode on in relative silence for a time. Another mile or so up the street and they began to reach the outskirts of campus. The streets were crowded on each side with more beer and tobacco stores, bars, and restaurants. There weren't too many zombies visible, but Brix did spot several lone ones staggering around in various spots in the street and on the sidewalks. They hardly constituted a horde, but then again, she'd thought the same thing earlier, during their flight from the accident scene. And somehow a horde had eventually formed anyway. There were enough of them around to warrant concern, at least.

She looked at Jason. "How much farther to the—"

There was a loud BANG!, and the steering wheel went spinning out of his hands as the car fishtailed across lanes of dead traffic, clipping the fender of an ancient Buick en route to the opposite side of the street. Brix screeched in fright as the car bounced up over a curb and careened into the parking lot of a convenience store. The car crashed to a halt as it collided with a gas pump, resulting in a rending screech of shredded metal.

Brix lurched forward then rocked backward into her seat.

She glanced in numb shock at Jason. "The fuck happened?"

He looked stunned, too, and could only shake his head. "Dunno. Blew out a tire, I guess. We're just lucky—"

There was another loud, cracking sound.

Something smashed into the dash between them, destroying the stereo.

They both glanced backward and saw the splintered glass of the rear window. The truth of what was happening hit them simultaneously. There was no time to discuss or debate the obvious. Someone was shooting at them and they were sitting ducks. Jason threw his door open and scrambled out of the car. Brix quickly followed suit. Jason dashed across the parking lot and climbed over a small, landscaped hill lined with bushes. Again, no time for debate and one direction was as good as another under the circumstances, so Brix followed him up the hill and into the parking lot of the bar next to the convenience store. Yet another shot rang out and sparks flew up from the asphalt near Jason as he raced at high speed toward the bar, which the marquee on the sign above the parking lot told her was called the Boro Bar and Grill. Beneath the establishment's name, spelled out in changeable block letters—TONIGHT ONLY! THE LIKES OF US & STALLION.

Local bands, probably.

She doubted either of them would actually be here tonight.

Show cancelled due to zombie apocalypse.

Three more loud rifle reports in rapid succession drove the thought from her mind.

A slug creased Jason across the right bicep, but he kept going. Brix felt like she was about to come out of her skin as she continued to follow him. Knowing a bullet from the unknown, unseen assailant could take her down any second was unbearable. She felt more helpless and scared and vulnerable than ever. And she knew one thing with absolute clarity—despite everything that had happened, despite the loss of her great love, she wanted to go on living. More than anything, she wanted that.

The front door of the bar came open as Jason reached it.

Actually, an instant before he reached it.

There was no time to ponder this new mystery. And no doubt at all as to the only path available to her now.

She followed Jason through the open door into the Boro Bar and Grill.

And then the door slammed shut.

TWENTY

He wished they would hurry up and kill him. And not just because the things they were doing to him were causing wave upon endless wave of mind-shattering agony. No, the real reason he craved death was because the memories were coming back. Previously they had hidden away in some remote, impenetrable corner of his mind thanks to an alcoholic blackout. But the intense pain had brought them screaming back to the surface, searing his consciousness with images so vividly lurid in their obscene sickness he would give anything to stop seeing them. Anything, including his life. Maybe even especially that.

Because how could he ever live with the knowledge that he had butchered Marie?

He should have guessed it from the beginning. He saw that now. How obvious it was. It was tragically absurd that he'd ever managed to convince himself some stranger had come into their apartment and done those awful things to Marie while leaving him completely unscathed. He had blinded himself to the truth. The massive quantities of alcohol he'd consumed was largely to thank for that, but now he was as sober as he had ever been and there would never again be any hiding from what he had done. The only solace available now was the sweet oblivion of death. He had no doubt these sick bastards would grant him that release eventually. But they clearly intended to stretch the process out as long as possible.

He sat at a round kitchen table. Long, thick nails had been hammered through his hands, pinning them to the table's surface. The flat heads of the nails rested flush with his bloody flesh. He was missing three fingers at this point, two from the left hand and one from the right. The stumps of his severed fingers were sickening blackened lumps. One of the guys, a tall blond guy the others called Rob, had cauterized the wounds with a welder's torch. A gorgeous young woman with hair an even brighter shade of blonde sat in the chair next to him. She was scantily clad, wearing only tight denim cutoffs and a bikini top. Her skin was flawless and her hair looked like she was freshly emerged from an expensive Hollywood salon. Except for the meat cleaver grasped lightly in her slender right hand, she looked like the poster child for the American youth beauty ideal.

Sometimes the others called her Mercedes, but mostly they called her Heidi. It was strange how they randomly alternated between the names. John supposed Heidi was her real name. Not that he cared. By any name, she was a sadistic bitch.

Heidi, still smiling, lifted the cleaver and placed the sharp edge against the pinky finger on his right hand. "Ready to say goodbye to another little piggy, Johnny?"

John sniffled. "Please . . . just kill me."

His crying inflamed their mocking laughter. Little did they know the primary source of his emotional misery was something other than their heartless cruelty.

In reality, he was no better than them.

The way her flesh yielded so easily to each thrust of the heavy butcher's knife had come as a revelation. The first time he had rammed it into Marie's body he'd been consumed with a storm of emotions. Rage, first and foremost. He had been out of work for so long. All he did was sit around the house and drink beer. He was drinking too much and getting too fat. He wouldn't easily be able to find another job if he kept on being a fat, drunken pig. These were some of the things she told him prior to her death. Normally she was so quiet, and so prone to keep things to herself. But not that day. That day she finally let it out. All her frustrations. All her disappointments. She'd had enough. She was thinking of leaving him. She couldn't go on living with someone so lazy. And so he had snapped. He was stronger than her. And she was so tiny. She never had any kind of chance. Despite his rage, he felt a great sickness at what he was doing in the beginning. But that subsided as the assault continued. It got easier each time he put the knife inside her. And easier still each time he ripped it from her body and saw the blood leap from the rents in her flesh. An unfamiliar, strange kind of madness rode roughshod over him for the duration of the assault. He'd never felt anything like it. And it allowed him to glory—to *gloat*—over the savaging of his wife's body, which concluded via the pulping of her head with the heavy lamp base.

After it was over, he'd thrown the knife under the bed. And had changed clothes. Somehow, despite the madness and savagery of it all, he'd the presence of mind to do that. He recalled thinking he might concoct some kind of cover story, but realized the forensic evidence would show the truth plainly enough. That was when the wild elation of what he'd done gave way to reality and despair. He sobbed and sobbed, truly regretful for what he'd done. Not knowing what else to do, he drank until he passed out.

Until he couldn't remember having done that awful, unforgivable thing.

Heidi abruptly raised the cleaver and slammed it to the table. John howled in agony yet again as the sharp blade punched easily through his little finger, separating it from the rest of his hand with a terrible ease that seemed fundamentally wrong. She swept the blade away from his hand, sending the severed digit spinning toward the center of the table. John's whole body shook from the pain. Then he convulsed again, harder this time, as Rob leaned in with the torch and applied the flame to his bleeding flesh. The agony was searing and for long moments made him forget all about what he'd done to Marie.

The aroma of sizzling meat assailed his nostrils and stung his eyes. But the smell had more than one source. His singed wounds were one, of course. His stomach churned as he watched another girl pluck the pinky finger from the center of the table and carry it over to the stove, where she dropped it in a pan with the rest of his missing fingers. He heard the snap and spark of spattered cooking oil, a sound repeated when she dumped in some more seasonings.

Heidi smiled. "Six little piggies left. Why don't you pick the next one to go, Johnny?"

He glared at her. "Go . . . to . . . hell."

Heidi tossed her long blonde locks and laughed as if she'd never heard anything so funny. "That's a riot. Wanna know why?" She leaned closer to him, her big, leering grin twisting in a way that conveyed a gleeful sadism and savagery. "Because I've got a long life ahead of me. I'm young and I'm gonna have a lot more fucking fun before I'm done. But you . . ." She rapped the edge of the cleaver blade against the table, laughing at the wince this elicited from him. ". . . *you're* the one who just bought a one-way ticket to hell, you fat bag of shit. Because you know what? I do believe in heaven and hell, Lord Satan and God above, and all the rest of that shit, too. But I don't fear damnation because I know Satan watches over me and sees that I serve him well. I'll have an exalted place in hell when my time finally comes. You, though, you're just a blubbering blob, a fucking waste of humanity. You killed your wife, sure, but Satan sees your regret. Eternal torment awaits ordinary, regretful sinners like you." Her eyes sparkled with a malign hatefulness. "An eternity that'll be beginning in just about, oh, five more minutes."

Despite the enormous pain still gripping him, John listened to the girl's speech with an increasing fascination of the morbid variety. He couldn't recall confessing to the murder of his wife out loud, but there'd been many moments of intense, agony-induced delirium, so it was hardly surprising. Also, he'd understood from the outset that he was dealing with a group of uniquely deranged and cruel individuals, but now it was clear they were far more unhinged than he'd even imagined.

"You're . . . Satanists?"

Heidi giggled. "Yes, silly."

The one called Rob lit a cigarette from a pack of Marlboros and blew a cloud of smoke over John's head. "From birth, boy. Folks raised us to follow the left-hand path." He tucked the pack of Marlboros in a shirt pocket and circled the table to hover over John's left shoulder. After blowing out another puff of rancid smoke, he held the lit end of the cigarette close to John's left eye. "Care for a toke, boy?"

John started shaking again. He was certain the kid meant to put the burning end of the thing out in his eye. Despite his terror, a part of him couldn't help being irked by the way a punk two decades his junior kept calling him "boy."

"Fuck you . . . boy."

Heidi scowled. "He's a lippy old fuck."

A grunt from Rob. "Maybe we should cut those lips off the fat son of a bitch."

Heidi gasped and smacked the table with the cleaver again. "Yes! Somebody get me a razor. I'm cutting his lips the fuck off."

The other girl moved away from the table, walking out of John's field of vision. He heard a drawer open somewhere behind him, followed by a sound of various metal things clanking against each other. Then the rooting-around sound stopped and the drawer was thrown shut. Heidi set the cleaver on the table as the other girl stepped back into view and passed her a long, thin piece of metal he recognized as an old-fashioned folding razor, the kind commonly used by men for shaving generations ago.

Heidi flipped the blade open. "Last time I used this I cut a guy's dick off and fed it to him. What do you think about that, Johnny?"

John looked at her and said nothing. The lit end of the cigarette was still an inch from his eye. He sort of wished Rob would stop fucking around and just jam the thing into his eyeball. Sure, it would be horrible, but at least that misery would distract him for a time from the no doubt even greater level of misery Heidi had in mind. But then Rob tapped ash from the end of the cigarette and pulled it away from his eye.

This should have come as a relief.

It did not.

Heidi leaned close to him again and placed the edge of the razor blade against his throat. "I bet you'd like me to open up your throat and just let you bleed out, huh?"

John sniffled yet again. A snot bubble emerged from one nostril and popped. "Yes. Please."

Heidi nodded. "Thought so. And maybe I'll do that." Her expression turned savage again. "But first those lips are coming off." A giggle. "And then they're going down your fat fucking throat."

A general round of deranged laughter from her siblings.

John opened his mouth to say something.

But a scream emerged in place of words as he felt a hot sting at the nape of his neck.

Rob and his fucking cigarette.

He tried to jerk his head away from the burning sensation, but Rob seized a handful of his hair and held his head in place as he continued to press the red-hot end of the cigarette against his sizzling flesh. Tears leaked from his eyes as the burning seemed to go on and on forever (even though it was likely only a few seconds). At last, Rob flicked the squashed-out cigarette butt to the table and relinquished his grip on John's hair. John sobbed through the pain, listening while the sadists gathered around him made fun of him for blubbering like a baby. In truth, the pain caused by the extinguishing of a cigarette on his flesh ranked considerably lower on the pain scale than most other things they'd done to him so far, but the cumulative effect of it all was grinding him down. Each fresh assault brought him closer to a breaking point. Soon his mind, unable to endure any more of this hell, would snap utterly.

He hoped so.

Because he didn't see how he could take any more of this and hang on to anything resembling sanity.

Heidi stood up and pushed her chair back. She glanced at Rob, who was still standing behind him. "Hold his head still again."

John whimpered.

More tears came.

Rob did as instructed.

Heidi smiled and slipped the edge of the razor inside a corner of his mouth.

And then, gripping his chin, she began to cut.

~

The door came open and the guy who had chased her through the woods slinked into the room. He was clearly trying to be stealthy and his attention was on the bathroom door the whole time. Though he wasn't wearing his mask and he'd changed out of his Leatherface wannabe clothes, Lashon knew he was the chainsaw guy from his build alone. He had a bulkier and more muscular physique than any of his siblings. No way would she have stood a chance against him in a direct confrontation. So it was a good thing she had moved into position behind the door as it came open, out of his range of his vision. She waited until he was fully inside the room and had taken his first step toward the bathroom before pouncing.

She launched herself at him and plunged the big knife into the side of his neck. He let out a squawk and swatted at her as she ripped the blade free of his flesh. A spray of bright red blood jumped from his wound as she reeled backward, avoiding possibly disastrous contact with his flailing fist by mere inches. Blood continued to spurt from the big gash in his throat as he spun about and gaped at her in terrified astonishment.

Lashon jammed the knife into his gut.

Tore it out.

Slammed it in again.

All in the space of just a couple seconds. Her struggle with Ashley had taught her valuable lessons. For instance, in life and death struggles, there is no value in hesitation. And even less in pausing for even an instant to listen to your conscience or weigh moral considerations.

Barry, as she recalled Ashley referring to this guy, took a weaker swat at her, but all this earned him was a vicious slash across an outstretched palm. He squealed in agony and staggered backward, panicked instinct propelling him away from the source of his injuries and pain. Lashon came at him again and his panic made him try to move faster, but his weakened condition soon betrayed him, causing him to trip over his own feet and tumble to the floor with a resounding crash.

Lashon fell upon him, straddling him across the waist as she delivered the death blow, a savage slash across his throat that tore it open nearly to his spine. She felt him twitch beneath her and then go still. Though she knew he was dead, she slashed at his throat again for good measure, nearly decapitating him this time. She'd seen enough cheap slasher movies to know it was best not to take chances with mad dog backwoods killers. They had a nasty, insidious way of coming back to life again and again, no matter how much damage had been inflicted upon their bodies. And she was living in a scenario almost literally ripped right out of one of those fucking movies, so insurance against an unlikely resurrection seemed doubly important.

She stared at his ruined throat, appraising her work and judging it good enough.

She stared at it some more, starting to frown.

Nearly good enough.

His head really was almost all the way off, but she decided almost didn't quite cut it, not in a situation like this one. So, grateful for the heavy blade she'd inherited from Ashley, she raised it over her head and brought it down as hard as she could, grunting as she felt it glance off the spinal column. She raised it up and brought it down again. And then many more times. Things went kind of blurry there for a while. By the time her frenzy subsided, Barry's head had been fully removed from his body and her hands were caked with blood again.

Two of them, she thought.

I've killed two of them now.

It seemed like a good start.

Knocking off two of these degenerates had emboldened a part of her. The savage, merciless part of her that had shamed her so in the wake of her assault on Greg. But now she felt a deeply compelling impulse to fully embrace it.

She disengaged herself from Barry's corpse and turned away from it to stare at the bedroom window. She fought against the storm of rage building inside her and tried to think in a logical way. That window was still the most sensible way out of this mess. And though she had killed two, several more formidable adversaries remained.

She couldn't hope to defeat them all.

Could she?

A sound of lightly treading footsteps in the hallway outside the open door decided the matter for her.

Don't hesitate. Never hesitate. Go!

She rushed through the door into the hallway and stood face to face with the one she had first known as "Grant." Ashley had called him Dylan, which was likely his real name. Either way, he was dead.

He stared at her in open-mouthed surprise for a moment.

Then he reached for the gun tucked inside his waistband.

Lashon knocked his hand aside and stabbed him in the gut several times in rapid succession, like a convict shivving a fellow jailbird in a prison courtyard. It was the kind of thing she had seen in movies a number of times. It seemed equally as effective in real life. She guessed sometimes movies got things right. She moved with Dylan as he fell back against wall behind him, keeping the knife shoved all the way up inside his body. He tried reaching feebly for the gun one more time, but she plucked it from his waistband and tossed it to the floor. She kept the knife in him a bit longer and moved with him as his eyes turned glassy and he began to slide to the floor. When she was satisfied he was dead, she pulled the knife from his gut and retrieved the gun.

Then she stood in the middle of the hallway and stared in wonder at her blood-covered limbs and mid-section. She was covered in crimson nearly head-to-toe and probably looked like the average teenage gorehound's hottest wet dream ever come to life.

Three dead, she thought.

I can do this. I really can. I can kill them all.

At this point she knew it was futile to resist the impulse, especially now that she had the gun. The gun was the equalizer, the one thing that possibly tipped the scales in her favor. Or at least balanced them just enough.

Her decision made, she turned away from Dylan's body.

And started down the hallway in the direction of the screams.

TWENTY-ONE

The clack of high heels and the white noise of bubbly female chatter made it difficult for Monroe to focus on what Lloyd and Tom were saying as he followed them down a long, dimly-lit concrete corridor. Three of the buxom vampire babes were trailing along behind him. They had traded in their bikinis for sexy party dresses and heels. Hearing them in this context—three gorgeous, vivacious ladies headed out for a night of clubbing—was so strange, knowing they had all participated in the act of ending his mortal life. They were astonishingly attractive and he would fuck any one of them given half a chance, yet he knew he could never actually *like* them. As he listened to their lilting voices and exuberant laughter, all he could think of was their fangs tearing into his flesh and how much it had fucking *hurt*. Okay, so technically he was one of them now. He nonetheless harbored a lingering resentment for what they had done to him. It was hard to feel any kind of real camaraderie with them. Same went for Tom and, to a lesser extent, Lloyd. He might have to fake some level of kinsmanship with the lot of them, either until he'd been among them long enough to feel it for real or until he managed to escape.

Huh.

There's a thought.

Escape had come to seem less vital after killing Marnie, mostly because his personal safety was significantly less of an issue. He was dead. That ship had already fucking sailed. Same went for Kira, according to Lloyd. She was the head vamp's new bloodsucking bride. The idea of getting out to summon some kind of help for her was a lost cause, as well. But there was a simple reason he had yet to fully abandon the notion of escape.

Freedom.

He didn't want to spend years hiding out in that weird underground playground these assholes called home. He'd asked Lloyd about that. Why they stayed. It had something to do with them being "sirelings" of Victor, the big boss vamp and owner of the mansion. They felt a loyalty to him. And a gratitude for granting them a kind of immortality. Not wanting to arouse suspicion, Monroe had pretended to understand this, but in truth he did not. He wanted to be out in the wider world, on his own and independent, as far away from this place and its stifling, confining weirdness as he could get.

So maybe he should try to make that happen tonight. They would be partying. And hunting. Stalking the neighboring city's hippest nightspots in search of the choicest prey. Their focus would not be on him, at least not much of the time.

A chance to bolt would arise.

And he meant to seize it when it did.

Lloyd glanced over his shoulder at him. He was frowning. For a fleeting instant, Monroe was confused, but then he realized the trench coat-wearing vamp had directed some comment at him and had not received a response.

Monroe gave his head a fog-clearing shake. "Whoa, sorry, sort of got lost out in the ether there. Say something?"

Lloyd smirked. "I get it. This shit's all new to you. Feels like a lot is happening really fucking fast. Am I right?"

Monroe shrugged. "Guess so. Just still trying to process it all, you know?"

"Yeah, yeah, I do, man, I do. Look, it's better at this stage to put it all out of your mind." He laughed. "Easier said than done, I know, but you should try. It'll make tonight more fun if you can do that." He craned his head around a bit further and grinned as he pitched his voice louder. "And fun is what tonight's all about, right, girls?"

The girls paused long enough in their rapid-fire conversation to let out identically shrill whoops of feminine enthusiasm.

Awesome, Monroe thought. *Vampire Girls Gone Wild.*

They arrived at the end of the corridor, stopping at a gleaming silver elevator door. Lloyd stabbed a button to the right of the door with a forefinger, then turned to address Monroe again. "Another thing, man. You're new at this hunting thing. Think of this first time as a learning experience. Let us take the lead while you hang back and watch."

Monroe was happy to hear this but thought it wise to feign disappointment. He sighed and scratched idly at his chin. "Damn. Shit, I guess you know best, but I was hoping for another taste of the good stuff."

"Blood, right?"

"What else?"

Lloyd nodded. "Not to worry. Our ride will be stocked with more gore-laced booze. Stronger shit than what I shared with you earlier. And if all goes well tonight, you'll have your own taste of whatever we bring home with us."

Meaning warm, fresh blood pumping direct from the veins of a live human being. Monroe recalled the ecstatic feeling that had consumed him while draining Marnie's blood. Though some part of him did still regret her death, he found himself salivating at the prospect of experiencing that again. But this surge of excitement was tempered somewhat by the knowledge that he might not return with these people tonight.

He smiled.

But so what?

Once he was free of this crowd and this place, he could hunt at will on his own. He could feed any time he felt like it.

There was a chime as the elevator door slid open. Monroe accompanied the others inside and moved to a corner in the rear. The girls were arrayed in front of him now and he couldn't help ogling their sleek, sexy forms as the elevator began its ascent. The black-haired, pale-skinned beauty directly in front of him was wearing classic black, a short and very revealing dress with clean, simple lines. There was a tattoo of a bat on her left shoulder, partly obscured by a thin dress strap. Not the most original tattoo choice for a vampire, but she was scorching hot, so she got a pass on that. The girl to her left had platinum blonde hair and wore a dress just as revealing, but hers was a shimmering, dazzling red. She filled out the dress wonderfully with amazing curves. The girl on the other side of Bat Tattoo Girl also wore classic black, though her dress was marginally more modest than those of her companions.

The electronic chime came again and the elevator door slid open, revealing a view of an underground parking garage. He saw dozens of cars, most of them luxury automobiles of varying types, with a few very sleek and dangerous-looking sports cars sprinkled here and there among them. As they exited the elevator, Monroe heard the purr of a finely-tuned engine as a long, black car approached from their left and pulled to a stop at the curb.

After a moment, he realized Lloyd was looking at him again.

"Sweet ride, huh?"

The car at the curb was one of the coolest-looking automobiles Monroe had ever seen. "Uh, yeah. What is it?"

A door on the driver's side came open and a man in chauffeur's livery popped out. He came smoothly around the car to open the doors for his passengers. Lloyd approached the car and paused for a moment with his hand on a doorframe. "This is a Rolls Royce Phantom. No better way to ride in style."

Monroe had to agree.

~

She was a lithe little blonde with a cute face and short hair cut in a pixie style. A colorful tattoo of a unicorn with a curve of rainbow above it adorned her slender right arm. The girl screamed again as Kira took a bite out of her right breast. She writhed in agony, but the two female servants Victor had summoned to assist held her easily in place. Kira swallowed the morsel of tasty flesh and clamped her mouth around the wound, groaning in ecstasy as she slurped down the blood. The female servants laughed as the girl sobbed and begged for mercy. Their laughter at the sound of her pain struck Kira as divinely decadent and only served to inflame her hunger. The women were voluptuous and gorgeous, one with flowing red hair and the other with short black hair and the palest complexion Kira had ever seen. The woman had joked about her "vampire tan." Her name was Aubrey. The redhead's name was Jenna. Both were vampires, but Victor had told her both would do anything she wanted, regardless of how degrading or twisted. Which was wonderful, because right now she had a head full of astonishingly twisted ideas.

Kira sat up and licked blood from her lips. They were situated atop a plush throw rug in front of the big fireplace in the massive master bedroom. A fire blazed beneath the stone hearth, casting a pleasant warmth throughout the room. "Aubrey, I'd like you to do something for me, if you don't mind."

Aubrey smiled. "I'm here to serve you, mistress. What would you have me do?"

As Victor's bride, she was their queen and they were expected to treat her as such. It was sort of hilarious, but she enjoyed it anyway. Her fixation on vampires had not been her only girlhood flight of fancy. Like so many other girls, she had daydreamed of being royalty. Of being a storybook princess. But being a debased vampire queen of blood was even better.

"I'd like you to dig out one of this cute little thing's eyes and feed it to Jenna."

"Yes, mistress."

The girl on the floor screamed again and whipped her head side to side in a desperate effort to avoid Aubrey's grasping hand. Kira clamped a hand under the girl's chin and forced her to stay still as Aubrey reached for her again. Aubrey had long, manicured fingernails painted a vivid shade of scarlet. The girl screwed her eyes shut as those lovely nails neared her quivering eyeball. But Jenna pinched the eyelid between thumb and forefinger and tugged it viciously open. The girl whimpered as Aubrey giggled and pushed her nails up under the outstretched eyelid. She started thrashing again as she felt the hard nails skim the surface of the eyeball. Kira shifted position and stretched a leg across the girl's midsection to straddle her.

The girl's eyes were both open now. The look on her face told Kira she knew further resistance was pointless. "Please . . ." She whimpered some more before continuing. "Please . . . don't do this . . . I'll do anything you want . . . anything . . . I swear."

"Hold on just a second, Aubrey."

Aubrey's fingers remained poised to dig, but she did not proceed. "Of course, mistress."

Kira smiled. "Do you mean that? Will you really do anything at all, no matter how sick and fucked up and wrong?"

"Yes. Anything."

"Do you have a family? Siblings? Parents?"

"Yes."

Kira pursed her lips and made a contemplative sound as she pretended to think it over. Then she smiled again. "What if I asked you to summon them here . . . would you do that?"

"Yes."

"My." Kira laughed. "You didn't even hesitate. Tell me this, then. Would you kill them if I said to? Would you butcher them? Chop their bodies into tiny pieces?"

Again, no hesitation. "Yes."

Kira nodded. "You know, I believe you would. I really do. I think you just talked me into sparing your life. That's how much I'd like to see that."

The girl sniffled. "I'll do it. I'd kill anybody you want or do anything you say if it means not dying."

Kira laughed again. "Well, now there's dying and then there's *dying*. I've learned there's a difference. I mean, look at me, I died and I'm still here."

Kira watched her expression change as the girl mentally connected the dots. "You mean . . . I'd become a vampire?"

"I think you're super cute and it'd be a waste to permanently snuff you. I've found I enjoy killing, so don't get me wrong, but I'd rather kill men. Their lives aren't worth as much."

Aubrey and Jenna both laughed at this.

The girl's face was shiny with tears. She choked back a sob and said, "Thank you . . . mistress. You won't regret this."

"Oh, I know, girl." Kira leaned in closer and tightened her grip on the girl's throat. "But you're still gonna lose that eye."

The girl sucked in a breath. "What? No. *NO!*"

Kira glanced at Aubrey. "Do it."

Aubrey's nails were still positioned beneath the girl's eyelid, which remained pinched between Jenna's thumb and forefinger. She never hesitated, plunging her nails savagely downward the instant her queen commanded it. The girl screamed again and writhed harder than ever. Kira laughed and rode her like a bucking rodeo bronco. She grew aroused as she watched Aubrey's middle and index fingers sink into the socket down to the second joint—and then down to the third. The girl was wailing so loudly at this point Kira thought her eardrums might burst. Aubrey dug her fingers around in the socket for a few moments, possibly longer than strictly necessary. Kira approved. She liked Aubrey's style, the way she was prolonging and reveling in the girl's agony. Aubrey seemed to sense this and glanced at her before finishing the job. The gaze they exchanged then was charged with an electric eroticism that was nearly as exciting as what they were doing to the girl on the floor.

Aubrey shifted position slightly and plunged her thumb into the other side of the girl's socket, eliciting yet another wail of delirious agony. Then the muscles in her hand flexed, her fingers tightening around the squishy orb as she began to slowly extract it from the socket. Slowly, so slowly, still drawing it out as Kira rode the bucking bronco again. The eyeball emerged at last from the socket, the stalk stretching to a thin strand before it popped and the bloody orb came loose.

The servant sat back and displayed her prize. "Done, mistress."

Kira relinquished her grip on the girl's throat and sat back to laugh and clap in delight. "Very good!" Then she glanced at Aubrey and Jenna in turn, smiling wickedly as her eyes glittered with further deviltry. "Now feed it to Jenna."

Jenna leaned toward her sister servant and held her mouth open wide.

Aubrey smiled as she leaned over the mutilated girl's head and pushed the bloody eyeball into Jenna's mouth. Jenna bit down at once, her sharp vampire's teeth pushing easily through the slippery tissue. Half the eyeball slid onto her eager tongue and she closed her mouth as she chewed slowly, making a groan of pleasure as she appeared to relish the taste. She was a vampire, so Kira was certain this was no act. She sort of wanted to eat an eyeball now herself. But Jenna opened her mouth again and quickly drew in the remaining piece of the girl's eye, slurping the end of the detached stalk between her pursed lips like a strand of spaghetti.

The show was over.

Kira had enjoyed it very much.

But she was far from done having fun with the poor creature quivering beneath her. There was still the matter of turning her into a vampire, of course. She didn't know how to do that yet and would either have to summon Victor or have one of these beautiful servants instruct her in the matter.

But first . . .

She pushed a thumb into the girl's empty eye socket.

The resounding screams that ensued were music to her ears.

~

The club's sound system was thumping, blaring song after song by dance pop artists he didn't recognize at skull-crushing volume. The sole tolerable refuge from the synth-driven bombast was in a row of semi-circular booths at the rear of the club, where the roar of the music was less overpowering. However, the booth occupied by Monroe and his companions was uncomfortably crowded. It had been fine until Tom and Lloyd had roped in a couple of admittedly attractive females between trips to the bar for more drinks. Six seemed the ideal occupancy for the booth. Eight was just too much. They were crowded in like . . . well, like something one might cram too much of into a tight metal container. Except that this was a booth and not a can of something. Monroe was a little drunk. Okay, perhaps a *lot* drunk. As a result, his mind kept spinning off into a lot of weird, random directions, thoughts and insights that started off with some glimmer of brilliance before devolving into something approaching insensibility. The table in front of him was littered with empty beer bottles and plastic drink glasses. One of the girls had foisted upon him something called a Mind Eraser. The concoction was true to its name.

The black-haired vampire girl with the bat tattoo was seated to his left at the back of the booth. Her name was Lilith. Monroe assumed this was some kind of alias. Her right hand was in his lap, high up on his thigh. She wasn't stroking him or squeezing him. Her hand was just *there*. Every now and then she'd give him a sly little look and go back to bobbing her head minutely to the music while power-inhaling yet another cigarette. Monroe had an erection so insistent it was painful. His discomfort was such he was tempted to ask her to take her hand away. But of course he did not. He was pretty sure he'd never wanted to fuck anyone quite so desperately. It was one of the many double-edged swords of vampirism. Everything was heightened. He was aflame with desire.

One of the stomping dance anthems came to an abrupt halt and a collective cheer arose from the dance floor. A sound of drunken revelry. Hearing it made Monroe smile. He had almost forgotten his earlier thoughts of escape. Almost. They were still floating at the periphery of his consciousness, but for now seemed distant.

Before the next song could start, Lilith leaned close to him, putting her mouth to his ear as she said: "Come with me. We're going for more drinks." She laughed softly. "At least that'll be the story."

Monroe couldn't help grinning. "Okay."

Lilith raised her voice as the next song started. "Up! We're going to the bar."

Everyone to her left shifted sideways, slithering out of the booth to make room for their exit. They then skirted the dance floor, heading straight for the bar. Monroe's swollen package attracted looks and occasional giggles from others coming and going in that direction, but he was too focused on Lilith's distractingly shapely form to much care. They reached the crowded area in front of the bar and kept going, bypassing the bar altogether. They detoured into a short, crowded hallway that led to the bathrooms. The people in the hallway were lined up awaiting their turns to relieve overburdened bladders and bowels. Lilith brushed right past them, roughly threading her way through the press of bodies to the door to the women's room. This elicited some angry reactions, but Lilith ignored all of it. Monroe hesitated at the door. He was a guy after all. He wasn't supposed to go in there. Lilith rolled her eyes at him and seized him by a wrist to drag him through the door. More angry reactions ensued. One woman, a tough-looking rocker girl in a leather jacket and torn jeans, tried to confront them, but Lilith silenced her with a look. The girl's face went blank. Then she turned away from them and walked out. Some weird vampire hypnotism thing, Monroe guessed, yet another vamp skill among many he had yet to learn. No one else attempted to interfere.

There was a row of stalls against the back wall. Lilith hauled him into one as it came open and the prior occupant strolled out. She threw the door shut and they stood face to face. The air in the stall felt superheated. Monroe knew her skin would feel hot to the touch. Warmth emanated from her body like waves of heat from a radiator. Her stare was electric and entrancing. Those plump lips, so glossy and wet and inviting.

Monroe couldn't take it any longer.

He put his hands on her waist and tried to pull her close.

She stopped him with a hand pressed flat against his chest. "No."

Monroe frowned.

What? You fucking cocktease . . .

It was an uncharacteristically non-chivalrous thing for him to think. Hardly surprising. He wasn't feeling like himself at all since the change. In fact, he kind of felt like a stranger in his own body. The impulse to swat her hand away and press the issue was a prime example of the alien thinking currently governing much of his actions. It was a thing the human version of Monroe would never have considered. But right now his frustration was such that the temptation was nearly overwhelming.

Lilith must have sensed some of this because her expression

softened some. "I'm sorry, I've led you on."

"Bitch."

He tried to move in closer again.

She stopped him again with a hand splayed against his chest. This time she let him feel her strength as she calmly drove him backward. Monroe said nothing, but was duly impressed. He was strong enough now to tear a human being to pieces, but she had moved him as easily as she would a small child. He supposed he *was* a child to her, in a way.

The softness had leeched from her expression. Now the angles of her striking face looked sharp enough to cut. "Tell me something. Were you thinking of trying to force yourself on me?"

Monroe said nothing. They both knew the answer to that question.

She grunted. "You get one pass on that. But only because I *did* lead you on. Try again and I'll rip your heart from your chest before you can blink. Understand?"

Monroe was still frustrated, but he knew what she said was no empty threat. He nodded and said, "Yeah. Sorry."

A hint of a smile teased the corners of her mouth. "No, you're not."

Monroe didn't return the smile. "So, if you're not gonna fuck me, you mind telling me why you dragged me in here?"

"Because I want you to have a chance, that's why."

Monroe frowned. "The fuck? Pretty sure you just told me I *don't* have a chance with you. Or . . ." His frown deepened. ". . . are you talking about some other kind of chance."

"Look . . . this is against my better judgment. It's stupid, really, that I'm even telling you this. I risk ruining everything."

What remained of Monroe's once-painful erection wilted. "Just spit it out, okay? The night's not getting any younger and I'd like to go find a girl I could actually fuck."

"Victor's mansion is being raided tonight by hunters."

Monroe frowned again. "Say what now? The fuck does that even mean?"

"A small army of heavily armed vampire hunters is hitting the mansion even now. Everyone there will be dead very soon."

Monroe said nothing for a long moment as he gaped in shock at her. He needed that time to even begin processing what she had said. Though starting to fade somewhat, his drunken condition wasn't helping matters any. He knew he had to focus and try hard to make sense of this. "Hold on . . . how do you know this?"

"Because I'm their inside man, so to speak."

"Like a double agent?"

She nodded, studying his expression carefully. "Exactly. I've provided the intelligence necessary to take Victor down. It's been in the works for over a year."

"Huh." Monroe shook his head again. "And you're telling me this because you want me to . . . have a chance. A chance to survive, is that what you mean?"

She nodded.

"But . . . why? Why single me out? What makes me special?"

"My guilty conscience."

"Are you fucking serious? Your conscience? You're a vampire. You don't *have* a fucking conscience."

She looked almost sad. "Typical baby vamp. You think you know it all already. Your conscience isn't dead. It's only been obscured by early-stage bloodlust. In time we learn to control that lust and more and more of our human aspect reemerges. Some of us choose to cope by suppressing the human part of our personalities, but it isn't easy. I have a lot of blood on my hands. A lot of innocents have died because of me. I was the one who finished you off in the hot tub, you know. The one who turned you." She moved closer to him and put a hand to his face. He was surprised to find himself trembling at her touch. "I had no choice. I did to you what I did willingly so many other times, and I'm sorry. So sorry."

Monroe touched the back of her hand. "So you're warning me because you feel guilty. Okay. What am I supposed to do now?"

She smiled. "You leave the club with me. A separate squad of hunters has been dispatched here to finish off Tom and the others. The driver who brought us here is waiting for us. He's another double agent. He'll take us someplace safe."

"Right. Safe. Okay. Safe is good." His eyes narrowed some as he thought of something. "And everyone at the mansion dies? Every human, every vampire."

"The human prisoners will be taken alive and debriefed, if possible. The corrupted human employees will be executed along with all the vampires in residence."

Kira.

She again seemed to sense his thoughts. "You can't help her, you know. It's already too late."

Monroe kept his expression blank and made himself nod. "Right. Nothing I can do against an army anyway."

That seemed to pacify her. "And what about Tom and Lloyd?"

"What about them?"

"You've been bonding with them tonight. Are you okay with them dying?"

Monroe shrugged. "Whatever. They're just characters in a bad movie anyway. Easy come, easy go."

"What's that supposed to mean?"

Monroe laughed.

Baby, you wouldn't believe me if I told you.

"Nothing. It's just a thing I say. Like a catchphrase."

"It's not a very good one."

"That's what everyone tells me. So . . . we gonna go now?"

"That's another thing. We had to wait for the other squad to arrive."

"So the others won't stop us from leaving, right?"

"Right." She glanced at the watch strapped to her slender left wrist. "They should be inside now. We can start—"

He had known the key to making it work would lie in catching her off-guard. So he waited, trying to sense the exact right moment. And then it arrived. The instant she believed he was on board with the whole scheme. He didn't hesitate. He couldn't. She was older and would make him pay otherwise. He struck with what he hoped was lethal quickness, slamming her head into the side of the stall as hard as he could. The blow would have crushed a human head. It only dented Lilith's. He pressed the attack, knowing he had to finish her fast while she was dazed.

Her eyes were glassy, but he could see them coming back into focus. He grabbed her by the throat and propelled her savagely backward, thumping the back of her head off the concrete wall behind the toilet. There was a sharp sound that might have been her skull cracking open, but that alone would not finish her. He thought of something she'd said and made a tight fist of his other hand, thinking he'd slam it through her chest to her heart, just as she'd threatened to do to him.

He drove his fist forward.

And in the same instant saw a smile spread across her face.

Oh shit.

A hand clamped hard around his wrist, stopping the intended blow cold. He looked into her eyes and saw they were again as sharp as ever.

"It's the girl, isn't it? Your friend?"

Monroe's hand was still clenched around her throat, so her words emerged as a strangled wheeze. He tried tightening his grip, bearing down with everything he had. He'd squeeze her head right off her fucking body if he could.

But she peeled his hand from her throat with disconcerting ease and smiled again. "So be it. You've used up the last of my good will. Now I kill you. Again."

She acted before he could even think about fleeing. One moment he was standing there in front of her, one hand paralyzed by her grip. The next instant he was flying backward at high speed, smashing through the stall door. He continued to sail through the air until his back collided with the edge of a sink against the far wall. Pain exploded throughout his body, agony ripping at seemingly every tendon as he pitched forward, cracking his knees and then his chin on the floor tiles. He pressed his hands against the tiles, feeling their crosshatched patterns against his palms, and tried to rise, knowing he didn't have much time if he hoped to survive.

He raised his head and saw the hem of Lilith's little black dress swaying as she walked calmly out of the stall. She stopped a few feet in front of him and he had a moment to admire the elegant turn of her ankles in her black heels. Then she raised one of those heels and stomped down on his outstretched right hand. The spiked heel punched through flesh and splintered bone. He screamed at the fresh agony and grabbed for her ankle with the hand that wasn't impaled. The room was chaos now. Other women in the room were screaming and scrambling to get out. One woman tripped and fell hard across his back, making him cry out in pain yet again. The woman stepped on his back once she got to her feet and got moving again, the sharp heel of her shoe gouging his tailbone. Yet another spike of searing pain. *Goddamn these women and their fucking lethal weapon footwear!*

Monroe's free hand was clenched around Lilith's ankle. He jerked hard at it to no avail. She began to grind her shoe against his hand, twisting the heel inside the raw wound and driving it in deeper. He screamed and beat at the floor with a fist.

Lilith laughed. "Thank you for this. My guilty conscience is clear now. And I'm actually enjoying watching you squirm. Now squirm a little more!"

She increased the pressure on his hand, grinding more viciously this time.

He screamed and begged for mercy.

"The only mercy you'll get is a fast death." She laughed again. "A second one."

Her shoe came away from his mangled hand. She grabbed him and jerked him to his feet. He'd been upright less than a full second when she spun him around and slammed him against the edge of the row of sinks. She wrenched an arm up hard behind his back. He was effectively immobilized.

"What's going on in here?"

Someone else came into the room. A woman, Monroe instantly knew from the sound of heels on the tiled floor. He cringed. If he somehow survived this, that sound would never again have any sexy connotations for him. Just memories of pain.

"Lilith?"

Monroe glanced to his left and saw the busty blonde vampire standing there in her shimmering red party dress. He hadn't talked to her much, but he'd heard the others call her Melissa. *Fuck it. Might as well give it a shot.* "She's trying to kill me."

Melissa took pointed note of his injured hand. "What's happening here?"

"Fucker tried to rape me."

"Bullshit."

Lilith twisted his arm harder, making him grit his teeth against the pain. "Shut up. It's true, Mel. Son of a bitch tried to force himself on me."

Melissa looked at Monroe. Her expression hadn't changed. She gave no indication of favoring one side against the other. "Is she telling the truth?"

"Well—" He grimaced as Lilith twisted his arm still harder, a not-so-subtle warning to keep his mouth shut about certain things. But she planned to kill him anyway, so fuck it. "It's sort of true, but she's leaving out the part where she told me about the army of vampire hunters she's been working with to—"

"*LIAR!*" She twisted his arm yet again and shoved him against the sink. "*Dirty fucking liar!*"

"Let the boy have his say, Lilith."

Lilith was seething with anger now. "*What!?* You can't believe his crazy fucking story! You *know* me."

Now something like a smile twitched the edges of Melissa's mouth. "Yes. I do. A little too well, actually." She looked at Monroe again. "Finish what you were going to say."

Monroe plunged ahead before Lilith could start screaming again. "She's a spy for the hunters. Double agent. They're hitting Victor's place tonight and mean to kill everybody there. Another squad was sent to take out the rest of you."

Lilith laughed at this, but Monroe detected a clear tinge of desperation in the sound. He hoped like hell Melissa heard it, too. "He's lying. You know he is."

"Let the boy go."

"What?"

"You heard me. Let him go. Now."

To Monroe's great surprise, Lilith relinquished her hold on him. Never one to question an unexpectedly fortuitous turn of events, he scurried immediately away from her and moved into position behind Melissa. He looked at his hand. The wound was still throbbing, but he was no longer in blinding agony. The wound even looked slightly smaller.

Melissa glanced over her shoulder at him. "It'll heal, don't worry. Get some fresh blood in you and you'll be good as new in no time." She shifted her attention back to Lilith. "Wish I could say the same for the rest of our friends."

Lilith turned pale. Paler than usual, anyway. It was the first time Monroe had seen her look scared. He took a nasty delight in seeing this.

Melissa moved a step closer to the other vampire.

Lilith started shaking, but remained where she was. It was as if she *couldn't* move.

Strange.

Monroe had no clue why Melissa would have such power over Lilith. He was just glad she did. Maybe it had something to do with the hierarchies of the vampire world, a subject that was still almost entirely a mystery to him. All he really knew was Melissa had saved his ass. Which meant he was Team Melissa from here on out.

Melissa took another step closer to Lilith, who was trembling all over now. She looked sort of like an animal trapped outside in a driving snowstorm. Another step closer and Lilith started to weep, tears cascading in rivers down her porcelain cheeks.

"Please . . . I'm sorry. Please . . ."

"They're all dead. All our friends and all your fucking hunter friends, too. I got lucky and spotted them just before they could close in. A second later and I would have been dead, too. Even so, it was a close thing."

"I'm sorry. So sorry . . ."

"Stop saying that. You're not sorry at all. You're only sorry you got caught. You fucking traitor bitch."

Melissa's hands snapped outward lightning-fast, like striking snakes, and seized Lilith by the back of the head and under the chin. She snarled like a beast and gave her hands a single savage twist. Lilith's head came free of her body with surprising ease. Despite his own close call at her hands, Monroe was surprised by the effect this had on him. He felt vaguely sick. Perhaps because it was so sudden and shocking and irreversible. Blood erupted fountain-like from the stump of Lilith's neck. Her headless body remained upright a moment longer before toppling over and crashing to the floor.

Melissa turned away from the corpse with a sigh. "So sad. I sired her long ago. It's why she couldn't flee from me or protect herself." A melancholy expression played across her features as she stared at the head clasped in her hands. She smoothed a lock of black hair back from its forehead in an almost gentle, affectionate way. "She was one of my special ones. One of my favorites. It's why I cut her so much slack, even when I suspected her heart wasn't fully in this vampire thing."

Monroe didn't know what to say. "That, uh . . . too bad."

Except that fuck no, it isn't. Ding dong! The bitch is dead!

Melissa held the head out to him. "Here. This is for you."

Monroe stared at her in silent stupefaction for a moment. Then he accepted the grisly gift, taking Lilith's severed head in his hands and cradling it gingerly. It struck him that this was the second severed head he'd held in his hands in less than a day.

My life has taken a really kind of fucked turn.

Melissa moved toward the bathroom door. "Let's go."

Monroe hurried after her. "Where are we going?"

She talked over her shoulder as they entered the hallway outside the bathroom and kept moving. Only now did Monroe notice that the constant blare of the dance music had ceased. Except for some corpses, the hallway was deserted. "Where else? Back to the mansion."

"But . . . Lilith said there'd be an army of hunters there. What can we possibly do against a fucking army?"

"Die, probably."

"Oh."

They emerged from the hallway into the area by the bar. Monroe glanced beyond the brass rail separating the bar area from the dance floor and saw evidence of carnage. Bodies and pieces of bodies. Great splashes of blood everywhere. "Victor sired me. I have to go. I need all the help I can get."

"You don't have to threaten me or anything. I'm going with you."

They hooked a left away from the bar, heading for the club's entrance. There was a sound of approaching sirens as they reached it.

Melissa looked at him. "Right. Come on then. We've got killing to do."

They walked out of the club.

THIRD INTERMISSION

Greg stood on the sidewalk outside the cineplex and scanned the parking lot. He saw the same smattering of cars he remembered from prior to entering the theater. There were maybe a few more now, but overall, it had been a sparsely attended night at the horror festival. Which was a blessing of sorts, as it meant only a few dozen people—at most—got sucked into this alien death machine masquerading as a decaying cineplex in a moderately bad section of an unassuming little college town.

Yeah.

Only a few dozen people . . . and one of them is Lashon.

Rather than departing immediately—as he knew he should—he remained on the sidewalk a while longer, staring out at the street beyond, watching the headlights of occasional cars go zipping by in either direction. He thought about the people in those cars and couldn't help marveling at how oblivious they were to the astonishing, horrifying thing happening in the middle of their town. Not one of them would ever suspect something so fantastic and insane could be happening right under their noses. And he could never tell anyone about it. They would think he was crazy. Or, even worse, the wrong person might get wind of his tale and he'd find himself being interrogated by black-suited men from some shadowy government agency.

No. No way. Fuck that.

For better or for worse, his lips were sealed forever. He'd be taking this secret to his grave. He stepped off the curb and started across the parking lot toward his car. The sooner he was in it and speeding away from all this weirdness, the better. His thoughts were on the nearly full bottle of Jameson's waiting for him in a cupboard back at his apartment when he was stopped in his tracks by a stray memory of Lashon.

It was from last year. From before things started go bad. Before she began to get so stressed-out by everything. It was his birthday. She had taken him on a seemingly aimless ride out to the country. It was a pleasant enough excursion along winding rural back roads and would have sufficed as a kind of birthday treat in and of itself. He had enjoyed her company that much back then. Just being with her was always enough.

But Lashon had more in mind that day than just a pleasant drive through idyllic countryside scenery. Just as he had become certain they had reached the official exact center of Absolutely the Middle of Fucking Nowhere, she took a detour down yet another side road. As they came around a bend in the road, the shroud of trees parted and he got his first look at the Starlite Drive-In. It was an outdoor movie theater, the kind his father talked of so glowingly when he was in one of his nostalgic moods. Only weeks earlier, Greg had told Lashon about that, mentioning how he had never been to one himself and then going on to say how sad it was there were so few of them left these days. And evidently she'd remembered because now here they were.

He'd had a big grin on his face as they pulled up to the ticket booth. "Holy shit! I can't believe this. Where'd you hear about this place?"

Lashon was smiling too as she paid for their tickets and drove on through. "The Scene." The Scene was the local free "alternative" paper. "Article last week about it. Thought right away about your dad's drive-in stories."

"And you didn't say a word."

"You have no idea how hard that was, boy-o. You better appreciate this."

He did.

They watched two movies that night. Second run horror films. Pretty good ones, too, unlike the low-budget pieces of garbage at tonight's horror festival. But the movies were a secondary pleasure that night. Then it was all about the setting, which for him was exotic. They munched popcorn and enjoyed each other's company. An epic make-out session led to lovemaking in the backseat.

"The best night of my life."

Greg grunted.

So now I'm talking to myself. Great. I'm crazy. Obviously.

As further proof of that, he turned around and started back toward the theater. He was going back inside. The decision had been made at a subconscious level, powerful instinct driving him back the way he'd come before he was even fully cognizant of what he was doing. His conscious mind caught up to what was happening seconds later, but even then his stride did not falter. He wasn't scared. Not really. Not anymore. This was the right thing to do. It was the only thing to do. He loved Lashon. Even after all that had happened, that was the truth and he couldn't just leave her to a fate like this. Probably it was already too late to help her. And probably the only thing he'd wind up accomplishing here would be to get himself killed or disappeared, too.

So be it.

It was the right thing to do. He had to *try*.

He stepped over the curb again and crossed the sidewalk to the theater entrance. After only the briefest hesitation, he pushed the door open and stepped inside again. The interior of the place remained the same austere all-white. He was mildly surprised it had not reverted to an illusory facsimile of a real cineplex lobby. It seemed sort of reckless on the part of whatever beings operated this strange facility, as did leaving the door unlocked. This posed troubling questions without obvious answers. Rather than pondering them any further, Greg began an exploration of the faux-lobby.

The plain white cubicle that had been the ticket booth was almost entirely featureless, with the exception of a thin slot in the front panel. The movie tickets had been dispensed through that slot, but a glance at the underside of the panel only deepened the mystery. He saw no device through which tickets would have been printed and fed. Frowning, he reached into his hip pocket to retrieve his own ticket. His frown deepened as he examined the blank white stub. He clearly remembered words imprinted on that stub, but it now appeared that had also been only illusion. He tried to conceive of technology sufficiently advanced to alter his perceptions to that degree and failed. And it struck him again how completely out of his depth he was here. He understood none of what was happening on any level and couldn't fathom how he might even begin to unlock the puzzle of this place.

But that didn't mean he was giving up. He had committed to a course of action and he meant to see it through to the bitter end. A check of what had been the concessions stand revealed more of the same strange featurelessness. There was no popcorn maker. Yet he remembered people in their seats gobbling popcorn as clearly as he'd remembered the words printed on his now blank ticket.

So strange.

Deeper and deeper down the rabbit hole.

Greg's attention was next drawn to the several tall protrusions jutting from the wall where the row of video games had once stood. He crossed the lobby to stand before one of the protrusions and stared at the strange pattern dancing across its black screen. He watched the colors swirl, coalesce, and break apart again before shifting his attention to the control panel in front of the screen. A single white toggle control and four white buttons arrayed around it. Not knowing what else to do, Greg grasped the toggle and twitched it to the left. Nothing happened. He twitched it to the right. Still nothing happened. Still grasping the toggle, he started tapping the buttons with his other hand.

Greg gasped as the floor beneath him abruptly lurched.

And then he was descending.

Startled, he turned in a shaky circle and saw that he was sinking into the floor. The panel he was standing on had detached from the others and was lowering itself toward some underground chamber. Instinct made him slap his hands against the nearest adjacent panel. The coward in him wanted only to crawl up out of this hole that had appeared from nowhere and then get out of this fucking place again.

But then he thought of Lashon.

And that magical night at the drive-in.

He let his hands slide away from the panel as he continued his descent into the unknown and the darkness below.

Somewhere beneath him he heard a faint sound of music playing.

Something he recognized.

Is that . . . Shriekback?

TWENTY-TWO

The interior of the bar was shrouded in oppressive gloom. Flickers of candlelight were visible through grime-smeared windows as a big, bearded man in a novelty tuxedo t-shirt hustled Brix and Jason through a small billiards room adjacent to the bar proper. Brix took immediate note of three other people sitting in booths as they entered the bar. There were three rows of booths. Two stood back-to-back in the center of the main room, while the third lined the nearest wall. One other person—a lean female with short, bristly hair—sat cross-legged on the floor between the rows of booths. The girl on the floor wore black jeans and boots and had several piercings to go with the multiple tattoos visible on her bare arms. She glanced up at them as they came in, her features twisting in a scowl.

"Nice going, Ben. You should have locked the fucking door."

Brix was taken aback. "The hell is your problem? We almost got killed out there."

The tattooed girl unfolded herself and rose smoothly from the floor. She approached Brix and stood toe-to-toe with her. "You think I give a shit? What's two more dead people in a world full of them?

What I give a shit about is the fact that you drew that crazy fucker's attention back our way after two days of peace. He'll be taking pot-shots at us all night and it's your fucking fault, bitch."

Brix gaped at her for a moment, unsure of how to respond. Part of it was that the girl was a good three or four inches taller than she was. And she was leaning in toward her and glaring down. The spell was broken only when Brix realized how deliberate and self-aware an intimidation attempt this was. The chick knew her height advantage alone would cause most other females to wilt under the pressure. And Brix had noted that everyone else in the room was male. She sensed instinctively that this lanky rocker chick had relished being the only girl in this little group of survivors.

So Brix smiled brightly and said, "Back off, skank."

Now it was the rocker chick's turn to gape in silent surprise. It was a deeply satisfying thing to see. But Brix gave her credit for a quick recovery. "The fuck did you just call me?"

"You heard me. And I don't like repeating myself. So, unless you feel like eating some of your fucking teeth, I suggest you . . . back . . . the . . . fuck . . . off. *Now.*"

The girl took a swing at her. It was a roundhouse punch thrown with no precision at all. Brix deflected the blow with ease and delivered a solid punch of her own that slammed into the soft flesh beneath the girl's sternum and nearly lifted her off her feet as it propelled her backward. Most of the men present—save for Jason and a heavily tattooed, long-haired dude sitting in one of the booths who looked like rocker chick's male counterpart—let out startled shouts and rushed to the girl's aid as she tumbled to the floor.

She angrily shoved them away and got quickly back to her feet. Brix was certain she detected a newfound respect in her expression. The girl put a hand to her sternum and winced. "You'll get yours, bitch. Just watch."

The bearded man who'd let them into the bar laid a hand on her shoulder in an attempt to placate her. "Come on, Dee, just chill, okay?"

Dee shrugged his hand away. "Keep your hands to yourself and do the same with your worthless fucking advice."

She dropped into the nearest booth and slid sideways along the leather-upholstered bench all the way to the back. "You'll all see," she said, reaching for a pack of cigarettes resting next to an overstuffed ashtray. "These twats will be the death of us."

Jason snorted. "I resent that. I'm a prick, not a twat."

This earned some genuine-sounding laughter from the other men in the room. Brix was glad to hear it. Some of the tension that had been building abruptly evaporated.

The tattooed guy—who was seated in the booth next to the one occupied by Dee—looked at Jason and lifted his chin. "You're bleeding, dude."

Jason glanced at his creased bicep, which was indeed leaking, though the wound didn't look very deep. "Just a flesh wound. I'll live." He shrugged. "Or I won't. Doesn't really matter much either way at this point."

Ben tapped Jason on the shoulder and moved past him toward the bar. "You may have a point there, son, but let's patch you up anyway."

Jason glanced at Brix, shrugged again, and followed the big man. "Try not to beat everyone up while I'm gone."

Brix smirked. "Can't make any promises."

Dee laughed. "That what you told your daddy when he asked you to stop sucking cock for a living?"

The tattooed guy and the other men present groaned in unison. Instead of snapping off an immediate retort, Brix dropped into Dee's booth on the opposite side of the table from her.

Dee frowned and blew out a puff of smoke, aiming it at Brix's face. "Go away."

"No. What's your problem anyway?"

"Already told you. Now fuck off."

Brix reached for the open pack of Marlboro menthols. "You mind?"

Dee's frown sharpened. "Hell yeah, I mind. That's my last pack."

Brix tapped a cigarette out anyway and wedged it into a corner of her mouth. She snatched Dee's lighter from the other side of the table and lit up. "Too bad." She exhaled her own cloud of smoke, pointedly aiming it away from Dee. "Normally I don't smoke, but it's been kind of a stressful day."

"How awful for you."

Brix just smiled. "Sarcasm. How unexpected. But you're right. It's been awful. My boyfriend was killed not even an hour ago."

"So? Am I supposed to pity you? Or empathize with you? We've all lost people. It doesn't make you fucking special."

Brix exhaled another stream of smoke and gave that a moment's thought. Dee had a point there. And, truthfully, she wasn't sure what she was hoping to accomplish here, except that something inside her made her want to confront the girl's enduring hostility head on.

"You're right. It doesn't make me special. And I sort of get your anger, I really do. But you know what? We're here now. It's a done deal. You should get over it and try to make the best of it."

One of the men who had tried to come to Dee's aid—a thin guy with glasses and longish hair—was still standing between the rows of booths. He nodded at this. "She's right. No point in crying over—"

Dee cut a thin-slitted glare at him. "No one asked you what you think, Jeff, so shut the fuck up."

Jeff's eyes widened behind his glasses. Brix could see the hurt there. The guy had a bit of a crush on Dee, she guessed. The poor idiot. He looked like he wanted to say something else. Instead he closed his mouth and turned away from them to slide into one of the booths lining the wall.

Dee made eye contact with Brix and mouthed a single word: *Pathetic.*

Brix didn't visibly react.

But it drove home just how much of an unrepentant bitch this Dee person was. Really, it went beyond mere bitchiness. She seemed borderline sociopathic.

Brix heard a shriek from somewhere behind her and shifted position on the bench to turn her head in that direction. Jason and Ben were behind the bar. Jason's arm was extended outward and Ben was pouring vodka into the wound from a bottle. As she watched, Ben dumped out more vodka and Jason cringed as it splashed onto his arm and dripped to the floor.

"Fucking stings like a motherfucker!"

Ben set the bottle down and reached under the bar to pull out a white scrap of cloth. "Means it's working. You don't want that shit getting infected." He tied the scrap of cloth around the bicep of Jason's still outstretched arm, then picked up the bottle again and took a healthy slug from it. He tipped it toward Jason and nodded. "To your health."

Jason snatched the bottle from him and took several deep gulps of his own. "Fuck. That hits the motherfucking spot."

Brix raised her voice. "Any beer back there?"

Ben glanced her way. "Plenty. None cold, though."

Brix shrugged. "Don't matter. Snag me some on your way back,

Jase."

Jase?

Did I really just call him that?

Weird, she thought, as she turned and faced Dee again. She and Jason weren't too many hours separated from having loathed each other on sight. And now here she was calling him by a nickname, the way a friend would. She guessed he was the closest thing she had to a friend now. Which was all kinds of sad.

Dee was smirking again.

Brix had a feeling she knew what was coming.

"Too bad about that dead boyfriend. But hey, at least you already had a replacement lined up."

Yep. There it was.

Brix wanted nothing more than to lean across the table and knock the smirk right off the cunt's face. But she had a hunch an immediate, violent reaction was precisely what Dee hoped to provoke.

Not falling into that trap, bitch.

She forced a smile instead. "So how long have you and your friends been holed up here?"

"Long enough. And by the way, I really don't wanna talk to you."

The tattooed man in the next booth chuckled and leaned far enough over to put his face in Brix's field of vision. He extended a hand and said, "Pay her no mind. Dee's a singer. Her mission in life is to come off as a lesbian Axl Rose. I'm Cade."

Lesbian?

Hmm. She might have to rethink some of her assumptions about Dee.

Brix gave his hand a brief shake. "Brix."

"The fuck kind of name is that?"

"Mine."

Cade laughed. "Fair enough."

Brix stubbed the cigarette out in the overflowing ashtray. "So, Cade . . . are you saying Dee is all bark and no bite?"

Dee grunted.

Cade laughed again. "Well . . . I wouldn't say that exactly. I mean, she *did* take a swing at you. Girl doesn't lack for guts. But sometimes she lets emotion override her common sense."

Dee raised a middle finger. "Go to hell, Cade."

Jason set four unopened tall cans of PBR on the table and slid into the booth next to Brix. "Miss me?"

Yeah. I did.

But rather than admitting that, she rolled her eyes and reached for one of the cans. She popped its tab and took a healthy slug of warm brew before saying anything. Then she set the can down and glanced at him, eyeing the cloth wrapped around his bicep. "You gonna be okay?"

He grabbed one of the cans and popped it open. "Shit. Fucking alcohol in the wound hurt more than actually being shot."

Dee laughed. "You assholes got lucky. Tucker's usually a better shot than that. He nailed the last dozen or so people to come through that intersection."

Brix frowned. "Tucker?"

Dee opened one of the beers, smirking at Brix. "Only fair. Beer for a smoke." She popped the tab. "Tucker's the shooter. Ex-marine."

"You know him?"

"No, I'm fucking psychic. Of course I know him, dummy. He was my roommate and drummer before all this zombie apocalypse shit went down."

"And how do you know it's him doing the shooting?"

"Because we've all seen him walking around out there with his fucking rifle. He knows not to come too close 'cause we've got a couple guns of our own. But with that rifle, he doesn't need to come close. It's got a scope."

Brix sipped more beer. "Why is he shooting at us?"

"Because he's using this whole breakdown of society thing as an excuse to get back at me. He's wanted me for a long time and I never let him be more than a friend. Stupid motherfucker. He knows I like girls. But some guys think they can get past that anyway. So now he's keeping me penned up and isolated in here. It's really fucking obnoxious."

Jason nudged Brix with an elbow. "You know why that crack shot missed us, right?"

Brix thought he was cracking wise in his usual way until she noted his sober expression. "Well . . . no, I've got no idea. Why?"

"It's because we're the heroes of the movie."

Brix looked confused for a moment—and then awareness dawned. "Oh."

Jason nodded. "You get it, right? It's the way it is in any flick. The bad guys take out people left and right. Until the protagonists come along and suddenly they turn into the worst shots ever. Like, can't hit the broad side of a fuckin' barn bad."

Now it was Dee who looked confused. "The hell is he babbling about?"

Jason ignored her and kept looking at Brix as he pursued the point. "The ones who do get killed? They don't matter. They're like extras, just part of the scenery. You're seeing the pattern, right? Like how that Wednesday 13 song came on as soon as that car we jacked started?"

Brix thought it sounded crazy.

But she also thought she was seeing the pattern, now that he was laying it out like this. This world they were trapped in didn't merely mirror the world of *Rise of the Dead*. She and Jason were actually living out the movie—or living *inside* the movie—and somehow they were inhabiting the starring roles.

Lucky for us. If we had been extras, we'd be dead by now.

Then it hit her.

Trevor.

He hadn't been one of the stars of the movie. Maybe he hadn't been something as lowly as an extra—after all, he'd featured in a few scenes prior to his demise—but he had clearly not filled one of the top-billed roles. And in the end, he'd only played a small part in moving the story along.

Just part of the scenery.

Molten anger possessed her at this thought. She wanted to find whoever was responsible for this strange experiment and tear his fucking head off. Or *its* head off, if it turned out the responsible party was not human.

Dee shook her head. "Awesome, Ben. You saved a couple of fucking crazy people. Happy?"

Ben and the man whose name she still didn't know—a heavyset short guy in a Melvins t-shirt—were standing next to their booth. They exchanged an unreadable glance. Then Ben shrugged and said, "Dunno. Don't sound too crazy to me. Ain't we all seen a million fuckin' zombie movies." He scratched his beard and looked thoughtful. "This shit *is* sort of like livin' in a movie." He looked at Jason. "That's what you're saying, right?"

Dee shook her head again. "I don't think that's what they're saying at all."

Brix looked at Jason, hoping he could read her carefully composed

194

expression and the warning in her eyes—*don't say another fucking word about this shit.*

Evidently Jason got the message because the next thing he said was, "Of course that's what we're saying. We're just tired and stressed. It's been a long fuckin' night."

Dee still didn't look like she was buying it, but she didn't pursue the subject further. Brix had a feeling she was holding any further comment in reserve as ammunition for later. The girl was playing the long game. She would wait for just the right moment, maybe a moment when paranoia among her friends was running high, and then she would revisit this exchange. And sow seeds of distrust among the rest of them.

Brix and Dee exchanged a long look.

Dee's by now familiar smirk was in place again.

She was definitely a Grade-A bitch. The look also told her she didn't give a damn that Brix knew because there wasn't a thing she could do about it. It was in that moment that Brix decided she and Jason had to get out of there and away from these people as soon as possible. Because Dee's manipulations posed a threat every bit as dangerous as the zombies wandering the streets of this ruined city.

Maybe more so because of the malicious intelligence behind it.

Tired of looking at Dee's smirking, knowing expression, she shifted her attention to Ben. "Speaking of the zombies, what's up with them? They converged on the last place we were holed up in and forced us out. Why isn't that happening here?"

Ben opened his mouth to reply.

Dee, of course, cut him off. "It's Tucker. He's picking off any who come near the bar."

Brix reluctantly glanced her way again. "But why?"

"Isn't it obvious? He doesn't want the fuckers getting to me. If anyone's gonna kill me, it's gonna be him."

"What about the rest of us?"

"He doesn't give a shit. He'll kill any of you if he gets a clean shot."

The conversation petered out from there for a bit. Brix soon felt the call of nature and nudged Jason to let her out. There was a short hallway to the left of the bar. Brix headed in that direction, assuming that was where the bathrooms were located. The assumption was correct. She entered one with the symbols on the door marked as unisex and closed it behind her. It was cramped and dark and, she sensed, not very clean, which made her grateful for the darkness. She left the door very slightly ajar, so she could see a bit by the flickering candle-light. She found the room's single toilet, confirmed the seat was down by touch, and dropped her jeans to sit down. She tried not to sigh too audibly as her bladder drained. When she was done, she felt for the paper roll she knew had to be there, found it, and tore off a few squares.

She was just zipping up again when the door opened and someone else came into the room. The door was open marginally wider now and she could see a bit better as more candlelight filtered in. Brix and Dee stood there staring at each other for a long and very tense moment.

Then Brix cleared her throat. "Step out of the way, please."

But Dee didn't move.

What kind of weird shit was she pulling now? Brix didn't know and didn't really want to know. The sooner she was back in the main room with the guys and away from this creepy chick, the better. She started to brush past her, but Dee slipped her arms about Brix's waist and pulled her into an embrace. Brix felt the taller girl bending her backward as she leaned into her, her mouth suddenly merging with hers, her tongue thrusting between her lips. Brix stood limply in Dee's embrace at first, too stunned by this turn to resist.

Dee went on kissing her.

And then Brix did something that surprised her, that went against any urge she had ever suspected she harbored. Her mouth started moving against Dee's mouth. And her hands went to Dee's back. Dee reacted with a groan and the kiss intensified. Brix realized she was genuinely aroused. This surprised her. She wasn't bisexual. It was a thing she had always known as surely as she knew the sky was blue and that the sun would always rise in the morning. She had barely ever even given the issue any thought.

Dee's other hand slipped beneath her t-shirt, probed urgently at her flesh

And she broke the kiss briefly to say, "You have no idea how hot it got me when you knocked me on my ass. You can hit me some more if you want."

Brix let the girl kiss her a few moments more, but her arousal was fading. Because a fresh piece of disturbing insight had invaded her brain. This inexplicable, out-of-character thing she was going along with was happening because it was what the movie wanted to happen. A bit of super-hot girl-on-girl action to titillate the guys in the audience. Okay, there was no actual audience (that she knew of), but she was seized by a belief that the basic principle was correct. So now anger was displacing arousal.

Time to put a stop to this shit.

Time to exercise some free fucking will and break from the goddamn script.

She broke the embrace and shoved Dee roughly backward.

Dee laughed and took this as additional erotic provocation. A direct reaction to the information she'd disclosed about her masochistic streak. She came right back at Brix and got shoved right back again. This evoked still more laughter, louder this time. It had to be audible to anyone out in the main room now. This embarrassed Brix even as it provided additional fuel for her anger. She didn't want anyone, Jason especially, knowing what had transpired here.

Dee came at her more aggressively the next time, propelling her backward and slamming her against the wall. Then her hot breath was on Brix's ear. "See? I can be rough, too. You like it, don't you?"

Brix made a fist of her right hand.

She would beat this crazy bitch unconscious if necessary.

But it wasn't necessary.

Because that was when the crack of the rifle resonated again after a long intermission.

She heard someone scream followed by sounds of chaos in the main room as everyone presumably dove for cover. Then there was another crack of the rifle. And another. And the tinkling sound of splintering glass. Brix jerked slightly at the sound of each shot, but Dee barely reacted. There were more shouts from the main room. And someone was screaming about someone named Gavin being dead. Gavin had to be the guy in the Melvins shirt. Poor bastard.

Dee put her mouth against Brix's ear again. "This had to happen eventually. Tucker got fed up with waiting me out. He's coming in close to finish off the guys."

"We have to help."

"Fuck that. Let them die. Then I'll just let Tucker have what he wants. That'll calm him down. Hell, he can have both of us." She laughed. "It'll be better that way. Tucker and his rifle protecting his lesbian girlfriends from the zombies."

And to think this bitch called me *crazy.*

Brix punched Dee in the side of the head with all the strength she could muster, sending the girl staggering sideways into another wall. That accomplished, she launched herself out of the cramped room before Dee could recover. She dropped to the floor to crawl out to the main room. Most of the candles had been extinguished, but she could make out the prone forms of the men on the floor between the rows of booths.

All of them except for Gavin.

Who sat slumped over a table in one of the booths, his brains leaking from a massive hole in his head.

She spotted Jason and scuttled rapidly toward him. They clasped hands as she reached him. She could feel his fear and desperation in the intensity of his grip.

"I think we're fucked, Brix."

Brix shook her head. "No. No way are we giving up. There should be a store room in the back. We'll get to it and find a rear way out." She tugged at his hands. "Come on. It's our only chance."

Jason tightened his grip on her hands. "He could circle around and pick us off back there, too."

"Maybe. And maybe not. But if we stay here, we're doomed for sure." She tugged at his hands again. "Come on."

But then Brix felt something heavy press into the small of her back, stopping her cold. She turned her head and glanced up to see Dee's shadowy form looming over her. That was her boot pressed against her back. "Stay where you are, you teasing bitch." And now Brix saw something else. Something that took her breath away. It was clasped by Dee's right hand and was aimed at the back of Brix's head.

A Glock. Much like the one she had owned.

Dee raised her voice to shouting level and addressed the unseen shooter. *"Tucker, it's Dee! Listen to me! I'm giving up! I've got the last gun these fuckers had. All you have to do is come in here and finish these people off, then you can have me. What do you say?"*

There was a brief, pregnant silence.

And then a deep male voice—closer-sounding than Brix expected; close enough to startle—responded: "All right. I'm coming in. Don't pull any shit or you're dead, too."

"You got my word. One other thing. Don't off this other chick. We could have some fun with her."

Tucker chuckled. He sounded closer than ever. "Oh, I know. Been thinking the same thing since she went runnin' up that hill."

Brix knew she had no choice but to act and act now. It might earn her a bullet in the back of the head, but she had to take the chance. The alternative wasn't worth contemplating.

She braced her hands on the floor and propelled herself upward with all her might. Dee let out a yelp as she was knocked off-balance. Tucker shouted, and as she surged to her feet Brix saw his big form come charging into the adjacent billiards room. Dee was facedown on the floor. The Glock was still clutched in her right hand. Brix couldn't tell whether she was conscious or not. No time to worry about that. Before Tucker could enter the main room, Brix fell atop her and wrestled the gun from her hand. Dee screamed and tried to grab it back as Brix brought it to bear on Tucker, who had just come through the door.

Tucker froze a moment. He looked stunned to find himself facing this end of a gun barrel. The moment was very brief. In the next he was fighting to get his rifle aimed at Brix. But he wasn't quite fast enough.

Brix's finger slipped through the Glock's trigger guard, rested on the trigger for only a microsecond.

Then she squeezed off a shot that slammed dead-center into his chest. Tucker wasn't a big man. He was actually slightly built. But there was a look of big surprise on his face in that last moment before he toppled dead to the floor.

Dee screamed.

She was still screaming when Brix aimed the Glock at her head.

Cade and Ben both yelled at her, beseeching her not to do it.

Brix's tone was unadulterated contempt. "You'd all be dead if she'd had her way. Fuck this bitch."

Dee stopped screaming. She looked up at Brix through eyes swimming with tears. "Please . . . I'm so . . . s-sorry . . ."

Ben spoke up then. "You can't do this, Brix. It's . . . wrong."

"The hell it is."

Brix put a bullet through Dee's tear-streaked face.

The bespectacled one Dee had called Jeff screamed and cursed her. Brix was sorely tempted to shoot him, too. Sorely tempted to shoot all these stupid motherfuckers, except for Jason. They weren't real, right? Not in the truest sense anyway. They weren't from her world. And this world wasn't real. Was it?

She sighed.

The only thing that stayed her hand was the simple fact that she didn't have real answers to those questions. She was only guessing at the nature of this fiction-derived world. Maybe it *was* real in its own way.

The sound of groans and thumps from the billiards room diverted her from this line of thought. She looked that way and glimpsed several shadowy forms through splintered windows. Staggering forms. Zombies. They had stayed offstage for this little dramatic setpiece, but now they were back in force. Of *course* they were. There was no other logical next act.

She looked at Jason. "Now would be a good time to get the fuck off your ass."

"Oh. Right."

Jason got upright and stared in the direction of the billiards room as the first zombie came lurching through the door. Brix shot it in the center of its forehead and it toppled backward into the zombie behind it.

She looked at Jason. "Let's find that back way out."

"Right. Good idea."

He stumbled after her in the darkness as they went searching for the exit.

TWENTY-THREE

The guy who had saved her from certain death-by-chainsaw in the woods was no longer screaming. The screams had given way to wretched-sounding moans punctuated by the occasional wail of unrelenting agony. The poor son of a bitch. Lashon's anger, already at fever pitch, ratcheted higher and higher as she listened to the sounds of her rescuer's anguish, achieving near-nuclear levels by the time she reached the bottom of the staircase.

The living room was empty and kind of dark, lit only by the low-wattage red bulb of a floor lamp. The red light was an odd touch. It gave the room a French bordello vibe. The only thing missing to complete the illusion was a few whores lounging around in slutty lingerie. Brighter light was visible through an archway at the far end of the living room. The sounds of suffering were coming from that direction. Lashon remained where she was a moment longer. She had one last chance to bolt from this place. The front door to the house was to her left, only a few long strides away. She could be gone from this place of nightmares and blood in a matter of moments.

Other sounds issued from the space beyond that archway.

Music playing at a low volume. Type O Negative's "Black No. 1."

A song she had always liked. Given the current context, she doubted she would ever again be able to feel the same way about it.

She also heard voices. Young and bright-sounding. Cheery. Laughter. A lot of it.

All so incongruous juxtaposed against her recent savior's blubbering pleas for the mercy of a quick death. Lashon's resolve returned. There was no real choice here. Just a solemn duty to perform. A favor owed. One she would repay in blood.

She had the knife.

And the gun. The great equalizer.

You can do this, she told herself yet again. *You really can.*

Kill them. Kill them all.

Lashon checked the automatic pistol's safety to confirm it was in the off position, exhaled a deep breath, and got going again. The living room's floor was carpeted, which masked the progress of her lightly-treading feet. She was thankful for that, at least. The creak of a hardwood floor might well have given the game away far too soon. She put her back to the wall as she moved past a leather sofa and neared the bright light shining through the archway.

The voices of the man's tormentors became clearer as she inched closer to the archway, an in-progress conversation resolving into focus above the swelling chorus of the Type O Negative song.

"That's a good boy, Johnny. Way to thoroughly chew every last bite of your meal. I mean, yeah, I had to take another little piggy from you to get you to do it, but in the end you came through like a champ." A girlish giggle. "You should be proud of yourself."

More laughter. The mocking approval of a sadistic audience.

And the low, pitiable wail of their prisoner.

Then the girl was talking again. "You should see your face. You weren't that handsome to begin with, but now you're one of the ugliest fuckers I've ever seen."

More of that awful, mocking laughter.

Lashon recognized the voice of the one speaking. It was the snooty sorority girl the others had called Mercedes. Based on her experiences so far, Lashon was certain her initial impressions of this girl had been false ones. She was no sorority girl, for one thing. None of them were the college students on a weekend getaway she had taken them for in the beginning. And no way was her actual name Mercedes.

The latter deduction was confirmed a moment later when the girl exchanged a few words with a guy who referred to her as Heidi. She recognized the male voice as belonging to the strapping, athletic-looking young man who had gone by the name Rick during their initial, brief meeting in the clearing outside. But apparently that had also been an alias, for Heidi addressed him as Rob. They had all been engaged in a kind of play-acting when she first came stumbling into their midst. Which struck her as a very odd thing for anyone to be doing out here in the middle of nowhere. Why assume make-believe roles for a likely audience of absolutely no one?

Lashon frowned as she thought about it.

Maybe it *did* make a weird kind of sense. She was currently residing inside of an alternate reality, one crafted via inexplicable means from a motion picture. These crazy assholes were maybe the mirror images of people from her world. In her world, though, those people weren't crazy at all. They were just actors. Professionals whose lives were built upon the ability to believably create false impressions, or rather the illusion of being someone other than who they actually were. So maybe there was some brand of very strange linking correlation between the two realities.

Maybe. And maybe not.

And maybe she was just over-thinking an admittedly intriguing question with no obvious answer while stalling for time. It was one thing to feel such anger that you felt compelled to exact bloody vengeance. It was another thing entirely to find yourself right at the precipice of that last moment of truth. Everything was heightened in this moment. Her heart seemed to be going a million miles an hour. Hell, a *billion*. The gun felt steady in her hands, more or less, but other parts of her body were trembling. She felt weak in the knees. Her breath seemed horribly loud as it went rapidly in and out. Sweat rose on her brow and slid down her temples.

Another female voice, one she didn't recognize, spoke up. "I'm bored, Heidi."

Heidi snorted. "So?"

"So this dude's done for. We should go get that hot chick Ashley stashed away in her room. She'll be more fun than Jigsaw Face here."

A brief, possibly contemplative silence.

Then a sigh from Heidi. "You got a point, bitch. Johnny can barely work up the strength to scream anymore."

Rob chuckled. "That black-haired bitch will scream plenty, I bet, especially when you start threatening to cut her titties off."

A laugh from Heidi. "Hell, that'll be nothing. Wait till I actually *do* cut them off. She'll be the loudest screamer we've had in a long time."

"I do love a good screamer," the other girl said.

"And I ain't had fried titties for dinner in a long-ass time," Rob added.

Even after all she had gone through so far, Lashon's stomach churned at that statement. Just when she thought she had plumbed the furthest depths of this band of psychos' sickness, yet another level of unthinkable depravity was uncovered.

"Go fetch the whore," Heidi said, presumably addressing Rob. "I'll open Johnny's throat for him while you're gone."

If she had been waiting for her cue, there it was.

Now or never.

She wheeled around and stood framed in the archway, with the gun extended in front of her in one hand and the blood-smeared butcher's knife clasped in the other. The faces of everyone in the kitchen turned her way in the same moment. Everyone including the man Heidi had called Johnny. Lashon's plan had been to start shooting right away. There was just no percentage in giving these people any time to react. But she found herself momentarily stunned into inaction at the sight of Johnny, whose hands had been nailed to a table. He was missing several fingers and the surface of the table was covered in blood. There was a scent of charred meat in the air and it was immediately apparent they had been cauterizing his wounds in order to extend his suffering. As awful as all that was, however, it was what had been done to his face that shocked her into temporary insensibility. His lips had been cut entirely away, leaving his teeth and gums exposed in a hideous rictus grin. Lashon felt sick. No amount of plastic surgery was ever gonna make that look right again. His bulging eyes stared a silent plea at her—*Kill me.*

They all stood there staring at each other for a frozen moment that seemed to go on forever. Lashon watched the expressions of the psychotic brothers and sisters slowly change from startled fright to anger as they took in her blood-soaked appearance. It appeared to hit them all in the same instant what must have happened. She had killed multiple members of their family. It was maybe the first time any of their many victims had gotten the upper hand. She was surprised to perceive real grief intermingled with their anger. She had believed these monsters incapable of actual human feelings unrelated to the base pleasures of sadism, but it was there all right.

Good. Fuck them.

The blonde girl she had heard talking to Heidi let out a shriek of rage and came charging at her from the left, wielding a frying pan raised high above her head. Hot cooking oil splashed out of the pan and traced a sizzling trail down the length of the girl's forearm. It had to hurt, but she appeared oblivious to the pain. Little lengths of blackened meat tumbled from the pan as well.

Fingers, Lashon thought.

Those are Johnny's missing fingers.

She swung the gun to her left and squeezed the trigger. The gun jerked hard in her hand, sending an unexpected shock of pain down her arm to her shoulder. But the bullet fired from the gun found its target, punching a hole through the girl's throat and staggering her backward. Lashon corrected her aim and fired again. The next round went right between the girl's eyes. Blood erupted from the back of her head just before she fell over dead. That left three of them. Heidi and the two guys. Big Rob and the slightly built guy who had posed as the boyfriend of "Mercedes" earlier in the evening.

"Get her!"

Heidi's shrill scream spurred the men into action. Both came barreling at her full-speed from opposite sides of the table. No time for thinking. Action time. Lashon aimed first at Rob, instinct telling her he was the bigger threat. She dropped the knife and gripped the gun's butt with both hands as she fired three rounds through his chest. They staggered him, but he kept coming, reaching her and falling upon her as she fired a final round up through his chin. Blood and fragments of brain and bone rained down upon her as the weight of his corpse drove her back through the archway and down to the carpeted living room floor. She heard Heidi screaming again as she struggled to get out from under the big body. Alarms went off in her head as she realized she had dropped the gun. She wrenched her head to the right and saw it on the floor within grabbing distance. She groped for it but an instant before she could snag it again it was scooped up by the sole surviving male member of the family.

He aimed the gun at her face.

So this is it, she thought. *I'm gonna die now.*

At least she had tried. She had gone down fighting rather than running off like a coward. And she had done a good thing by ridding this world of most of these goddamn psychopaths. She stared into the face of her probable killer and remembered the others had called him Blake. Yet another alias, most likely.

"Don't do it, Blake."

Okay, maybe not.

She saw Blake's hand shaking as tears leaked from his eyes. More genuine human emotion. Still so strange from the likes of someone so evil. Just seeing those tears made it all worth it. Even her own death. This prick *should* suffer, at least a little. His forefinger trembled on the trigger. His need to kill her was a palpable thing, an almost living presence there in the room with them.

Heidi moved into view to stand next to him. She wrapped a hand gently around his own and eased the gun's barrel away from Lashon's face.

A strangled sob tore out of his throat. "*She has to die!*"

"I know, I know," Heidi said in a soothing tone. "Shush now, baby." She stroked the back of his hand in an oddly intimate way considering they were brother and sister. "She *will* die. I promise you that." And now one of the wickedest, most insidious grins Lashon had ever seen curved the girl's mouth. "But I've got something special in mind for this murdering cunt."

Blake choked back another sob. "Y-you do?"

"I do, baby. I do." The wattage of that insane smile cranked higher still. "We'll deal with her down in the cellar. Now roll that slab of dead beef off her."

Blake did as instructed and Lashon sucked in a great, gasping breath as the weight of the corpse was removed. But this instinctive physical relief was short-lived as Heidi squatted on her haunches to leer down at her.

"I bet you feel pretty good about yourself, huh? Going all kill crazy like that on my family. Bet you feel all fucking *badass*." She dropped to her knees and leaned even closer. "Yeah, you do, I can tell. But let me tell you something, bitch. That's all gonna go away once you're hanging from a meat hook in the cellar."

Blake did a strange thing then.

He giggled.

He sounded like a demented little girl. For some reason, Lashon found this as disturbing as any of the admittedly unnerving things Heidi had told her.

Oh fuck. Maybe I made a mistake after all . . .

Heidi stood up. "Give me that." She pried the gun from Blake's dangling hand. "Now drag this whore down to the cellar."

Blake grabbed Lashon by the ankles. A moment later he was dragging her through the archway back into the kitchen. She clawed for purchase on the floor, her fingernails skidding over the grooves between the tiles as she futilely sought to impede Blake's progress. Next she tried kicking her feet free from his hands, but this effort proved just as ineffective. She heard Johnny voice some unintelligible sound of protest as Blake dragged her across the floor. It earned him a slap across his ruined face from Heidi.

She screamed at him. "*Shut up, you fucking Frankenstein!*"

And then she laughed.

Lashon lifted her head and saw that she and Blake were headed toward a closed door in a far corner of the kitchen.

The cellar door.

And, beyond it, the meat hook Heidi had promised was waiting for her.

Lashon's eyes filled with tears as Heidi hurried past her and opened the door for Blake, who dragged her through it onto a wooden landing. He jerked her to her feet and positioned her at the edge of the landing.

Then she screamed as he threw her down invisible stairs.

Down into a deep, deep darkness.

The next thing she was aware of was pain.

And a lot of it.

TWENTY-FOUR

The sound of many sirens approaching fast kept getting louder, but thus far no flashing lights had appeared in the wide four-lane street beyond the club's large parking lot. That would be changing any moment now. Monroe hoped like hell their escape window would remain open long enough to get gone from this place before that happened.

He followed Melissa at a fast trot through the parking lot, banging his hip more than once as they wove between the long rows of parked cars. The black Rolls Royce Phantom was parked diagonally across two spaces at the far end of the last row of cars, which abutted a concrete divider separating the dance club's lot from the parking lot of a small strip mall. As they neared the car, Melissa put on a burst of impressive speed, becoming a barely visible blur zipping through the night.

When she became visible again, she was standing next to the Phantom's driver's side door. Monroe heard a tinkling of safety glass as she punched a fist through the window, reached deep inside with both hands, and pulled the screaming, bleeding chauffeur back out through the window. Monroe figured she'd spent at least a moment grilling the traitorous human servant for information regarding details of the assault on the mansion. They would need to know as much as possible about what was happening in advance in order to formulate an at least remotely viable counterassault plan.

But Melissa had a different agenda, apparently.

She slammed the pleading chauffeur against the side of the vehicle and used a fist again to punch a hole through something—this time straight through the man's abdomen, which yielded to the blow with shocking ease. She dug around in his abdominal cavity for a moment as his screams rose to higher and higher registers. Then her bloody fist emerged from the gaping hole in his gut wrapped around a length of intestine. She pulled at it and pulled at it like a woman unraveling a spool of thread. That was gruesome enough, but she wasn't finished yet. She looped the man's guts around his neck twice and then shoved the end of the length of guts into his mouth.

Monroe's mouth hung open as he watched this bit of insanely over-the-top depravity.

God . . . damn . . .

This all happened in a space of seconds. She looked like a demon at work. Monroe supposed she sort of was a demon of sorts. Which kind of made him one, too.

She tossed his corpse aside and looked at Monroe. "What are you staring at? Let's get out of here."

Monroe closed his mouth. "Right. Of course."

They got in the car. The keys were still in the ignition. Melissa cranked the engine to life, put the car in reverse, and punched the gas. The car lurched twice as its front and then back wheels bounced over the chauffeur's body. Melissa's face was a mask of intense concentration as she shifted gears again and put the gas pedal to the floor. The Phantom's tires squealed loudly as they patched out with the car's front end aimed at the sidewalk. They bounced over the curb and onto the street, earning blasts from the horns of several angry motorists as they crossed the lanes of moving traffic. Melissa paid it all no mind as she cranked the wheel hard to the left and got them pointed in a more or less straight direction again.

They were speeding away as Monroe glanced at the mirror on his side and saw the first flashing lights appear in the distance. He gulped. There were a lot of them. He looked away from the mirror and saw more flashing lights approaching from the other direction. Melissa never slowed down as she blew by them all. Monroe clutched the door handle in a death-grip as the Phantom's speed soared to felony-level recklessness. He may even have screamed a time or two as they rocketed through a busy intersection without slowing. This time he heard more than the horns of agitated motorists. He heard a crunch of metal. And then another. And another. Another glance at the mirror showed a column of flame rising into the air behind them.

Holy shit.

"Um . . . I think there may be a cop or two on our trail now. You're sort of leaving behind an unmistakable path of carnage."

She kept her eyes on the way ahead. "I don't care."

"Right. Of course not. I'm just sayin' . . ."

Now she looked at him, frowning. "What?"

Monroe frowned, too. "Um . . . what?"

"You said you were just saying. Saying what?"

Monroe closed his eyes a second.

Give me strength.

He opened his eyes and looked at her. "Nothing. Just a stupid expression. Look . . . I know we're off on a serious mission of vengeance type deal here, but, uh . . . any idea what we're gonna do when we actually get back to the mansion. Do you have, like . . . a plan?"

Her gaze went to the road again. "My plan is to kill as many fucking humans as possible before they take me down."

Monroe kept frowning. "Oh. Well . . . that works. I guess. By the way, how you dealt with the chauffeur . . . that was some hardcore fucked up shit."

She glanced his way again, arching an eyebrow this time. "Problem with it?"

Monroe gave his head a brisk shake. "No. No, no, no. Hell no. All I meant was wow, but that was totally fucking crazy. But in a cool way, of course."

"I was very angry."

Monroe turned his head aside a moment so she wouldn't see the reflexive roll of his eyes.

No shit, lady. You were like the fucking She-Hulk or something there. On crack.

He looked at her again. "You really think we're gonna get killed trying to stop these people?"

"Probably. From what we know, they had the numbers and the element of surprise. It may already be too late to do anything about it."

Though a part of him—that still-lingering remnant of his humanity—wanted very much to help Kira, the colder, vampiric side of him felt ready to embrace the notion of futility. Maybe if things looked sufficiently hopeless once they arrived back at the mansion, he might stand some chance of convincing Melissa to abandon any thought of retaliation and take off with him. They could start over again somewhere else, maybe establish and build a vampire colony of their own similar to the one reigned over by the rich old vamp.

Except . . . hold on . . . why follow the blueprint set here at all?

It was kind of a weird deal, after all.

"Can I ask you something?"

"Make it fast. We'll be there soon."

"Why in fuck did Victor keep a nest of attractive, young-looking vampires in that fucking weird underground adult playpen type of place?"

"Why not?"

"I hadn't thought of it like that."

She glanced at him, frowning again. "Is this really the kind of thing you want to know right now? We could be dead—*really* dead—in a matter of minutes and you want to discuss trivial things?"

"Forget I asked." Monroe's eyes got wide and he cringed backward into his seat. "Look out!"

Melissa's head snapped back toward the road. She saw what was coming and jerked the steering wheel to the right just in time to avoid a full-on rear-end collision with a stalled Camry. The Phantom's fender instead clipped the Camry's rear bumper. The Phantom careened out of control for a fraction of a second as it shot toward the guardrail beyond the road's right shoulder. She wrestled the car back under control with amazing quickness. Those vampire reflexes at work again. Monroe felt certain a human driver would have gone crashing through the guardrail to the embankment below.

Melissa's hands were gripped very tightly around the steering wheel now, her eyes locked on the road in front of her. "How about you keep the chatter to a minimum from this point on?"

"Good idea."

They drove on in near silence for maybe twenty minutes. The only sounds were the hum of the high-precision engine and the roar of the wind audible through the shattered window. Somehow Melissa had shaken their police pursuers.

During the silence, Monroe did some thinking. He had a theory on the underground vampire nest, one he was relatively certain hewed pretty close to the truth. A truth Melissa's "why not?" response addressed rather aptly, now that he thought about it. The model for this world was a bad B-movie. He kind of kept forgetting that in the midst of all the excitement. And very often in those movies things sort of just happened. Odd, random things. For no good reason. Or for almost logical but totally insane reasons, as in any typical Troma film. This little mystery was sort of like that. Or it wasn't. She was right, though. It didn't really matter much, so he decided to stop thinking about it.

Which was a good thing, as they were nearly out of time.

They came around a bend in the wildly curving, tree-shrouded road and Victor's multi-story mansion loomed into view. This was the first time Monroe had gotten a really good full-on look at the thing. It was massive. The kind of abode you usually only saw in movies about absurdly super-rich people. It was very gothic and ominous-looking.

Monroe said, "Gulp."

Melissa looked at him. "Did you just say 'gulp' out loud?"

"Yep."

"Thought so."

Melissa slowed as they neared the gate to the towering iron fence surrounding the property. The gate stood open and a number of vehicles were parked haphazardly in front of the mansion. These were all nondescript black vans with tinted windows. Some were parked on the lawn. One had slammed into a statue of some sort, knocking it over. Pieces of marble were scattered across the circular drive.

Monroe heard sounds of shooting from inside the mansion as they stopped just outside the gate. He also heard screaming between rounds of gunfire. Whether it was human or vampire in origin, it was impossible to tell.

Melissa and Monroe exchanged a troubled glance.

Monroe said, "This is not good. They seriously arrived in force."

"They do seem to mean business."

Melissa stared at the mansion and thought things over a moment longer.

Then she backed the Phantom up, executed a quick three-point turn, and headed back the way they had come.

Monroe hoped his relief wasn't too obvious. "Probably the only real option, I guess."

Melissa grunted. "Oh, we're not running."

"We're not?"

"No."

"Oh . . . well . . . good. I guess."

If Melissa noticed his reluctance, she didn't show it. "There's a little access road we passed on the way in. It'll take us to a secret rear entrance."

Monroe suppressed a groan.

Of course it will. We are so fucked.

Minutes later they were speeding down the very dark and narrow access road. Monroe didn't see how Melissa could see well enough to keep them on course in the depths of such darkness. More advanced vampire skills, he guessed. Still, it was a harrowing journey. He would have prayed to God to keep him safe until they arrived at their destination, but he knew how much of a joke that was. He was a vampire. A monster. A killer.

God, if such a being existed, didn't care about him.

Not anymore.

A dim light ahead pierced the darkness. The promised rear entrance, probably. Monroe's mind had barely formed this thought when the already much-abused Phantom crashed through a closed gate with a ringing screech of rending metal.

~

Victor came striding back into the master bedroom only moments after the first faint sounds of gunfire erupted. His gait was purposeful but unhurried, the set of his features conveying grim determination but no panic. Kira was still cradling the corpse of the one-eyed blonde girl she had failed to turn into a vampire despite careful coaching from Aubrey and Jenna. She had gotten carried away and had bitten out too large a chunk of her tender throat. Determined to make the best of a plan gone awry, Kira had endeavored to consume every remaining drop of blood from the girl's body, a goal she had nearly achieved by the time the mysterious assault on the mansion began.

Victor took in the sight of her blood-drenched nude body and gave a terse nod of approval. "Good. You'll have your strength up. You'll need it."

"What's happening out there?"

"An attack by an army of vampire hunters. We need to leave this place. Now."

Kira let the dead girl's ravaged body slide from her arms to drop with a thump on the floor. "I need clothes."

"No time." He snapped his fingers at Aubrey and Jenna as he crossed the room to stand before a painting hanging on the wall by the fireplace. "Girls, escort your mistress to the helipad at once. Protect her at all costs."

The servant vampires made sounds of assent and each seized Kira by an arm. They dragged her to her feet and steered her toward the bedroom door. Kira allowed them to lead her away, but she turned her head to address Victor en route to the door. "Where are we going?"

Victor felt along an edge of the painting and triggered a hidden latch. The painting swung away from the wall on hinges, revealing a safe with a combination lock. Victor quickly spun through the combination, opened the safe door, and began removing documents. He flipped through some of them as he addressed Kira. "Somewhere safe, my bride. I have several other uncompromised residences in various parts of the world. That's all you need to know for now. The rest can be arranged once we are safely away from this place."

"But—"

But there was no more time for interrogation. Aubrey and Jenna dragged her out into the corridor and steered her to the left. Kira glanced over the ornate, polished railing at a scene of carnage and chaos two stories below. A number of Victor's black-clad security goons were tangling with an opposing force of men and women also clad in black. The invaders swarming through the massive foyer also wore black ski masks and were armed with scary-looking automatic weapons. Victor's men fought bravely, but they were outnumbered, even with many of the vampires in residence fighting alongside them. The guns of the invaders chattered endlessly as body after body fell beneath the fusillade. Most shocking to Kira was how easily the bullets blew apart the bodies of vampires.

Aubrey was right behind her and seemed to sense her thoughts. "I've seen this before. Wood-tipped bullets."

"Where the fuck have you seen this shit before?"

Aubrey gave her a less-than-gentle push in the back to get her moving again. "During the war. Keep moving."

"War?"

"World War II. In Europe."

Right. Of course. Aubrey looked like a gorgeous young woman barely more than twenty. But she was a vampire. Which meant she could be hundreds or thousands of years old. But the ongoing rattle and chatter of the guns was a powerful reminder that existence as a vampire could easily be cut short.

She picked up her pace as she followed Jenna's enticingly nude backside down the long hallway. The gorgeous vampire's long red hair trailed backward behind her, a flowing vision of beautiful crimson, as she shifted to a run and met the first invader successfully able to breach the third floor. The enemy combatant's lithe figure marked her as female. She screamed as Jenna grabbed her and lifted her above her head. The masked woman whipped her arm outward, raking the railing with a wild hail of automatic fire. Kira and Aubrey cringed back against the wall, miraculously avoiding being struck by ricocheting bullets. Jenna let out a shriek of rage and flung the woman back down the staircase, bowling over three more masked assailants in the process.

Kira and Aubrey followed her as she got moving again.

As they passed the staircase, a stray round fired by one of the fallen assailants ripped through Aubrey's skull, sending a spray of red arcing through the air. Kira stopped in her tracks and stared in paralyzed shock as the body of her beautiful servant tumbled dead to the floor. Then she glanced down the staircase and saw one of the fallen assailants struggling to get to his knees. He paused for an instant and looked right at her. His eyes looked dark and hateful behind the holes in his mask. Kira was briefly possessed by a wild impulse to fly down the stairs and rip him apart. She was enraged. She hadn't known Aubrey long at all, but she had nonetheless felt a very strong sisterly connection with both her and Jenna. They were sisters in blood. And now that connection was gone. Dead. A beautiful creature's long existence wiped out by a single fucking bullet.

The assailant shoved the body of a fallen comrade away from him and began to bring his weapon to bear. Another second longer and she might have been just as dead as Aubrey, but Jenna grabbed her by an arm and pulled her out of range just in time. Wood-tipped bullets thunked into the wall behind where she had been standing an instant later. They continued down the long hallway, Jenna pulling her along at a pace nearly faster than she could match until they arrived at a metal door.

Jenna let go of Kira and yanked at the handle.

The door didn't budge.

Kira grimaced. "Locked. Shit."

She glanced behind her. More men and women in black masks had reached the top of the staircase.

Jenna saw them, too. Her hand was still on the locked door's handle. "I've got this. Duck."

"Huh?"

"Duck, goddammit!"

Kira dropped to her knees and cringed again as Jenna ripped the door off its hinges, lifted it above her head, and sent it flying down the hallway. To Kira's astonishment, the door flew as straight and true as a missile fired from a silo. Its bottom edge slammed into the midsection of the lead invader with tremendous force. The impact killed him instantly as blood exploded from his mouth. The door then flipped over and crashed into more of the black-clad invaders coming up fast behind the dead man.

Jenna took Kira by a hand and pulled her through the space formerly occupied by the metal door. The short passage beyond was cloaked in darkness, but Jenna seemed to know exactly where she was going. Seconds later they were ascending an equally dark set of stairs.

"Where are we going?"

"To the roof."

An explosion resounded somewhere behind them as they banged through another door and out into the crisp, cool night air.

FINAL INTERMISSION

There had been no time to ponder his expectations of whatever was waiting for him beneath the phony cineplex. However, had there been sufficient time, he doubted his mind would have conjured visions of anything remotely like what he actually saw. As the translucent floor panel continued its slow descent, a winged albino monkey floated past him. The monkey laughed when it saw his expression of bug-eyed wonder. Then it zipped away into the neon purple sky. A sky that appeared to stretch on forever. The clouds drifting lazily through the air above him were a radioactive shade of green. Greg knew what he was seeing couldn't possibly be real, but it sure as hell *looked* real. The only flaw in the illusion was the rectangular black hole in the sky directly above him, which corresponded in size to the floor panel upon which he was still standing. It looked sort of like a horizontal monolith floating in midair and was out of perspective with everything else.

All very trippy, no question.

Enough so to stir serious doubts regarding his sanity.

But questions of sanity gave way to queasiness when he glanced down and noted that the still-descending floor panel appeared to be many hundreds of feet above the ground. Perhaps as much as a thousand feet. Or higher. This was another thing the rational part of his mind recognized as almost certainly being illusory. No way was there an underground world of such scope and bizarre wonder lurking beneath the little college town he and some one-hundred thousand other souls called home.

Or *anywhere*, for that matter.

Again, though, the illusion was so perfectly rendered it challenged the things his rational mind insisted it knew. An intense attack of vertigo assailed him as he stared at the ground far below. He was overcome with a nearly irresistible impulse to get down on his hands and knees and cling to the panel for dear life.

Bile touched the back of his throat and sweat formed on his brow. *Oh, fuck it.*

He got down on his hands and knees and peered over the edge of the panel. A panoramic view of a gorgeous countryside extending toward the magnificent, gleaming spires of a distant city took his breath away. Gently rolling hills and a vast expanse of lush forest dominated the landscape. More winged creatures swirled about in the sky above the towering treetops. Some resembled the flying albino monkey he'd already encountered, while others were reptilian with fearsome wingspans. The winged reptiles resembled drawings he had seen of pterodactyls. Only larger. These creatures looked fully capable of snatching a man up in their jaws and flying away with him. Greg couldn't help whimpering at the thought. Some of the creatures weren't very far away.

Not real, he told himself. *They are not fucking real at all. Just remember that and you'll be fine.*

He whimpered again as one of the winged reptiles peeled away from the forest and swooped into the air above him to wheel about like a vulture circling dead meat. Except that wasn't quite right. Because vultures had nightmares about creatures like this thing. *Not real, not real, not real.* The creature squawked and flapped its long wings, causing a gust of very real-feeling hot air to rustle Greg's hair.

Fuck. I am seriously gonna pee my pants in a minute.

He closed his eyes and prayed for the thing to go away. Minutes passed. When he opened his eyes again, the creature had vanished. *Wow, magic.* He was also much closer to the ground, a few dozen feet high instead of countless hundreds. Seconds later he sat up again as the panel at long last completed its descent. It set down near a single set of railroad tracks winding away toward the distant city.

Greg frowned as he wondered what his next move should be. Perhaps he should follow the railroad tracks to the city and see if he could find any answers to this mystery there. Or he could just stand here a while, maybe wait and see if the panel would rise again and return him to the abandoned lobby of the faux-cineplex. Because in the last few minutes he'd had ample reason to reconsider his resolve to somehow help Lashon. He was up against a power beyond his comprehension. Things had seemed hopeless before, but now he had a fuller appreciation for how well and truly fucked the situation was.

He decided to attempt something. He jumped straight upward as high as he could, hoping the release of pressure would cause the panel to ascend again. It remained right where it was, an incongruous translucent white slab pressed flat against the dusty ground by the railroad tracks. He frowned. Well, there was something else he could test, at least. He knelt at the edge of the panel and pressed the tips of his fingers to the ground. His frown deepened as he moved his fingers in the dust, feeling the grit of the dirt against his skin. Well . . . it certainly *felt* real enough.

The implications deeply disturbed him. As he saw it, there were just two possibilities. The first was that this strange realm was real after all, which would mean he had somehow been dropped into a world straight out of some warped fairy tale. Such places were fun for children (and some adults) to read about in fanciful stories, but the notion of one of them rendered tactile and real was kind of terrifying. The lone other possibility was no less unsettling. And that was that he had been right from the beginning and everything he was seeing here actually was part of some comprehensive and powerful illusion. The technology necessary to create an illusion so thorough right down to all the textures, sights, and smells had to be advanced beyond anything humans could even begin to fathom.

Which meant—

He was jolted out of this line of thought by the toot of a train whistle. A glance to his right showed a train engine trailing a single coach car approaching at a moderate speed. He hadn't even heard the damn thing coming up, yet it was almost upon him. Also audible was the unmistakable chug of a steam engine. Yet no steam emerged from the chimney at the front of the locomotive or anywhere else. So here, at last, was a chip in the otherwise perfect veneer of a masterful illusion. The train slowed as it neared him, rolling to a complete stop as the passenger coach pulled up alongside the floor panel.

Well, this was weird.

No weirder than anything else so far, but still . . .

A door opened in the side of the coach car and a little person with green skin dressed in a tiny tuxedo appeared at the top of a short set of steps.

Greg couldn't help gaping at him.

Oh, come on. You've gotta be shitting me.

The green man grinned broadly and called out to him in a jocular voice. "Greetings, Greg Nelson! Dr. Ominous requests the pleasure of your company!"

Greg said nothing. He just stared.

The man's jolly grin faltered slightly. "Did you not hear me, Greg Nelson?"

"Oh, I heard you. Listen . . . are you a fucking leprechaun?"

"No, I am not a fucking leprechaun. I am a little green man with a rapidly dwindling sense of humor. Now, will you please board the train? You do not want to keep Dr. Ominous waiting."

"Dr. Ominous? Seriously?"

The little man sighed and pinched the bridge of his nose. "I didn't want it to come to this, but I suppose force will be necessary."

"Whoa, hold on. No, no, no. Here I come. No force required."

Greg stepped off the floor panel and approached the train. The little green man didn't look like much of a threat, but appearances didn't mean much in this strange place. He had no doubt the diminutive green person could unleash an impressive degree of force and fury should circumstances warrant it. And that was a scenario he'd rather avoid.

The little man stepped aside as he climbed the steps and boarded the train. The door squeaked shut behind him and the train started moving again. A man sat behind a large wooden desk at the rear of the coach. Greg couldn't see him because he was reading a newspaper held open in front of his face. Well . . . he had assumed this Dr. Ominous person was a man. But maybe not. He saw chipped black nail polish on the fingers curled around the edges of the newspaper. The newspaper itself had to be some kind of prop. Just another piece of the illusion. It was a copy of a 1960's edition of the New York Times. The headline was about a military escalation in Vietnam. It was an odd detail he might have fixated on if not for the wealth of other, vastly stranger things vying for his attention. Prior to boarding the train, he had noted windows lining the side of the coach. Now there was no sign of them. Instead there were several large screens displaying what appeared to be images from gruesome horror movies. On one screen, an attractive blonde girl was leading a group of frightened-looking people across a dark parking lot while trying to avoid zombies. Fascinated, he watched as she calmly and expertly blew away members of the shambling army of undead. On another screen, naked women covered in blood were running down the hallway of a very large house, possibly a mansion.

And on another screen . . .

Greg's heart almost stopped.

Lashon . . .

She was on her back in a dark room. She looked unconscious. The angle of the view changed and he saw other people in that dark space. Bodies.

Hanging from hooks.

A deeply resonant male voice spoke. "Have a seat, Mr. Nelson."

Greg continued staring at the screen, his heart racing as he silently willed Lashon to wake up and get the fuck out of that hellish-looking place.

He heard a crinkle of newspaper as the man's voice spoke again. "You want to help her, Mr. Nelson? Then do as I say. Have a seat."

Greg reluctantly turned away from the screens and looked at the person seated behind the big desk. So "Dr. Ominous" was a man, after all. He looked about sixty and had a wild corona of puffy white hair ringing a shiny bald scalp. He had bright rouge on his cheeks and wore smudges of poorly-applied green eye-shadow. His eyebrows had been tweezed to flare in an exaggerated way. He wore a white lab coat over jeans and a Church of the Flying Spaghetti Monster t-shirt. A stethoscope dangled from his neck.

Oh, boy. We're in full-on loony land.

Despite his misgivings, Greg crossed the room and settled into a seat opposite the desk. "How do you know my name?"

"Simple. An examination of your personal effects while you were unconscious in the theater."

"I see. And let me guess. We're not actually on a train headed off to Oz or wherever. Right?"

"Correct."

"And your name isn't actually Dr. Ominous."

"It is as far as you are concerned."

"Fair enough." Greg cranked his head as far to the right as he could without actually getting out of his chair and watched the blonde girl shoot yet another zombie. Then he frowned as he faced Ominous again. "Those things happening on the screens . . . is any of it real or is it all as fake as that demented La-La Land you subjected me to?"

Ominous steepled his fingers and rested them on his ample chest. "It is all very real."

"And the danger they're facing . . . that's real, too?"

A nod. "Indeed."

You son of a bitch.

"If they die there . . . wherever *there* is . . . then they die for real. Right?"

Another nod, this time accompanied by a very small, inscrutable smile. "Quite so."

Greg felt tired and very confused. He wanted this to all go away. Wanted to wake up and have it all have been a bad dream, the way things sometimes happened on TV shows or in bad movies. Yet he had a feeling that wasn't in the cards here. He had to see this game through to the end, for good or ill.

He looked Ominous in the eye. "How is that even possible?"

"Are you familiar with the many worlds theory of quantum mechanics?"

"Vaguely."

Ominous chuckled, though his eyes remained coldly appraising. "Very simply, it posits that all possible alternate timelines and histories are real, each consisting of its own world. This is only highly debatable, unverifiable theory as far as most in the scientific world are concerned. I, however, know it to be truth." Another chuckle empty of actual humor. "I confess to having an unfair advantage. No other human scientist has access to the dimensional-manipulation technology with which I have conducted my experiments. Using means that became available to me through a set of fortuitous circumstances, I have mastered the ability to open passageways to and from the alternate worlds. Do you understand, Mr. Nelson? Do you fully appreciate what I'm telling you?" Ominous leaned forward now—rather *ominously*, Greg thought—and braced his elbows on the edge of his desk while keeping his fingers steepled. "I have solved many of the riddles of the fabric of existence itself, a fabric I can manipulate and bend to my will. I am become God."

Greg nodded at this.

Rrrriiiiiiiiight.

"So . . . again, let me see if I have this straight . . . there are other worlds, say, where the Nazis won World War II or where the American Revolution was defeated?"

"Of course. And I have visited many of them. I can access them whenever I wish. It has been fascinating to witness the alternate ways human history and technology has advanced—or not, in some cases—along different timelines. But you are not yet grasping the true genius behind my discoveries. The level beyond anything imagined possible by any of the theorists." Ominous gestured at the screens behind Greg. "Anything imagined and given some marginal degree of shape and form in our world—the stuff of low-budget cinema, for instance—can be made manifestly real along other planes of existence."

Huh?

"Say what now?"

"It is as I have said. I am become God. I am a creator of worlds. And not partially formed pseudo-realities or merely very advanced virtual environments, such as you encountered on your way to see me. I'm talking about actual *worlds*." There was a manic, dangerous gleam in the man's eyes now. He looked truly mad. "Fully realized worlds with millions of years of richly detailed history and countless billions of human lives lived out upon them." He laughed at this. "All derived from the stuff of fiction."

"How the fuck can that be?"

"Incomprehensibly advanced alien technology. Think of each fiction-derived world as a computer program. The foundation for each is a bit of basic code identical from one reality to the next. But from that code, endless permutations are possible."

Greg thought of the bizarre theater workers he had encountered upon entering the fake cineplex. "Man, I fucking *knew* aliens had something to do with this shit. But why in fuck would these goddamn aliens share their super technology with you?"

Ominous smiled. "They are somewhat inscrutable, but here is my perception. They have long observed us, fascinated by the slug-like progress of our own advances. Some among them noted my own work along these lines was becoming more advanced than that of my peers. That it showed potential to eventually move beyond the realm of theory. They wanted to see what I could do with a bit of help."

Greg stared at Ominous for long moments without saying a word.

How dearly he wished to wipe the smug expression from the madman's face.

"You're an asshole, Ominous."

"Geniuses throughout history have ever been labeled such. It bothers me not at all."

"But you're toying with the lives of innocent people."

Ominous shrugged. "*Insignificant* innocent people."

The remark made Greg fume. Lashon was one of those so-called "insignificant" people. *You bastard. You fucking bastard son of a whore.* "Can you bring them back? The ones still alive?"

"Of course."

Greg waited a beat before saying, "Will you?"

A cryptic shrug. "That depends."

"On what?"

"On you."

Greg's brow creased. "But—"

Ominous pulled open a drawer from his desk and extracted an object that made Greg's eyes go wide with alarm. He cringed and gripped the arms of his chair. Ominous slid the drawer shut and placed the object on his desk. It was a handgun. A large-caliber revolver. From another drawer, he produced a bottle of expensive whiskey. Maker's Mark. He set the bottle next to the weapon. The demented scientist smiled again. "I propose a game."

Greg relaxed only a little. "A . . . game? What kind of game?"

Ominous snapped his fingers. "O'Dell! Glasses!"

Greg sensed movement somewhere behind him and in a moment heard a rattle of glassware. The little green man moved into view and went up on his tiptoes to place two rocks glasses on the desk.

Then he was left them again.

Ominous looked right at Greg as he poured whiskey into the glasses. "The rules are simple, Mr. Nelson. If you win, the surviving members of tonight's audience—including those currently locked in limbo—will be returned to your world. You will be free to depart this place and live out your lives."

"And if I lose?"

"If you lose, the girl in which you showed such interest will remain where she is, where she will likely die. As will you. Because what I'm proposing, you see, is a friendly game of Russian Roulette."

Greg eyed the big revolver atop Ominous' desk.

And reached for a glass of whiskey. He tossed the booze back in one go and set the glass down again. "How can you possibly bring them back if you lose? You'll be *dead.*"

"There's a code. O'Dell knows it. And he knows how to input it. It's my final failsafe. If I lose, he will do what is necessary to fulfill my end of the bargain."

"Fuck me. O'Dell is real?"

Ominous laughed. "As real as you or I. Only his current appearance is illusory."

Greg thought it over a moment more before saying, "I don't get why you would do this. Why risk everything on a deadly game of fucking chance?"

"Because I can. Because the possibility of losing, regardless of how slight, makes me tingle pleasantly in my nether regions."

Gross.

"And maybe because I know I cannot lose. I am become God, remember?"

"If you can't lose, then where's my incentive to play along with this insanity?"

Ominous shrugged and spread his hands. "Because maybe I'm wrong. Probably not, but one must allow for the possibility. And because what other choice do you have? You quite literally have *no* other hope of rescuing the lovely young woman you so admire."

Greg stewed on it for some moments, trying to perceive any way things might possibly work out in his favor. All the while, he remained all-too-aware he might be squandering the last few remaining moments of Lashon's life.

Ominous poured another inch of whiskey into the empty glass and pushed it toward him. "What do you say?"

Greg again downed the whiskey and gestured for Ominous to pour him some more.

Then he summoned a fatalistic smile.

"Fuck it. Let's play."

Ominous laughed and nodded approvingly.

Then he picked up the revolver and put it in his mouth.

PART 3

THE MAN BEHIND

THE

CURTAIN PRESENTS...

THE FINAL

CHAPTER!!!

What he needed to summon here was a force of will beyond anything he had ever managed in his life. The effort needed would necessarily be monumental, the kind of thing only the most desperate people would ever attempt. Badly wounded soldiers on a bloody battlefield would know this kind of desperation. He and the young woman he had saved once before were locked in an apparently hopeless fight for survival. The enemy had the upper hand and was clearly not inclined to display any degree of mercy.

It's all down to me, John thought. *And it doesn't matter how much it fucking hurts, I've got to do this.*

The only surviving members of the psycho family were down there in the cellar with the girl. He could hear them screaming at her and occasionally laughing in a wild way that chilled him to the bone. They sounded like patients in a mental institution whacked-out on powerful drugs. He looked at the blood smeared all over the table and thought about what had been done to his hands and face. His nostrils twitched again at the acrid odor of burnt meat. The source of that horrible smell was his own flesh, the missing parts of him they had cooked.

His fucking *fingers.*

He had six left.

Maybe just enough. *Maybe.*

The girl had shown up with her gun before they could take the rest. Before they could finish him off. She had made a valiant effort. It took guts to do what she had done. Amazing guts. But it hadn't been enough and now she was about to die. She could have taken the easy way out, could have fled from this place while they were all still preoccupied with torturing him, but she had tried to help instead.

He was a worthless, cowardly fucking murderer and deserved to die.

She did not.

And helping her might not quite qualify as an act of redemption—there could be no real redemption in light of what he had done—but it was maybe as close as he could hope to come. John stared at the flat heads of the nails that had been hammered flush against the backs of his hands.

They had left him alone up here in order to tend to the girl.

He was obviously no longer considered any kind of threat.

Well, let's just see about that, you fucking assholes.

He tensed the muscles in his arms and mutilated hands and tried hard not to scream as he tried to pull his hands from the table.

~

There were many panicked shouts and sounds of people banging into things as Brix and the others barged their way through the bar's dark back room. The bearded man named Ben had been a bartender here and was trying to direct them to the right place. His guidance was helping, but it was impossible to avoid so many invisible obstructions. Brix screeched in frustration as she knocked over a case of beer bottles that shattered on the concrete floor and instantly filled the tight space with an intensely hoppy aroma. Broken glass crunched beneath the soles of her boots and she nearly slipped in the spreading pool of beer, but a strong hand closed around her arm before she could take a spill.

A voice right in her ear: "I got ya."

Jason.

There was no time to thank him. The zombies had followed them into the back room and someone bringing up the rear—she thought probably it was the tattooed man named Cade—started screaming in agony. Though she couldn't see anything, it was too easy to imagine what was happening thanks to the countless living dead movies she had seen. They were tearing him apart, just like in a Romero flick, pulling out his intestines and pushing them into their slavering mouths. Devouring as much of his warm flesh as they could ingest. But there were too many zombies and one man wouldn't be enough of a meal for them all.

Brix pulled free of Jason's grip and pushed ahead, one hand clutching the gun and the other held in front of her to feel for the wall she knew had to be there. After a few more tense moments of groping, she found it and began to pat its surface in search of the door. There were more shouts from Ben as more things were knocked over in the dark and more bottles shattered on the floor. The zombies weren't just getting closer, they were almost upon them. And Ben was too panicked now to be of any further help. Brix kept her hand on the wall as she moved carefully but quickly to the right. She could hear Jason slapping his hands against the wall as he tried in the other direction. Ben was screaming now. It was impossible to tell whether this was purely from fright or if the zombies had caught up to him. Either way, there was nothing to be done about it. Being effectively blind pissed Brix off. She preferred to fight, not grope around helplessly this way. And now her frustration was reaching a crescendo. She had bumped up against shelving of some type. She had reached the end of the wall without finding the door. And Ben's screaming was louder than ever. A cloud of despair hung heavy about her, waiting to engulf her.

Jason let out a jubilant shout. "*Found it!*"

There was a faint screech of metal and then the back door was standing open a dozen feet to her left. Jason's bare-chested form stood silhouetted in a rectangle of fortuitously clear moonlight. Brix had probably been right by the damn door when she had opted to go this way.

Ben was on his hands and knees in the middle of the floor. His hands were bloody from clutching blindly at broken glass. A slender female zombie in the tattered remains of a little black dress was right behind him, reaching for him. Brix shot the dead bitch in the head and rushed forward to help Ben to his feet. Then they followed Jason through the door out to the rear of the building. There were more zombies outside. Many more than she had seen in the area prior to entering the bar. Of course it would be that way. Moaning, staggering living dead converged on them from both sides of the building.

The three of them exchanged jittery glances.

Brix could see they were all thinking the same thing—*what now?*

She focused on Ben. "You work here, right? Where can we go?"

The bartender had his eyes on the approaching front line of zombies and could only whimper in response.

Brix slugged him in the shoulder. Hard. "Ben! *Where* can we go?"

"Dunno. But . . ." He indicated the crowd of zombies approaching from the left side of the building. ". . . my car's parked over yonder. We'd have to get past those things somehow."

"You've got your keys?"

"Yep."

"Then let's do this." A quick glance at Jason. "I'll shoot as many as I can till I run out of ammo. We'll fight our way through the rest. Punch them. Kick them. Knock them on their fucking zombie asses. Whatever it takes."

Ben's face was grim. "We're about to die."

Jason nodded. "Maybe. But we'll go down swinging."

No more time to talk. The zombies were too close.

Brix brushed past Jason.

Raised the gun.

And started shooting. Reanimated corpses dropped like slow-motion bowling pins. Then the gun was empty and they were in the thick of a battle to the death.

~

The Phantom slammed through the rear gate and shot across a fenced-in area behind a wing of the mansion. Monroe glimpsed tennis courts flashing by to his right and the dim shape of what might have been a swimming pool somewhere beyond. The area they were passing through now was a courtyard, with a beautiful garden in its center and some marble benches ringing it. A piece of the double-sided gate had come off its hinges in the crash and now rode atop the Phantom's hood. Melissa seemed unfazed by the violence of their entry into the courtyard. Of course. The only thing on her mind was getting to Victor, the vampire who had sired her. Which made Monroe think of Lilith. If she had told him the truth, he had been her sireling. He had no reason to doubt it was true. She had told the truth about everything else. Yet he had felt nothing for her like the overriding loyalty Melissa apparently felt for Victor. There had to be more to whatever was driving Melissa than just the blood connection to the vamp who had turned her.

"Um . . . are you in love with Victor?"

The question startled Melissa. She lost control of the Phantom for a moment as her head whipped toward him. There was another long and loud screech of rending metal as the side of the Phantom scraped one of the marble benches ringing the garden. She stomped on the brake, bringing the ravaged car to a squealing halt in the middle of the courtyard. The piece of the gate slid off the Phantom's hood and hit the courtyard's cobbled surface with a metallic rattle.

Melissa's eyes were narrow, dangerous-looking slits. "What made you say that?"

Monroe wanted to run and hide. It didn't matter where, just so long as he got away from those predatory eyes. "It was just a guess. I didn't mean to, you know . . . offend you or anything. If I did—"

"Shut up."

"Right. Shutting up now."

She continued glaring at him in that unnervingly fierce way a few more moments. Then her expression softened. "I do love him."

"Look, we don't need to talk about it. I was wrong to bring it up. Really."

"I love him and want to be his bride."

Jesus. Why did I have to say anything? Me and my stupid mouth. She's just gonna go on and on about her fucking heartbreak or whatever while the whole goddamn world is falling down around us.

Other sounds penetrated now that the car was no longer in motion. There was a faint popping noise he initially thought was fire-crackers. But that made no sense and an instant later he realized he was actually hearing distant gunfire. A recognition that did nothing to soothe his jangling nerves. He also heard a loud *whoop-whoop-whoop* he soon identified as the rotors of a helicopter. He leaned forward a bit and glanced upward through the badly splintered windshield. He caught a glimpse of the spinning rotors just over the edge of the mansion's roof.

Melissa touched his arm. "Your friend, Kira. She took what's rightfully mine."

Monroe looked at her, frowning. "I think Victor's the one who did the goddamn taking. You wanna be mad at anyone, be mad at him." His frown deepened. "You're not gonna hurt her . . . are you?"

"Depends. There may be a way we can both have what we want."

"How?"

She told him what she had in mind.

Monroe nodded. "Let's do it."

~

Ominous smiled in a grotesque way around the barrel of the revolver stuck in his mouth. With his garish makeup and corona of wild white hair, he looked like a crazy, suicidal clown. He was still smiling as he applied pressure to the trigger and the revolver's cylinder began to turn. Greg watched with a kind of morbid hope as it rotated. He would love nothing more than to see an abrupt end to this terrible game of cruel fate. He sat on the edge of his seat and watched the gun's hammer snap backward and then forward. But all that happened was a flat click as the hammer failed to land on the live round that would have sent the mad doctor's brains exploding out the back of his head.

Ominous chuckled as he removed the gun from his mouth and pushed it across the desk toward Greg. He then poured more Maker's Mark into Greg's empty glass. "I imagine you'd like another brace of alcohol prior to taking your turn. Just think. It could be the last drink of your life. You'll want to savor it."

Greg snatched up the gun.

Opened his mouth wide to receive the barrel's length.

And squeezed the trigger.

He only became aware of how hard his heart was thumping when the hammer made that flat click again. He let out a relieved breath as he carefully removed the gun from his mouth.

Ominous clapped his hands together three times, in a slow, mocking way. "Bravo, Mr. Nelson. Have to say I approve. That took balls the size of Mars. I shouldn't be surprised. It took gloriously massive balls to come back for the girl. I was watching you on another feed, you know, as you were standing outside the theater. Most men in your position, having made good their escape, would have fled immediately. I'd bet my balls on it. People in general are more inclined to save themselves rather than attempting an act of almost certainly futile heroism."

Greg grunted. "I guess I'm not most people. And you have a really weird balls fixation."

"I was touched inappropriately as a child."

Why am I not surprised?

Greg glanced at the weapon still clutched in his hands. A crazy idea occurred to him. A notion so compelling he nearly acted on it. The gun held a single live round. He could aim the gun at the crazy man and simply squeeze the trigger repeatedly until it fired.

Ominous laughed heartily. "You could not be more transparent, Greg. May I call you Greg? I feel as if two men engaged in a game in which the stakes are life and death should be on a first name basis."

Greg shrugged. "Knock yourself out, Ominous."

"Excellent. And you may call me Eerie."

Greg arched an eyebrow. "Eerie?"

"My full name is Doctor Eerie von Ominous."

No. No, it isn't, you fucking fruitcake. I don't know what your actual given name is and I don't give a damn.

"I'll just keep calling you Ominous, if you don't mind."

"You can call me whatever you like, just don't call me late to dinner."

Greg groaned at this lamest of lame old jokes.

The mad doctor's expression sobered as he eyed the gun. "I'd advise you not to attempt anything stupid. Possibly you would succeed in killing me, but O'Dell would then immediately kill you. Isn't that right, O'Dell?"

The little man , still hanging out somewhere behind Greg, said, "Damn straight."

Ominous nodded. "And your woman would remain where she is." His eyes twinkled as he leaned forward a bit to lend extra emphasis to his next utterance. "*Forever.*"

Greg set the gun on the desk again, exchanging it for the replenished glass of whiskey. "I'll play by your rules, Ominous." He smirked. "Even if I think the game is rigged."

"You wound me. I am an honorable man, I assure you."

Like hell.

Ominous pulled the gun toward the center of the desk, where he gave it a twirl, like a kid playing a game of Spin the Bottle. He laughed yet again when it stopped spinning and wound up pointed roughly in Greg's direction. "Not at all portentous, I'm sure."

Greg sipped more whiskey and didn't reply.

Ominous kept smiling and tapped his fingers in a jaunty beat on the desktop. He clearly was drawing out the next stage of the game. Because he was having fun and didn't want it to end too soon. The evil fuck. The tapping of his fingers became more manic until he slapped his hand on the desk and barked a command at the little man. "O'Dell! This party needs tunes. Cue the Mix of Diabolical Awesomeness!"

Greg squinted at Ominous. "The what?"

A maniacal cackle from the doctor. "The Mix of Diabolical Awesomeness!"

"That's what I thought you said."

He heard O'Dell moving around behind him for a moment and then music was emanating from hidden speakers. Shriekback's "Nemesis" again, a song he only knew thanks to a mix CD made for him by an older cousin years earlier.

Ominous pushed back from his desk, stood up, and started dancing manically around like the certifiable lunatic he was.

Greg helped himself to more whiskey and waited with failing patience for the game to resume.

~

The tumble down the stairs left her in tremendous pain, though miraculously no bones seemed to have been broken. There was, however, some serious internal discomfort as she tried to rouse herself from the cellar's concrete floor, so maybe she did have some cracked ribs. She winced and bit back a cry of pain as she braced her hands on the cool concrete and tried to push herself up. But her strength was at a very low ebb and all she could do was whimper in frustration as Heidi and Blake came clomping down the wooden cellar stairs.

Lashon glanced up and saw their forms partially illumined by the light pouring in from the door to the kitchen. The faint light also allowed her to glimpse other things. There were other people down here with her. People who looked like they were floating in midair. A stench of decay hung heavy in the air and hinted at a darker truth regarding her silent companions.

Blake and Heidi reached the cellar floor.

There was a click and a low-wattage red bulb—like the one Lashon remembered from the living room—popped on, revealing a half dozen bodies in various stages of decomposition hanging from meat hooks. One body looked relatively fresh. The dead man's face looked vaguely familiar. He had on a t-shirt depicting a scene from an old horror film called *Basket Case*. Lashon wondered why he should seem familiar. Then it hit her. She had caught a glimpse of him in the audience for *Chainsaw Maniac*. So she and Johnny hadn't been the only unfortunate souls transported to this nightmare place from the theater. The blood-tipped point of the steel hook protruded grotesquely from the man's chest. It had taken great strength to impale the guy that way. A thing like that had to have been done by either Barry or

Rob, who were both dead now.

Heidi screamed and came running at Lashon.

In her weakened state, there was no time to react or defend herself as Heidi kicked at her, burying the point of her shoe in the soft flesh just beneath her already banged-up ribcage. "Take that, you fucking filthy whore!" Another savage kick, even more painful. "And that!" And yet another. "And that!"

Blake came up behind Heidi and placed a calming hand on her shoulder. "That's enough."

Heidi shrugged his hand away. "You're not the fucking boss of me!"

She kicked Lashon several more times before finally breaking off the attack.

Lashon sucked in a great, gasping breath and then sobbed. She wanted to defend herself. Wanted more than anything to fight back. But her body just wouldn't cooperate. She had never been in so much pain.

It's hopeless, she thought. *They're gonna kill me and there's nothing I can do about it.*

She rolled onto her back and stared up at the dangling bodies of the crazy family's earlier victims. There were two more hooks she could see that had no bodies hanging from them. Though it was obvious neither Heidi nor Blake possessed massive upper body strength, she supposed it was possible they could get her onto one of those hooks if they worked together. She imagined her body sliding onto one of those steel points and wanted to cry.

Heidi saw her staring at the hooks and laughed in a cruel, heartless way. "Yeah, bitch. That shit's gonna hurt like a motherfucker. You wouldn't believe the fucking noise people make when they get put on those things."

Blake grinned. "Oh, she'll believe it when she feels it for herself."

Then they were both laughing.

Lashon choked back another sob and glared at them. "I hope you both rot in hell."

Heidi giggled. "They always say shit like that sooner or later. Never stops being fucking funny."

Blake's reply to that was more laughter.

Then Heidi slapped his chest with the back of a hand. "Enough. Let's do this bitch."

Lashon cringed and tried to scoot backward as the leering siblings came at her with grasping hands.

~

The nails were too long and thick to extract from the table, at least with his hands in such a mangled condition. But there was one other possible solution. It would mean even more nerve-shredding pain, but what was more pain to him at this point? Part of his face had been cut away. The shredded, bloody flesh framing his mouth was a raw, twitching mass of live wire nerves and misery. Every twitch of his mouth or facial muscles sent countless more jolts of punishing agony sizzling through him.

There could be no level of pain higher than what he was already experiencing.

So fuck it.

John set his teeth and began working his hands side to side, digging the heads of the nails deeper into his flesh. It hurt. More than he'd anticipated. But he kept working at it. He meant to do this thing regardless of the cost. And after a while it began to work. The wounds in his hands opened wider and he began to pull his hands upward again. The nail heads sank into the meat of his hands and scraped against brittle bones as his hands began to slide up the shafts of the nails.

His hands came free with moist, sickening plops.

The pain was incredible. Had he thought he'd reached the upper limits of his pain threshold? Really? How delusional. Because he had been seriously fucking wrong. His hands felt as if they were on fire. *Again*. Even so, he experienced an accompanying thrill of exhilaration. He had done it! He was fucking *free*!

But the sense of accomplishment was short-lived. The much bigger task—saving the girl—was still ahead of him. And it still looked impossible, even in light of the amazing thing he'd already done. There were two of them. Two healthy, whole, completely nuts young people. And he was just one much weakened, not exactly whole middle-aged wife killer. The odds against success were steep. To understate on an epic level.

He would try anyway.

What else was left for him?

The cleaver Heidi had used to take his fingers sat at the edge of the table, where she had abandoned it in the wake of the girl's gunblazing arrival. John reached for it with his left hand—the one with the most fingers remaining—and picked it up. It was wet with his blood and almost slid from the three fingers the hand still possessed. But he curled those fingers as tightly as he could and maintained his grip on the handle.

Next he slid out of his chair—careful not to scoot it backward on the floor, for fear of making noise—and began a slow, careful approach toward the open cellar door, through which he still heard the siblings screaming and laughing at the girl he meant to rescue. When he reached the door, he poked one eye around the jamb and peered down into the cellar. Though she was wobbling badly, the brother and sister had the girl up on her feet now and were tossing her back and forth between them, alternately shoving her and backhanding her across the face. They taunted her with dark promises of the nasty things they planned to do to her and screamed the vilest insults John had ever heard. Many of the worst came from Heidi, which didn't surprise him. She had orchestrated his own torture, after all. He wanted to run screaming down there and hack her into a million little pieces with the cleaver. But the one called Blake had the gun tucked inside the waistband of his jeans. So, though it frustrated him to no end, he would have to wait for an opening.

He could only hope there would eventually *be* such an opening.

And then, like a miracle, one arrived.

The brother and sister eventually tired of smacking the girl around and started talking about getting her up on one of the meat hooks. Some debate regarding how to do this ensued. Neither sibling was tall or strong enough to do the deed on their own. They would have to work in tandem. Heidi ordered Blake to head back up to the kitchen to fetch a stepstool stored in the pantry.

Had he still been capable of it, John might have smiled then.

Instead, he stepped back and waited for the brother to come up the steps.

~

The paralyzing terror Ben had displayed prior to wading into the fray was displaced by screaming, savage fury. He punched zombie after zombie and bowled over others by knocking some of the larger ones into the ones behind them. Jason fought with equal levels of ferocity and desperation. Brix did what she could once the Glock's clip was empty, but she didn't possess a comparable level of strength. Still, she managed to contribute as they worked their way around to the other side of the building, where Ben's car was parked. They were making progress. She caught a glimpse of the blue Firebird he'd said would be in the last slot by the sidewalk. So close, but still so far away with so many zombies remaining in their path. Even in the thick of battle, she had to wonder where they had all come from so suddenly. It was almost as if they had all been hiding out somewhere nearby, perhaps inside the neighboring buildings, just biding their time until some secret signal let them know it was time to show up for the climactic zombie battle scene.

She felt the outstretched fingertips of a zombie touch her from behind and wheeled about to slam her fist into the space where she assumed the thing's chin would be. But the zombie was too tall, many inches above six feet. Her fist bounced harmlessly off its desiccated chest. The big zombie reached for her head with one of its oversized hands. Brix did the only thing she could think of by kicking out at one of its knees. There was a crack of splintering bone and the thing went toppling over. Though the giant was an impressive size—to say the least—it had been in a more advanced state of decay than many of its undead brethren.

Jason screamed something at her.

She turned away from the crippled giant and discovered that she was surrounded by living dead. Panic burned inside her at the sight of all those open mouths and teeth and outreached, questing hands. The moans of the zombies rose to a higher, louder pitch. They seemed to sense that they had her and would soon be feasting on another fresh meal.

Then the one directly in front of her was yanked backward and slung to the ground. She saw Ben's intent face appear through the gap as he urged her forward with a desperate hand gesture. Brix didn't need any extra encouragement. She shot through the gap before it could close again and followed Ben as they hurried to catch up to Jason, who was only a dozen yards from the Firebird.

Brix tugged at Ben's shoulder. "Your keys. I'll make a run for the car while you guys hold these fuckers off."

Ben dug them out of a hip pocket and tossed them to her.

Brix caught the keys on the fly and did the only thing she could—she rammed straight into the crowd of zombies still standing in their way, shouldering them aside like a fullback on a football field. It worked. She managed to bull her way through the tightest press of living dead bodies and slipped on through to the other side. There were still other zombies between her and the car, but she easily eluded them by zigging and zagging across the parking lot en route to the

Firebird.

She flipped hurriedly through the keys as she reached the driver's side door. The motherfucker had a bunch of goddamn keys. Too many. It was like a maintenance man's key ring, for fuck's sake. Luckily, though, she was able to quickly identify what had to be the key that would open the old car. It was significantly longer than the rest of them. She jammed it into the lock and gave it a twist.

The door popped open.

She couldn't resist a shout of jubilation.

Fuck yeah!

She dropped into the car behind the steering wheel, yanked the door shut, and leaned across the seat to unlock the other door. A glance at the rearview mirror as she slipped the key inside the ignition showed that Jason and Ben had elected to emulate her near-suicidal plunge straight through the thick of the zombies. She held her breath a moment, waiting to see if they would emerge through the other side.

They did.

Hallelujah!

Brix fired up the engine and put the car in gear as the guys came racing across the parking lot toward her. Jason reached the Firebird first. He got the door open on the passenger side and came barreling into the front seat of the car. Ben, who now had a deep, oozing gash down his right arm, shoved the seat forward and dove into the back.

Jason pulled the door shut and looked at her. "*Go! Fucking go!*"

Brix didn't need to be told again.

She stomped on the gas and the Firebird went flying backward. It's rear end collided with a couple of zombies, knocking them over as she hit the brake pedal and changed gears. Another burst of gas and they were out in the street and speeding away from the Boro Bar and Grill. Brix barely slowed down as she hooked a right at the first intersection, put the gas pedal to the floorboard again, and kept going.

Jason let out a whoop and slammed a fist against the Firebird's dash. "We did it! We fucking did it!"

Brix grinned and nodded. "Yes. We did. Holy shit."

Ben groaned and sat up in the back. Brix glanced at the rearview mirror and saw him crane his head from left to right and back again before shifting his attention to her. "You're heading back into town."

"I know."

"Why? Thought you wanted to make for the interstate."

"I did at first, but I got to thinking." She glanced at Jason, who looked just as puzzled as Ben. She had a hunch that might change once she told him what she had in mind. Ben wouldn't get it. He was a part of this zombie-infested alternate world and would only think she was talking nonsense. But Jason might understand. "We're heading back to the theater."

Jason looked intrigued, but still puzzled. "We are? Why?"

"It's the only way. Don't you see? We can keep trying to survive in this place, where some new menace is always around the corner, just like in a fucking movie, or we can go back to the source of this shit and see if we can figure a way home."

Ben made a sound of disgust. "Again with this movie crap. You talked this same kind of shit in the bar. What's wrong with you people?"

Neither Brix nor Jason replied to this right away.

But they exchanged a lingering glance that communicated much as they continued speeding back into the heart of the city.

Jason shrugged. "All right. Okay. Might as well take a shot."

Ben made that disgusted sound again. "You know what would be great? If one of you assholes would tell me exactly where we're going. That's what."

Another glance at the rearview mirror. "The Sunshine 6 cineplex on Memorial Blvd."

Ben snorted. Then he laughed. "What? Come on. You're pulling my leg, right? That dump has been closed for years. Tell me where we're really going."

"The Sunshine 6 cineplex."

"Well, that's just about the stupidest damn thing I've ever heard. Why would you do that?"

"It doesn't matter. You wouldn't understand if I tried to explain." Brix met his gaze in the rearview. "Look, we're not kidnapping you or anything. You can have your car back once we get to the theater and then you can go anywhere you want."

A lengthy silence unfurled after that and lasted until they arrived at an intersection the green directional signs at the corner marked as Memorial and Clark.

Ben made a clucking sound as they turned left. "Crazy. Just crazy. I'm supposed to just abandon y'all to your fate."

"That's about the size of it."

Yet another sound of disapproval from Ben. "Crazy. I don't know what else to say, man. You're both out of your fucking minds."

That was a point Brix couldn't dispute.

What she had in mind was probably doomed to failure.

But she meant to try anyway.

~

The song playing now was one Greg didn't recognize. It was some demented-sounding thing about all women being bad, a sentiment he couldn't really endorse. Except that, given the singer's delivery of the lyrics, it seemed as if the notion wasn't being put forth as a negative thing. The singer seemed to relish the notion of a "bad" or dangerous woman. Greg couldn't help thinking of his own enduring obsession with Lashon even in the wake of her attack on him. Maybe, much like this apparently deranged singer, he was also drawn to women with a dark or "bad" streak. Ominous appeared to love the song, because he was again bounding about, doing one of his ridiculous, rhythmically-challenged dances. Watching him, Greg couldn't believe someone as goofy as Mr. "I Am Become God" held the fate of the woman he loved in his hands. Or that he was capable of anything at all other than perennial first place winner of the official Craziest Person In All Fucking Creation contest. He had to work at keeping one fact front and center, and that was the knowledge that Ominous was putting on a show for him. His loony exterior masked a far darker brand of inner madness.

The song ended and Ominous dropped into the big leather chair again. He laughed and mopped sweat from his brow with an already-wet handkerchief. "I've got dance fever, son, and there ain't no cure!" Another wild burst of laughter, followed by a big sigh. He perked up when a new song—obviously by the same band as the "All Women Are Bad" people—started. "The Cramps! Gotta love 'em. Am I right?"

"Right."

Ominous picked up the gun, put it in his mouth, and squeezed the trigger.

Click.

He set the gun on the desk in an incongruously nonchalant way and leaned forward in his chair with a peculiarly avid look on his face. "They say music soothes the savage beast. But is that really true? Personally, I find that a lot of music, particularly the really good stuff, *stirs* the beast. Wouldn't you agree?"

Greg didn't say anything at first. He was still trying to process the fresh disappointment of yet another dry-fire of the gun. By his calculation, they were down to just two chambers. One plugged and one containing—ostensibly—a live round. The next time he put the gun in his mouth, he would have a 50/50 chance of either living or dying.

Ominous grinned in an irritatingly knowing way. "Getting down to the real nitty-gritty, aren't we?" He pursed his lips, nodding thoughtfully. "Listen, you may not believe this, but I like to think of myself as essentially a fair guy. Go on, scoff if you like, but it's the truth. So I'll offer you one last chance to opt-out. You can abandon the game and leave this place. You can live to see another day, and many more days beyond. This is your lifeline. Do you want to take it . . ." And now he pushed the gun to the edge of the desk again. ". . . or do you want to continue?"

Greg stared at the gun.

Sweat formed on his own brow as he thought it over. It shouldn't even be a question. He had come this far. Risked this much. But shit was getting real now.

50/50.

One click away from death.

Maybe.

He had been brave. Really fucking brave. No one could say otherwise or much blame him for taking the opt-out Ominous had offered. Then he thought of his last glimpse of Lashon in that basement of horrors and knew there was still no real choice.

He picked up the gun and put it in his mouth.

Then, for the last time, squeezed the trigger.

~

Lashon toppled to the floor again when a blow from Heidi's closed fist connected solidly with her chin. The slaps and backhands blow she and her brother had been meting out had been bad enough, but this was the hardest blow she had taken yet. The crazy bitch had deceptive strength. She looked like a sorority girl, but punched like a champion welterweight. She had probably had a lot of practice knocking people around. Lashon ached to lash back at her, but she had absorbed too much punishment with no opportunity at all to recuperate.

She rolled onto her side and stared at a row of shelving. The shelves had square compartments and in each was a jar containing preserved body parts. She saw eyes and hands and tongues and genitals floating in formaldehyde. Each compartment contained three or four such jars. There had to be several dozen of them in all. Christ, how many people had this demented family butchered over the years? Too many. She no longer thought of these sickos as phony people. No longer thought of this world as not real. It was real enough, all right, regardless of whether it was derived from a work of fiction on another plane of existence. They were real, and all the people they had ever killed had been real. It made her sick to think of it.

All those lives . . . wasted . . .

Heidi squatted next to her and grabbed her roughly by a shoulder, then rolled her onto her back. "You ready to hang, bitch?"

Lashon sniffled. "Please . . ."

Heidi's features formed a pinched expression of mock sympathy. "Please. Oh, please, please, please." She said this in a lilting, sing-song voice. Then she laughed. "Not so tough now, huh, killer? Keep begging. It's music to my ears."

Lashon sniffled again, but said nothing in response this time.

Heidi snapped a backhand slap across her face. "Beg. That's an order."

Lashon still said nothing.

She got another, even harder slap for it. "You're making me very angry. You should beg. Maybe I'll kill you fast if you do."

"I don't believe you."

Heidi laughed. "Why would I ever lie? Oh, I know." She put a forefinger to her cheek and made her eyes go wide. "Because I'm *crrrrrrrrraaaa-zzzyyy!*"

She cackled in a gleeful, manic way meant to emphasize the point. Not that it needed emphasizing. Lashon was already fully convinced of the girl's utter madness. It was something in their genes, a tainted strain of DNA that had poisoned them all from birth. Not that this excused anything any of them had done.

They all deserved to suffer.

To *die.*

But she'd had her chance to finish them off and had blown it.

Heidi leaned in close so that their faces were separated by just inches, dropping her voice to a whisper. "You know, it's possible to hang alive on one of those hooks for hours. Rob was real good at placing motherfuckers on 'em just right so they'd suffer as long as possible. Blake and me aren't as strong as our dead brothers, but we're gonna try our damnedest to make it as bad for you as possible. What do you think about that?"

Lashon's eyes misted. "Fuck . . . you."

Heidi giggled. "Oh, but I might fuck *you*. With a broom handle." She was leering at her again. "While you're hanging up there, all help-less and shit. What do you think about *that*?"

Lashon's mouth came open, but whatever she had been about to say remained unspoken.

Because that was when something came crashing down the stairs.

~

The guy couldn't have been any more oblivious when he came through the door into the kitchen. He was wearing a shit-eating grin that belied the grief he'd displayed over his lost family members not so many minutes earlier. Maybe his grief had been exaggerated. Or just reflexive and not something he felt so intensely below the surface. Or maybe it was because he was crazy and crazy people never went long without having some new sick thing on which to focus their malignant energies. Things such as smacking the girl around and ter-rorizing her with hints of even more fucked-up degradations to come. Whatever the explanation, John was grateful, because the man's dis-traction spelled his doom.

John chopped him across the throat with the cleaver. He then pulled the man into a rough embrace and wrestled him away from the door as blood jetted from the gaping wound in his neck, blood that soaked the front of John's already blood-drenched shirt. The man struggled against the embrace for a moment. Until John's left hand reared back—and then snapped forward, burying the cleaver in the back of the man's skull.

Then he struggled no more.

John allowed himself only the slightest moment to catch his breath. He had to keep acting fast if he hoped to save the girl. His desperate attempt was close to working beyond his wildest hopes, but the girl was still down there with Heidi, with whom he would have to deal as quickly and as brutally as possible. Because she was as danger-ous all on her own as the rest had been put together.

He plucked the gun from the man's waistband.

Steered the corpse back over to the cellar door.

Allowed himself a last moment to steel his nerves.

And then tossed the body down the stairs.

~

Melissa went over the makeshift plan again as they rode up together in the service elevator. The sound of gunfire, seemingly so close as

246

they had entered the mansion from the courtyard, was now inaudible. The silence in the self-contained space was so perfect it was almost possible to believe the battle raging throughout the house wasn't actually happening.

But Monroe knew better.

People were fighting and dying out there, vampire and human alike. It was a crazy thing to realize he was in the middle of a kind of war, but it was the truth.

"That helicopter is waiting to take Victor and your girl away. I'm banking on us getting there ahead of Victor. I know him. He's methodical. He'll make sure he has everything he needs and that every base is covered before he leaves. I'm thinking that'll still take a few more minutes, regardless of the danger."

"You're *hoping* it'll be a few more minutes."

Melissa snapped a glare at him. "Obviously. And if I'm right, I'll put you in the 'copter and send the pilot on his way with you and the girl."

Monroe frowned. "Okay, so . . . what? Another 'copter comes in to take you and Victor away?"

"That's what I'll tell the pilot. He's human. I can make him believe anything."

"So what's your way out? If there's not another 'copter . . ."

Melissa looked at him, a sad smile dimpling the corners of her pretty mouth. "There's not another way out. Victor and I go down together once the hunters breach the roof."

"Hold on. Surely there's room on the 'copter for all of us."

Melissa shook her head. "There isn't. And Victor wouldn't let you come along even if there were room. This really is your only hope. And Victor wouldn't abandon his new bride in favor of me. We'll die together, but at least we'll *be* together. The way it should be."

"Jesus."

The elevator car came to a stop and the door dinged open. The sound of the helicopters rotors was almost deafeningly loud as they hurried out into the cool night air.

~

They were more than halfway across the roof of the building when Kira saw something strange. The door to a service elevator located next to some A/C units over by the edge of the roof slid open. This in itself was surprising. Not to mention frightening. She expected to see black-masked hunters come swarming onto the roof with their automatic weapons blazing. Instead she saw Monroe and some woman in a red party dress come running toward them.

Jenna banged into her as she stopped in her tracks a couple dozen yards from the helicopter and its whirling, noisy blades. "What are you doing? Keep going!"

Kira ignored her, calling out to the friend she'd figured was permanently lost to her. Submerged but still powerful feelings came surging back to the surface. "Monroe!"

Jenna grabbed her by an arm and tried to drag her toward the helicopter.

Kira shrugged free of her and went running toward Monroe. She saw that his eyes were brimming with tears as they drew close to each other. Her own eyes were moist. This was another thing that surprised her. She had assumed she was beyond feeling this kind of human emotion, but here it was.

And she was so happy to feel it.

Not just happy. *Joyous.*

Jenna started screaming at her as they embraced and kissed with a passion that was pure and more wonderful by far than anything she had experienced with Victor. There had been pleasure with Victor. She couldn't deny that. But it hadn't come from a place of true feeling. Of real love. *This* did.

Jenna's screeching and gesturing became ever more animated.

And then it abruptly ended.

Kira broke the clinch with Monroe long enough to see that the woman in the red dress had torn Jenna's head from her shoulders. She felt a reflexive but short-lived burst of anger. Short-lived, because somehow she knew this stranger wasn't an enemy. She had come here with Monroe and he seemed to trust her.

That was good enough for her.

The woman and Monroe exchanged a few quick words. Last instructions. And goodbyes. Her name was Melissa. Kira was happy to know who she was. It was good to be able to properly thank an unexpected savior. But there was only time for a single word of thanks. Because after that Melissa had a last piece of business to tend to before they could depart. She stepped up into the helicopter and had a word with the pilot. When she reemerged, she evidently spied something that troubled her because her expression changed. Her eyes opened wide and her mouth dropped open.

The hunters? Had they finally breached the roof?

No. Kira sensed the truth without having to turn her back. Victor was somewhere back there, on the far side of the roof. Only Victor could terrify a creature as fearsome as this Melissa. Kira's eyes brimmed with tears again.

There isn't time to get away. He'll stop us.

But he didn't. For the first time that during that long, long night, something finally worked out in their favor.

Melissa hustled them into the helicopter.

And as it rose slowly into the air—too painfully slow by far to suit her—Kira watched in helpless, sick wonder as the only vampire in all the world who might possibly be Victor's match went to meet her death at his hands. It was over before the helicopter banked away from the mansion and flew away into the night. Melissa lay dead and broken at Victor's feet as he stood there and stared up at the receding helicopter. He didn't flinch when the hunters at last broke through the reinforced steel door behind him. And he didn't move as the heavily-armed killers swarmed the roof and bore relentlessly down upon him. Her last sight of the proud vampire was of him standing like that, watching his bride fly away into the night, forever lost to him now. It was the right thing, what had to happen, she knew that. Yet still it tore it at her. Kira clutched at Monroe's arm and buried her face against his shoulder, spilling tears of sorrow and regret.

And yet she also felt something very close to happiness.

Monroe was with her again.

Sometimes, she thought, *we really do get the happy endings we deserve.*

~

There hadn't been many zombies in the area right around the cineplex in those first confused moments after their arrival in this world and fortunately that was still the case. Brix spied a handful of staggering mobile corpses as they came screeching into the parking lot, but the living dead presence here was nowhere near as thick as what they had so narrowly eluded down by the university. In fact, it seemed as if there were significantly fewer present than she remembered from several hours earlier. Brix suspected many of the more agile zombies in the area had attempted to pursue them and had simply not returned, because why would they? There was no more food to be had here. Well . . . not until now.

She spared the burned-out hulk of her truck a quick glance as she sped toward the cineplex. It again struck her as odd that it was there at all. Or that Jason's car had been here. She and Jason were not from this world, so it made no sense. Unless they had counterparts here, natives to this world whose lives were mirror images of their own, and some reason other than seeing a movie had brought them to this place at the onset of a zombie apocalypse. Or maybe the presence of the vehicles had something to do with the proximity to the dimensional-shifting event and some kind of mystical link between humans and their possessions. She guessed either explanation was possible, even as tenuous as they seemed, but she pushed the question from her mind because there was a larger issue to contend with now.

She guided the Firebird to a stop at the curb outside the theater and glanced at Jason. "You ready for this?"

He grunted. "Not really. But fuck it, you're right. What else are we gonna do?"

Brix twisted in her seat to look at Ben, whose wary expression told her he still believed he was riding with a couple of world-class whack jobs. "Good luck to you, Ben. And sorry for the detour. We wouldn't have gotten this far without you."

Ben's expression turned sour again. "Still don't get what you're hoping to accomplish here." He waved a hand at the boarded-up old theater. "If it's a hideout you're after, there's got to be better places. Not sure you're even gonna be able to get in there."

"You got a tire iron or crowbar in your trunk? Anything we could maybe use to pry off those boards?"

"Yeah. And you can have it. But this is suicide. Ain't many of those things around just now, but could be that'd change in the time it'd take you to get into that dump."

"It's a chance we'll have to take."

Ben shifted in his seat and swiveled his head side to side for a quick survey of the living dead presence in the vicinity. Still weren't many around, but a few had turned in their direction and had drawn marginally closer, though the closest was still dozens of yards away.

Now he looked at Brix again. "We've got a little leeway here, looks like. A little time. So I'd like to hear the real reason behind this and all the weird shit you've been talking. I think you owe me some kind of explanation. And before you say a word, I don't want to hear anything but the no-bullshit truth. I don't care how crazy it is."

Brix exchanged another glance with Jason. He didn't say anything, but she felt certain his tired, resigned expression mirrored her own feelings. Ben was right. He had saved her life more than once tonight. She owed him an explanation. A true one, even if it accomplished nothing other than confirming his doubts about their sanity.

She glanced through the rear window to appraise the closest zombie. It was a female in a hospital gown and it was still moving at a pace not even a snail would envy. No real danger there. At least not yet.

She looked at Ben. "You remember me talking about my boyfriend back at the bar, right? Well . . . earlier tonight, like hours and hours ago, we came out here to meet some of his friends for a movie . . ."

Ben listened to the quickly-related tale with a careful expression that betrayed nothing. When she had finished bringing him up to speed, he let out a tired breath and rubbed at his eyes before saying, "Well, that is definitely some crazy shit you just told me."

Brix shrugged. "I told you—"

He laughed, cutting her off. "But it ain't any crazier than zombies overrunning the whole goddamn world. Listen . . . let's say you're not crazy at all. I mean, let's just suppose. And if what you say is true . . . and *if* you can get into this place and somehow figure a way back to your world . . . what do you think the chances are of taking me back there with you?"

Now Jason turned in his seat to look at Ben. "Slim and fucking none, brother, most likely."

Brix didn't say anything at all. She suspected Jason was right, but she had no way of knowing one way or the other.

Ben stared at the hands folded in his lap for a moment, nodding to himself as he mulled it all over. Then he looked at them, a small, fatalistic smile touching the edges of his mouth. "Back the car up."

Brix frowned. "What?"

"Back the fucking car up, girl."

"Why?"

"Because you're ram it right through the front of that fucking theater. *That's* why."

Now Brix was smiling, too. "Right on."

She turned away from him and got settled behind the wheel again. She glanced at Jason. He nodded and reached for his seatbelt. That struck her as a good idea, considering what they were about to attempt. She got strapped in and heard Ben doing the same in the back. Then she put the car in reverse, put the gas pedal to the floorboard, and sent the car rocketing backward halfway across the lot. There was a loud thump as the Firebird's rear end sent the nightgown-clad zombie sliding across pavement.

Brix moved the gearshift to the slot marked D.

She looked at Jason again and reached across the seat to clasp hands with him. "Sorry about wasting your girlfriend earlier."

Jason shook his head and clutched her hand tight for a moment. "Sorry she wasted your boyfriend. Maybe this isn't the right time to bring it up, but maybe if we make it through this, we could, like, go out or something."

She smiled and gave his hand a final squeeze. "It's a date."

She faced forward again and stared at the boarded-up building. "Here we come, motherfuckers."

"Ready or not," Jason chimed in.

"Yee-haw," was Ben's contribution from the back.

It sounded sort of sarcastic, but in a good-humored way. Which was amazing in light of all they had been through. And in light of the overwhelming evidence of death, chaos, and destruction all around them. But Brix guessed that sometimes you had to laugh in the face of darkness in order to keep it from consuming you.

She let out a breath.

Tightened her grip on the steering wheel.

And put the gas pedal all the way down again.

Brix kept smiling even as her body instinctively braced for impact. The theater's boarded-up entrance loomed large within seconds. In another second the car's wheels bounced over the curb, rocking them violently in their seats. And then they were all screaming as the car's front end smashed through the entrance and into the darkness beyond.

~

This is it, John thought. *My moment of truth.*

Tears brimmed in his eyes as he started down the stairs to the garishly-lit cellar below. But the tears weren't for him or for his own life, which he knew for certain was within its last moments.

I'm sorry, Marie.

Sorry I killed you.

Sorry you didn't find a man truly worthy of you.

Sorry for everything.

The immense sorrow added additional fuel to his rage as he neared the bottom of the stairs. Heidi's face was a mask of shock as she knelt over her brother's lifeless body.

Good.

I hope it hurts, bitch.
Hope it hurts like hell.
He raised the gun and started shooting.

~

Lashon was astounded by what Johnny had accomplished. The guts it took to have gotten himself this far was beyond comprehension. The man was a fucking hero. His dramatic reappearance reignited her hope for a single exhilarating moment.

Until he started shooting.

She couldn't fault him for trying to take out Heidi immediately. But, thanks to his injuries, his hold on the gun was awkward at best. Heidi scampered away from him as the first few shots missed and the slugs ricocheted off the cellar's concrete walls. One passed through the skull of the unfortunate young man in the *Basket Case* t-shirt, sending a spray of brains out the back of his head. Lashon did the only thing she could do with bullets bouncing around in the closed space—she curled into a tight, quivering ball and hoped no stray fragments of lead would come ripping through her flesh. When she opened her eyes again, Heidi was over by the shelves containing the gruesome jars of pickled body parts and shriveled organs. Johnny hobbled closer to her and tried to steady his aim for a more effective shot. Heidi reached into one of the compartments and pulled out a jar containing what looked like a brain. She raised it over her head and heaved it at him just as he finally managed to squeeze off another shot. The bullet nicked her shoulder and sent her crashing backward into the shelves.

Unfortunately for Johnny, Heidi's aim had been true as well. The big glass jar hit him square in the face and exploded on impact. He screamed and dropped the gun as he fell to his knees, swiping clumsily at his eyes with his mutilated hands. There were shards of glass embedded in his flesh, including a large fragment protruding from one of his eyes. He had been at least temporarily blinded.

Heidi unleashed a scream of rage and frustration as she braced her hands against the shelves behind her. She pushed herself away from the shelves with sufficient force to cause several more jars to come crashing to the floor, where they shattered and spilled their sickening contents. Blood was leaking from the hole gouged across the top of Heidi's shoulder, but Lashon was crushed to realize it was nothing like a fatal wound. Poor Johnny. He had tried so hard, struggled so valiantly . . . all for nothing.

Lashon knew she should make a grab for the gun. But she was still too weakened and was too far away. Heidi snatched it up within seconds and started screaming again as she aimed it at Johnny's bleeding face. The words spewing forth from her mouth were too shrill to understand. She nonetheless clearly had some choice things to tell Johnny, regardless of whether the poor bastard could understand her through her molten rage. Lashon hoped the bitch would keep up the verbal assault a while longer yet. Because though the gun was lost to her, something else was not.

Blake's body had landed almost within grabbing range.

She eyed the cleaver in the back of his head with an intensity of focus that cut cleanly through her pain. She coveted that goddamn cleaver. Wanted it more than she had ever wanted anything else. She summoned what remained of her strength and crawled closer to the body. Her hand closed around its handle just as Heidi's screaming was reaching its apparent apex. She gave it a savage yank and it came loose with a grind of splintering bone. In the same instant, the boom of the gun resounded in the cellar again and Lashon didn't need to see what had happened to know her hero was finally dead.

I'll do her for you, Johnny, she thought. *I fucking promise.*

She got to her feet with a howl of pain and took a lurching step toward Heidi. A glance at Johnny's prone form dead on the floor—with a growing pool of blood spreading out around his head—enraged her enough to return her strength to near-normal levels. She took a steadier step toward Heidi and began to raise the cleaver.

Heidi laughed. "Stupid bitch. You're done for and don't even know it." She raised the gun again and aimed it point-blank at Lashon's face. "Goodbye, whore."

She squeezed the trigger.

Click.

Her expression of insane glee slowly faded, giving way to a frown as she stared at the gun. But she kept it aimed at Lashon and squeezed the trigger again.

Click.

Click, click, click.

"Empty." Lashon smiled. "Used your last bullet on a blind man. Who's the stupid bitch now, you fucking cunt?"

Heidi dropped the gun.

She shook her head in dismay and held her hands up in a warding-off gesture. "No. Please."

Lashon kept smiling. "That's right. Beg."

Heidi whimpered and a step backward. "Please."

"Good, good. Keep it up. Maybe I'll be merciful."

With her next backward step, Heidi's foot landed on something big and slimy that might have been some poor dead bastard's diseased liver. Her mouth opened in a big surprised O as her feet went out from under her and she went crashing to the glass-strewn floor.

Lashon was done playing with the evil bitch. She pounced immediately, straddling her to pin her to the floor as she raised the cleaver high overhead and brought it down with every ounce of savagery she could muster. The first chop split the girl's face open to the bone. She writhed and screamed, pain galvanizing her as she tried to buck Lashon off her body. But Lashon would not be budged. She brought the cleaver down again, this time slamming it into her throat. The girl's eyes jittered in their sockets and her body twitched. Blood leaked from the corners of her mouth even as larger gouts of gore spurted from the wound to her throat.

Lashon still wasn't satisfied.

She chopped at Heidi's face and throat many more times. By the time she was done, the dead girl's once very beautiful face was an utter, ugly ruin. Given what she had done to Johnny, this seemed only right. At last, she arrived at a moment where it felt like it was enough. Her rage had been expended. Now she just felt tired. Weary almost beyond reckoning. She tossed the cleaver aside and staggered to her feet.

She turned in a slow circle, taking all the madness in one last time. The bodies hanging from the hooks. The hideous things that had been done to those poor people. The many jars still remaining on all those shelves. Those trophies of horror and atrocity. And, worst of all, Johnny's poor, violated body sprawled on the cold, hard floor. She went to him and knelt by him to mutter a few words of sincere gratitude for all he had sacrificed.

Then she got up and walked out of there.

She emerged from the house and stood for a time on the long porch, wondering what her next move should be as she watched the first rays of the sun already peeking over the horizon grow brighter. The cooler she remembered from earlier was still propped atop a table in the middle of the porch. She flipped open its top and saw a few cans of beer still floating in cool water. She plucked one out, shook off the excess moisture, and popped the tab.

"Here's to you, Johnny," she said, with a slight tilt of the can.

Somewhere a bird twittered prettily. The sound made Lashon smile. There was still beauty in the world, after all. Nothing could ever erase that, including any amount of horror.

Nothing.

She stayed there a while longer, drinking and thinking.

~

The man who called himself Doctor Ominous was no longer doing his impression of a jolly, delightfully mad evil genius. If anything, his expression betrayed an unexpected shade of sadness as he stared at the corpse slumped in the chair opposite his desk. Greg Nelson had been right, of course. The game had been rigged from the start. Ominous had known precisely how many clicks of the revolver's trigger would spin the cylinder around to the single live round it contained.

O'Dell cleared his throat. "A-hem. Should I, uh . . . dispose of the remains?"

Ominous steepled his fingers and kept his eyes on the face of the man who had dared to challenge him. His hands were hanging slack by his sides, but the gun was still wedged inside his mouth. There was a messy spray of blood and brains decorating the middle of the control room, which now no longer resembled the interior of an old timey train coach. Rarely in his life had the doctor witnessed displays of courage on this level. It was a thing to be admired, no doubt. And yet what had his courage earned the young man? Nothing. Not a damn thing at all.

A shame.

Empathy was an emotion Ominous rarely experienced. He didn't much give a damn about other human beings. Never had. It was curious he should feel empathy now, even in light of Greg Nelson's admirable sacrifice.

And yet . . . he did.

"Doctor?"

Ominous blinked and gave his head a shake to clear the mental cobwebs. He looked at O'Dell, whose illusory leprechaun appearance was no more. In truth, O'Dell was fair-skinned and stood a few inches taller than six feet. It had amused Ominous very much to craft an illusion so far removed from the man's reality.

He waved a hand at the dead man. "By all means, dispose of the body. But . . ." He trailed off, chewing on his bottom lip as he began to entertain a concept so foreign he could scarcely credit it as originating from his own brain. And yet here it was. "Before you do that . . ." He waved his hand again, this time indicating the screens on the wall. "Reset the continuum. Bring them all back."

O'Dell's expression betrayed genuine surprise for a fraction of a second. Then he was all business again. "Of course, doctor. Many of them are dead already, of course."

Ominous nodded and drummed the tips of his fingers together as he began to swivel back and forth in his chair. "Of course. But bring back the ones still living. And . . ."

He stopped swiveling and trailed off again.

O'Dell cleared his throat, prompting him. "Yes, doctor?"

"I imagine we could access a plane of existence where another version of Greg Nelson yet lives."

"Probably."

"A variation on our own world where the difference is so slight as to be negligible."

O'Dell nodded. "You already know you can do that, doctor."

Ominous snapped his fingers and sat forward, suddenly more buoyant than he had been at any point since the last moments prior to this Greg Nelson's demise. "And that is precisely what we shall do! We will bring another Greg Nelson here, dropping him smoothly into the life formerly occupied by *this* Greg Nelson!"

"Right. Um . . ." O'Dell cleared his throat again, a touch more nervously this time. "To what end, sir?"

Ominous smiled. "I'm feeling magnanimous, O'Dell. A version of Greg Nelson will have a chance to reconnect with his girl. We'll even tamper with the replacement's brain a bit, allow him to believe he experienced what this Greg Nelson experienced tonight." His grin broadened as he warmed to the idea. "Albeit with an alternative outcome."

The alternative concept that had been niggling at his brain was . . . mercy.

So truly foreign and strange a thing.

And yet . . . not without its small pleasures.

He began to rock in his chair again as the Mix of Diabolical Awesomeness shifted to a new song, "Death Comes Ripping" by the Misfits.

The music moved him. It always did.

Stirred the beast, as he'd told Greg Nelson.

He got up and danced around the room, slipping and sliding in the blood and gore.

~

Out of the darkness and into the light . . .

~

Darkness gave way to blinding light as the Firebird blew through the theater's entrance and passed through what seemed like empty space for a moment—a moment during which consciousness faded and the fabric of reality itself ceased to exist. Then the world coalesced around them again and the car was hurtling through a wide-open white room that bore a passing resemblance to a movie theater lobby. Then the Firebird slammed into an obstruction that had once masqueraded as a movie theater concession stand and ground to an abrupt halt.

Still rattled by the crash through the theater's entrance, the three of them looked around at their strange surroundings in dumbstruck wonder.

Then Jason said, "Goddamn. This is like some space odyssey bullshit up in here."

Ben leaned forward to poke his head between seats. "Please tell me the rest of your world doesn't look like this."

Brix shook her head. "I'm not sure this *is* our world."

Jason turned fully around in his seat and frowned at something.

Brix followed his gaze, shifting around in her seat, too. "Okay. That's strange."

Ben took a look as well. "Could someone explain that to me?"

Brix shook her head. "Nope. Not me."

Jason grunted. "Me, either."

Though there were signs of damage caused by the Firebird's careening path through the lobby, the theater's entrance was intact. But Brix remembered the explosion of glass and wood planks as the front end of the car had gone crashing through. Still, it was impossible to deny the evidence of her eyes.

Then it hit her.

The crash had occurred somewhere else. In that *other* world.

And this thing that had disguised itself as an ordinary-appearing theater was somehow the facilitator. This white austerity surrounding them was the truth beneath the surface, along with its hints of an otherworldly, incomprehensible reality-warping technology.

Brix said, "Guys, I've got a great idea."

Jason looked at her. "Yeah?"

"Yeah. Let's get the fuck out of here."

Brix tried to start the car, thinking she'd just get it turned around and go crashing through the entrance again. But the engine wouldn't turn over.

Brix smacked the steering wheel. "Fuck it. Abandon ship."

They bailed out and commenced a mad dash for the theater's front doors. Which, astonishingly, were unlocked and yielded easily to their touch.

~

One moment they were embracing in the rear compartment of the helicopter as the bird flew off into the deep darkness of the night. Then a bright flash obliterated the darkness and the next thing they knew they were in the parking lot outside the theater where the whole nightmarish evening had begun.

Monroe recognized at once that they really were back in their own world. And yet things hadn't simply been reset. He saw other people wandering about the parking lot in a daze. A few of them he recognized from his brief time inside the theater. Strangers who had stood on line with them for tickets and popcorn. Some of them looked like they were in shock. Some were crying. Some were covered in blood. Kira was still wrapped in his arms. Like many of the others, she was blood-drenched.

She was also nude.

She shivered in his arms as she nervously scanned the surroundings. Then she looked at Monroe. "We've got to get out of here."

He nodded. "I know. You can wear my shirt. It'll be something at least."

"That's not what I mean. Look." She jerked her head in the direction of the brightening horizon. "The sun's coming up. And we're still . . ."

Monroe was confused for a moment.

Then awareness dawned.

Shit. She's right.

"We're still vampires."

It was true.

Everything that had happened over in that other world actually *had* happened. They had become vampires there and so they still were here.

Kira clutched at his shirt. "I don't want to burn. I don't want to die, Monroe."

"We're not gonna burn. I promise."

There had to be a car somewhere nearby they could steal. Kira's car was here, but it was useless for now, as her keys were still back in that other world. Monroe scanned the parking lot again, searching for a likely victim. After a moment, he spied someone perfect, a very woozy-looking middle-aged man in a ragged-looking t-shirt attempting to open his crappy Dodge Neon.

He took Kira by the hand and led her in that direction.

"Come on," he told her. "We'll catch a ride to my place and have a drink along the way."

She smiled at this and clutched his hand tighter.

"This will be fun," she said, almost cheerily. "We're probably the only real vampires in this world. There probably aren't even any hunters to worry about."

Monroe thought she was probably right. This *would* be fun. The future suddenly seemed very bright indeed. Or, he reflected with a smile, as bright as it could for creatures who would have to spend the remainder of their very long undead existences living under the cover of the night.

~

Most of the Late Night Horror Show survivors had already wandered off by the time Lashon rematerialized in the parking lot outside the theater. Though she would never realize it, there had been a slight delay in her return to her proper world. A delay necessitated by certain arrangements that had to be made.

There was just one other person there to commiserate with upon her return, a slightly plump woman in her thirties who claimed to have survived a wild night of being chased around by flesh-eating zombies. Lashon had no reason to doubt the tale. She and the woman wound up being the only two witnesses to the ultimate fate of the Sunshine 6 cineplex. Or, rather, what appeared to be its fate.

The woman frowned as she puffed at a cigarette. Lashon thought it odd she'd somehow held onto her smokes through a zombie apocalypse, but she guessed she'd seen stranger things over the course of the last dozen hours.

She realized she sort of wouldn't mind a smoke herself and said so. "What is it? Something wrong? Something else, I mean."

The woman tapped a cigarette from a nearly empty pack and passed it to Lashon. "The theater . . ." She nodded in its direction. "Is it sort of . . . *glowing?*"

Lashon turned to look at the building.

It wasn't glowing. Not exactly.

No.

It was . . . shimmering. Turning translucent. Fading in and out of existence. Or just turning invisible. Or just going somewhere else. Somehow.

And then it was gone.

The two women stood there a while longer, puffing on their cigarettes and staring at the empty space formerly occupied by some kind of alien thing or other that had pretended to be a movie theater.

Then the plump woman flicked her cigarette butt away. "Well. There's something you don't see every day."

Lashon nodded. "You're right about that. Your car here by any chance?"

"Yep."

"Reckon you could give a girl a ride?"

"Sure."

The woman drove Lashon back to her apartment building. They exchanged very few words along the way. Though they had shared similar experiences, no mystical bond of any type arose as a result of their journeys through nightmarish other worlds. Instead there was an unspoken but understood mutual desire to forget any of it had ever happened. The woman dropped her off at the curb outside her building and drove away without another word.

Lashon started toward the building, but came to a sudden stop when she spied Greg Nelson sitting on a bench outside the front door. She was immediately apprehensive, but then he smiled and waved when he caught her eye. A wild stew of emotions churned inside her at the sight of that smile. He wasn't a bad guy. Never had been. He just hadn't known when to back off and leave her alone. And there was the issue of what she had done to him. Which was not good. Not good at all. Seeing him now triggered fresh pangs of remorse. He seemed so happy to see her. She had assumed their relationship was dead forever, but was it possible there was still hope?

Well.

There was only one way to find out.

He stood and waited right there for her as she went to meet him.

BIO

Bryan Smith is the author of numerous novels and novellas, including *68 Kill*, *Slowly We Rot*, *Depraved*, *The Killing Kind*, and *Kill For Satan!*, which won a Splatterpunk Award for best horror novella of 2018. He won a second Splatterpunk Award in 2020 for *Dirty Rotten Hippies and Other Stories*. He is also the co-author of *Suburban Gothic*, written with Brian Keene. A film version of *68 Kill*, directed by Trent Haaga and starring Matthew Gray Gubler from *Criminal Minds*, was released in 2017. He lives in Tennessee with his dogs Mac and Roxie.

Other Grindhouse Press Titles